LYNDEE'S SAVIORS

Men of Montana

Eileen Green

MENAGE AMOUR

Siren Publishing, Inc.
www.SirenPublishing.com

A SIREN PUBLISHING BOOK
IMPRINT: Ménage Amour

LYNDEE'S SAVIORS
Copyright © 2013 by Eileen Green

ISBN: 978-1-62740-368-9

First Printing: July 2013

Cover design by Harris Channing
All cover art and logo copyright © 2013 by Siren Publishing, Inc.

ALL RIGHTS RESERVED: This literary work may not be reproduced or transmitted in any form or by any means, including electronic or photographic reproduction, in whole or in part, without express written permission.

All characters and events in this book are fictitious. Any resemblance to actual persons living or dead is strictly coincidental.

Printed in the U.S.A.

PUBLISHER
Siren Publishing, Inc.
www.SirenPublishing.com

DEDICATION

I would like to dedicate this book to my Dad who I admired so much. His dedication to achieve his goals is what has driven me to this spot in my life that I have reached my first goal in my writing.

I would also like to dedicate this book to my friend Big John who supported me in everything I did.

Both men will be greatly missed in my life. I will always love you both.

LYNDEE'S SAVIORS

Men of Montana

EILEEN GREEN
Copyright © 2013

Prologue

The wooden door separated from the metal hinges that held it to the frame as it collided haphazardly against the perpendicular wall to the right with a crash. A scream emerged from the only occupant in the room as a tall man stepped into the space where the door had rested just seconds before. Black jeans hugged his muscular thighs, black leather cowboy boots with a silver toe cap on his feet while a black long-sleeved T-shirt stretched across the broad shoulders, which nearly spanned the width of the doorway. Long black hair pulled back into a leather tie at the base of his thick neck framed his face that expressed his anger and hatred for the woman in the room. To complete the wicked ensemble, a police badge was lodged into the black leather belt at his waist and a gun was held in his large right hand.

The woman had been sitting on the couch watching CNN on the flat-screen TV mounted to the wall at the end of the room. She cursed herself that she hadn't been as thoroughly prepared for this situation as she should have been. Reaching for her purse, which was her first instinct, she didn't make it that far as the gun in the man's hand expelled a bullet silenced by the small device on the end of the barrel. Again she screamed as the metal piece of shrapnel struck her well-formed left bicep as the man rushed toward her, his fist making contact with her jaw before she could move, and she slumped to the back of the nice piece of furniture she sat upon, all reality slipping from her mind.

* * * *

Sound echoed within the woman's head as dizziness swam within its darkness. Soreness within her head caused her to keep still though other parts of her body ached also. Trying to move her hands, she found they were manacled above her head, a numbness already setting in so she wasn't sure how long she had been left in this position. As she tried to do the same with her feet, she found they too had been secured in place, in a spread-eagle fashion. The surface beneath her was soft so she assumed she must be on a bed.

Soft cloth covered her eyes while a cloth was wedged between her lips, her tongue swiping against the material as she realized the situation she was in. The memory of the brute storming into her apartment came back to her, and a chill ran through her as she knew she would die soon. However she knew he would take her body before he did so as he had threatened to do many times in the past.

A sound alerted her as if a match had been struck and then the confirmation came as she smelled the sulfur a moment later. Since she was blindfolded, her senses were heightened as the fuzziness began to dissipate within her brain and her sense of survival told her to lie still as not to let the pervert know she was awake.

A breath was expelled right next to her right ear before she heard a whispered, "Are you awake yet, my dear?"

When she didn't move in response, an evil laugh emerged from the man and she felt him lean over and place a kiss on her slim neck. Revulsion bubbled in her stomach and she had to force herself to remain still and not wretch at his touch. His lips moved up to her ear again as his hand covered her nearly bare, ample breast, which spilled from the sides of the shirt she wore. "I can't wait until you are awake so I can fuck you over and over again. If I like what you can provide me, I might just let you live as my slave and keep you here forever."

* * * *

Philip moved away from the bed and went to sit in one of the battered leather recliners in front of the fire that he had started in the hearth. Orange-red flames began to lick at the logs he had placed in them before he had gone to retrieve his prize. Now he could relax until she woke and he could have his way with her. Mesmerized by the flames, he rubbed his enlarged cock beneath the fabric and zipper of his jeans, eager to thrust it into his captive's mouth, cunt, and ass again and again, quenching his thirst for the woman he had wanted for so long before she had screwed him over.

Glancing over at the queen-size bed in the center of the room of the cabin he had rented, her hands and feet had been secured to the brass head and foot boards. He had left her clothed in the jogging shorts and skimpy tank she wore. Before he had picked her up at her apartment, he had checked and found she wore no undergarments, which had his dick instantly hard, but he knew he would have to wait until she was awake before he would take her. He wanted her to be fully conscious as he fucked her, wanted her to know who was in control of her until she died.

She was a feisty thing as he had seen while he worked with her. The little thing had fight to her, which he liked in his women, and he couldn't wait until she fought against him as he took her as that would make the experience more enjoyable for him. He couldn't wait until she woke.

Rising, he made his way over to the refrigerator and grabbed a bottle of beer. Popping the top as he made his way back to the chair, he detoured past the bed and laid the cold bottle upon her breast, watching the nipple rise beneath the material involuntarily. Chuckling, he returned to his seat, absorbing the heat from the burning logs as the night was turning cold here in Western Montana and it was just the end of August. His arrogance that no one would find them was running high at the moment since neither one of them were from the area and he knew that he had her all to himself.

Chapter One

Three miles away from the cabin in a renovated farmhouse, Trey and Storm entered the living room, removing their cowboy hats and dusting their jeans off before sitting in their respective black leather recliners in front of the large stone fireplace which had stood for over a century. A fire had already been started by their housekeeper, Martha, who could be heard in the kitchen preparing their dinner. It had been a hard day of rounding up the cattle from the southern end of the ranch to bring to the breeding pens near the barn. Both men were so tired that neither of them really felt like eating but knew they needed to replenish their bodies with nourishment as there was more work to be done the next morning.

Each man toed off their boots before the woman that had cooked and cleaned for them since they were children discovered they had worn them into the house, as she would chastise them much like their mother would have. The woman had remained on with the two after they had come of age and even after their parents had been killed in a car accident seven years prior. She called out from the kitchen as she knew them well, "You better have removed those boots before you entered the house! I just vacuumed before y'all came in! Dinner will be ready in fifteen minutes! Get Austin over here!"

"Yes ma'am," they replied in unison as Trey picked up the remote and pressed the power to turn on the fifty-inch flat panel TV mounted over the fireplace, ignoring her request to call Austin. Flipping through the channels he landed on a sports channel, broadcasting a baseball game from Denver. It wasn't that they were really into sports since there were no professional teams in the state, but it was a way to wind down after a day on the range. A few minutes later the screen door opened and slammed against the wall, letting in the tall man who was their foreman and cousin.

"Supper ready yet?" he asked, plopping down onto the matching leather sofa to the right side of the fireplace.

"Not quite," Trey said, tossing the remote onto the small round table between the two recliners. Raising his voice slightly for emphasis, he answered, "According to the boss lady, about another ten minutes or so."

A loud "humph" was expelled from the kitchen as the announcer on the TV began an excited tirade announcing the ball flying through the air and the crowd cheering, catching the men's attention. Watching the game through the excitement of the homerun to the next couple of pitches, supper was finally announced and all three men crowded into the kitchen and around the sink to wash up.

Martha stood at the end of the granite countertop, arms crossed across her chest in irritation. "Why do y'all have to wash up in here all the time? There are perfectly good bathrooms and a mudroom for you to do that in."

Chuckling, the men finished up, dried their hands, and crowded around the small table in the breakfast nook that had been built as an addition for their mother. It jutted out from the kitchen with a bay window effect on the outer wall, though the windows themselves were floor to ceiling and faced the western mountain range. The sun was setting at the moment, though none of them paid any attention to it as they began serving up the bounty that sat upon the table.

"I hope y'all remember I'm leaving in the morning for my cruise," Martha said, playing with the food on her plate.

"We did," Trey said soberly. "I hope you have a wonderful time."

"We'll miss you greatly," Storm said setting down his fork. "You deserve it after you raised us and all."

"Perhaps you'll find the man of your dreams while out on the high seas," Austin joked.

"The man of my dreams doesn't even know I exist," she said discouragingly. The boys knew she was thinking about Tom at the steakhouse in town. She had had her eye on him for some time, but he was always too busy to pay any attention to her.

"Oh, he notices you," said the youngest brother jokingly, taking a bite of fried chicken. "He's just afraid of you."

The two elbows, one from each side, slammed into his chest and the foot that kicked from beneath the table surprised him. "Ouch!"

"Have some respect for the old woman, will ya," Storm said. "She can't help it if she's mean."

He felt the kick from her foot on his shin also, though he remained silent. There were many bruises on their legs from their housekeeper as the trio of men didn't know how to hold their tongue around her. Like a mother to them, but also a bit of sounding board to their many dilemmas and pranks, they knew how far to push her and when to back off. Now was the time to back off.

"Who's taking you to Butte to the airport?" Trey asked, shoveling a mouthful of mashed potatoes into his mouth.

"Ginger is. She'll be here at five in the morning."

Noticing her melancholy mood, the three men watched her out of concern. Trey nudged Storm to say, "Is there something wrong Martha?"

Rinsing her dish off before setting it in the dishwasher, she sighed loudly before letting the tears begin to fall. "Yes. I'm going to miss you guys."

The trio of men stood up to their full heights of over six feet and surrounded the woman who they held in such high regard within their home. They respected her even though they threw their barbs at her occasionally. She was a part of their small family and always would be.

"Martha," Trey started, lifting her chin with two large fingers. "We are going to miss you greatly as Storm said, but you have been here every day for us since Mom and Dad died. You put up with us day in and day out. You deserve this vacation. You deserve to have fun. Let your hair down, live a little."

Pulling the middle-aged woman into his arms, Storm hugged her like he did his own mother many years ago, "Yes Martha, though I wish you would have let us pay for the trip. You deserve it for putting up with us."

"And what am I supposed to spend my money on then?" she joked, her face smashed against the dusty shirt spanning the man's wide chest.

Murmurs made their way around the three men but none could really give an answer. Pulling away from Storm, she let the other two men hug her before going over and clearing the table. As she began to rinse the dishes, she began going over a list of things for them to follow. "There are casseroles in the freezer in the garage for you. One for each night I'm gone. I'm sure you can fend for yourselves for breakfast and lunch. Just take out a casserole each morning and let it thaw and put it in the oven for about forty-five minutes to cook. Except for what you are wearing, there are enough clean clothes to last the two weeks I'll be gone. I'll do the washing when I return. Just pile any mail I get on the stand inside the door of the cottage. If I have a problem with a ride home, I'll call you on your cell to arrange something, but otherwise you should be all set."

"Yes ma'am," the three agreed.

Each man stepped up to kiss her on the cheek before going and settling down in the living room. A somber mood hung over the room as the evening wore on and finally none of them could stand it anymore and each went to their own rooms.

Martha had been a stable fixture in their home as long as they could remember. After Trey and Storm's mother and father had died, they depended on her more and more as the woman of the house. Sure they had their share of women, even bringing some home and going as far as sharing amongst themselves, but no one could ever take the place of dear, sweet Martha. She would be sorely missed in the house for the next two weeks.

* * * *

At the cabin in the woods, Philip had fallen asleep in front of the warm fire, his cock finally deflating enough to let his body rest. He had been in an emotional and physical turmoil for three days now, anticipating the demise of the woman who occupied his bed. A noise brought him fully awake, hoping his captive was awake, but he realized he had dropped the empty beer bottle onto the braided rug beneath his feet. Standing, he quietly made his way over to the old brass bed situated in the center of the room.

The woman in the black tank top with the spaghetti straps and the black jogging shorts lay in the same position. Worry settled over him as she hadn't regained consciousness yet. Perhaps he had injected too much of the sedative into her. But that was the only way he could have transported her safely on their journey and kept curious eyes off of them.

Eyeing the colorful tattoo that peeked out of the armhole of the tank starting at the side of her right breast and snaking down her side to disappear beneath the tank again, he was curious to see what the design actually was and where it ended. He had never imagined this petite woman who pretended she was so quiet and demure would have a tattoo, let alone have one that was actually on her tit. He felt his dick stir in his pants again and knew he had to move away from her or he would take her while she was still asleep and that wasn't what he wanted to do. He wanted to fuck her savagely for what she had done to him, to show her that he wasn't a man to mess with, but he needed her awake to make his point.

Adjusting his burgeoning cock in his jeans, Philip made his way to the door and stepped out into the cold night air. Closing the door behind him, he stood, breathed in the clean air, and sat in the pine Adirondack chair next to the door on the small porch, absorbing the quietness that surrounded him. It was so different than the city noises he was used to, along with the smog that was beginning to pollute the air where he lived. He missed the hustle and bustle of the city, but he would be returning soon enough, after he completed this personal mission.

Philip had been enjoying his break on the porch for about fifteen minutes when he heard the rattle of metal on metal. Launching himself from the pine chair, he rushed into the cabin, letting the door slam open. Adrenaline pumping through his body and with a rush of cold air, he entered the cabin smiling. "I hear you are finally awake, my dear." The struggles within the metal police cuffs and the tossing of her head from side to side, along with the screaming behind the gag showed she was afraid, and well she should be. She had discovered he was a dirty cop working for the mob, and she had enough on him to put him away for life. He couldn't let that happen so he was going to have to take care of her the only way he knew how, but first he was going to enjoy her delicious body.

He stood still, letting her anticipate his next move, letting the fear rise within her. With discipline, he kept his hands at his sides, his breathing steady, though he felt his cock throbbing against the zipper of his jeans. The cold air had kissed his captive's body as her nipples hardened under the skimpy material that covered her breasts and goose bumps danced along all visible flesh, though he hoped the fear caused it more than the cold.

Philip watched as quiet anticipation finally got the best of her and she began to struggle against her metal prison, pulling hard on the cuffs on each one of her limbs, while her body thrashed about as much as it could against the bindings. She screamed through her gag. The cursing was muffled, though he could still make out the words she spat out.

"Now, now," he chastised with a chuckle, letting his fingers brush lightly along the side of her breast that protruded out from the confines of the tank top. "Those are not words to be used by a lady."

Trying to move her arm up to brush him away, she caused her bandaged bicep to hit his forearm and she cried out in pain, remembering he had shot her before he hit her. Again she cursed at him through the gag, which caused him to chuckle then grasp her breast and squeeze tightly, causing her to cry out again. Bending down so his mouth was next to her ear he whispered, "You can fuss all you want, Lisa! I intend to have what you have to offer under these clothes, the same way you offered yourself to your customers. You've shunned me enough while working for the boss, and now I intend to take what I want from you."

She must have found what he said funny for she tried to suppress a giggle but wasn't able to. Her body began to spasm as her laughter bubbled to the surface.

Philip stood straight staring down at his prisoner as if she had lost her mind. He pulled his hand from her body and ran a hand over his face in confusion. The longer the laughter continued he felt she was mocking him so he reached out and slapped her cheek.

"Stop it, bitch!" he shouted at her, causing her to laugh harder. His face became redder with each passing moment until his mental rage overtook his body and he lashed out with his fist and slammed it down onto her jaw.

The laughter stopped and her body went still immediately as she slipped away into unconsciousness again from the impact. Anger continued to build within the man, and lashing out, he struck the headboard once, twice, and then a third time as he tried to release the emotion that had control of his body and mind. Frustrated that he let the vixen get to him, he growled at her before stomping back to the chair in front of the fireplace and sat back down. Staring into the flickering flame that had diminished over time as the logs became smaller, he tried to control himself, breathing in and out deeply until he felt at ease at hurting her again. Eventually sleep overwhelmed him and his body relaxed, though his mind remained sharp.

Chapter Two

Sunrise caught the Goodall brothers and their cousin Austin starting up the mountain path west of the ranch house to find some cattle that had wandered up that direction. GPS tags had been attached to the animals at birth so they knew how to track them without searching the entire twenty-five thousand acres for them. If their father was still alive, they would be working the old-fashioned way at the ranch, but after he passed, the boys brought it into the 21st century. Also, it would give them the opportunity to ride into mountains that had allured them day after day. Though exploring had evaded them due to their day-to-day chores.

They had risen before Martha had and actually had breakfast ready for her when she came in to tend to the task. This was her vacation and there was no sense in her working first thing in the morning on her first day off. After seeing her off with her friend Ginger, they saddled up their horses and set off so they could see the sunrise as they started up the trail. Sitting for a moment to watch the pinks, purples, and gold rise from the mountains across their valley gave them each a promise of a new day, a new adventure that awaited them as it did every morning.

A cell tower sat about five miles south on their property so they were able to get a signal on their smartphones for calls and to track the cattle through the GPS tags so all three of them were able to go after them. The other ranch hands remained around the barn and house to perform the chores that needed to be done while the three family members were gone for the day. They hoped to return before nightfall with the stray cattle as the tracker indicated they were about two and a half miles up the trail near one of the streams.

* * * *

Philip woke with a start, confusion setting in when he saw the fireplace before him as this wasn't his apartment, but then remembered where he was. Standing, he stretched the kinks out of his tall body before looking over at the bed where his captive lay. She wasn't moving so he made his way over to her to see if she had regained consciousness after he had slugged her the previous evening. As he approached, he heard her pleas through the material stuffed in her mouth for a gag.

* * * *

Her hearing was enhanced since she couldn't see behind the blindfold so she heard his boots on the floor getting closer and closer. The need to pee had risen greatly since she had awoken a while ago. She hoped he would be considerate enough to let her use the restroom and not have to embarrass herself by relieving herself in the bed. She didn't hold out much faith as the man was ruthless and uncaring as she had found out when he killed a prostitute he had hired because she had bit him on his penis when he got too domineering.

Struggling against the restraints and talking into the cloth she hoped he would try to discover what she wanted. Feeling his hand on her right breast she went still but kept trying to talk. In a moment she felt him pull the gag down to lie on her neck.

"I…I need…" She tried to speak but the dry, cottony feeling wouldn't leave her mouth as she tried to gather saliva.

She felt him next to her, but he had become still. Was he getting ready to rape her? What was he waiting for? She knew he was a sadistic bastard and that he would most likely antagonize her psyche before he took her and killed, but could her nerves withstand the waiting?

After what felt like hours, where her heart pounded against her ribcage, she heard him move. The sound of his boots on the hardwood floor and the movement of his clothes took him away from her. She heard what she thought was a refrigerator open and close before he made his way back to her.

Since she didn't have her sight, she heard what she thought was a top being unscrewed from a bottle. Next she heard his throat swallowing and her mouth dried even more at the thought of him drinking something. In the next moment, she felt the cold top of the bottle on her lips. Opening them, she felt the comforting of cold water splash the desert that was her mouth. Swallowing as quickly as possible for fear of choking on the liquid in her position, she was allowed this three times before he pulled the bottle away from her. Water dribbled from it as he pulled the plastic bottle away from her. Apparently he didn't care if he spilled some on her.

As the cold drops landed on her top the woman felt her nipples contract at the sensation. She knew Philip's eyes would be ablaze with sadistic desire. He had made no qualms about wanting to fuck her when she worked for the mob, even saying it with those exact words. An involuntary shudder ran through her, knowing she was at his mercy for him to perform his deepest desire. A struggle in her bindings caused Philip to laugh out loud before pouring some more water into her mouth.

When her mouth was wet enough, she tried to speak again, though this time with coyness. "I need to use the restroom."

Fear engulfed her when Philip grasped her chin in his large hand and leaned in close to her. Pressing his hand together against her face had her thinking he was going to hurt her and fear consumed her. "If you even think of trying anything, little girl, I will snap your neck in two and then fuck your dead body! Is that clear?"

Nodding quickly she whispered as she fought down the bile threatening to come up. "Yes."

Blinking as bright light punctured the darkness she had been in for God knows how long, she watched as he pulled the key from his shirt pocket. He set about unlocking the manacles on her legs, moving around the footboard to do so, then he began on her left wrist then moved on to the right one. The first three manacles were left attached to their respective metal posts but he left the right one on her wrist.

Before she could stand on her own, he pulled her up by her shoulders, and once on her feet he took a step behind her and let his large hand come up around her throat and squeeze it, not giving her a chance to move on her own. His other hand wrapped around her waist as he began to push her in the direction of the bathroom. Once there she thought he would leave her to do what she needed to do but he released her and stood against the counter watching her, to her aggravation.

It was hard for her to answer nature's call with an audience but she was able to finish. After she pulled her shorts up he grasped her again in the same fashion, one hand on her throat and the other around her waist as he escorted her back to the bed. Taking her wrist with the handcuff still on it, he attached it to one of the spindles on the headboard, the click echoing throughout the room, causing the lady to flinch.

She watched him go over to the kitchen where he fixed some food. Quickly Lisa took in her prison. Grasping the handcuff she quietly tried to pull on it and found the spindle was loose, which caused her heart to soar and she began to plan. Looking over at the mountain of a man in the kitchen, she saw his gun sticking out of the waistband of his jeans. He had put the key back into the pocket of his T-shirt, and now she had to figure out how to get both away from him.

Reaching over, she moved the spindle back and forth until it came loose, and she slid the closed part of the handcuff out from under it though left her hand near the headboard to keep up the pretense she was still bound. Shifting slightly, the sheet beneath her moved to help cover up the handcuff so she hoped she'd be able to pull this off.

Philip came back around to her, handing her half a sandwich, which she took with her free hand, and he watched while she wolfed it down as he knew she was hungry. When she finished, he handed her the other half, which she fumbled and dropped to the floor. Philip backhanded her face before reaching down to pick up the mess, forgetting for a moment how close he was too her.

Lisa pulled the Glock from his jeans and rolled herself across the bed before Philip could pull himself up to stand. She was on her feet and both hands on the trigger when he realized what had taken place.

"You will not hurt me again, Philip McKnight! And when I am through with you, you will regret the day you ever laid a hand on me," she said with such venom that it even shook her. "I am going to expose you to the police and they will have you in jail faster than you can think about it and that's if your mob boss doesn't get to you first."

During her tirade, Philip began to slowly move around the footboard of the bed and toward her. Backing up, she kept the gun trained on his chest as she inched toward the door. When her back hit it, she used one hand to open it while the other remained on the trigger, not taking any chances of turning her head away from him. She back stepped onto the porch and that was when Philip took the opportunity for an attack.

He lunged for the door as it began to slowly close, thinking she was already running, but she heard him and pulled the trigger. A groan escaped his lips and she knew she had hit him. Turning, she began to run down the path through the thick trees blindly, not knowing where she was going.

Fearing for her life even more at this point since she had shot him, she ran faster, her hair flying around her face, the gun still in her hand in case she still needed it. Weaving in and out of the trees she could hear his grunting behind her, and she turned once to see where he was and found he was faltering on the path so she picked up her pace.

She didn't know how long she ran but she began to get winded and a sharp pain developed in her abdomen. Sweat ran off of her body and trickled down her face from her hair. The higher elevation did nothing to relieve her breathing and she began to get dizzy. The lower branches of trees and the bushes scratched at her exposed flesh as dirt began to stick to the sweat. Between the sweat and the dizziness, she didn't realize she had wandered off the path, and when she felt no ground beneath her foot at her next step, she knew she was going to fall, though how far she didn't know.

A scream escaped her lips as she tumbled down the embankment to the dry streambed below, hitting rock after rock and bushes along the way. Her head struck a boulder and everything went black.

* * * *

"Did you hear that?" Austin asked as the gunshot still seemed to echo through the forest.

"Yeah," Trey said, chirruping his horse to speed up. "Poachers?"

Storm's mouth thinned at the thought of someone poaching on their land, and he followed his brother and cousin up the mountain trail in search of whoever had a gun on their property. He had rented out the cabin on a moment's notice, and he hoped that he wasn't going to have problems with the man who had paid him in cash.

They were about a mile and a half from the cabin so hopefully they would have their answer soon. After moving quickly for about half an hour, a woman's scream echoed through the small canyon, causing the men to halt their horses.

"Doesn't sound like too far away," Austin said then prodded on. "Let's go."

Picking up the pace again, they found the footprints of someone heading down the trail, dodging in and out of the tree line. Odd. Austin backtracked a bit and found where the tracks led off a bit from the trail and then where they disappeared over the side of the embankment.

"Over here! Looks like someone took a tumble!" he shouted back to the boys.

In a flash he was off his black and white appaloosa and heading down the hill. Trey and Storm slid from their horses when they came up next to their cousin's and both peered over the side and watched the man jumping from rock to rock. At the bottom he stopped, abruptly staring at the ground, and said, "Ah, shit!"

Bending down, he felt the neck of the woman he found beaten and battered by the forest that she had run through. Feeling the telltale sign of life beneath his fingers, he moved her head slightly and found the lump, along with some blood behind the right ear. Her tank had become skewed during her tumble, and her right breast was exposed, showing the head of a green-and-yellow dragon near her nipple as if it were going to bite it. The dragon's body disappeared under the material and guilt struck at him at the thought that he wanted to know how far it went.

Feeling her limbs he found them to be intact and also came across the handcuffs still attached to her right wrist, so looking up at the top of the embankment he called out, "She's pretty banged up! I'm going to try to bring her up!"

"You need help?" Storm called down to him.

"No. There's too many rocks on the way up. It'll be too difficult for two people to carry her. But just wait 'til you see her!"

The two brothers glanced at each other, curiosity now peaked. It took about five minutes for Austin to appear with the petite bundle slung over his shoulder and by then the anticipation was eating at them. He never should have teased them about her looks because by the time the man arrived with the woman, they were both tripping over themselves trying to get a look.

The tall, dark man knelt to the ground and carefully laid the woman down on the dirt, his hand resting behind her head so it wouldn't jar her any more than her body already was. Straightening up her clothes as not to reveal too much of her delectable body, as they all had been raised with manners, he stood again to face his cousins.

"I'm going to check the surrounding area," he said, looking up the path. "Something had her spooked and I don't think it was just the sound of a gunshot."

The brothers nodded in agreement as the man walked up the hill, following the footprints in the dirt. Storm made his way to his horse, pulled out a first aid kit from one of the saddlebags, and returned to the girl, finding Trey feeling under her to see if those loose-fitting shorts had a pocket.

"No pockets mean no identification," the younger brother said discouraged, more to himself than his brother. "I wonder who she is."

Storm knelt down beside her and opened the plastic kit. Taking out a small square package he tore it open and pulled out the gauze then held it against the bleeding lump on the side of her head. A moan escaped her lips at the action, though she remained unconscious so that told Storm at least she was able to feel it, at least deep in her subconscious mind.

Trey took in her full lips, though split in several places, along with her slender neck and down to where the excess flesh of her breasts fell out to the sides of the tank top. He wondered what color her eyes were under those long lashes but would have to wait to see when she woke up. He noticed the bruising on her cheeks, and reaching down he moved her head to the left and to the right, concern striking first and then an overwhelming anger that boiled up from deep within him.

"Hey bro, look at these bruises," he pointed out. "Looks like the imprint of a fist or two on this cheek and then over here, looks like someone backhanded her."

Storm noticed the cuffs and, pulling her arm out from next to her body, held it up so the free end dangled down. Confusion set in. In shock, he let out a confused exclamation. "What the hell?"

"A prisoner?" Trey asked. "Dressed like this with bruises like that? No wonder she ran."

Setting her arm down gently, Storm looked at her lovely face and saw what was beneath the dirt, cuts, and bruising. His blood boiled within him that anyone would treat a lady like this. He thought briefly of the man he had rented the cabin to but knew investigating would need to wait until this woman was settled in at the Circle G and tended to by Doc Anderson and then conscious enough to let them know what had happened to her. It was too much of a coincidence that the cabin was about a mile away from this exact location.

A twig snapped from behind them and they both stood to attention, reaching for the firearms they kept at their sides until Austin came into view. "Sorry guys. I should have said something."

The two brothers squatted again next to the woman, both shaking their heads in disgust. The action wasn't missed by their cousin.

"I'm surprised about the handcuffs myself. What else have you found?"

"She's still unconscious. We need to get her home and get Doc out as soon as possible," Storm said. "She's been beaten. Give me your phone, Trey."

Handing over the small device, Storm set it into camera mode and began snapping pictures of the woman's face and body to record what she looked like when they found her along with the handcuffs. If she was a prisoner, they needed to cover their own hides, but also, if she was a prisoner, she didn't deserve to be beaten up.

The surprise came when Trey pulled her toward him so his brother could take more pictures and they found the puncture wounds to the neck. Snapping more pictures, the men became more irritated with what they found.

When they were finished Storm handed the camera back to Trey and then mounted his horse. Austin picked the woman up as easily as if he were picking up a bag of feed. He then handed her up to Storm, who sat a bit back in the saddle and sat her in front of him, his arm around her chest to hold her up. The others mounted up and they rode down the mountain.

* * * *

Philip had nearly reached his prey when he heard the horses arriving so he had to hide behind a large tree a few hundred yards away. He watched them bring up his captive from the ravine and then take pictures of her before setting off. He needed to get those pictures from them and needed to get Lisa away from them for his life now depended on it. Either the cops would get him for his crimes or the mob would kill him. He knew he should have killed her in her apartment and not let lust rule his body.

Chapter Three

The doctor was waiting outside the ranch house on the front porch, sitting in one of the chairs, feet up on the railing, when the small group rode up. Several ranch hands rushed out to take the horses to cool them down and settle them back into their stalls. They knew if Doc was there the bosses would need help. Shock registered on their faces when they saw the woman slumped against Storm, but they quickly gained their composure and went about the tasks at hand.

Austin took Lisa into his arms before Storm dismounted and went up to the porch to greet Doc Anderson. Once Trey had met up with them they all entered the house and Storm motioned for Austin to take her to the only room available, which was their parents' old room. Neither of the boys had felt it was right to take the room so they had left it as a guest room.

Laying her on the side of the large king-size bed Austin stepped away, letting the doctor have to do an examination. The three men watched anxiously as the man looked her over. The older man didn't say a word when he saw the cuffs and examined her other wrist. They watched him check the bandage on her left upper arm and find the bullet wound, which had been cleaned. He seemed to be infuriated by the marks from the manacles on her legs. The lump on her head seemed to be a concern, and when the doctor checked her pupils, they noticed her eyes were shaking.

Standing, he shook his head. "I don't suppose you'll let me take her into the hospital?"

The three men glanced at each other. They had talked on the way back to the house and came to the conclusion that they all wanted her. It wouldn't be the first time they had shared a woman, so that wasn't a problem between them, but they all knew they needed to protect her from whatever demon was trying to hurt her. They knew she belonged with them and she had been a long time coming to them.

Storm stepped forward. "Doc, she has been through a terrible ordeal, and unfortunately we didn't find the person responsible for this so I think it's best she stay with us. We can protect her here. Just let us know what we need to get for her."

"She has a concussion and she needs to remain in bed at least for a couple of days even if she regains consciousness soon. There will be dizziness and possibly vomiting. The pain will be great but no painkillers until her eyes stop jittering. Clean her body gently. I'll be back in two days to check on her. Trey, you should know what to do with her."

"Yes sir," the trio said in unison.

"If you need me, call me any time and I'll be out as quick as I can," Doctor Anderson said as he shook hands with each of them.

"And guys..." They looked at him. "Be gentle on her. Give her some time to adjust."

Shocked expressions floated through the trio at the statement, but they weren't too concerned about the old coot. They knew his secrets as well.

The older gentleman left them alone with the woman who had them hard as steel all the way home. Trey found the trip difficult with the task he needed to perform on the way back, and Storm had his own difficulty holding the woman, his arm lying beneath her breasts, tempted to let his hand splay across them but kept himself in check. Austin couldn't get the image of the handcuffs from his mind. Was she into bondage? Could she fulfill that desire of his, of theirs? Did someone get too overzealous in a scene and spook her? But what about the fact that she had been shot? They all their own thoughts dealing with the woman but when all was said and done, it was up to them to protect her and to seduce her.

The men split up to perform tasks. Storm went into the adjoining bathroom and began to run warm water in the sink while Trey went to the kitchen, put on a pot of coffee, and retrieved a large bowl to take back to his brother. Austin gathered some towels and washcloths from the linen closet in the hall, along with some extra blankets. He also grabbed a clean T-shirt from his room, thankful that Martha had done the laundry.

After filling the bowl with warm water, the men converged on the bed, surrounding the woman. At first none of them knew how to start with their task. Even though they desired her, they respected the fact she was a woman, and since they didn't know her, guilt swept over them about undressing her.

Slipping an arm under her shoulders, Austin lifted her torso and let Trey gently remove the dirty black tank top, allowing her breasts to spill free from their loose confines. Taking a wet washcloth Austin wiped down her back, making sure to remove all traces of dirt, pebbles, and foliage that had stuck to her body, while studiously trying to avoid staring at the white globes topped with luscious dark-pink nipples that had hardened in the cool air.

Trey began to wash down one side of her while Storm washed the other, each man being as gentle as possible. Moans emanated from the woman and the men were unsure if it was from pain or something else in her subconscious, especially when their hands cleaned her breasts. Her nipples puckered even more at their ministrations while the men salivated at the sight. Each of them had to readjust themselves within their tight jeans before continuing and knew this was going to be a long night.

The tattoo caught their attention. The green-and-yellow coloring contrasted with the black lines. As Austin had seen before, the open mouth of the dragon was near her nipple as if it were going to enjoy the delectable hard nub, and as they followed it, it wrapped around her ribcage, moving across her back. Its tail ended up on her left ass cheek, the pointed tip as if an arrow pointing toward her anus. The men traced it with their hands, lost in the moment, amazed that such an innocent-looking woman was so decadent with the art.

After cleaning her all over, they dressed her in the T-shirt that Austin had provided, though she looked so lost within the large garment. Austin brushed her hair gently, remembering the way his mother loved to have hers done when he was younger. He had loved to brush her long, dark hair that came down below her rear as he was always eager to please her after his father left them. The memories weren't good from his childhood, but he was thankful that his aunt and uncle had helped them out so there were some good recollections interspersed with the bad.

When they finished cleaning her up, Storm pulled the sheet and blanket down while Austin picked her up and moved her to the center of the bed. Replacing the sheet and blanket, Storm laid down on her right side while Austin sat on the left. Trey left the room to gather up some much needed food along with coffee to help keep them awake. Returning about half hour later, he returned with a tray piled with sandwiches, chips, cups of coffee, and some treats for dessert as they hadn't had a chance to eat out on the trail.

Settling down on the end of the bed, he set the tray at the end of Lisa's feet so the others could easily reach it, and they ate in silence, watching their patient. The room remained silent as the shadows moved slowly as the day outside turned into dusk and then night. A bedside lamp was turned on and the men remained, though Austin had returned the tray to the kitchen when he had checked with Kevin, the ranch hand he had left in charge in his absence to make sure everything was running all right, before returning to the room, to their woman.

* * * *

The woman slowly woke, confused from her surroundings. This was not her apartment. She didn't remember how she got there but she saw the three men in bed with her. Her head hurt though she didn't know why, and she hoped the men hadn't hurt her.

Flashes of her life came into her head and it frightened her. Moving her hand up to her head, the cuff clanked on her wrist, causing all three men to jump up. Their quick movement frightened her as she instinctively pulled herself into a ball, remembering that someone had hit her before.

A soothing, husky voice to her left sounded near her ear as Austin put a hand on her hip. "Sshhh, little one. We are not going to hurt you."

"Can you look at me, darlin'? Please?" Storm asked.

Slowly she pulled her arms down away from her head and looked into the light-blue eyes that belonged to one of the most handsome men she had ever seen. The concern in them caused a calm to settle upon her body and she felt she could trust him. Letting her eyes take in his features, she found his blond hair was straight down to his shoulders, which were wide beneath the shirt he wore. His bottom lip was full but she couldn't see the top lip under the mustache he sported and the thought of him kissing her caused her pussy to leak and her nipples to harden.

Turning to her left, she found a darker man watching her intently. His dark-brown eyes bore into her as if searching her soul, while a smile played at his full lips. A lump on the bridge of his nose testified to the break he had suffered, probably while playing football, and his high cheekbones were something any woman would kill for. His long brown hair spilled down to his waist and she wondered what it would be like to wrap her hands in it or have it drape across her naked breasts while he sucked on her nipples. He, too, was broad in the shoulders, his hand large with thick fingers that were splayed on her hip.

At the end of the bed, at her feet was a man with similar looks to the one to her right, though he had dark-blond hair that came to right above his shoulders. His green eyes flashed with delight, but she also saw desire there. He sported a scruffy beard as if he hadn't shaved in a few days, which was becoming on him. He, too, was solidly built and she wanted to see what these men looked like without their clothes.

Looking back at Storm she tried to sit up but found that a dizzying feat so stayed where she was, relaxing and stretching out her body. "Where am I?"

"You are at our home. We found you in the mountains after you fell down a ravine. What is your name?"

Opening her mouth she started to speak, but closed it again quickly when she couldn't remember. Confusion ruled her features and the men took it as stubbornness.

"We're not going to hurt you," Austin tried to reassure her. "We are trying to help you."

Tears welled in her iris-colored eyes as she looked from one man to the other and then landed back on Storm as he gathered her in his arms.

"It's okay, darlin'. We promise not to hurt you. Were you running from someone? Did someone hurt you?" Storm asked.

A sob escaped her throat as her right arm flew around his shoulder, hugging him close to her. "I can't remember what happened! I can't even remember my name!"

* * * *

Storm let her hold onto him as his right hand splayed on her waist, reveling in the fact that they were each getting to touch her in some way as a comforting gesture, though causing him to use as much willpower necessary to keep from laying her down and ravishing her body. Austin moved closer, his hips barely touching her ass cheeks as he ran his fingers up and down her spine while Trey moved up and stroked one of her legs that stuck out from beneath the massive tee she wore.

They had all seen the tattoo and the curvy hips along with her waxed cunt. Her breasts were bigger than what a girl her size would normally have, and they wondered about implants though it didn't look like it, but only time would tell. Storm liked big breasts, liked to suck on them and bite them. He had always been a breast man. Trey was the pussy man. He could spend hours eating a woman's pussy, giving her orgasm after orgasm, while Austin was an ass man. He loved to bury his long, thick cock into a woman, and after seeing the tattoo pointing the way to her little puckered hole, Storm knew how much that enticed the man.

When she finally calmed down, Storm laid her back on the bed. Looking down at her he wanted nothing more than to kiss her full lips but had to restrain himself for her sake as well as his own. They needed to take care of her, protect her. "Are you hungry?" he asked as he stood.

* * * *

Nodding, she again tried to sit up as he left the room. This time the dizziness wasn't so bad and Austin propped up pillows behind her so she was comfortable. Taking her hand in his, she was shocked to see how it dwarfed her own but delighted in how the callused skin felt good against her soft skin. She could tell these were men who worked for a living, though she had met many a man in her line of work that did.

The thought frightened her. Her line of work? Flashes of memory floated through her mind. She was dressed in skimpy dresses along with other women, made up to look trashy, high stiletto heels strapped to her feet. What the hell? That wasn't her at all. Shaking her head she tried to get the images to leave her brain but instead caused the dizziness to get worse, and she leaned back into the pillows, eyes shut tight.

This action wasn't lost on the two men remaining in the room and Austin's other hand came up and began caressing her cheek. "What is it, little one? Did you remember something?"

Nodding sadly, the tears rolled down her cheeks at the memory. Disbelief at what had been revealed through the flashback hurt her to the core as she felt she was stronger than that. But then why did her body react to the three men who had rescued her the way it had. Perhaps she was mistaken.

"My name is Lisa," she said between sobs. "I think I am a prostitute!"

She felt Austin grab her up against his hard chest, hugging her to him in an offer of comfort. Oddly, she felt as if she was home in his arms, but the revelation was unnerving for her. She could only accept his comfort, though for how long?

Concern struck her though when she felt Trey rise from the bed and storm out of the room. Could he not deal with her so-called profession?

* * * *

Storm heard Trey making his way down the hall, passing the kitchen, and letting the wood and screen door slam behind him.

Popping his head out the door of the kitchen, Storm watched his brother angrily leave the porch and stand out in the driveway talking to someone. Something had happened that had pissed his little brother off. Going back down to the bedroom, Storm took a beer for each of the men and a glass of water for their patient. Entering the doorway, he saw Austin cuddling their woman and instantly he assumed his brother was jealous.

Setting the beers down on the bedside table next to Austin, he sat on the bed and rubbed the bare leg of the woman in his cousin's arms, again having to restrain himself. "What's up?"

Her sobbing, which seemed to break Austin's heart, could still be heard against his rock-hard chest. Turning his head, Austin mouthed, "Talk to Trey."

Anger and frustration consumed Storm as he stood and made his way out to the front yard, his boots pounding on the wooden floor. When he reached his little brother, he grabbed his arm and twirled him around, demanding, "What the hell is going on?"

Trey faced his brother and held up a finger to wait a moment, listening to the person on the other end of the phone. Storm began to seethe with anger and impatience until Trey finally said his good-byes and hung up.

"Again, what the hell is going on?" he practically shouted. Then not waiting for an answer he said, "I go to fix dinner and next thing I know is you are storming through the house and that little woman is crying! Now tell me!"

Trey took a deep breath in what seemed like an attempt to remain calm. Holding the phone in his hand, he said, "She apparently had a flashback. She thinks her name is Lisa and that she's a prostitute."

"That's ridiculous." Storm gave a short laugh then sobered. "Isn't it?"

Showing his brother the phone, Trey spoke quietly. "I sent her picture over to Connor over at the sheriff's station. He's going to see what he can find out. If she is what she says, perhaps we can keep her here so she doesn't get into any trouble with the law. Especially since it looks like she already had a brush with it."

"Oh, she's staying here, little brother. Make no mistake about it. Lisa is going to become our woman, our wife, and we will be the last men she ever fucks again," Storm announced with confidence. "Let me know what Connor finds out. Come back as soon as you can."

Storm left Trey in the cold yard to do what he needed to do to help them find out who their new woman was. Stomping back into the house, he let the screen door slam behind him.

Chapter Four

In the kitchen, Storm threw a tantrum with any object that got in his way—serving spoons, a trivet, even a pitcher that he was going to make tea in. Once he had calmed himself, he pulled the casserole out of the oven and put it on the tray along with paper plates, silverware, and a loaf of sourdough bread with some butter and carried it to the bedroom.

Upon entering, he found Austin lying on the bed with Lisa cuddled up to him, her head lying on his chest, her hand splayed on his hard abs. His cousin was smoothing her hair that sprawled across the pillows while she lay with her eyes closed though still swollen from crying. When she heard him enter she opened her eyes and watched him move toward the bed and set the tray down. Rising slowly to avoid the dizziness, she rose up to her knees and faced Storm.

"I'm sorry that I made you mad," she said softly. "I'm not sure what is going on with me, but Austin said you guys were going to help me."

"We'll do our best, darlin'," he promised as he laid his palm on her cheek. When she moved her face into the gesture, he had to take a deep breath and will himself to be gentle. Leaning down, he let his lips cover hers briefly before pulling away. He didn't want her thinking they wanted her only because of her declaration of who she was.

To occupy himself, he picked up the serving spoon and a paper plate and started to serve up the food that thankfully Martha had had the foresight to cook for them. Buttering a piece of bread and placing it on top of the casserole, he handed it to Lisa, who scooted back up to sit up against the pillows next to Austin, who by that time had sat up. Knowing his cousin could get his own food, but feeling he needed to keep his hands busy, he served him up and then fixed his own plate before going over and sitting in the rocking chair in the corner facing the bed.

The action wasn't missed by either occupant of the bed. When he looked up he saw Austin glaring at him and Lisa watching him curiously.

"I'm not going to bite, you know," she teased. A smart-ass retort didn't pop into his brain quickly enough so with a sigh he went to sit next to her on the bed. He watched her wiggle her ass a bit and settle in between her two rescuers. While they ate, Storm thought it would be a good time to go over some rules with her.

"I know you have questions for us, and there are questions we have for you, but for now, you need to rest and do as you are told. You have a concussion. You are to stay in bed unless one of us is with you. You could pass out or fall down without help. Also, you were shot in the arm and will need to be careful of the wound. You don't have to be afraid of any of us here, or out on the ranch. We will protect you," Storm explained patiently, expecting her to argue.

"Also, you are to let us know as soon as you have any more memories surface," Austin added. "We are trying to figure out who you are and where you came from. Also, someone went to a lot of trouble to get you out here to hurt you, so they most likely are still out there looking for you. You need to stay in the house even after you are well enough to move around. Is that clear?"

He held her attention, looking straight into her iris eyes. At first his words seemed to spook her, but she nodded slowly in understanding. Both men noticed a shiver running through her and wondered what she was thinking about.

Setting their plates on the nightstands, they both moved in closer to comfort her. Austin ran his hand up her back under the sheet of gold that hung from her scalp, stopping at the junction of her neck and shoulder. Storm cupped her chin and moved it around so he could cover her mouth with his. This time, he licked across the seam of her lips, asking for permission to enter, and when she opened to him, he was ecstatic. His tongue slipped through, past her teeth, and slid across hers as a moan sounded in her throat. Breaths became ragged as the desire built within each of them.

Taking her plate from her and placing it on the night stand, Austin kissed the skin of her shoulder where the tee had slipped down and made his way up her neck, nipping along the way. He ended at her ear where he traced the shell of it with his tongue before biting her earlobe, which caused her to jump a bit, but his hand on the back of her neck along with Storm's hand on her chin kept her grounded.

Storm's hand moved down from her chin along her neck and then down to splay across her chest, remaining over the cotton material of the tee as his mouth soon followed. Austin moved up onto his knees and moved his mouth around to capture her lips and thrust his tongue into the depths of hers as if he was afraid she would disappear. Their tongues dueled for dominance but he won as he sucked hers into his mouth.

With his hands on each shoulder he turned her toward him while Storm let his hand slip lower to capture a hardened nipple between his thumb and forefinger. Squeezing it caused her to mewl in Austin's mouth, which led both men to go further. Storm let his mouth cover her breast through the material, and he began to suck upon the hardened pebble, drawing it into his hot, moist mouth as his hand covered her other breast, gently squeezing the round globe. Her back arched, thrusting her chest out to him to use her breasts as he saw fit.

Both men groaned as the air perfumed with her arousal and were spurred on until the fall of boots stopped at the door.

"What the hell is going on here?" Trey exclaimed.

* * * *

Coming to their senses, Storm and Austin pulled away from the equally shocked Lisa as Trey took in the scene. Her lips were swollen with desire, her neck and chest red from the scratch of his brother's mustache, while a wet spot on the tee clung to her wet, erect nipple where Storm's mouth had been. His cock engorged in his jeans, knowing he wanted to be doing what the others had been doing, but he knew at least one of them needed have a clear head and figure out what was going on with their woman.

"Am I the only sane one here? The woman was just attacked and she has a concussion. She's been shot and God only knows what else she's been through and you two are in here taking advantage of her? Doc said she needs to rest. Are you trying to hurt her more?" Trey yelled. "I've been outside trying to get information on her and you always tell me I'm immature! Jesus, guys! Let her rest and recuperate. After that we can see what happens!"

Sitting back against the pillows Lisa shyly looked at each of them slowly, "I'm sorry. I didn't mean to be a distraction to you."

Trey watched as Storm and Austin sheepishly rose from the bed, guilt written all over their faces. Austin licked his lips as if he could still taste her there before he had to readjust his crotch. The man smiled down at the woman, "No. It wasn't your fault. We shouldn't have done that."

When her face flashed her disappointment he continued.

"Not that we didn't want to. We do. We shouldn't have tried anything until you are well enough to move around on your own. Until the Doc gives you a clean bill of health and hopefully you remember who you are."

Storm nodded his agreement though obviously he had been left high and dry after this little predicament. Trey knew there were going to be two cold showers tonight. Both men picked up their plates and left the room, leaving Trey to watch over the beauty.

He made his way over to the nightstand where he picked up a plate and handed it to her. He noticed her hands shook with nervousness. Picking up one of the beers, he made his way over to the rocker and sat down. Popping the top he lifted the bottle to his lips and let the cold liquid make its way down his throat, which was dry after shouting at his brother and cousin and the way the girl in the bed was watching him.

Leaning down to rest his elbows on his knees he thought that this was the first time he had been nervous in front of the opposite sex. Her iris eyes watched his every move, which was unnerving him. Taking another swig of beer for fortitude, he ran his hand down his face in frustration.

"Sweetie, you need to eat. You need to build your strength back up and then rest."

"I'm sorry. I didn't mean to upset you or cause problems with your brothers," she said as she looked down at her plate. Then she looked up shyly. "Jeez, I don't even know your names."

With a look like that, Trey knew there was no way she was a prostitute. She was too innocent-looking for that. It made him happy at that thought. "I'm Trey. My brother is the one with the mustache and he's Storm. Austin is our cousin."

"All of you live here?"

"Yes. Storm and I have lived here all our lives. Austin moved in when our parents died to help run the place. He was actually the one who hauled you up the ravine. He said you were really heavy, too." He smiled mischievously.

"What?" she exclaimed before she realized he was joking. A smile appeared on her face, which Trey was happy to see.

Trey was watching her intently and saw her smile disappear as she began to think to herself. Her teeth worried her lower lip, and he knew what she was thinking after what had happened between herself, Storm, and Austin.

"You are not a prostitute!" he said adamantly. "Something is horribly wrong here and someone has done a number on your head."

Raising her head to face him, a tear slid down her cheek as she asked quietly, "Then why did I like what they did to me? What both of them were doing to me?"

Trey's heart seemed to break at that moment with just one teardrop. A sigh was released from the man, not sure how to start the explanation, but he needed to clean up what his brother had started. Usually it was Trey that started on the ladies, but for some reason, Storm and Austin took matters into their own hands tonight, though it proved that all three of them were of the same mind when it came to the beauty before him.

"Out here we are alone most of the time. We have learned to share our women. They are a little few and far between out here. That way we are all happy and we don't fight over them. We tend to like the same type of women, which really helps.

"We all instantly knew we wanted you when we saw you. It was hell watching you all the way down the mountain hoping you would wake soon. Then when Doc said you had a concussion and said you had been shot, we were all so angry. We wanted—" he said before he corrected himself. "We want to know who did this to you and might likely kill them when we find them."

"I think it all goes beyond just one or two people," she said innocently before her hand went to her head in pain.

Trey stood and stepped to her side quickly. "Are you okay? Did you remember something?"

Shaking her head, she said, "I'm not sure. It seems like my brain is trying to tell me something, but I can't seem to wrap my head around everything."

Sitting next to her, Trey innocently laid his hand on hers, his fingers touching the metal of the handcuff. "It'll all come back to you eventually. It'll just take some time."

Standing, Trey started to leave but Lisa grasped his hand. "Please don't leave me. I promise I'll be good."

"I'll be right back. I need to get something and then I'll come back and stay with you during the night."

He was gone for a few minutes. Returning to the bed, he sat down and took her hand in his, and slipping a key into the lock of the handcuffs, he popped it and the metal teeth let go, letting the device fall to the blanket.

Exhaustion seemed to overtake her as she tried to reach over to the nightstand to place her plate on it but couldn't reach so far from the middle of the bed. Trey took it from her along with the handcuffs and placed them on the bedside table. Standing again, he removed the tray from the table, exited the room, and returned a few moments later after depositing it in the kitchen. Stepping to the nightstand, he turned off the lamp and made his way around to the other side and turned off that lamp also.

Sitting on the bed, he removed his boots and let them fall to the floor with a thud before leaning back against the headboard and taking the petite woman into his arms. Her head was on his chest and her hand splayed across his hard abs as a light mewling emanated from her as she snuggled against him. He heard her soft snores a few moments later as she had fallen asleep, and he tried to move himself down on the bed to get comfortable but was too afraid he would wake her so he opted to be uncomfortable for a while.

Chapter Five

Austin was the first to rise the next morning as it was his custom to make sure his men began working when they were supposed to. It was still dark with just a tinge of gray beginning to paint the eastern horizon. The chill in the air was ignored by him in his T-shirt stretched across his wide chest but was noticeable when he entered the barn and found the twelve men inside wearing their winter coats. Those would be shed as the day went on, but for now they needed the protection from the worst of the seasonal elements. Winter was going to come early this year, his body told him. A great way to keep their little woman warm was in bed with them making sweet, passionate love to her day and night. That warmed him more than any coat could.

Normally he would join in the daily work, but he was anxious to get back to the house to check on their newest addition to the family. After issuing orders he made his way back to the house, put on a pot of coffee, and made his way to the back bedroom, bumping into Storm as he exited his own room. The two stepped over to the door and peaked into the master bedroom and could make out the forms of both Trey and Lisa lying next to each other as the light from the hallway illuminated the darkness. They were spooning, Trey with his back to the woman who had a hand on his hip in a possessive pose.

Stepping back, the two men made their way to the kitchen before Storm let out a breath of irritation. "Damn that little shit!"

"Which one?" Austin asked, sitting at the table.

"Trey, of course. He came in all righteous last night acting like he was our boss and telling us to stop loving on our woman, and then he goes in and sleeps with her?"

Austin had to be the optimist at this point. "Perhaps they just fell asleep talking. I'm sure that he was the perfect gentleman to our guest. He did have a good point, that she did just have a nasty fall and injured her head. I can't imagine the headache she must have."

"Or the pain in her arm where some bastard shot her," Storm seethed. Austin watched Storm rush from the room and returned a few minutes later fully dressed with boots on. Pouring himself a cup of the black brew from the pot that had just finished dripping, he mumbled he'd be back in a little bit and left the house, letting the screen door slam shut in his wake. Austin just watched him go, though he knew something was bothering his cousin.

For the first time in a long time, Austin felt like an outsider. Trey was working with the local sheriff's department to find out Lisa's true identity while Storm seemed to be working on something else about the woman. He was sure it was an oversight that Storm hadn't thought to include him, but it still hurt, just like back in school when he would be chosen last for activities because he was a Native American, though in these parts it wasn't a bad thing to be, now. When high school came along and he joined the football team and drove them to three state championships and three regional championships, he showed them that he was more than an outsider.

Standing, he moved to the coffeepot and poured himself his own cup and sat back at the table. He often wondered if the only reason he worked here was because he was related to the boys but deep down inside he knew it wasn't true. Running his hands through his long, dark hair in frustration, he knew he had to stop self-sabotaging himself.

"Shit!" he exclaimed, thinking he was alone until a noise caught his attention at the doorway of the kitchen.

Looking up he found Lisa leaning against the doorframe watching him. His T-shirt hung down her body, one shoulder on, one off. Her hair was mussed up and her eyes puffy with sleep but to him she was beautiful. Standing, he pulled a chair out for her for her to sit before moving toward the coffeepot. "Coffee?"

"Yes please," she answered with a yawn. "Do you have cream and sugar?"

"Yup."

The tall, muscular man watched her shiver involuntarily as he set the mug down in front of her along with the pint of half and half and the sugar bowl, wondering what she was thinking. Returning to his seat, he took a sip before asking, "Did you sleep well?"

Nodding, she continued to watch him through lowered lashes. "What made you upset?"

The right side of his mouth turned up a bit. "Nothing. I was just thinking about you and this situation. You have all of us doing things we don't normally do."

Raising her eyes to him fully, coloring flushing in her cheeks, she said, "Then perhaps I should leave. I don't want to inconvenience you guys or cause you to fight amongst yourselves."

"That's not what I meant," he said, cupping his hand over hers and feeling the electricity that passed between them. "I just mean that everyone is trying to help you and it just has us doing things we don't usually do. Trey, for one, is usually carefree and he was trying to protect you last night, and Storm is the one who has everything under control, and he lost it last night, as did I."

"And what about you, what are you doing differently now that I am here?"

"I should be out making sure my men are working and not slacking off. Instead, I want to be by your side to protect you and make sure you get well."

Austin felt the shudder this time that traveled through her body moments after her gaze turned wistful. "Are you sure you are all right?"

She nodded. "Yes. I just keep getting little images flashing in my head. I just can't put them all together. It makes my head hurt, too."

Patting her hand, the one that he wanted to have holding his cock soon, Austin spoke breathily. "It'll come in time."

"That's what I said last night," a sleepy Trey said coming into the kitchen. "It was happening last night also."

Feeling a bit sinful at the moment, Austin looked at Lisa with a glimmer in his eyes but asked Trey, "Did you behave yourself last night, pup?"

Trey gasped at the question, probably more from the embarrassment of being called a nickname he hadn't heard in years. Austin and Storm were two years older than him, and when he was little, they started calling him pup since he reminded them of a puppy who would follow them around. The name stuck until a few years ago when he finally stood up to them and threatened them that if they called him that again he would kick their asses.

Looking at Austin, Lisa defended him. "He was a perfect gentleman. He didn't even give me a kiss good night."

Possessiveness seemed to overcome Austin's younger cousin for Trey bent over and let his mouth cover Lisa's gently at first. As the two battled for control of the kiss, Austin watched the heated display lustfully, his cock growing behind the zipper of his jeans. He remembered how lethal her kiss was from the previous night and his body screamed for him to go over and join in, but Trey was a gentleman the night before so he gave them this moment. The sound of boots stopping at the door seemed to break the spell the two were under, and they broke away from each other as Storm entered. Austin watched as guilt seemed to seize both Trey and Lisa. Trey stood quickly and moved over to the kitchen counter and poured himself a cup of coffee. Lisa lowered her eyes and took a long drink of coffee, which he was surprised she didn't spill with how much her hands were shaking at the moment.

Trey returned to the table and sat at Lisa's free side, and Storm, a look of confusion on his face, sat across from Lisa. Austin tried his best to hide his merriment in the whole situation.

Storm looked at Lisa and smiled. Apparently he remembered he was a gentleman and in a ménage, there could be no jealousy. His actions pleased Austin.

"Good morning," Storm greeted her. "How are you feeling?"

"Good. Thank you."

"I want to show you some pictures and I would like to know if you remember being there. Would that be all right?"

Austin saw the tentative moment she took before nodding, knowing anything could trigger her memory, and he was afraid they would lose her. What if she was married or had kids? None of them had thought about that last night, but it had to be done.

* * * *

Reluctantly, Storm slid pictures of the cabin over to the woman. Looking at all three men before looking at the pictures, she knew there could be a two-edged sword effect. If she remembered her life before now, she might be able to control the spiral her life had obviously taken. Yet there was the possibility that it would take her away from these three sexy men who caused liquid to form in her slit by just being in the same room with them. Swallowing hard, she picked up the first picture and examined it.

A brief image flashed through her head when she saw the picture, but something was off about it. The furniture was arranged differently so perhaps it wasn't the same cabin. Shaking her head, she set the picture down and picked up the second picture. The bedroom scene registered as she tried to put scenes together in her mind. Her hands began to shake and a sob escaped her throat and tears welled in her eyes.

Memories of being manacled to the brass bed flashed quickly through her mind as if she was watching an old flipbook she and her friends had made in school when they should have been studying. Remembering the terror that swept through her caused her to drop the picture and stand quickly, turning away from the men.

They all stood and surrounded her, hands on her shoulders, arms, and waist. Trey spoke first. "What did you remember, baby?"

Unconsciously she rubbed her wrist where the handcuff had been, remembering the feel of it. "The bed, it was downstairs. I was handcuffed to it. My arms and my legs were shackled to it. I remember waking up that way."

"Were you alone?" Trey asked quietly.

Nodding, she spoke softly with a sob. "At first I was. I couldn't hear anything. I was blindfolded and gagged. Then there was a man. He was large and he had a gun. He was telling me what he was going to do to me. I was so afraid."

Fear engulfed her as the memory flooded her and she sank to the floor before any of them could catch her. "He said he was going to take me over and over again before he killed me!" she wailed.

* * * *

Austin went to his knees and gathered her up in his arms. She had gone limp with the statement, as if her body couldn't take the impact of the realization. Standing and picking her up, he hugged her close to his chest as his shirt absorbed the tears she was shedding and made his way back to the room they had given her. He knew the others were right behind him.

Laying her down in the bed, he toe-kicked off his boots and laid down beside her and pulled the covers up over them before pulling her into his arms. Her face pushed into his chest as if hiding her shame or fear, he wasn't sure. Looking over at his cousins, his eyes pleaded with them for no more questions at the moment and with a nod, they left the room, closing the door behind them.

"Sshhh, little one," he crooned to her. "You're safe. We won't let anyone hurt you."

Laying a kiss on the top of her head, he felt her body start to relax, though a sob would emerge now and again until she stopped altogether and he knew she had cried herself to sleep. He hoped Storm and Trey were going to follow up on this information soon, but for now he was going to stay with this vulnerable, fragile woman that held his heart captive and had his cock so riled up.

Agony tore through Austin for the next couple of hours as the woman in his arms slept, his body aware of every nuance that emanated from her. From her aroma to her softness against his hard body down to her soft breath fluttering against the cotton shirt he wore. He could hear Storm and Trey moving around in the house and talking softly to each other. He wished he could be in on the conversation, but he needed to be near Lisa to calm any fears she might have upon awakening.

* * * *

Lisa woke, her eyes puffy from crying and her head against a hard, wide chest. Her hand slid down with her movement and brushed against the hard bulge beneath the jeans of the man she half-lay upon. Heat rose in her face as she looked up with guilt into the face of Austin, who was watching her intently. He smiled at her, his eyebrow lifting in curiosity.

Moving his hand up to her chin, he lifted it up and lowered his mouth to hers, peppering her lips with his before she moaned and leaned up to offer her mouth willingly. His mouth covered hers furiously, bruising her lips under his as his tongue pushed its way into her mouth while his hand slid down her throat.

When his hand covered her breast and squeezed, she tried to move up even more, letting her thigh slide over his, her hand still lying on the mound that had grown between his legs. Electricity shot from her breasts down to her pussy, which wept as he continued to squeeze her breast as her breath became ragged. A gasp escaped her but was absorbed by Austin's hot mouth at the feelings surging within her that she had never experienced before.

* * * *

Austin felt the gasp and pulled away slightly, looking into her eyes. Amazement and fear mingled within the iris eyes before her lashes lowered as if shyness overtook her. Though if she was a prostitute, which he didn't believe, then why was she so coy, almost shy about him touching her?

"I'm not going to hurt you, little one," he said, laying kisses on each eyelid. "We are not going to hurt you."

Eyes still lowered, a whisper emerged from her lips. "I know. I'm just afraid of everything else."

Pulling her tighter to him, her breasts flattening against his hard-chiseled chest, he let his lips capture hers again, sucking on her bottom lip. His hand slid down her side, passing through the in-curve of her waist, then over her hip and down to where his T-shirt came to her thigh, letting it slip beneath the cottony material. Slowly his fingers, barely grazing the skin, moved up her thigh, the material bunching up on his forearm as he went. He stopped at her hip, letting her adjust to what was about to happen, and when he didn't feel any resistance, his hand glided inward to the apex of her thighs where it was denuded of hair.

The feel was foreign to him as the woman he had been with in the past kept their pubic hair intact, but he reveled in the silky feel of her skin. Letting his fingers move lower, they slipped into the moist folds of her slit and over the hard nub of her arousal. Her breath hitched and the thrust of her hips into his hand encouraged his ministrations as he ripped his lips from hers. He had to have her naked, to feel her skin against his.

Sitting up and taking her with him, he pulled on the hem of the T-shirt from around her hips up and over her head, freeing her large breasts to his hungry eyes. Tossing it aside, he didn't hear it hit the dresser or the knick-knack as it fell as he pulled his own shirt from his body and let it fall where it may before he lowered his lips again to hers.

Letting his one hand return to her silky nether lips, his fingers slipped into the wet folds along each side of her clit. Lisa's hands grasped his muscular shoulders, one to hold onto him and one to feel him, letting her fingers caress the muscles beneath the silky feel of his smooth skin. Austin moved his lips from hers and trailed his tongue along her cheek moving toward her ear where he licked the shell and felt her shudder with the motion. Capturing the lobe between his teeth, he gently bit down on the soft flesh, enjoying her as she moaned in pleasure. His fingers still teased her clit but not enough to move her into the frenzy that would drive her toward orgasm.

* * * *

Lisa felt the tingling between her pussy lips and she let her legs spread for the man before her, but as she did so, she also felt the bed dip behind her and to her right. Pulling her head away from Austin's, she saw a naked Storm and Trey moving toward her. Anticipation grew within her as did trepidation as she couldn't remember being with multiple men before, but if she was a prostitute, she was certain that would have been in the job description.

They looked magnificent in their naked glory. Their shoulders and chest were sculpted with muscle while the skin was tanned from the sun. She could picture them working out on the range without their shirts on and it sent more moisture to her pussy. Their waists were tapered but only rightfully so with well-defined abs that would set any woman's mouth drooling. She couldn't see an ounce of extra weight on them.

Their hips were lean as their hipbones protruded slightly, melting down in Vs down to what amazed her the most. There, rising from the pubic hair, were their penises, standing up hard, long and thick. Each mushroom-tipped head seemed angry and hot as they were near purple and the long vein that ran up each shaft bulged out, the side veins not as predominant. A pearly drop of pre-cum topped each tip. She couldn't remember if she had seen anything so beautiful before or so big and she swallowed hard as she salivated beyond belief. They seemed to be pointing upward to their beaming faces, which showed their desire for her.

The three men each were fisting their cocks eagerly, though she didn't know what that meant. Below each cock was a heavy sac, each hanging low, between their muscular thighs. Her tongue swept out to lick her lips hungrily. From their thighs, their legs tapered down, and she slowly moved her eyes back up their bodies, stopping again at the core of their desire then upward. Their lips were pursed together as if they were trying to restrain themselves. Their eyes were hooded with pure lust. She gasped.

Storm leaned over and kissed her shoulder, letting his lips nip tenderly at her skin as Trey took a foot and began to kiss and lick his way from her toes on up. Austin returned to her earlobe, his teeth grazing the flesh, a shiver running through her body.

Moving her hand back and up, she moved it to feel Storm's face as he continued to kiss her shoulder and then she moved it into his hair, reveling in the softness there. His own hand moved around and grazed the side of her breast and she gasped. He moved up her neck, licking as he went and then across her cheek, his mustache tickling her skin as he went. Moving her head toward him, she offered her lips to him, which he hungrily covered, devouring the pouty flesh while his tongue thrust inside.

Further down the length of the bed Trey was slowly moving his mouth and tongue up her leg. He was now at her knee, and as he started up her thigh, she instinctively spread her legs wider, giving his head room to maneuver, especially when his palm slid onto the opposite thigh. As he got closer to her slit, she heard a growl emanating from his throat.

Austin cupped the back of her head while Storm gently pushed her chest down so she was reclined upon the bed in a more relaxed position, a position where they could pay homage to her delectable body. Storm's lips still had hers captured while his hand moved down between her breasts before tenderly grasping her left one and rubbing the pebbled nipple between his thumb and forefinger. Her body arched at the sensation and his mouth absorbed her mewling.

Trey had reached the spot where her thigh transformed into her pussy lip. Lisa heard him breathe in deeply, erotic tingles shooting through her body at the thought of him actually smelling her juices. His hot breath was right there as she could feel it fanning her wetness. When she felt his tongue touch her folds then plunge into the dark moist hole she clutched her pussy closed at the invasion, moaning into Storm's conquering mouth.

Austin moved his lips down her throat to her other breast and licked up the slope to the pink, hard tip, teasing it with the end of his tongue before closing his mouth over it and sucking as much as he could into his mouth. Pulling her mouth from under Storm's she cried out at Austin's action, amazed that so much of her breast could fit inside his mouth and what he was doing felt amazing. The tongue in her pussy was out of this world, she thought, until it slowly moved up to the hard nub at the top of her slit and began to lick at it.

Thrusting her hips caused the heel of Austin's hand to press down on her lower abdomen while Trey held her hips down with both hands, his fingers keeping her open to his mouth. Storm rose up while looking down at her. With hooded lids his gaze moved further down her torso. She watched as he lowered his mouth near her nipple and began to lick a path along her skin, which she figured was the dragon for he stopped where her back met the mattress. Ripples of delight ran along the area he had just traced. "I've been wantin' to do that since I saw it, darlin'," he whispered wickedly. "Soon, I'll trace it all the way to the end."

Her breath caught in her throat with that declaration before he retraced the wet path he had made back up to the nipple before catching it between his teeth. Lisa's hand captured both men's heads at her breast, holding them to her as if never to let them go. Her fingers slid into their hair, reveling in the silkiness of Austin's long, silky tresses and the slightly rougher texture of Storm's.

Down below she felt Trey's mouth cover her clit. He began to suck on it as hard as he could while sliding two fingers into her depths. They moved within her and passed a spot that caused her whole pussy to tighten. He must have known he found that spot for he began to move his fingers against it. As they moved faster and faster, she raised her hips and began bucking against his fingers and face as if she was trying to fuck them.

"Oh, fuck!" she hissed at the sensations that were shooting through her body from all the places these men touched, especially from what Trey was doing to her. She felt the tight coil within her groin get tighter and then it seemed to explode within her, shooting out shock waves all through her body. Her cream seemed to shoot from her depths, coating Trey's fingers and leaking out onto his hand. Her luscious body convulsed with each shock wave that rolled through her body. Her scream erupted from deep within her as she rode the waves of orgasm until they began to subside, though her pussy still pulsed around Trey's fingers. Leaving her clit for a moment, he lapped up her cream from his hand as if a cat lapping up milk from its bowl.

"God, you taste wonderful," he said before returning his attention back to her pussy. Again he sucked on her clit while his fingers continued their onslaught on her G-spot, and it was barely a minute before she felt her pussy walls shudder around his digits again. Arching her back off the bed, taking all three men and their mouths with her, she was screaming as her orgasm consumed every cell in her body.

Riding the wave of climax downward, the men pulled away from her, watching the satiated look on her face as her breathing began to slow. Trey let his tongue drag across her skin from her pussy all the way up to her mouth as he captured it with his. She tasted herself on him and moaned at the flavor, treasuring the way he savored her mouth.

Her eyes flew open and found his green ones watching her as she felt the head of his hard cock pushing at the folds between her legs. Running her hands on his chest, she moved them up to his shoulders and around to the nape of his neck and held him tight as if he were going to float away. She felt him spread her legs with his knees and adjusted to his girth as he pushed in once, then twice. She let out a whispered plea against his lips. "Fuck me, please?" Seeming unable to hold back, he thrust hard into her and buried himself deep within her.

Her scream of pain was unexpected to all of them as her hips tried to dislodge him from atop her body, though her pussy clinched him to remain where he was. Trey tried to move away from her, but her arms were thrown around his waist and she held on dearly to him. Raising his upper body from hers, bracing himself on his arms, Lisa watched the emotion in eyes of dread. "Shit! She's definitely not a prostitute!" he exclaimed, not certain what to say.

Chapter Six

Austin and Storm both moved to face her, each questioning Trey in unison, "What was that all about?"

Trey hung his head in shame as she watched him through tear-filled eyes, fearful he would stop since he was upset with her. Shaking his head, still shocked by what he found, he closed his eyes to avoid watching her with his announcement through clinched teeth. "She was a virgin."

Shock rocketed through Lisa at the pained announcement. How could that possibly be? Glancing around at three handsome faces, she found they were equally as stunned, though Trey's expressed pain.

"I am so sorry, sweetheart," he said looking into her eyes, guilt written on his face. "I didn't mean to hurt you."

"I know," she whispered, kissing his chest. "If I had remembered, I would have stopped you, but this is going to be a learning experience for all of us at this point. But for what it's worth, I really do love the way your cock feels in my pussy right now." The last sentence laced with a bit of sass.

Trey sucked in a breath through his teeth though smiled at her declaration. "I don't want to hurt you more."

"You're not hurting me anymore. The pain is gone and I really want you to fuck me, now!" she demanded, biting into his chest.

Smiling, he leaned down and kissed her mouth sweetly before moving up and kissing the end of her pixie nose and then each eyelid. Slowly he began to move inside her, letting her adjust to him. Pushing his upper body back up she locked eyes with his as his thrusts became harder and quicker within her, and with each thrust, he would twist his hip slightly as it came in contact with her clit, adding a jolt to the already aroused nub. Her moans began low within her throat as he began to pound into her pussy. She felt her vaginal walls begin to spasm around Trey's thick cock right before her womb seemed to explode, and she screamed out beneath him, trying to hide her face in his chest as he yelled out from his own orgasm.

Slumping down over her she found he tried not to land fully on her but still managed to cover most of her body with his. She kissed his chest smattered with brown hair, her tongue flicking at his nipple. Hissing, he raised back up. "Woman, you are evil."

A giggle escaped her as she laid her head back down and looked up at him sweetly. "Whatever do you mean?"

Trey kissed her once more before rising from the bed while Austin, who had undressed by this time, took his place at her mouth. Austin captured her lips in his, his tongue slipping between her teeth to caress the insides of her satiny mouth. His hand caressed her breast while Storm positioned himself at her entrance, his hard cock throbbing and hot against her soft folds. The tip rubbed against her clit, sending sharp pulses through her pussy and causing her to squeal in delight before he moved his shaft down and into her. Her hips bucked upward, letting him slip in easily though she was tight. Spreading her open with his size he thrust in and out until he was in as deep as he could go, his full balls flush against her derriere.

Once seated fully within her depths, Storm rolled over so she was laying on top of him, her pussy grabbing at his dick to keep him fully seated inside of her. Placing her hands on his chest, which was as wide and muscular as his brother's, she let her hands and eyes examine him. His skin was lighter even though it was still tanned, and there was blond hair peppering his pecs and abdomen. She could feel it as it made its way down to his groin, circling his cock and balls. Leaning up to a half-sitting position, she felt herself sink further down onto his cock, the root pressing against her clit. Experimenting she ground her clit against him. Groaning, she smiled down at him.

"I'm not hurting you, am I, darlin'?" he asked, concern lacing his voice.

Her fingers tweaked his nipples then watched them harden as hers did when aroused. "No. I'm fine. I feel alive, and at the moment very full."

Austin had risen at her side. She felt his fingertips trace the tattooed dragon from its head at the side of her breast, all the way around until it ended at her ass crack. He began to rub his finger up and down the crevice as he nearly growled near her ear. "You'll be fuller in a minute, little one."

Her breath caught in her throat at the realization of what the large Indian meant, and she clinched her ass cheeks together, which caused her pussy walls to squeeze vise-like on Storm's dick.

"Oh, darlin' that feels wonderful," Storm said huskily. "I know you are still new to this, but relax. Let Austin do his thing and we'll both make you very happy. Besides, I don't want to have this over before it gets started."

Storm grasped both breasts and firmly squeezed while his thumb flicked against the peaked tip of her nipples. Trey had reentered the room after cleaning himself off and Lisa saw him hand Austin a tube. The lid popped on the tube and she felt Austin's hand on her puckered hole along with a cold liquid. Bucking forward briefly at the temperature, Austin's hand on her hip pulled her back, and she felt his finger moving slowly into the hole that she felt was dark and taboo. With Storm's hands showing love to her breasts and Austin's hand on her hip, rubbing in circles, she felt Trey put his hand down and began strumming her clit. Austin had his entire finger buried deep within her anus and began to slow pump in and out of her as if he was fucking her. Finding the act not as unpleasant as she thought, she began to relax her ass muscles and wanted to move back on his digit, but his hand on her hip stopped her. After a minute, he added another finger and stroked her with both digits before stopping and scissoring them inside of her, trying to stretch her out. All the while, Lisa took deep, breaths to calm her anxiety and absorb the pleasurable pain the man was inflicting on her, especially since he had big fingers. After a while the pain turned to exquisite pleasure and finally she was able to move back against his thrusts.

Disappointment washed over her when he pulled his digits out from her, but it was short-lived when she felt more coldness at her entrance as Austin's thick, hard cock met the puckered hole. He began to push in, feeling her clinch against him again.

"Storm!" was all he said before his cousin began tugging her down to his chest by her breasts, a growl erupting from her at the sensation. The cock at her back entrance continued pushing in while Austin's other hand rubbed up and down her spine in a soothing motion, which helped take her mind off some of the pain as did the two hands clutching her breasts. Trey's fingers continued to caress her clit as he bent and let his mouth caress the sensitive spot between her shoulder and neck, letting his teeth nip at her in between the kisses.

"Bear down on me, sweetheart," Austin ordered. "Try to push me out."

Following his instructions, Lisa pushed with her muscles. With what seemed like a pinch she felt the tip of his cock push through the outer ring of muscles. As if he sensed her uneasiness since her breath had become ragged, he held still, letting her become adjusted to the foreign object in her butt.

She figured he must have been in some discomfort for he barked out through clenched teeth, "Trey, you need to stop for a minute, buddy, while I get inside."

A sob escaped Lisa as Trey did as he was told, causing her impending orgasm to subside quickly. Wanting to please these men, she breathed deeply, in and out as she had been taught in yoga. Again, she pushed the image aside and felt the cock push further inside before it stopped, his balls against her perineum.

Austin pulled out slowly, driving Lisa wild as her ass tried to hold onto the hard shaft. When only the tip was left resting in her ass, she whined, thinking he was going to leave her. Instead she heard him growl before she felt droplets of perspiration land on her back.

"Oh, man, you feel so tight, baby! Now we are going to fuck you so hard, you'll never want anyone else to ever touch you again," he swore as he began to piston in and out of her.

Storm let go of Lisa's breasts and she moved her body back up as he began his own rhythm, which was the opposite of his cousin's thrusts. One moved in while the other moved out, each stroke moving up that mountain of sensations that every woman strives for, while Trey began rubbing the nub at the apex of her slit. She felt her pussy weeping around Storm's cock, and she leaned back against Austin's hard chest, letting her arms move backward to capture his neck and pull his head to her shoulder where he placed his mouth upon the soft, pale flesh there and began to suck on it. Trey latched onto her nipple and began to suckle it.

She never knew sex could be this wonderful. The fullness within her consumed her as she wondered where each man ended and where she began. The nerve endings within her pussy and ass were on high alert and these men were stroking every one of them. Chills rippled through her body with each stroke of their cocks and she reveled in the feeling. Her throbbing clit felt swollen and angry with each stroke of Trey's fingers sliding over it, but it felt like heaven. Her womb was heavy but welcoming, needing this onslaught of love and attention. It had been unused for too long. Lisa's core was alive now and she knew she could never go back to having nothing touch her there.

With so many sensations building within her from all over her body she felt like her body was going to splinter and then she felt her pussy throb wildly then shoot electrical pulses outward to all nerve endings in her body. Her head tossed back against Austin as she screamed her release before she felt both men thrust hard within her together and hold themselves there. They each shouted out their own release as they shot stream after stream of hot cum deep within her, filling her with their seed. After a few moments, Lisa and Austin collapsed onto Storm, all energy spent.

Satiated, Lisa basked in the glow for a few moments before she began to gasp for air as Austin had forgotten he was actually lying on her. "Ah, Austin, I can't breathe."

The man reluctantly pulled his deflating cock from her ass and rolled to his side, leaving her backside cold in the morning air, the moisture from their combined perspiration cooling quickly. Shivers ran through her and before she knew it, Trey had plucked her from Storm's body and carried her into the en suite bathroom and set her down on the side of the large spa tub.

Starting the water, he made sure it was warm enough before motioning for her to climb in. It thrilled her that he watched her sink slowly into the liquid, making sure she got in safely. He gathered some towels before joining her. Flipping a switch, the jets within the tub came to life, causing the water to bubble around them.

* * * *

Watching her settle against the back of the tub, Trey hoped the warm water and bubbles would help her relax. Trey sat to her right to make sure her injured arm didn't fall into the water and just watched her serene face, letting his hand run up and down her forearm. He was pleased she had opened up to them so freely but worried that once she regained her memory she would be upset that he had taken her maidenhead. Would she hold it against them for making love to her, especially all three of them? They knew nothing about her and that began to scare him.

Before long, her breathing was steady and he knew she had dozed off from being in such a relaxed state and she continued that way as Storm and Austin came in to join them. He had motioned for them to be quiet before they stepped foot in the tub, which each had nodded in understanding.

Her breasts seemed to float on the water, moving with the bubbles that burst against them, capturing the staring eyes of each man. They were each lost in their own thoughts as they watched their woman sleep and they knew they would need to talk about what happened, not only with her, but with each other.

* * * *

"Lisa, you are going to meet with two men from out of town tonight. They want to take you to dinner, so you need to dress conservatively, decent dress, not too much cleavage showing, high heels, your hair done up nice. Under the dress you are to wear nothing but a garter belt and stockings," the tall man with dark hair instructed her from behind his desk. "The boss wants these guys to be happy, do you understand?"

She sat on the couch wearing denim daisy-dukes and a white blouse unbuttoned to show her ample cleavage tied into a knot under her breasts. One bare foot bounced in the air from her leg that was crossed over the other knee, an ankle bracelet attached to her slim left ankle. Her hair was pulled back in a ponytail while long spiral earrings hung from her ears. Sapphire-blue nail polish painted her finger and toenails.

Nodding her head at the man, she felt nervous around him and she rose from her seat to leave. He was in front of her before she could make it to the door, blocking her body with his. She was eye level with his chest and a shiver of fright shot through her, hoping he didn't know her secret. His hands grabbed her upper arms, "Don't ever walk away from me, Lisa! You are going to start giving me what I want, do you understand me?"

Glaring up at him she tried to pull away from him. He may have been her pimp, but he had no right to demand she give herself to him. Besides, she was filled with repulsion every time she found him watching her.

"You will never get a part of me." She hissed, trying not to show fear or pain. "When the big guy tells me to, then believe me, I will give it very grudgingly!"

The openhanded slap to her cheek was quicker than what she gave him credit for, and at that moment, she thought if she had had her gun, she would have shot him.

Chapter Seven

Her eyes flew open and her body twitched with a start at the memory flash. This one had been the most information her brain had processed since she had awoken in the bed yesterday afternoon. With astonished faces watching her, she felt conspicuous, but safe. She trusted these three men, and after seeing how that one man treated her, she knew she needed to depend on these three even more as they were the only people she knew at the moment.

"Did you remember something?" Austin asked, rubbing her calf soothingly.

Nodding, she breathed deeply before starting. "I was given orders to entertain two clients. The man I took orders from grabbed me and slapped me. I remember wanting my gun to shoot him."

Chuckles came from all three men before Trey looked into her eyes. "And that's all you remembered?"

Nodding, she wrung her hands in frustration. "I'm sorry. I don't want to be a burden to you."

Trey motioned for Austin to take his place. Still rubbing her leg, Austin moved toward her, letting her put her arm around his shoulder along the side of the tub. Trey had moved and was getting out of the tub. As he moved, his muscles bunched in his chiseled ass and thighs, which Lisa found fascinating. She watched the rivulets of water move down his tanned, muscular body as he grabbed a towel and wrapped it around his waist, hiding his firm ass from her view. He exited the room, leaving her sitting between Storm and Austin, who were both rubbing their hands up and down her legs.

"Your skin is so soft, darlin'," Storm whispered into her neck, taking nips with his teeth. She felt the goose bumps rise on her skin at the gesture and his hand moved up to her breast, caressing it gently.

"If you were a virgin, little one, have you ever sucked a man's cock?" Austin looked at her as if he knew the answer.

Shrugging, she let her head drop so they wouldn't see the tears that had welled up in her eyes. She felt so alone between the two hunks next to her who knew who they were and they were strong to boot. They had each other. They had a family.

* * * *

Storm's fingers touched her chin and turned her gaze up to his, gasping at the tears within the most beautifully colored eyes he had ever seen. "Please don't cry. We know you are scared. Hell, we're afraid of what is waiting out there for you. We are here to protect you, to keep you safe."

Austin's heart broke seeing her like this. They should have never made love to her and he had no right to ask if she had even sucked a man before let alone seen a man's dick. Standing up, he started to exit the tub. "Fuck!"

Before he could get his leg fully over the edge, he felt her hand grab his. "Please don't go."

Turning, he looked down at her sad face, embarrassed that his cock was hard, aching for her to hold it, to put her mouth around it. Kneeling before her, still holding her hand, he lifted it to his mouth and kissed the back of it, seeing her shiver at the contact.

"Why are you mad at me? Did I disappoint you in the bedroom? Did I not do it right?" she asked, trepidation filling her.

Shaking his head as he turned her hand over in his so her palm was facing up before he kissed it and then let his tongue slide over the roughness, he said, "No. You did nothing wrong. You were wonderful. I would love to be able to make love to you all day long, but we never should have made love to you. You weren't ready and we don't know enough about you to take you like that. I'm so sorry."

Lisa rose to her knees to be face-to-face with Austin while Storm let his hands rub along her back, nodding his head in agreement with his cousin. She pulled her hand from his and along with her other hand, captured his face in her delicate hands. "Please don't apologize. I am honored that you shared this part of your life with me. I feel safe with you all and know you wouldn't do anything to hurt me deliberately. Be patient with me until we find out who I am, please? Apparently I'm new to all this emotion stuff."

The man's large hands went to hold her at the waist before turning his head to lay a kiss on one of her hands. "I promise. We will protect you and we will honor your wishes with patience."

"Thank you," she said meekly. "I hope I pleased you."

Storm rose onto his knees behind her and pressed himself to her as Austin tilted her chin up to look at him. "You were absolutely wonderful, sweetheart. I hope you will be able to say that we pleased you with our lovemaking and that we didn't hurt you or overwhelm you."

Leaning up, she kissed his lips lightly before turning to do the same to Storm. "You were perfect gentlemen, except for the one part, but that's expected. I hope Trey isn't upset with me."

"No. Actually I hear him on the phone. I'm sure he'll be right back," Storm said kissing her shoulder. "But for now, let's get you cleaned up and get some breakfast in you before you die of starvation. It is our place to make sure you are well provided for."

Austin picked up a washcloth and some soap and began washing her body from her neck on down, being careful of the bandage on her arm. Gently he washed her breasts, paying a little extra attention to the nipple area, one at a time, before gliding the cloth down her stomach, letting it dip into her navel. She giggled and tried to pull back but bumped into Storm, who let out an amused laugh against her neck. Austin proceeded to move down between her legs, cupping her nude mound, pushing the soapy washcloth between the folds there and cleaning their seed from her body.

Motioning for her to stand, Austin soaped the cloth again and as she stood he began to wash her thighs. When he got down to where the water pooled around her knees, he handed the cloth off to Storm, who started from the bottom and washed the back of her thighs, up to her butt, moving in a slow, circular motion across hemispheres and then between her crack. "Sit," he commanded, and as she did, he continued up her back and then around her neck and shoulders.

Picking up the spray nozzle, he started the water so it would activate it and then proceeded to rinse off all the soap from her petite body. When that was done, he wet her hair, set the nozzle aside and then lathered shampoo into her long tresses, taking his time to massage her scalp.

* * * *

Giving herself over to these men to bathe her body felt so relaxing and tantalizing she thought she could get used to this treatment. Perhaps, even if they found out who she was, they would still want her. A thrill rushed through her body at the brief thought. Shaking her head of the thought, she knew she would have to take it one day at a time to see what the future would bring.

Little moans escaped from her as she reveled in the care the two men had given her, and she watched them try to keep their arousals under control. She needed time to rest after the morning they had enjoyed. And they all needed nourishment, so she let Storm rinse her hair of the shampoo, apply the conditioner and then rinse that out also, after which he squeezed as much water as he could from the heavy length. When they finished, Austin stood and grabbed two towels, handing one to his cousin, who had stood to help dry her off.

Each man putting out a hand, they helped her to stand and then to step out of the tub onto the plush cream-colored mat in front of it. Storm began to squeeze the towel around her hair, letting the cotton material absorb the remaining water, while Austin dried her body. When they finished, they led her out into the bedroom, and Austin led her to the antique vanity with the triple mirrors on it and sat her on the small bench in front of it. Gently he began to comb her wet hair, starting at the bottom first so there were no snarls to cause her pain.

Never before could she imagine a man so tall and muscular could be so gentle when combing a woman's hair. Her first thought had been she couldn't remember a man doing that at all for her, but then she swallowed that thought quickly as she couldn't remember much of anything. She giggled involuntarily at that, and when the comb stopped briefly, she glanced at Austin in the mirror and lowered her lashes in shyness.

She noticed his hardened cock bob quickly at the glance and tried not to stare at it while he attended to her, though it was hard not to. Did she really have that much power over his body? She could never imagine that.

"I know we said we needed to get breakfast," Austin said huskily. "If you want to try anything, you're welcome to it. Or if you have any questions…"

Her eyes flew open to meet dark-brown ones in the mirror, Austin's gaze smoldering as he held the comb in midair. They moved down to the now-hard cock that seemed to point straight up to his navel. His balls hung low with the weight of them, and she found it fascinating that while Storm had hair down to his pelvic region, Austin did not. His chest was smooth also. Interesting, she thought as she tried to remember Trey's body.

Turning on the bench, she came face-to-face with the thick length of the dark cock that beckoned her. The tip was purple and a bead of cream topped it. Licking her lips, she leaned forward and licked up the side of it, letting her tongue stop just short of the tip. He groaned.

Putting her hands out, she moved them to his thighs and pulled him toward her so she could capture it in her mouth without moving. Leaning her forehead against his washboard abs, she moved her mouth down to let the tip slip in her sweet cavern without letting it touch her lips just yet.

Her hot breath covered his cock before her lips did, and actually, her lips didn't surround him until the tip tapped the roof of her mouth and then they gently folded inward. Tasting his pre-cum on her tongue, Lisa moaned before sliding her lips further down his shaft, until her nose touched the junction between cock and groin. Austin's hand wove into her hair on the back of her head and pulled her back slightly.

"Easy, little one, take it easy. I know this is all new to you so just take your time."

Her lips came to just under the lip of the mushroom-shaped head where her tongue swept over the tip again, savoring in the taste of this man she trusted with all her heart. Sliding back down, she began to fuck his cock with her hot mouth, mewling in her throat at her newfound talent.

* * * *

Austin's eyes met Storm's fascinated ones in the mirror as his cousin sat on the bed watching their woman enjoy sucking cock for the first time. She was enthusiastic with her ministrations, putting her all into it. Austin felt as if he were in heaven as he let his eyes close in the eroticism of it all, letting his head fall back while his other hand threaded through her long wet hair, holding her head still. His hips began to piston against her face as he lost himself in the moment, moving in and out of her hot moist cavern of sin. He felt Lisa's hands move to his ass and dig her nails into the flesh. A growl emanated from him as his thrusts gained speed, feeling his balls tighten and begin to move up toward his spine. Boiling man-juice shot from his balls as he held himself against her, his cock at the back of her throat. He felt as if his dick exploded down her throat, the stream seemingly never-ending.

When he was spent and he began to deflate in her mouth after she cleaned him with her tongue, he pulled out of her mouth, stumbled backward to sit on the edge of the bed. Looking down at her sitting shyly on the bench in front of the vanity, licking her swollen lips, he smiled. "God, you are wonderful!"

A blush stole up her neck and face as she turned to look back at the mirror. She went to pick up the brush, but her shaking hand stopped right above the object. Staring at her reflection in the mirror her face went from one of well fucked to one of fear within a second's time.

A heart-wrenching sob ripped from her throat and her body began to shake uncontrollably. Storm was up and off the bed in a heartbeat and kneeling beside her, his hands pulling her into his.

"Baby, what happened?" Storm asked, concern lacing his baritone voice.

Austin had seen the change also and put his hands on both of her shoulders, watching her face in the reflective surface. Tears squeezed from her closed eyes and trickled down her cheeks and he began to worry.

"Lisa, look at me," Austin ordered. When she didn't respond, his hands gripped her shoulders tighter and in his strictest Dom voice he said, "Damn it, Lisa! Look. At. Me."

Her iris-colored eyes flew open and connected with his in the mirror. They were glistening with her tears but the fear he saw there was overwhelming.

Austin stood and knelt down beside her and was pleased that she followed his gaze in the mirror until he was in front of her and then she looked directly at him, though fearful. It killed him that she had to experience the flashes of memory and that they hurt her, but if they were going to help her, she was going to need to be totally open with them and let them help her with her past, no matter where it led them. Moving his hand up, he laid it gently on her cheek, caressing her with his thumb, captivating her total attention.

"You are never to ignore any of us when we speak to you," he said with authority. "We need you to share your feelings, your thoughts and your wishes with us so we know how to help you, now and in the future. It is for your own well-being and for ours. Do you understand?"

She nodded and swallowed a sob. "Yes, sir."

"Now, darlin', what did you remember?" Storm asked, drawing her attention to him.

"Trey must have been mistaken about me not being a prostitute," she said, sadness filling her voice as she lowered her eyes and bit into her lower lip in frustration.

"Why do you say that? He would know if you had ever had sex before. A woman's body doesn't lie about that," Austin said.

Lifting eyes to look back at Austin, she sighed. "I was thinking about how you have all taken me in ways that I didn't let other men take me and my pimp was always trying to force himself on me. He thought because I worked for him, that he could take what he wanted from me."

The three cousins being as close with each other as they were they were able to read each other pretty well. Austin watched as Storm was perplexed over the woman before them. He knew he was certain Trey hadn't made a mistake, but to Lisa, the images within her mind's eye seemed very real. Something just wasn't right.

"This is the second time you have had a flashback of a pimp. Is it you could be mistaken about what kind of work you did for him?" Storm asked.

Sobbing, she tried to pull her hands from Storm's but not succeeding. "I just don't know. Everything is coming back in little bits and pieces and it's hard to try to put everything together, but I remember being in his office and him telling me that I had to entertain two men and that I had to make them happy. Then he tried to push himself on me before I could leave. I'm just so confused!"

Austin watched as Storm lifted her hands to his lips, kissing each of them. "This is confusing for all of us, sweetheart, but we'll get through this and find out the truth. I promise."

Austin wiped the tears from her cheeks before leaning forward and kissing her gently on the lips. "I agree with Storm, but for now, we need to get you dressed and fed. You need your strength and after this morning, I need some sustenance. You zapped my strength with your body and mouth."

A giggle emerged from the lips that minutes ago were wrapped around his cock, and it warmed Austin's heart to hear it. It sounded nice to hear her happy after what had transpired in the past couple of days, and he hoped he would hear more of it in the future. He hated that she looked confused and sad and that she was uncertain about anything in her life. He vowed that he and his cousins would do everything they could to help her find out who she really was.

Content to watch now that his desires had been quenched, at least for the time being, Austin watched as Storm helped her stand then took her in his arms before his head lowered to hers, capturing her lips beneath his. His hands moved down her back to her ass, caressed the rounded globes and then pulled away, nibbling her full bottom lip before releasing her. "Let's get dressed."

* * * *

As if anticipating their impending need of clothes, Trey entered holding some clothes that upon seeing caused Austin and Storm to groan before breaking into big smiles. The latter men chuckled before leaving the room, leaving the door open. Trey, who had dressed while he was out of the room, handed the clothes to Lisa, who held them up to her body, one item at a time. The pants were too long and big for her body, but the sweater would at least fit as more of dress than top. If she had a belt, she could gather the material at her waist so it didn't look so much like a sack on her petite body. Trey watched as her mind worked itself around the clothing situation. He wished they hadn't given all their parents' clothes to charity. His mother had been petite. Perhaps a few inches taller than Lisa, but her clothes would have fit. Now as it was, there was nothing left of clothing or personal effects, but it had taken some time. They had been gone a long time and there was no sense keeping any of it around. With a snap of his fingers, he had a thought and left the room quickly and returned as quick with a long black jewelry box.

"Try this," he said, opening the box.

Confusion lit up her features as she looked at the box Trey held, but once she saw the content, a long chain necklace lying against the black velvet, she must have understood. Her eyes twinkled as she lifted the thirty-six-inch gold chain from its resting place, unhooked the clasp, and then wrapped it around the waist of the sweater, letting the unused portion dangle down. Turning to look up at him, Trey saw the hesitant smile. "There is just one thing missing."

"What's that, sweetheart?"

Almost too shy to say to a man, she whispered as if someone else would hear her. "Panties."

Smiling, he moved his hand up to caress her cheek, saying, "I'm sorry for that, but as you can tell, our housekeeper is a bit bigger than you and her panties would just fall off of you, so for now, no panties. We'll go shopping later this afternoon after our chores are done and get you some new clothes, though, you are welcome to prance around here naked all day if you wish."

A blush bloomed on her cheeks with the last sentence. Trey watched the way her eyes twinkled at whatever her passing thought was and a sly smile appear on her lips. Damn she was sexy! Especially knowing she didn't have anything on under the sweater and that they were going to take her shopping like that really had his cock twitching in his jeans.

Taking her by the hand he led her down the hall to the kitchen where he had already made breakfast. While he used his Bluetooth device, he was able to multi-task, prepare the meal, and still write down notes. Bacon, eggs, hash browns, and toast were piled high on plates and set on the table. Escorting her to a chair, he poured coffee into mugs at all four place settings and set the pot on the table so everyone could serve themselves seconds if needed. Storm and Austin came in a few moments later, both of them eyeing Lisa's outfit.

"Well, look at you, darlin'," Storm complimented, kissing the top of her head before moving around to the chair in front of the window. "You look very lovely this morning."

Austin also kissed the top of her head but let his hand brush down a short length in her hair before taking his seat. "Yes, you do, but since you fill out our housekeeper's clothes better than she does, we may have to fire her and hire you on in her place."

The blush appeared again so she busied herself with taking a piece of toast from the plate. "Oh, no thanks. I'll keep my job any day. It's rewarding and I don't think it is as stressful as taking care of you three men."

As she buttered her slice of bread, it took her a moment to register the silence, and she looked up to find all three men watching her guardedly. "What? I enjoy my job."

Austin's hand came to rest on her forearm. "And what job is that, Lisa?"

Chapter Eight

"My job at the…" The thought was right there, but she couldn't quite remember. They all knew she didn't mean as a hooker, but that's what her memories all led to, though there was something missing.

Tears filled her eyes as she tried so hard to finish her sentence but wasn't able to. Releasing a sigh, Trey retrieved the notepad from the island top and set it down on the table.

He seemed to be nervous as he looked at his notes.

"Does the name Dwyer mean anything to you?"

Thinking, she shook her head negatively.

"All right," he said. "How about the name Preston McMillian?"

Again, she shook her head.

"I am a deputy with the local sheriff's department. I've been on the phone trying to get a name on you or something since we brought you in yesterday. We've been working on towns within the area or at least the state, or possibly even a tourist, but there wasn't anything."

Storm and Austin served up the food while Trey was explaining.

"When you had the flashback in the tub about your pimp, I called in some favors from the State Police. You have been identified as Lisa Dwyer. You live in Denver and work for a man named Preston McMillan. I don't know what is going on with this information, but it does indicate you are a prostitute, which I know for a fact you are not."

Standing, she turned her back on the trio and made her feet take a couple of steps, her feet feeling as heavy as her heart felt at the moment. She didn't remember any of this, but Trey had the proof, which was her record. After Trey's exclamation of her being a virgin, she had hoped against hope that her memory had been playing tricks on her, but she knew now it wasn't. Her head began to try to process this news, and what was she going to do now?

"Denver? How did I get up here? You have proof that I work for this guy? What do I do now? Do I go back there?"

She stopped babbling when all three answered in unison to the last question, "No!"

Turning, tears still in her eyes, though it warmed her heart to know they didn't want her to go back to her old life, she said, "I can't stay here."

Stepping up to her, Trey put his arm around her shoulders and guided her back to her chair. He didn't force her to sit but let his hand gently guide her back to her seat where he insisted she sit, which her body accepted. Kneeling next to her, he took her hand in his free hand. "I have already told you that I will get to the bottom of this. You are not who you think you are or what the files say. I feel it in my heart and in my gut. You will stay here with us for however long it takes to figure things out."

"Trey's right, little one," Austin began, placing his hand back on her forearm. "We already promised to protect you and that we will do no matter what. Even if you were a prostitute before, which I know for a fact you weren't, you are not going back to that life. It isn't safe for you."

"Hell," Storm put in, "if we have to change your name we will. If you'll let us, we will keep you on here on the ranch, and you don't have to deal with the outside world at all."

Surprise lit her face. "You mean I would stay here like a fugitive?"

All three men laughed as if they thought she had watched too many westerns and dramas. Trey stood, accepting a plate of food that Austin had filled, and placed it in front of her. "No. You would not be a fugitive. As far as we can tell, you are not on the lamb from the law but from someone else who wants to hurt you."

"Like I said, you are welcome to stay here as long as you want," Storm said with a grin. "You make us all very happy and we don't mind having you around."

Trying to hide her smile by taking a bite of bacon, she said, "What about your housekeeper? I'm sure she would be shocked to find out you are harboring a hooker in your home."

"I want to ask you one question before we put this subject to rest," Austin said, going serious. When she nodded, he continued, "Do you feel like a prostitute?"

Thinking about the question and what she had experienced when Trey made love to her earlier, she shook her head.

"Then, I want you to stop referring to yourself as one. We have gone beyond being friends and protectors here. We are claiming you as our woman and we are not going to let anything happen to you. Do you understand me?" Austin spoke with authority.

His tone frightened her as well as sent a thrill to her pussy. She couldn't let them get hurt if someone was trying to hurt her but she didn't want to leave them either. For the first time in a long time she felt she belonged somewhere, though she didn't know why. Also, she didn't understand why she responded to Austin's forcefulness since it seemed to thrill her to give up control to him and his words seemed to go straight to her pussy and her nipples, causing them to pebble. Even now, she shifted in her chair to help relieve the throbbing between the folds between her legs.

Nodding, though keeping her head down and looking at her plate, she said, "Yes. I understand."

"When I ask you a question, Lisa, you are to look at me when you answer. Communication is important in any relationship, and we need to be able to read your eyes, not just hear the words come from your lips."

Looking directly at the darker man, she took in a deep breath, "Yes, sir."

Austin leaned over, captured her chin with his hand, and lowered his mouth to hers. The kiss was gentle, not what she had expected from him, which surprised her. After a few pecks, he pulled away, let go of her, and picked up his fork. "Let's eat. We have things to do today."

They all dug in. Lisa was surprised at how hungry she was after she helped herself to another helping of eggs and hash browns. After they finished, she and Trey cleaned up the kitchen and he pulled the casserole out of the freezer for supper later that night.

* * * *

Pushing clothes aside on a clothing rack in a super store in Kalispell, all three men looked for items that their woman would look good in. Jeans, skirts, tank tops, and blouses filled the shopping cart. When they found something they liked, they just threw it in. They didn't even ask if she liked it. Trey picked out bras and panties for her, proud of his selections of lingerie. They let her go to the shoe section and pick out what she wanted. Boots were the order of the day for living on the ranch. Two different pairs of cowboy boots, one in black and one in pink and white, were chosen while leather booties in black were added to the collection. Sneakers were also chosen so she would have something to wear in the house.

When she insisted that there were too many items in the cart, Storm told her not to worry about it and to just let them spoil her. She giggled and gave in, knowing that it was a losing battle to argue with them. The lack of nightwear concerned her but Austin made her blush when he told her that she wasn't to wear anything to bed.

Sundries were the next on the list as she would need her own shampoo and conditioner for moisturizing and frizz-control, along with body soap and lotions. Hair accessories were added to the basket that was so piled up she feared they would need to get a second one. She wasn't sure when her monthly would arrive so she picked up some items for that to be prepared.

Making their way over to the grocery section they picked up food items that would be needed since there was another mouth to feed. Snacks were selected and she insisted they get plenty of ice cream as that was her downfall at night while she was relaxing. Wine and beer was added to the bottom of the cart so they didn't have to come back here for a while.

Heading toward the checkout stand, Austin accidently ran into a shopping cart that emerged from a side aisle. The tall woman pushing the basket stopped abruptly as she was the one at fault but wouldn't admit it. "Watch it, you fucking moron!"

Recognition struck her features, moving from angry to flirty and coy in a heartbeat. "Well, if it isn't the Goodall boys, and Austin! What are you all doing here?"

Observant, Lisa watched the men's expressions transform from happy to irritable as quickly as the woman's attitude changed. They each looked at each other as if questioning one another silently on who was going to answer her.

Austin spoke up. "Hello, Angela. We're here shopping for our new girlfriend, Lisa. She needed a few things."

Lisa had noticed that Austin had spoken with a bit of distain, as if he didn't really like the woman. The change in attitude from the other two wasn't missed on her either. Instantly she knew there was a history with this woman, and she wondered why they weren't with her now. Tall and fit with fiery red hair that lay in curls to right below her shoulders, she was someone men took a second glance at. She had green eyes with specks of gold beneath long red eyelashes while her mouth was a magnificent red bow, the kind that offers a man a full-mouth kiss along with other hidden talents. She wore blue jeans along with a red tank top that showed off her arms and shoulders covered with freckles. Red cowboy boots adorned her feet, though Lisa thought it was a bit too much red color on the woman.

* * * *

Angela looked Lisa up and down, which wasn't a big stretch given her stature. Jealousy and hatred burned through the woman. How was this little tart going to fulfill the demands of all three of these men? She looked like she was too high maintenance for them from the way the shopping cart was piled up. Also, where had they found her? The outfit she wore looked like it was a reject from the eighties.

Through the awkwardness, she remembered the conversation her brother Connor, who was the sheriff, was having earlier with someone on the phone. He must have been talking to Trey about this woman. Triumph twinkled in Angela's eyes when she realized this petite woman with her men was a hooker. "So this is the little hooker from the big city," she purred evilly. "How is she in bed? Is she better than me?"

* * * *

Glares and growls emanated from all three men with the statement while a gasp escaped Lisa's lips at the hateful woman's statement. Embarrassment engulfed her fully as redness flooded her facial features. Tears stung her eyes as her feet began to move. The entrance to the store was blurred within her vision as she ran toward it. She had to dodge several carts and multiple people before she finally reached her destination, and once there, she searched out the black dual-cab pickup they had arrived in. Cursing when she found the doors locked, she climbed into the bed and lay down on a blanket in the back that had been placed there for whatever reason.

Hidden from people in the parking lot, she cried quietly, hating that someone else knew the truth about her, and not just anyone, but a spiteful woman that apparently had slept with the men in the past. How was she supposed to look the trio in the eye again, knowing that other people now knew they were sleeping with a prostitute? Leaving was her best option. She wouldn't subject them to the rumors and backstabbing that was inevitably going to surround them.

After a while a man's voice near the truck interrupted her pity party. It was authoritative and for some reason familiar. Leaning up a bit, she peered over the side of the tailgate and saw a tall man, a bit taller than her three, with long dark hair pulled back and tied in a leather piece. His back was to her so she didn't recognize him but was intrigued on why he was so familiar. As people approached him walking to and from their vehicles, he held out a picture and inquired if they had seen the woman in the photo. Everyone who looked shook their heads and some even went as far as ignoring him or avoiding him altogether. She could tell he was extremely irritated when this happened. His shoulders tensed and his stance caused him to look like he was going to pounce on them. Evil emanated from his body and she ducked back down, knowing deep inside she couldn't be seen by him but didn't know why.

Holding back her sobs, she lay quietly until she heard the three men approach the truck. The man had approached them. "Excuse me. Have any of you seen this woman?"

* * * *

Austin took the picture from the man, glanced at it, and held himself in check to avoid giving away his feelings. He handed the picture off to Storm, who responded the same way before passing it onto Trey, who spoke for the three of them, his lazy drawl tense. "Nope, can't say that we have. I'm sure we would have remembered seeing a woman like that. Why are you looking for her?"

"She is my niece and was kidnapped a few days ago by her boyfriend. We think he was trying to take her north of the border."

"Sorry pal," Storm said, unfeeling at the bold-faced lie. "We haven't seen her."

Pushing the cart full of plastic bags to the truck, Austin turned. "Why don't you give us your number in case we see her so we can give you a call? I can't stand it when men take advantage of a helpless woman."

Austin's tone was flat and tinged with anger even though he tried to control it. He wanted to take this man down right there in the parking lot but knew that to protect Lisa they had to do this right. He accepted the business card from the man tersely, shoving it in the front pocket of his jeans before grabbing bags and quickly placing them in the truck bed. The slight movement at the tailgate caught his attention and he saw his woman lying there terrified.

"By the way, what is her name?" he asked as he continued to put bags in the bed.

"Lisa," the man answered without hesitation.

"And yours?" Trey asked guardedly.

"Philip. Philip McKnight."

Lisa had to cover her mouth with her hand to keep from crying out. The name was familiar but she didn't know why, but she knew it wasn't a good name to remember. God, she hated that she couldn't remember things!

* * * *

When Austin had all the bags in the truck, he turned to the man, trying to hide the hatred in his brown eyes that had turned nearly black. "We'll be in touch if we see her. I hope you find her soon."

The man stepped away from the truck, heading toward some more patrons of the store that were walking to their car, asking them the same questions he had asked the men. As the trio moved toward the cab of the truck, Storm and Trey both glanced in the back and saw their woman half covered in plastic bags. Nonchalantly they piled into the cab, Storm in the driver's seat while Trey was in the passenger seat and Austin sat in the back seat. Starting the engine, Storm pulled forward since there wasn't a car parked in the space in front of them and drove to the opposite end of the parking lot. There, Austin got out and helped their petite bundle from the truck bed and into the seat beside him.

Cuddling up to the large man's side, Lisa hid her face against his chest, as if ashamed that she had let Angela get to her. "I'm so sorry about that."

"You were not the one in the wrong, she was," Austin said, tilting her chin up to look him in the eyes. "Angela is a self-centered bitch who felt scorned because we no longer wanted her."

Surprise lit her face at Austin's statement as thoughts seemed to swirl in her brain. Then another emotion crossed her face as if she was uncertain of something.

Austin saw the emotions sweep through her as her facial expressions morphed from one to another. He knew there was going to be an issue with the way things went down at the store and he intended to stop it before it ever got started.

"Look at me!" he ordered. She hesitated. His hand reached out and slapped the side of her hip since that was all he could come in contact with. Her head shot up. "Angela is nothing to us. She is the sister of Trey's boss and thought she could charm her way into our lives. She wanted us so she started coming around and flirting. We are men and weak when it comes to women, so we took her. It lasted for about a month and then we found out she was also sleeping with some other men. We dumped her immediately.

"She thought we were going to marry her even after what we found out, so she is bitter. That part of our life is over. We want no one but you, and we want you in our lives for the rest of our lives. You will not be pushed aside once we find out who you are. It doesn't matter what you've done in the past. If you are a criminal and the law is after you, we'll stand by you no matter what. Even if we have to set up conjugal visits, we will be there for you. Is that clear?"

Austin saw a quick flash of fear in her eyes before it was replaced with a twinkle as she answered, "Yes."

Surprise filled him when she pressed her lips to his as her hand splayed across his chest. Grabbing both her arms he squeezed and she cried out, as he had forgotten about her gunshot wound. He quickly let go and caught her up in his arms, careful of the hidden injury. "Jeez, little one. I am so sorry. I didn't mean to hurt you."

Tears filled her eyes and her bottom lip was between her teeth as she was trying to breathe through the pain. Laying her head on his chest he relished the gesture as if she were a small child looking for comfort. His heartbeat was pounding against the inside of his walls as if trying to escape, as he internally chastised himself for hurting her. A sigh escaped her as he kissed the top of her head before glancing down and seeing the blood spreading across her sweater sleeve.

"Damn it!" he swore, more to himself, but Trey looked back at him as Storm tried to see what was going on through the rearview mirror. Austin chided himself as he realized she had passed out from the gripping pain he had caused her, especially right after the lecture about them protecting her and taking care of her.

Trey instantly removed his shirt, shuffled around in the front seat to face backward, and proceeded to wrap the material around her delicate arm. Austin gently pulled her fully into his lap, cradling her against his chest. He ran his hand soothingly up and down her thigh and that's when he found out she was sans panties. Hearing Trey's chuckle, he knew that his cousin was aware of what she wore, or didn't wear, which he should have realized he knew since he was the one who'd dressed her. His cock throbbed with need at the thought of her walking around the store the way she did. He would have loved to been there helping her try on her shoes.

Feeling wretched for even thinking those fanciful thoughts after hurting her, he tried to calm his libido down some, though resting his hand on her bare hip while she slept felt right. They should have mandated that she didn't wear underwear while around the house.

Damn! Why was he thinking like this? He knew that he had fallen in love with the small bundle in his arms, and he knew hell or high water wasn't going to keep him from her. He heard Trey on the phone arranging for Doc to be at the house when they arrived but his voice sounded so far away. Focusing on his love, he buried his face into her neck to keep his cousins from seeing the tears in his eyes.

Chapter Nine

Storm had seen the action in the rearview mirror and his heart broke for Austin. They all knew he hadn't meant to hurt her and he was certain that Lisa would understand, but since he was a child he had hated to hurt anything. It was one of his strong suits, especially after he had accidently killed a puppy he found. He had been so ecstatic about the little bundle he found in the woods, and as he was trying to race home to show his parents, he had taken a tumble and had landed on the little fellow. Perhaps that was why he was so taken with taking care of Lisa. She probably reminded him of that puppy— small, fragile, and alone.

"Doc will be waiting when we get home. He was upset that we took her on an outing so soon, so expect a lecture when we get there," Trey said, sounding stressed and deflated. They had had such a wonderful morning that they all had forgotten about her injuries and that she had a concussion. Yeah, there would be hell to pay for this. They'd be lucky if Doc didn't take her to the hospital and keep her there until she was fully recovered.

By the time they arrived back at the house an hour later the bleeding had curtailed and the little bundle had woken. Austin wouldn't let go of her, his hand still resting on her naked bottom beneath the sweater. Her hand had moved down to his rock-hard stomach while she just watched his face, trying to reassure him that it was all an accident and she was all right.

Déjà vu came back after the truck pulled up in front of the house, and Austin carried their little woman into the house and into the master bedroom, laying her on the bed. The doctor was already there, sitting in the living room watching a sporting event on the television as he waited for them. One of the ranch hands felt the man didn't need to wait outside like he had the last time. When they had arrived, he followed the trio into the bedroom, placed his bag on the bed, and waited for Trey to remove his own shirt that helped absorb the blood. Taking his pocket knife from his pocket, he cut away the sleeve of the sweater so Doc had access to view the damage.

After introductions were conducted since she had been unconscious the first time he attended her, the older man examined the wound after he cleaned the area. Apparently when the flesh had been squeezed, one of the wounds had split open. When Doc removed a syringe from its packaging and drew medication from a small vial, Lisa became agitated.

* * * *

Waking in a stupor, she looked around trying to get her bearings. Leather upholstery rose up to her right with piping that reminded her of the back of a car seat. Looking downward along the length of her body, she saw her hands were handcuffed and her legs tied at the thighs and at the ankles. The handcuffs were tied to the rope around her thighs, and then looking further down, she saw the window in the door. Yes, she was in a car. Panic rose within her as she saw the scenery beyond the glass of tall trees and blue sky scattered with white puffy clouds. They weren't moving at the time, which frightened her even more.

The door behind her opened quickly and a man's face came into view. Trying to twist around to get a better look at him, he lowered his head to hers. His lips covered her in a carnal, wicked way, though it wasn't a loving kiss. She tried to pull away from him but was too weak to move. Rising up he laughed roughly as he clutched one of her breasts in his hand, squeezing until she cried out. Bile rose in her throat and she tried to swallow it down, wanting to be strong and not show too much fear. When he pulled his hand away, he forced her head to the side but before she faced the back of the seat she had seen the syringe. Kicking out with her legs, she tried to scream but he placed his hand over her mouth before plunging the hypodermic into her neck and then pushed the plunger down until all the liquid it contained was now rushing through her bloodstream.

Tears rolled down her temples and to her ears as she felt the effects of the drug. As she glanced at the window at her feet, the trees began to waver as did the clouds in the sky before the darkness that had started on the outer reaches of her vision quickly began to overtake all of her sight. Everything went dark and the last thing she heard was his dark, harsh voice. "I will take that body over and over again until I have tired of it. Then I will kill you."

* * * *

Whimpers began as did the tears at the memory. In a crab-like motion, she began to crawl back on the bed until she hit the headboard then panic slammed into her like a freight train. Turning her head from side to side she looked for an opening to escape the needle that had been coming at her, but a man was standing on each side of the bed. Her knees pulled up to her chest and her arms instinctively wrapped around them, as if shielding her body from the impending danger.

Lisa watched as the doctor pulled back with the syringe. He must have been concerned about her abrupt panicked state. Austin and Trey each climbed onto the bed, one on each side, facing her. Storm was beside the doctor, concern written on his face. He began caressing her leg as if he was trying to soothe her, but it didn't matter. She couldn't seem to get her body to stop shaking or the tears to cease as she sank further into her manic state.

"Would someone like to tell me what's going on? Why is she so terrified?" Doctor Anderson ordered.

With a heavy sigh, Storm turned to the older man. "She doesn't remember who she is. She doesn't remember what happened to her. Every once in a while, a memory flash hits her but this is the most terrified she has looked after having one. I'm assuming the memory must have been too much for her."

Doc looked at each of the men one by one and then let his kind eyes land on Lisa. "Why wasn't I told this?"

"She didn't wake until last night and by then we were dealing with her getting used to us. This morning we made sure she bathed and then since she didn't have any clothes, we took her shopping. The day kinda just got away from us and then this happened," Storm explained nervously.

Through her tear-filled vision, Lisa could see the doctor thinking for a moment before he spoke. "Can you leave us alone, boys? I would like to deal with Lisa alone for a few minutes."

Somberly, Austin and Trey rose from the bed and exited the room with Storm trailing behind them. Lisa watched as they slunk from the room as if children in trouble, but trepidation filled her as the doctor watched her. He replaced the cap on the end of the hypodermic needle and placed it on the nightstand, her eyes ever watchful of his actions.

"Now, little lady," he started, looking around the room and spotting the rocking chair. Moving it to the side of the bed he sat, thinking it would be best to sit there instead of the bed since she seemed to be wary of him. "Are those boys taking good care of you?"

Tears still shimmering in her eyes, she looked at his hands, afraid to look at his face. His hands were folded in his lap. In answer to his question, her head nodded.

"Good. They are good boys. Sometimes a little rambunctious but they are good boys for the most part. I'm sure they are paying a lot of attention to you?" He chuckled and went on, as it was a rhetorical question. "Storm said you can't remember very much. The memories you are having, does your head hurt when they come to you?"

She let her eyes move up to his kind gray eyes under the salt and pepper eyebrows. How did he know about her head hurting? He smiled at her. He reminded her of her grandfather. As a child on warm days he would take her to the beach at the edge of the city and they would play in the water and have a picnic with her mother and grandmother.

A sharp pain shot through her head. This was the first time she had thought back that far. Before the memories were more current so this was probably a good thing that was happening to her though the pain wasn't.

"Another flash of memory?" Doc asked, leaning forward after seeing the crease between her eyebrows.

"Yes." She swallowed hard. "You remind me of my grandfather."

Smiling, the older gentleman rose to his feet. "A lot of people tell me that. Unfortunately, I don't have grandchildren. My daughter is a little younger than you. She's in college in Chicago right now. She was a blessing to me and my late wife since she was so long in coming to us."

A release on her emotions let her legs slide down to rest straight out in front of her and her hands rested in her lap. "I'm sorry to hear about your wife. How long were you married?"

"Thank you. Forty-five years. She passed a year ago. Breast cancer got her." The emotion was heavy in his voice as he spoke about his dear wife. He must still miss her.

"My grandfather passed away a few years ago. I wasn't able to go to the funeral because of work. I was in too deep on a case and couldn't get away." Gasping, she looked at the doctor. "I don't know why things just pop into my head like that."

"That's good. It's good when things come back to you just by having a conversation, instead of forcing yourself to remember. You are on the road to mental recovery, my dear. Now for the physical side of things," he said, sitting on the bed next to her legs. "I was going to give you a local anesthesia so I could stitch up your arm. Would you let me do that?"

A wary glance at the needle sitting on the bedside table caused an involuntary shudder to zip through her, but she also knew it was best for her and she felt she could trust the doctor. Nodding, she sat forward so he could have room to administer the aid she needed. After he stitched her wounds, he also checked her eyes and her reflexes. The wound on the side of her head was healing nicely, he stated, and if the boys in the front room would leave her arm alone, that wound would heal as well.

"Have you taken any of the pain meds I left for you?"

Shaking her head, she responded, "No. I really don't want to either. If they make me drowsy, I don't want the memories coming back and then not be able to make sense of them."

Helping her up from the bed, her arm freshly bandaged and the tears completely gone from her eyes, he offered, "If the pain becomes too much take half a pill or just make sure one of the guys are around to help you when you wake. Then you can tell them all about your dreams. How does that sound?"

"Good. I hope I didn't drag you away from something good on a Saturday afternoon." She smiled apologetically.

"No. I was just building some new bookcases for my office. I don't like the pre-fab ones and I love to work with my hands."

"Well, I'm sorry that we took you away from that. Can you stay for dinner at least?"

Packing up his bag he chuckled. "I know Martha is away and I'm afraid of what these guys would serve for supper."

Moving up close to Doc, she lowered her voice. "Martha left two weeks' worth of casseroles in the freezer for them. So I'm sure you're safe. Trey cooked breakfast this morning and it wasn't so bad."

Chuckling, the doctor placed his hand in the small of her back as he escorted her out into the living room where the men were waiting. All the bags from the store had been brought in from the truck, the groceries put away. As perfectly mannered gentlemen, they stood as she entered the room and Austin examined the newly bandaged arm.

"You okay?" he asked lowly.

"I'm fine. Doc and I have come to an understanding and as long as one of you put the casserole in the oven, we will have a guest for dinner." Three sets of eyes stared at her and she felt the flush on her cheeks. "What? We interrupted his woodwork on a Saturday of all things. I think we can offer him some dinner."

"You've been here all of two days and you are already bossing us around," Storm teased before making his way to the kitchen. "Doc, there is liquor on the bar. Help yourself."

Not sure what to do at that point, she watched as Austin and Trey picked up the plastic bags piled near the front door and took them to Lisa's bedroom. Returning to Lisa's side while Doc Anderson helped himself to a glass of scotch, Austin slipped his hand into Lisa's. "Let's go get you changed into something more comfortable," he suggested.

If the older gentleman hadn't been there, the blush wouldn't have colored her cheeks, but for some reason she felt awkward that he knew she had succumbed to the men's advances. Or did he? Was it possible he just thought they were truly trying to help her? Leaning up to Austin's side, she murmured, "I can get dressed by myself."

"I know. But it'll take a few minutes to go through all the bags of things we bought for you. I thought it would be quicker." He smiled down at her adoringly.

At that moment Lisa felt the love from these men. The proclamation that they wanted to protect her and love her was very real within that moment in time and her heart seemed to burst with it. Her life had been in such turmoil in the past five years that she couldn't even go to a loved one's funeral. Tears pooled in her eyes. The action wasn't missed by Austin or Doc, but the former pulled her into his strong arms and held her, as if willing his strength into her tiny body. After a few moments, he must have sensed her embarrassment for he led her down the hall to the room and sat her at the end of the bed that was now covered in all the clothes they had bought her while he crouched down before her.

"What's wrong, honey? Did I embarrass you too much?"

Shaking her head, her breath hitched a moment before she looked into his almond-shaped brown eyes. She hadn't noticed the tiny gold flecks that lay within the darker color. The whites of his eyes were more of an ivory. High cheekbones accentuated his eyes and gave him an exotic beauty, which she found striking. Raising her hand up to cup his cheek, she leaned forward and brushed her lips upon his full ones.

* * * *

Trey watched the loving interaction from the bathroom doorway as he returned from putting away her sundries. The range of emotions in his cousin was something he had never witnessed before. They ranged from concern to tenderness to love to admiration. It affected him being just a few feet away from them as his cock seemed to have a mind of its own. Not wanting Lisa to know he had seen anything he stepped back into the confines of the bathroom for a few moments.

* * * *

Lisa's eyelashes fluttered several times against her cheek as the moment turned into seconds after she pulled away from Austin. She reached for his hands and pulled them into her lap. "You are so lovely, so caring. You did embarrass me a little bit but now I see clearly how much you care for me. I had to see it in your eyes for me to believe it. I know you will never intentionally hurt me and accidents happen."

"We all…" She stopped him with a finger to his lips.

"I know you have told me that you will protect me, but I know that life isn't a guarantee. I don't know how all this is supposed to work out, but I feel safe with you guys. I didn't believe it until now but now I do and I will accept your love, now and for whatever the future brings us. I can't guarantee what'll happen after I regain my memory, but I won't be afraid of you guys anymore."

At a loss for words, Austin just stared at her, a smile lifting the corners of his mouth and giving him a more relaxed look than before that stirred something within their little woman. Austin watched Trey emerge from the bathroom again, and as if unable to keep from being touched by the scene he moved in behind her, leaned a knee on the bed, and slid his arms around her shoulders, burying his face into her hair. "We will always love you," Trey murmured.

Retaining one of Austin's hands in hers, she lifted the other and held onto the arm that was crossing the front of her shoulders, rubbing it lightly. "I know," she whispered.

After a few minutes, Austin stood, "We need to get you dressed so Doc doesn't think we are being rude. It's not nice to invite someone to supper and then desert them."

Lisa undid the clasp on the necklace that had worked as a belt all day and handed it back to Trey, who laid it on the dresser. Since Austin was the one who had had to hold her all the way back from town knowing what she hadn't been wearing under the sweater, he helped her stand then reached for the hem and gently pulled it up over head, careful not to hurt her arm. When she stood before the two men naked, Austin couldn't speak for Trey, but he had to remind his cock this was to be an innocent encounter to help her dress not throw her on the bed and ravish her.

Trey picked up a pair of blue jeans along with a pair of pink bikini panties. Helping her step into each of them, Austin picked out a matching pink lacey bra and a green T-shirt, and once her bottoms were on, he helped her into the bra. Chuckling at his task, he looked up to find Lisa looking at him with a crook in one eyebrow silently asking the question, "What is so funny about my backside?"

"I'm not laughing at you, honey. I just realized I have taken many a bra off a woman, but I have never put one on one."

A hand came out to slap him upside the head and he was surprised to find it was Trey's. "She doesn't need to hear about our past dalliances with the opposite sex, you moron!" the younger man chastised.

Placing her hand on his arm, Lisa looked up at Trey. "It's all right. I know you guys haven't waited around your whole lives for me to show up. I know there have been other women, and to tell you the truth, I'm happy that you had those times because it helped you know what you like and don't like. Not like me who apparently doesn't know anything about sex."

With a smile that he hoped would touch her soul Austin lifted her chin to gaze into her eyes. "But from what I've seen so far, little one, you have done a good job at satisfying us. There are no complaints and we'll have a long time to discover what you like and don't like. It's all trial and error. Just like life."

Unexpected by Austin, Lisa jumped up into his arms, hugging his neck while her legs circled his waist. He had noticed Trey stepping forward so she wouldn't fall from him before he got a good grip on her. Austin grasped her ass willingly, just to be able to hold those luscious globes within his hands, while Trey's ran up and down her spine in a loving, soothing gesture. He knew he wanted to make sure she knew how much she meant to them, but he didn't want her to think this was all about the sex. He was surprised when after a few moments, Lisa pulled her head back a bit to look into his face before she kissed him. Her tongue searched out his briefly before turning and doing the same to his cousin. When she ended the kiss, she let go of her grip around his neck, and he and Trey guided her back down to her feet before they finished dressing her.

Barefoot was the theme at the moment as the men removed their boots and all three padded back to the kitchen where they found Storm and Doc Anderson talking about horses and their therapeutic attributes to disabled kids. Storm must have told Doc he knew of a few people in Colorado who had set up programs on their ranches for such a purpose and were having great success. "I'll get in touch with my friend in Denver who sets up excursions for the kids in the area to one of the ranches outside the city. Perhaps he can let us know what we would need to get set up."

A gasp resounded in the room and Austin turned to Lisa, who was pale, her pupils in her eyes so dilated that her color was gone.

Chapter Ten

It was welcoming to be sitting outside in the warm sunshine without being a "working" woman who was dressed for business with obnoxious makeup, hair, and perfume. Like any respectable man really liked that, but that was what the business was about. She hated it, but it was her job. The women weren't that bad. Friendships weren't something that you trusted in her line of business as it was a cutthroat one. Everyone wanted the one job that they thought would rescue them from this low-end life, but for most it never materialized. For many, it was a death sentence either by the pimp or by the addiction of the bottle or the drug of choice. For a few, the death sentence was that they never escaped from this life and continued to do their job until their bodies were old and worn out. Occasionally, one died from diseases that they weren't protected against. Shameful that so many women took this road in life.

Sitting across from her was John. A cryptic phone call stating to meet him for coffee sent her happiness scale soaring. Knowing it was going to be a few hours of reprieve from everyone else in her life at the moment had her smiling like she had just won the lottery. Coffee the way she liked it was sitting in the open place at the table as she arrived, and as a gentleman, he rose until she sat and then he returned to his seat. She shook his hand in case someone was watching her before she sipped from her caramelized hot beverage.

"How's it going? Anything interesting?" he asked, taking one of her hands in his and running his fingertips along the palm. He was old enough to be her father. Black hair with gray at the temples, kept cut short. No facial hair. He had piercing green-blue eyes that reminded her of water in the Caribbean that she had seen in pictures, under black eyebrows that always seemed to be looking deep inside of a person, which was probably why he was good at his job. Thin lips that always reminded her of how her mother pursed her lips when she was angry with her, but when he smiled, he made you feel comfortable. Strong chin and a Grecian nose highlighted the rest of his face. She knew that he knew how to treat a lady by how he always stroked her hand when they would meet up. That he always had her favorite coffee ready was also a good sign in a man.

Leaning toward him as if she was going to kiss him, she lowered her voice. "I'm supposed to meet up with Alexander Markova. I've never met him."

Running his hands through her hair, he said, "He owns a trading company, a software company, and several other ventures. He's been a bane to our existence because he avoids everything. It's almost like he has someone on the inside."

"He's having a party out at his ranch tonight outside of Lyon, near Crater Lake. A bunch of us girls are supposed to be going. A limo is supposed to pick us up at six to head up there."

"That's another one of his 'charitable' uses of his ranch. He has a foundation setup there that lets physically and mentally challenged children go out there and ride the horses. It's supposed to be therapeutic for them. Be careful. You know how to get a hold of me." Standing, he leaned down and kissed her on the lips chastely, which she always hated but had to do.

Watching him walk away, she finished her coffee. As she was getting ready to stand, she felt as if someone was watching her. The hair on the back of her neck stood on end and a chill ran up her back while fear gripped her. She had to wonder who it was but acting as normal as possible, she stood, tossed hers and John's cups in the trash can, and began to walk back to her place of employment.

* * * *

Her hands were at her temples as the pain struck with the extended memory. Austin and Trey, who were still at her side, caught her as she began to sink to the floor, sobs racking her body. Fear and frustration ran through her as a long, pitiful, hurtful wail escaped from deep within her. It hurt to remember but it was getting to be that she didn't want the memories as she was afraid they would take her away from her men. The flashes were so confusing that she couldn't make heads or tails of them. She just wanted them to stop.

* * * *

Austin bent slightly and put his arm under her knees, pulling her up against his chest, and followed an already retreating Trey down the hallway. In her room Trey began pulling the new clothes from the bed, tossing them into the closet while Austin laid her on the bed. Storm and Doc were right behind them, the black bag already in the doctor's hand. He pulled out his stethoscope and listened to her heart and then checked her eyes for dilation. Pulling a syringe from his bag, he again filled it from a vial and flicked the plastic before pushing up and letting a small bit emerge from the thin needle. He injected the needle into her arm as the trio stood looking down at her, their tiny, fragile woman.

Austin looked at Doc pleadingly before getting a quick nod of approval from the man and then he lay down next to her. Pulling her against him he wrapped his arms around her, letting her head rest on his bicep. Beginning a gentle rocking motion, he put his mouth near her ear. "Hush, little one. We're here for you. It's going to be okay."

* * * *

After administering a sedative, Lisa's body gave into the medication as her eyes closed. He knew she had been fighting the pain for too long now. Doc saw her body begin to go limp, her sobs begin to subside as she lost the fight to stay conscious. Standing, he put his tools of the trade back into his bag and then left the room. The brothers followed him out, turning off the light as they closed the door behind them.

In the living room the doctor went over and poured himself another drink. Downing half of it, he turned to the concerned men. "She's still in a lot of pain from the head trauma, but she's trying to be strong and not take any of the medication. She told me that she's afraid to take it because she is afraid when she wakes up she might not remember any dreams she has. I don't think it's the dreams that are getting her. It's the normal conversation that is triggering her memory and it's hurting her."

"She thinks she is a hooker. She's not. That much was proven this morning," Trey said. "I put some feelers out there and there are arrest records indicating she is. She has a criminal record, but I can't believe any of it. She's ashamed of what she is."

"That's not what's hurting her," Doc said, downing the rest of his drink. "I mean it is literally hurting her. When she has a flash of memory, it's like hitting her head over again. Either we need to get that memory of hers back or we're going to have to keep feeding her painkillers."

Sitting down in one of the recliners, Doc ran his hands up over his face and through his hair in frustration. Storm sat in the other recliner while Trey sat on the leather couch. It was a few minutes before anyone spoke.

"I need to get up to the cabin tomorrow and check it out. Since we found her up that way I have a suspicion about that place," Storm thought out loud, then turned to Doc. "If we take an ATV up there, can she go with us? Perhaps it may trigger another memory."

Thinking briefly, the doctor sat back, crossing his leg across his knee. "I think I would enjoy a ride up the mountain with you guys. Since tomorrow is Sunday, I don't have anything to do so do you mind if I ride along? I could be useful if Lisa has any problems."

Storm patted the man on the arm. "Of course you can come along. You don't ever have to use her as an excuse to get an invite. You're welcome out here at any time. Now, let me check on supper."

"Does this mean you are going to stay tonight, Doc?" Trey asked.

Nodding, he smiled. "Yes. Do you have a spare room?"

"You'll have to sleep in Austin's room. He'll probably stay the night with Lisa. We'll change the sheets before you head to bed. There's a TV in there attached to the satellite so you can make yourself at home. We'll get you a set of clothes also," Storm said from the kitchen as he pulled the casserole out of the oven.

* * * *

Lisa's steady breathing was welcoming to Austin as her sobs from earlier broke his heart. The love for this woman filled him so contently that he thought his heart would burst within his chest, but the pain she was in sank to the opposite level and he was surprised that a human heart could take such a toll. He had never been a violent person, but right now, he couldn't wait to find out who had hurt her physically and mentally and beat the shit out of him, if not more.

With a light hand, he smoothed her lovely long blonde hair down her back as he still rocked her. He knew a relationship was more than sex, and even though his cock wanted to be embedded deep within her, he relished just holding her, to let her know he was there for her no matter what. Thinking back to just a little while when she declared her trust in them caused him to smile. Little Lisa had come into their lives so unexpectedly but had turned their lives upside down. He knew they all loved her and he hoped she would soon reveal hers to them, as her mouth might not have declared it, but her body and emotions had.

Later that evening Storm brought Austin a plate of food, some water, and a soda, turning the small bedside lamp on so he could see. Explaining Doc's presence in the house and their planned excursion for the next day, Austin said he'd have her up early and ready to go.

* * * *

Near dawn Lisa stirred, her body stretching out against the hard, warm, muscular body of one of her men. Feeling her nipples pebbling beneath the sheet when she moved, she became aware that someone had removed her clothes. The room was dark so she wasn't sure who was behind her, but their arm was draped over her waist, their clothing still on as she could feel the shirt sleeve against her skin. Turning over, she faced the man sliding her hand up his chest to where his shirt opened into a V. The skin was smooth beneath the material and she knew Austin was embracing her. Leaning up, she let her lips lightly touch the skin and felt a shiver rush through him.

In a flash she was on her back and he was poised above her, resting on his forearms on both sides of her head while his knee insinuated itself between her legs. His long black hair fell in a curtain on both sides of her face, providing an intimate setting. Smiling down at her, he whispered, "I've been waiting all night for you to wake up. Are you all right?"

"Yes. The pain was so bad and the memory was so shocking. They keep coming more and more and they scare me," she said lowly, ashamed she wasn't able to control her thoughts.

"Why? Are they that bad?" he asked, letting his mouth caress her ear.

"No. Not bad. They're confusing. Plus, I'm frightened of them."

"What do you mean?" he whispered, his tongue sliding down her neck toward her shoulder.

Moving her head aside and giving him more access to her delicate skin, she moaned in delight. "I'm afraid you won't want me if you find out who I really am, and I'm afraid the memories will take me away from you."

Nipping the sensitive spot where neck and shoulder meet, he chuckled. "That will never happen. We don't care what or who you were in the past. We see who you really are when we look in your eyes. You will never disappoint us and we won't let the past take you from us. I promise you that, little one."

Shivering in the dark beneath his body, she placed both hands on his chest and began to unbutton his shirt. Pulling the hem from the waistband of his jeans, she let her hands slide up the smooth skin, over the ridges of his abs, her thumbs dipping slightly into his navel as they traveled upwards. Her fingers spread when they reached his pecs, reveling in the muscles beneath and how they seemed to twitch with her touch. His breath hitched as her fingers ran across his nipples, which she found hardened to tiny nubs. Smiling in the dark, she pressed her thumbs against the round discs, rubbing around in circles.

Groaning, he moved his mouth over to hers and demanded entrance with his tongue. Opening to him, she felt his tongue slide inside past her teeth and over her tongue. He devoured her mouth, his tongue roaming over the roof and along the insides of her cheeks before he began to suckle on the organ within her mouth. She took her hands off his nipples and pushed them up to his shoulders, pushing the material of his shirt backward to prompt first one arm and then the other to lift up for its removal. All the while, he continued to possess her mouth.

Letting her hands roam back down his sides, she encountered the waistband of his pants, and moving around to the front, he sucked in a breath, his abdomen pulling inwards. Unfastening the first button at his crotch caused another groan to emanate from him as he took her mouth harder. When the second and third came loose he pulled away from her, rising up on his hands, and then the fourth one slipped through the buttonhole and he growled.

Her hands gently pushed the denim downward, though his hand went down to protect his hard length from being caught up in the material. With the jeans down around his thighs, his hard heavy cock tapped her leg, and her hand moved down to try to pull it into her grasp.

Lisa was surprised and confused when he grabbed both her wrists in one large hand and moved them above her head, pinning them down to the bed. He slipped in between her thighs though remained still even though she was trying to fight the bond. "Be still, little one. You need to wait. Otherwise you will not get to enjoy anything."

"Can't you let go of my hands? I want to touch you," she whimpered with need.

"No, I like you struggling below me. One of these days I am going to tie you down to the bed and fuck that pretty little pussy 'til you pass out from coming. Then my cousins will do the same." He chuckled when he heard her gasp. "Does that turn you on?"

Her body had stilled at his comment of tying her up and he feared she had a bad memory until she leaned up and licked his chest. A hiss escaped him as she made a physical challenge with her tongue. "It does turn you on. You are a little vixen, aren't you?"

"You'll just have to see if you get the chance," she verbally challenged.

She felt him move up slightly as the hard mushroom tip of his cock was at her wet entrance. He seemed pleased that she was already aroused and wet for him, though he hadn't touched her with his hands. With a reluctant look, Austin removed his hand from her wrists before grunting out an order, "Keep your hands where they are or I will have to hold you down again, understand?"

His words struck her core, excitement near bursting within her. Lisa didn't think her breasts could swell any more than they already had or that her nipples could be so hard, but what surprised her most was that more liquid pooled within her channel, causing her hips to begin to writhe under his groin. Leaving her hands where they were, she knew this left her breasts thrust up toward him, and if there had been more light in the room she was sure he would have appreciated the view immensely. Grasping handfuls of the sheet, she held on for she knew this was going to be quick and hard from the way he was panting.

* * * *

Rising up briefly, Austin canted his hips closer to her sopping pussy. He could smell her cream wafting up to his nose as she undulated beneath him, causing his dick to become a rod of steel that he was going to use to ram into her over and over until she cried out his name and everyone in the house heard it. He didn't care at the moment. The moment she had relaxed in his arms the previous evening he had to endure this raging hard-on and now he was going to take care of it.

Resting his hands on both sides of her right above the shoulders, he let his cock resume its position at her entrance, and then with one push of his hips, he buried himself deep within her. A moan escaped her as did her breath. Waiting a moment, he let her regain her composure after that swift movement, and when he felt her hips rising up to him in invitation, he began to move outward until just the angry purple tip rested at her sweet opening. Pulling his chiseled ass and hips back, he rammed into her. Repeating the motion over and over again, he felt her hips thrusting up to meet his as her breathing came in pants. Her silky walls tightened against him with each movement until he felt the muscles begin to flutter around him and she seized up, squeezing at his shaft, and with one final thrust, he felt his seed shoot from his tip and he let out a roar. He heard her cry out his name as her cunt milked his cock over and over until nothing was left, his strength drained. She was his Delilah to his Samson. Going down to his forearms, he let his chest rest upon hers, her hard nipples poking against his skin in wanton invitation. Her pussy wept with his seed and her juices around his cock, and his heart sang with the feeling of joy that he had created the flood within her sweet channel.

The room was beginning to lighten slightly as light began to permeate the curtains covering the large window and now he was able to see the serene look upon her cherubic face. Iris eyes glittered as she gazed up at him, her love for him radiating within their depths. Leaning down he gingerly kissed each of her eyelids, then her nose and lastly, her lips. His lips teased and then nibbled at them, just loving her.

Gazing up into his face as the light pooled within the room, she could see the adoration in the strong man's eyes above her even through the silky veil of dark hair that hung from his head. Lifting her hand she let her fingers comb through the tresses that tickled against her shoulders and neck. "I love your hair. It's beautiful," she whispered.

"As is yours," he whispered back, kissing her chin. "You are a very beautiful woman and I am so glad that I can claim you as mine. You will always belong to me, to my cousins, and we will do everything in our power to make you happy."

Lifting up, she spread light kisses up his sternum then along his right clavicle to where it met his arm and then headed back in the other direction, though this time she licked her way across to the other side. He tasted manly. There was a bit of saltiness from him perspiring during their lovemaking, but there was no taste of cologne or aftershave that she had tasted before on men. She had at least participated in a petting session. Austin was all male and she loved that about him. As her lips began a descent toward the small disc that sat on the edge of one of his pecs, he pushed himself up to rest on his hands.

"I wish we could stay like this for many more hours, little one, but we have a small trip to make today. Storm has arranged four-wheel transportation up to the cabin so we can check out if there is any evidence of you being held there and also if there may be a chance of a memory trigger for you. We need to get dressed and then have breakfast. Otherwise, I really would love to keep you in this bed and fuck you until you are exhausted."

Even in the dim light she knew he could see the flush that rose to her cheeks. A giggle escaped her at the thought of his erotic words but fear also rose within her at the thought of more memories coming back to her. It frightened her as to what direction they would take her life, but she also worried about the pain that accompanied them. He had seen the change of emotions in her eyes and let his arms move under her shoulders and in one swift move, rose to his knees bringing her up to rest in his lap holding her tight to his chest.

"We will be there for you as will Doc. He invited himself along because you seemed to have touched his heart with your love. As I'm sure you probably do with everyone you meet. But if there is any problem, we will help you."

Breathing in deeply, she held the breath for a few seconds before she remembered to exhale. "I'm sure you will be right by my side if I should need you. Thank you. I hope we can return to where we left off when we get home. What should I wear?"

"Clothes," he joked which brought a gasp from her. He didn't seem the joking type. "I think we would be too distracted if you wore nothing. We'd never even get out of the house."

Kissing his chest, she giggled. "I wouldn't mind that, though I'm sure the kind doctor would be embarrassed."

A chuckle emanated from deep in his chest and she discovered that when he wasn't so serious, he could let his barriers down. The planes and angles on his face softened while his eyes glinted with happiness and love. She saw that look most of the time when he was with her. Little fingers of thrill rushed through her when he looked at her like that. It wasn't like the dirty, lustful way that other men tended to look at her. This was love and it warmed her heart. It was the same when Storm and Trey looked at her in the same way, and she felt loved, desired and mostly, she felt as if she truly belonged to them.

"I think just jeans and one of those thermal shirts you got. Wear the down vest over it because it will be cold up there and then take a jacket. You can wear a pair of the sneakers you got," Austin said as he placed a kiss on the tip of her nose, "or a pair of your boots."

The door opened slowly, the visitor expecting the two lovers to still be asleep. The duo looked over and found a slightly surprised Storm peeking in. Austin rose to his knees and scooted off the bed. "Get up properly and help her take a shower, cuz."

Chapter Eleven

The door closed behind Storm as he walked to the foot of the bed and eyed the little bundle lying naked in the center of the large expanse of rumpled sheets. Even through the slowly lightening room, he could tell her lips were swollen from his cousin's kisses and her breasts were red from his ministrations while her dark-pink nipples stood up hard and pebbled, admitting their arousal. He was certain her sweet pussy lips were slick with her own juices along with Austin's, which sent pulses to his already throbbing cock. Her long blonde hair fanned out on the pillow, giving her an ethereal, angelic look about her.

Lisa watched Storm standing at the foot of the bed watching her. Smiling coyly, she stretched her body languidly as a yawn hit her. When her legs spread wide with the stretch, she saw his tongue dart through his lips in desire and his eyes look wild, feral. The bulge in front of the flannel pajama bottoms mirrored the blatant desire in his emotions. He wore no shirt and she had to wonder if he had just thrown on the pants as a gesture of modesty for her and the doctor, but he looked so inviting standing there.

Rising onto her hands and knees, she moved in a slow crawl toward him, her eye on the prize between his thighs as she could see it twitching beneath the material. Once in front of him, she laid her lips on his abdomen in an openmouthed kiss, her tongue licking the ridges that resided there. As petite as she was, she didn't even have to move from her position to move her mouth over to his navel. She circled around it several times with her tongue before kissing the actual nub of the remnant of his birth within the shallow dip there. The hiss above her let her know she was getting to him and she smiled to herself with the power. Letting her tongue move lower, her hands led the way by hooking into the elastic waistband of the flannel pants and began to lower the material. Careful to pull the front out further from his body so as not to catch on the hardened, throbbing object of her desire, she slid the pants down to his knees.

Leaning down she licked at the sac that hung low between his legs. It was swollen with his desire and it tightened even more as she pressed her lips to it. Sucking in carefully, she pulled one ball in, worshipping it with her tongue, leaving the coarse hair there plastered to the skin. The fingers on one hand moved back and ran along the tender line between his balls and the puckered hole, giving him cause to gasp aloud. Smiling to herself, she moved over and sucked the other ball into her mouth, showing it the same attention she had shown the other one. Her fingernails moved back and forth along the perineum, which caused his balls and cock to throb even more, his breathing heavy. She looked up at him, his eyes hooded in lust as his hands sought out her head.

"Oh, darlin', please take me," he pleaded. "You are much too good at that."

Running her tongue up the length of the hard shaft before her, she continued to watch his face and delighted in the expression she saw there. Lust and desire mingled together and when he looked down at her, love showed through, causing her heart to skip a beat and she inhaled sharply. Cream dripped from her pussy down her thighs while her breasts, which didn't seem to be able to swell any more, did. Happy that she could make him feel this good she leaned forward and licked the tip of his swollen cock, tasting the pre-cum that had emerged from the small slit there. Kissing the tip, she let her lips slide down around the tip then down the side slowly engulfing her man's cock in her hot mouth. When he hit the back of her throat, she glanced down to see that only about three-quarters of his velvety steel rod was in her mouth.

Her groan reverberated around his swollen cock. "Stop, baby. Just hold still a minute," he ground out through gritted teeth.

Obeying his command, she held still with mouth and hand while he tried to gain control of his senses and his cock. Man, did she really have this much power? No wonder the girls made good money doing this. Too bad the pimp got most of it, she thought.

The pain shot through her head with the thought, but she wasn't going to ruin this for her or Storm by revealing what had just happened. She just had to learn to deal with it and not let it frighten her. They would all help her with this and protect her from whatever brought her to them. Even if it was the devil himself that brought her to these three loving men, she would have to thank him for that.

* * * *

Storm knew the moment she had a revelation as her mouth tensed but a moment later it relaxed again. Fear rushed through him that she would pull away and not finish what she had started so he was relieved when she just sat there, waiting for his permission to let her resume her dalliance with his cock. When his balls didn't seem to be pulling up into his spine, he hissed. "Okay, baby. Your mouth is so hot, make me come."

Her tongue flattened along the underside of his cock and slid up it as it followed her lips until it rest right beneath the head. Moving it, she let it swirl around the top, tasting his essence there before beginning her descent down toward his balls again. As she did this, she again let her fingernails run along the seam between his sac and his asshole. She felt him tense, his cheeks clinching together. "Uh, uh," she moaned around him as she tapped his cheeks with her fingers. She knew that they would do the same to her if she had tightened any of her openings against them.

Drawing in a deep breath, Storm relaxed his ass cheeks. Through his adult years he had been given many a blow job before, but not one of them included having his asshole played with. He wasn't trying to keep her from playing there. It was so erotic and it sent pulses throughout his groin he thought he'd cum to soon. Placing his hands on her shoulders he began to rub them down each side of her spine, her back arching for him at the sensation. With the comparison of his height to hers, he was able to bend slightly as she still moved her head up and down on his cock and reach her buttocks as they swayed with her movements. Relaxing her butt cheeks, she moaned against him.

She removed her mouth from him. "That feels so good," she said before moving her mouth to his balls. Kissing and licking at them, she loved how they hung down, ready for her mouth to suck them in, which she did, worshipping one at a time before gliding her wet tongue up his cock to take him deep in her throat again. He groaned at the action. With his hands on her ass, he pushed her toward him and then, squeezing the flesh there, pulled her back slightly, helping her to fuck him.

Lisa let him lead her body as she moved in and out on his cock, relishing the smoothness of the hardened shaft and how it fit well in her mouth. She felt wanton as her ample breasts swung beneath her body, the nipples lightly grazing the rumpled blanket and sheet. That action sent pulses down her abs into her cunt, which throbbed to be touched. Slick juices ran down her thighs, which she rubbed together, rubbing her pussy lips together. The action squeezed her clitoris and she felt the tingle deep within her. Each movement Storm made drove her pussy into a deeper frenzy. She moaned at the sensation, which caused his cock to swell even more. His hips began to piston in and out of her mouth, rocking her body between his groin and his hands.

One of his large hands slipped between her thighs through the moisture that was leaking from her slit and found her clit. Rubbing it, he moved his middle finger in circles, driving her on a collision course with her impending orgasm. Her finger pushed through the tight muscle at his puckered hole and slid in up to her second knuckle, and she began to move it back and forth. Apparently he liked it, for she found when she did that, he bucked even harder and she had to be careful not to let him gag her. After about a half a minute, she felt his balls tighten beneath her chin and his cock throb within her mouth before he thrust one last time, held her body to him, and climaxed within her hot mouth. His seed shot from his cock and down her throat several times. Though the size of him pushed to the back of her throat was a daunting task she tried to drink all of his offering down, and as a bit of his spunk leaked from the side of her mouth, she felt as if she had failed him.

She didn't have time to think too hard on it as she felt his finger speed up on her clit and then a hard slap on her derriere struck and the coil deep within her sprang, sending out tentacles of sensation throughout her body, and she cried out around his cock. Her pussy seemed to radiate outward as if trying to overtake her body, though she knew it remained in the same place. She was surprised it could cause her to feel so content and the thought struck her that he had slapped her! He had really slapped her ass and that is what had sent her over the edge of the climactic cliff.

Storm slowly slid his hands back up her back and to her shoulders where he gently tried to push her off of him so he could look into his woman's eyes, but she was still bathing his softening cock with her tongue. Pulling her finger out of his ass he let out a deep breath and she moved her hand to the bed. "God, darlin', you really do treat me good," he smiled down at her.

Pride swelled in her chest as she finally removed her mouth from his member and looked up at him shyly, afraid he would be disappointed that she missed some of his seed. He moved his hand to caress her cheek as she licked her lips, cleaning the taste from them. He moved his thumb over, swiped at the small drop of his cum at the corner of her mouth, and spread it on her bottom lip while she gazed up at him. Licking her lip again, she felt his thumb there and tasted his cum. Drawing the digit into her mouth, she sucked on it briefly before he pulled it out. Thinking he was angry with her, she started to back away when he reached out, pulled her up to him, and covered her lips with his own. His tongue pushed through to duel with her own as he held her face in his hands, reveling in the taste of her, and for the first time, the taste of himself on her tongue.

Pulling himself up to his full six foot three inches, he stood before her, love shining in his eyes. Thinking how this little woman had managed to twist them all around her little finger and forage a way into their hearts so quickly was surprising. Little did they know the day they went out to find several head of cattle, which were still wandering around on the mountain, that they would come back with the love of their lives. He could spend days just kissing her but knew they needed to get going.

"Let's get you into the shower and cleaned up. Did Austin tell you we are going on a little Sunday drive?"

Bewilderment in her iris eyes raised up to his, she asked meekly, "You aren't mad at me?"

Confusion crowded his mind, trying to figure out why he should have been angry at her. Was it because of her breakdown last night in the kitchen? No. Couldn't be. Did he miss something? Letting his hand go back to her cheek, caressing it lovingly before kneeling down in front of her still perched on her hands and knees, he asked, "Why would I be angry at you, darlin'?"

Lowering her eyes, she felt vulnerable with him nearly undressed before her, love shining in his eyes. "Because I wasn't able to take all of your cum."

Blond eyebrows lifted in surprise at her comment, and then with a shake of his head in disbelief, he moved his hand down to her chin and gently forced her to look at him. When her eyes met his, he was saddened to see tears pooled there. God, what kind of life had this woman lived through before she arrived? They needed to get her memory back as soon as possible and get her out of this living hell she was in. Standing, he stood on the remains of his pajamas pooled around his feet and stepped out of them. Moving his hands down to her waist, he lifted her as if she weighed nothing more than a small child and sat her down on the foot of the bed. Sitting next to her, he returned his hand to her chin, lifting so she'd see his eyes, though they remained closed, and then kissed each eye, catching the tears that dripped down with his lower lip then sliding his tongue on his lip. "Yum. Salty." A small smile crossed her lips though her eyes remained closed.

"Darlin', look at me, please." A moment passed before she gave in to his request. Her sad eyes broke his heart. "I would never be mad at you because you can't take all of my cum in your mouth. I know I am a big man and that most of the time I can be quite overwhelming, not just in size but quantity as well. I loved your mouth around my cock. You made me crazy with what you did to me. I have never had a woman put a finger in my ass before. It was heaven for me. I was more concerned that I came before you did but once you got going in my ass, I lost all control. I'm sorry about that."

Her smile grew bigger at his compliment, but that he apologized for bringing her to her climax later than his confused her. "I'm sorry," she said, crossing her arms in front of her. "I don't understand. You want a woman to have an orgasm? Before you do?"

A gaping mouth was not what she expected to see but Storm's reaction was a total shock. Trying to regain his composure, he closed his mouth and then shook his head, trying to shake his thoughts into rational ones. "Oh, honey, we really have so much to teach you. Of course a real man makes sure his woman climaxes before he does. That's what it means to take care of a woman. We make sure her needs are taken care of before our own. Not just sexually, but in everyday life also. Why does that surprise you?"

It worried him that he put out the question for he knew what was about to happen, but he had to do it. It seemed like the only way she was to remember anything was by holding normal conversations around her and they seemed to trigger memories. Bracing himself, he waited for the fallout of what was sure to be a recollection for her.

* * * *

"Just once I would like to come while having sex," the redhead said, sailing into the room. Lisa sat on the couch leafing through a magazine. "All these guys want to do is come and they don't care if you get off or not. I'm tired of going home and getting myself off every night. If the money wasn't so good I'd leave here and find myself a boyfriend that would take care of my needs before his own."

"Oh, like those are really out there," the dark-haired beauty in the barber chair exclaimed. "I don't think there is a man alive that will get a woman off first. Even in all the porn movies the woman never comes. At least in the gay porn both the guys get off. So, all the way around, the men win when it comes to sex. Just get used to it. What do you have to say about it, Lisa?"

Looking up at the two women, so vastly different from each other, not only in looks but in opinions and personalities, she knew she would have to put in her opinion. The dark-haired woman dominated the room and Lisa knew she hung on every word any of the girls said while they were together because she would report it back to their boss. All the girls hated when Bridgette was in the room as they had to monitor their actions and their conversations.

"I agree with Bridgette on this one, Lani," she said, addressing the fiery redhead. "I don't know any man that wants a woman to come before them. They just want you to suck them off or just stick their dick into you, fuck you until they are done, and then get up and walk away."

Damn, she was good! Pride swelled within her until she saw the tears in Lani's eyes. The girl was eighteen and fresh from a farm in Kansas. Their boss had picked her up six months prior while she was still seventeen, a runaway on the street in Topeka. Dirty and starving, he took her in, promised her the land of milk and honey, and brought her here and began to pimp her out immediately. At first she was terrified until the money began to come in and she had something she could call her own, even though she really didn't know how much their boss made off of her. For what she brought in for him, she only received about twenty percent. Lisa knew he got fifty percent and the rest went to the hierarchy of the organization. In general, since the clientele were more upper class, wealthy business men, and the exchange of money was done between their boss and the men. The women had no idea how much was paid for them. Lisa was inadvertently made aware of the payout to the girls when her boss had gotten drunk one night and bragged to her about it.

Lisa was sorry that she had hurt the girl but there was no other way around the conversation. The girl had to know the truth, but also, she didn't want to give Bridgette ammunition to take to their boss about her. She couldn't afford to lose this job at the moment, but most importantly, their boss had taken to showing her too much attention lately and she didn't need that right then. She had to concentrate on the bigger picture here.

The door opened and a plump blonde entered, smacking on her gum. She was the epitome of the term hooker and blonde bimbo all wrapped into one. Bleached blonde hair usually teased up and piled high with hairspray, Lisa would swear the woman used a can of hairspray a day. E-cup-sized tits adorned her chest which the girl had paid a pretty penny for. She was determined to snag one of her clients as a husband so she was also living in a fantasy world. Plopping down on the couch next to Lisa, her breasts bouncing with the action, she turned to Lisa. "Boss wants to see you, sweetie."

Exasperated, Lisa stood. "Great. Wonder what he wants right now?" she said before she exited the door.

* * * *

Storm wrapped his arms around his lady before the memory set her off into tears. The gasp that emerged from her before she relaxed against him sent a chill through him. Since he had been observing her nuances and could now read the distant look in her eyes that meant she had reverted within the confines of her memory, he knew that he had to catch her before she fell into the tears that would surely follow.

His hand soothingly smoothed her hair down from her crown to her shoulders and then back again repeatedly in an attempt to calm her. Snuggling deeper against his warm chest, Storm reveled in her hand moving across the expanse of his wide chest and shoulders, as if reveling in the strength beneath the skin. He could tell the memory seemed to be teetering on the edge of her consciousness as her hand caressed his chest, but it seemed to elude her. Kissing the top of her head, he laid his chin on the spot. "Do you want to talk about it?"

"It's just so confusing," she answered lowly. "I know what Trey said about me being a virgin, but I keep seeing myself sitting around talking to a group of hookers and sometimes talking to my pimp."

"Perhaps it was a suggestion that was placed in your head, or perhaps you are a reporter or a writer doing research," he threw out there, not wanting to upset her any more at the moment. "Anyway, we need to get showered. Can I join you?"

"Will we actually get clean or get dirtier in there together?" she giggled against him.

"We have a guest waiting for us, so I promise to be on my best behavior," he said as he scooped his hand under her knees and drew her up to his chest, carrying her into the bathroom. Setting her down, he reached into the shower stall, started the water, and then looked around.

"Where are those bags from yesterday that we brought in? We need one to put over your arm." It was a rhetorical question but he watched her think for a moment before she ran naked from the room. He heard a door open and then the rustling of plastic bags and then watched the door for her return. When she returned, he got a show of her breasts bouncing with her movements. He nearly had to bite his tongue to keep a groan from escaping his lips.

Standing still, she patiently let him wrap the plastic around her arm to allow her bandage to stay dry. "Did you know one of you guys threw all my new clothes into the closet? Now I'm going to have to iron everything," she said in mock irritation.

"We'll help you," Storm said, finishing the plastic bandage. "I'm sure they aren't all wrinkled. Besides, the dryer we have is pretty top of the line.

Toss them in there for a few minutes and then hang them up. That's what Martha does for most of our clothes."

Placing his hand at the small of her back, he escorted her into the walk-in shower stall tiled from floor to ceiling in white tiles with black tiles around the edges of the walls and at the top and bottom edges. A rain showerhead was suspended from the ceiling and there were several showerheads situated on the two walls perpendicular to the shower door. To him, it seemed as if she was surprised at the opulence of it. Storm helped her wash her hair and rinse it before taking a washcloth, soaping it up and then washing her body, taking extra care around her breasts and then her pussy and ass.

Surprised hit him when she laid her head back on the tile, soft gasps escaping her lips as he bathed her. He refused to let her bathe him, as he would never have gotten out of the shower at all, so she stood and watched him instead. His dick was semi-hard as she would gaze at it and lick her lips. At that point, he felt they may have created a sex monster, but that would be a good thing since there were three of them.

When he finished, he turned the water off and stepped out onto the bath mat in front of the shower. Grabbing a towel he wrapped her hair up first, piling it on her head, and then retrieving another towel he dried off her body. "Go get dressed," he said, patting her on the derriere as she sashayed into the bedroom.

Drying himself off he looked at himself in the mirror, debating whether to shave or not, but since they were going up into the mountains, it didn't matter. Wrapping the towel around his waist, he gazed at himself in the mirror, giving him cause to contemplate whether they were doing the right thing taking her to the cabin. It could be nothing, but his hunches usually panned out and he hoped this one did. Running a hand over his face, he took a moment to regain his composure before heading into the bedroom.

The clothes that had been pushed into the closet the previous night were now scattered on the bed, and his woman was shuffling through them. Storm leaned against the doorframe and watched her as she studied the items, debating which would be best to wear. Choosing a black pair of jeans and a burgundy thermal T-shirt, she set those aside and then chose a red lacey thong pair of panties and a matching red lace bra that he knew wouldn't cover much of her at all. Thick white socks really spoiled the look that had caused the towel to tent in front of him, but he knew she would need them with her shoes, no matter what she wore.

Clearing his throat in frustration, he said, "I'm going to get dressed. Will you be all right?"

Smiling brightly she answered, "Of course. It'll take me only a few minutes to get dressed."

Sauntering out of the room, Storm made his way to his own room.

* * * *

A few minutes after he had left, Trey made his way into her room, lightly knocking before he entered. She had just finished dressing and was sitting on the edge of the bed pulling on her socks as a pair of black running shoes sat next to the bed. Trey grabbed the comb and an elastic band from the dresser before climbing onto the bed behind his woman. Taking the towel, he blotted at the long blonde tresses he loved. Once he felt they were dry enough, he began to comb out her hair, careful not to cause any pain when he ran across a tangle.

"I love how you guys all take care of me," she whispered, enjoying the attention.

"We love to do it for you, baby. We love you so much. Somehow you swept in and stole all our hearts." He had finished combing her hair and began doing a French braid along the back side of her head, trying not to pull too tight. Once the hair fell below the scalp, he continued braiding it and then tied it off with the elastic band. Now her hair would be out of her face while they made their journey.

Turning to face him she lifted up to kiss his lips. "Thank you. How do you know how to braid a girl's hair?"

"A girl taught me," he said sassily as he replaced the comb on the dresser.

Turning quickly, she knelt on the bed facing him as he stood next to the dresser. "Who was the girl?" she asked softly.

The smile he had on his face slipped away quickly when he realized he had hurt her feelings. Apparently love was something new to her and she was actually jealous. Kneeling in front of her he placed two fingers under her chin and lifted her face so she could meet his eyes. At first they remained downcast. "Look at me." When she didn't look up right away, he became a little more demanding as he had seen his cousin do with her. "Look at me, baby girl!"

He loved how she responded so well to their dominance, for her blonde-fringed eyes flew up to look into his. He saw sadness there, but he also saw her jealousy.

"Baby, first, I don't want you to ever be jealous of any of the women we dated in the past. They are part of the past and we don't want anything to do with them. We love you and want you to stay with us. We'll take care of you, protect you"— his voice softened— "and make love to you whenever we can. Second of all, my cousin Abby taught me how to braid hair. She was a year older than me and she teased me relentlessly. She was Austin's sister."

Lisa seemed to notice as he choked a bit on the last sentence. "Was?"

His eyes became misty at the thought of his cousin. "When she graduated high school she had enlisted in the Army. Five years ago while she was stationed in Afghanistan, her convoy was hijacked and those who survived were taken hostage. The women were repeatedly raped and then when they were done with them, they killed them."

Moving closer to him, she threw her arms around his massive shoulders. "Were you two very close?"

He nodded, afraid if he talked she would know he was crying. Burying his head into the nook between her shoulder and neck, he nuzzled her, giving himself an excuse to have his face on her shirt so it would help blot the tears. It took a minute to regain his composure, though he hadn't fooled her. Laying a kiss on her neck, he said, "As close as what Austin, Storm, and I are. She was a year older but we were in the same grade in school. It was a shock when the man from the Army came to tell Austin."

"I'm sure it was. I know whenever I have to go tell a family member that a loved one has died in the line of duty, it's very difficult."

Storm had told Trey and Austin that if she remembered anything to just hold her, soothe her before she became too emotional. Holding her, he waited for her to say something or even cry, but she didn't. Thoughts began to run through his brain and he knew he needed to talk to the Sheriff. "You okay?"

"Yes." She nodded. "That was weird."

Pulling gently away from her, he said, "Let's go get something to eat and head out. I think today may be a day of surprises."

Chapter Twelve

After the small group enjoyed the breakfast that Trey and Austin had put together they made their way out to one of the barns. At first Lisa was confused. She thought they said they would take ATVs so why were they heading to the barns? When Storm and Austin rolled the large doors aside, she saw that this barn held equipment. She was surprised to see a Bobcat parked inside along with a Backhoe and a Ditch Witch. Along one wall eight ATVs were parked in a row. Next to them were some dirt bikes, and she had to wonder what kind of work on a ranch would require their use. Storm, Austin, and Trey climbed onto three of the ATVs, started the engines, and drove them out in front of the barn. Storm came back for a fourth one and parked it next to the ones already outside. Afterward, they closed the doors back up.

Austin stepped up to Lisa. "You're going to ride with me."

Looking at the compactness of the vehicle she had to ask, "Is it safe?"

Gazing into her eyes, his hand came up to caress her cheek before kissing her lips. "Do you think I would do anything to intentionally put you in danger?"

She knew better than to question him but he was so big that he took up a lot of space on it. Shaking her head, he took her hand and walked her over to the all-terrain vehicle and climbed on. Motioning for her to get on behind him, she did. Finding a foothold, she shimmied her butt around on what remained of the seat to get comfortable and wrapped her arms around his waist. The three other men climbed aboard their motorized steeds after Storm and Trey slung backpacks on, and they all headed out to the west.

They followed a dirt road that went beyond the house for about a half mile and then they came to a stop. Storm got off his ATV and unlocked a gate, rode through, and then let the others through before locking it back up again. After continuing, they rode for another half mile before they began an ascent into the mountains. The oak trees that dotted the landscape on the flatland around the ranch became dense, and pine trees became more popular among the foliage. They followed the path that had been developed over time. Occasionally, Austin would point something out to Lisa that he thought might be of interest to her but mostly she hung on to him.

He was happy with the situation of her riding with him. Her hands clasped together on his hard abs right above his crotch. Her breasts were smashed into his back, and when they hit a rut, he felt them move up and down or smash further into him. They thought it would be better for her to ride with him since he was more surefooted when it came to the vehicles, though they all knew how to ride. He was surprised at how well Doc handled himself.

The trip took about an hour as the path ambled through the forest and in some places dipped or the grade of the ascent or descent was deeper than in other places. If this was the area where they had found her, she could only imagine what their ride was like carrying her on horseback.

The cabin came into view. It was an A-frame with a nice porch along the side of it. A couple of Adirondack chairs sat on it, a nice place to relax and take in nature. Windows climbed from the first floor all the way to the roofline, broken only by the rock chimney that ran up the height of the building and then some above the roofline. This was a beautiful place, Lisa thought to herself, though apprehension filled her body to the point she was shaking. At first she thought it was from the vibrations of the vehicle, but once it stopped, she knew better.

Carefully Austin climbed off and turned to his woman. Her face was pale. He had felt her shaking behind him and knew this had to be hard on her. Gathering her in his arms, he pulled her against him, her face buried in his shirt at his stomach. Running his hand down her hair, he tried to soothe her as much as possible. Storm and Trey noticed what was going on and came over to them.

"She's scared," he told them, almost in a whisper. Both men let their hands run up and down her back until they all could feel her calming down. Once she was composed enough to let them know she was all right, they helped her off the ATV and get control over her legs as they had been spread so wide for so long.

Storm and Trey took off their backpacks and each opened them up, and to Lisa's surprise, they pulled out three handguns. Each keeping one, Storm handed one to Austin before he began to give instructions. "Trey and Austin will go in first to make sure it's clear. Once they give the okay, Doc, Lisa, and I will head in. Lisa, I want you to be careful inside and I want you to stay with one of us at all times. If you remember anything let us know right away."

Nodding, she slipped her hand into his left one, leaving his right hand free for his gun. Austin and Trey made their way to the door and held their gun up straight in the air so it was pointing to the sky. Trey tried the door. It was unlocked and he pushed it open. Moving their guns down to aim in front of them, they entered cautiously. Clearing the first floor, Trey moved to the staircase at the back of the cabin. As quickly as they had cleared the first floor, Trey had cleared the second, which was basically a loft. Coming back down the stairs, he shouted out the door, "Clear! Come on in!"

Storm pushed the gun into the waistband of his jeans and started toward the door. When they arrived he growled at the hole in the door. Upon examination, the wood splintered inward and he had to wonder what had caused that. He wondered what else would need to be repaired. Pushing the door open, he entered before Lisa and found the interior as it should be except for the bed. Surprised it looked decent he had only to frown that the renter had moved the entire bed, frame, headboard, and footboard included, down to the first floor. Odd, but just like Lisa had described.

Lisa knew everyone was intently watching her. Doc was behind her and she nearly jumped out of her skin when he spoke.

"Trey."

Trey made his way over to him. "What's up?"

The two other men turned to see what was going on while Lisa moved closer to the bed, sweat beginning to bead on her forehead. Her heart had begun to pound within her chest and her head. As Trey began to take pictures of the kitchen and anything of importance, Lisa tried to steady her breathing.

Flashes of the day in this room began to appear in her memory.

Being cuffed to the bed.

The man threatening her of her impending rape and murder.

Her escape.

It was all coming back to her and it frightened her as if it was happening again.

Backing away from the bed, Lisa turned abruptly, and before any of the men could stop her she was out the door running blindly down the hill. Darting through the trees and brush, she seemed to be in a déjà vu moment, which frightened her even more.

A skittish rabbit darted out in front of her, and as she tried to avoid it, she stumbled. When a strong arm grabbed her around the waist she began to scream, trying to fight off the person behind her. She was lifted off the ground as the man's other arm caught her around her chest and she bent her head down to bite it. As her teeth sank down, she tasted blood.

"Jeez, woman!"

The arm around her chest was pulled away though the arm at her waist remained, but as she kicked backward and caught the man on his shin, he stumbled and they both fell to the ground. The man rolled so he wouldn't land directly on top of her. She felt herself turned toward him and hauled to her knees as he rose to his own while his hands spanned her waist.

Adrenaline still pumping through her veins, she felt threatened even though the demanding voice was familiar. "Lisa, look at me!" she heard him say to her as her fists struck at him blindly. After her fist struck his chin she felt herself being shaken.

"Damn it, Lisa! Stop! Stop it or I will put you over my knee and blister your bottom!"

Fear that someone would hurt her again had her trying to strike harder. When she struck his cheek this time, he grabbed both her wrists and held them together as he leaned further away from her. With his free hand, he grasped her chin and forced her to look at him. "Little one, you need to stop! I am not trying to hurt you!"

Austin's voice penetrated her hysteria as her eyes finally focused on the muscular man before her with the beautiful, long black hair. The planes and angles of his face were tight while his dark-brown eyes looked black with anger. She stopped fighting him, though her body visibly shook. Her iris eyes were wild with fear as they searched his face for comfort. Releasing his hold on her wrists, he drew her to him, wrapping his strong arms around her and held her as she cried against his chest.

"He broke into my home and he shot me and hit me," she started in between sobs. By that time the others had arrived. Trey hit some buttons on his phone and held it out toward her. "Whenever I would wake up he would stick a needle in me and I'd go back to sleep. I knew we were in a car but didn't know where we were going. When I fully woke, I was handcuffed to the bed. He said he was going to fuck me until he had his fill and then he would kill me. I knew I had to get away. When he took me to the bathroom and then handcuffed me back to the bed, I was able to work it loose.

"I pretended I was still cuffed. When he was trying to feed me, I grabbed his gun and tried to leave. He came after me and I shot him. I was the one to put the hole in the door. I'm sorry about that." She turned to Storm, who caressed her cheek lovingly. "I ran for a while. I could hear him chasing me. I remember taking a step and there was nothing there and I fell down the hill."

"You're okay now, little one," Austin said, kissing her head. "We're glad you remembered that."

Silence except the wind blowing in the trees surrounded them. Trey bent down to get closer to her. "Do you remember anything else? Who you are? Where you are from?"

Grasping onto Austin's shirt with one hand, she held out her hand to Storm who accepted it. Now that her memory had returned, she was terrified she was going to lose them. Trey continued to hold his phone toward her. Doc Anderson stood against a tree watching and listening.

* * * *

"My name is Lyndee Dwyer. Actually, Agent Dwyer. I am with the FBI." The pregnant pause was for the men to control their shock before she continued. "We have been trying to pull down an organized crime boss in Denver for about seven years now. I had just been accepted to the FBI when I was approached to go undercover as a hooker. It took me almost a year to catch the attention of the pimp that worked for him and I have been there ever since."

Austin had to ask the question that apparently everyone else was thinking. "How did you manage to have sex with men if you... Well, you know... You're not supposed to have sex when you are undercover," he was finally able to say, though couldn't get the other sentences out. He was beet red and she chuckled at that.

Sheepishly, she said, "I always had another hooker that looked like me go in. They wouldn't usually know me so I got away with it for a while. In the past year everything started falling apart with my cover. The pimp was starting to get suspicious. While I was trying to deal with him, I discovered he actually was a detective in Vice so he was playing both sides. I found out he was pushing the other pimps and hookers off the streets as his department came down on them, but he was able to operate easily off the grid for the crime boss. The day he busted me I had a meeting with my supervisor and I had told him that there was to be a party at the big boss's house that night and we were all going. Preston, Philip, my pimp, must have followed me. When I went back to the house we all shared, he called me into his office. He told me that he knew that I was giving information to the cops about him and he would be keeping an eye on me at the party. He told me then he was going to enjoy fucking me and making me pay. I fought him off and went back to the room the girls and I worked out of, waiting for a job."

All four men snickered at the comment of waiting for a job, though her three men looked angry as her story continued.

"We were taken to the boss's ranch that night by limo. The boss apparently has horses which he uses for therapy for children with disabilities."

"That's why you freaked out when you heard me talking to Doc about the same thing," Storm interjected, now fully understanding her action the previous night.

Nodding, she licked her lips and they knew she was getting nervous about the rest of the story. Austin was smoothing her hair down while Storm was rubbing her thigh while she straddled his cousin. "When we got there I tried to remain as inconspicuous as possible so no one would choose me but then when the raid went down, I was caught just like the rest and then hauled in to the Denver PD. Preston, I mean Philip, was at the ranch by that time also and was arrested. My supervisor bailed me out, declaring he was my father, but really he had pulled rank. We thought since it was nighttime that everyone would be held until morning so I went home to my apartment. Philip somehow managed to get out and came after me. I was so stupid that

I wasn't prepared for him when he burst through my door. I was exhausted and couldn't get to my gun in time."

Trey spoke finally. "It wasn't your fault. You know damn well he would have found a way to get to you no matter what. I'm just glad he didn't manage any further damage to you. Is there anyone you need to get a message to?"

"Yes. My supervisor needs to know I'm all right and where I am and that Philip is out there somewhere with a bullet wound looking for me."

A sharp intake of breath sounded next to her and she turned to look at Storm as he reached into his back pocket. Pulling out his wallet, he pulled out the business card that had been given to him yesterday at the store.

"Damn it! I should have read the damn thing!"

"What is it, honey?" she asked, taking it from him. Recognizing the logo of the Denver PD she looked further down and saw the name. Philip McKnight. Fuck! Now it made sense. She had heard his name at the store when she was hiding in the truck, but it didn't register with her amnesia. Plus, she hadn't recognized him from the back with the quick glimpse she had of him, though there was something familiar about him. Damn it!

"I can't believe that he has done all this. Why not just run away and hide? Change his name, his appearance. I can't believe he would add homicide to his list of crimes," she said sadly. "I didn't even know he was a cop until earlier this year."

Still holding his phone, Trey reached out and caressed her other cheek. "Sometimes people see dollar signs and they get greedy. I can't believe you actually got a ringer for yourself. Remind me not to cross you, baby. I don't want to be on your bad side."

Turning her head slightly, she kissed the palm of his hand, smiling. "Was there enough blood to get samples of?" she asked, going into investigator mode.

"Yes. We'll also need pictures as this is now a crime scene," Trey said, standing. "Doc, we'll need your fingerprints once we get back to town. Both Austin and Storm's are already on file, as are yours, baby."

Storm and Trey helped Lisa, or rather Lyndee, up to her feet while Austin rose to his own. Holding his arm gingerly where she had bitten him, Lyndee noticed the wound. "Oh, honey, I am so sorry," she said, holding onto his hand. "I was back in the moment when Philip was chasing me and I thought you were him."

With his good hand, he reached down, cupped his hand behind her neck and drew her to him for a kiss. Desire rested there as did concern and she knew the reason for that. Her men would be just as concerned about losing her as she was of losing them. She knew she would have to restructure her whole life now that it had been turned upside.

Doc stepped forward and examined the bleeding wound. "Damn woman, you don't need a gun!" the older gentleman said. "You just need to bite people. Your dentist must be so proud of you."

The jocularity broke up some of the tension as the group made their way back up to the cabin. Once there, Trey began to take pictures of the interior while the doctor got a knife and a plastic baggy and scraped some of the blood splatters from the counter top. Also, the sheets were stripped from the bed and placed in trash bags. A beer bottle was retrieved from the trash can outside and placed in another baggy. Everything was then placed into another trash bag and tied onto the back of Trey's ATV before he climbed aboard.

The other three men climbed aboard their machines and Lyndee swung up behind Austin. Taking off, she took one last look at the cabin over her shoulder and shuddered. As they made the descent down the mountain, a thought struck her, and she tapped Austin's shoulder to get his attention. When he stopped he turned to her. "What's the matter?"

"I had his gun when I fell. Can you take me to where you found me?"

The others had noticed the halting of the ATV and swung back around to see what was going on. "We're going to where we found her."

"I took all the pictures I needed to there," Trey said.

"I have to go back to find something," she said, her personality braver than what it had been an hour ago.

Austin led the way and when they came to the spot next to the ravine, she climbed off and examined the ground. Sure enough, there were her footprints and then one footprint but not the corresponding match to it. Slowly climbing downwards, she went from rock to rock, examining the areas around them until she got to the bottom. Blood marked the area where she had lain and she glanced around. Spotting something under a bush, she stepped over to it, pushed the foliage aside and found what she was looking for. The Glock that had probably saved her life. Double-checking the safety on it she tucked it into the waistband on her backside, climbed back up the hill, and resumed her place behind her domineering man. On the trip back to the house, she had time to think about the three men.

Austin was domineering, which sent a thrill to her pussy whenever he spoke in that tone. He was a bit rougher than the other two when it came to his lovemaking but she liked that. Several times he had threatened to spank her and that caused her cunt to weep just like it was doing at the moment. She feared that by the time she got off the vehicle she would be embarrassed by a wet spot between her legs. Hugging him tighter, she laid her head on his shoulder.

Storm was more controlling in his lovemaking. It was like he didn't want to hurt her. He had been able to read her enough to know when to hold her close during a memory trigger and the same with sex. She enjoyed that part of him.

Trey was the wild one. Oh, he could be funny and mischievous as he had been the previous day at the store, but she found he could be quite serious, especially when it came to his job. She was surprised he was a cop. She expected something totally different of him, like a waiter or a rodeo clown, or even a bull rider in the rodeo. A person who didn't care what kind of job he held.

* * * *

As the machine's engine ceased, Lyndee jerked awake. She had been exhausted by her excursion into the past and had dozed off. Austin had held onto her hands when he felt her body relax behind his, worried she would fall off. Climbing off the vehicle, he pulled her to him, bent slightly, and slipping his hand beneath her knees, carried her into the house and to her bed. Storm and Trey watched the retreating form as he disappeared into the house and even a few moments afterwards.

Doc came up between the two men. "So, what are your plans with this young lady? I would hate to see you hurt her."

The two men slowly turned toward him in shock, but Storm was the one who was able to find his voice first. "What do you mean, Doc?"

"You are all obviously in love with her and she is very much in love with all of you. I won't admit to understanding it, but please, give her time to recuperate from this debacle. I don't want to hear you have broken her heart in any way."

"You won't, Doc. We do love her and she understands it. We'll do right by her. We promise," Trey said, patting the man on the shoulder. "She has a good friend in you, lookin' after her and all."

"She's been through hell and back with this. I think now that she has her memory back, she'll be okay."

Glancing back at the house, the brothers spoke in unison. "We hope so."

"Well, thanks for an interesting time, boys, but I'm heading home. Call me if you need me," the man said as he walked to his small pickup. He had already put his doctor's bag in the cab earlier that morning, so he was ready to go.

Trey went into cop mode quickly. "Hey, Doc, don't forget to go into the Sheriff's office and have them take your fingerprints. I'll be sending a team up to the cabin tomorrow."

The older man had opened his door and was climbing in. "Will do, Trey."

"Let's get these in the barn and then I'll need to get to the office," Trey said, climbing back onto the vehicle.

"Are you going to be taking Lisa with you?"

"No. She needs to rest before all the questioning and interrogation begins. I'll try to get anyone interested to come out here so we don't stress her out too much. Plus we can all keep her in our sights since we don't know who to trust. As it is right now, I'm not sure she knows who to trust either."

Climbing onto his ATV, Storm nodded his agreement. His brother may irritate the daylights out of him sometimes, but when he was in cop mode, he was a different person. Storm would never admit it out loud, but he was proud of his brother. Their parents would have been proud of him also.

Chapter Thirteen

The two put away all of the ATVs before heading into the house. Trey made his way to Lyndee's room to see if he could get some alone time with her before he went to the office. Knocking on the door lightly, he heard her sweet voice bidding him entrance. Austin was just coming out of the bathroom, and glancing at his cousin he gave him a knowing smile. Leaning over, he kissed his woman on the lips. "I'll be back later. I think the cop wants to interrogate you now."

Waiting until the door closed behind him before moving, Trey watched her face. There was weariness there as it had been a trying day for her, but he also saw raw desire. Stepping to the bed, he kneeled on it next to her. "I know this has been a trying day for you, so if you want to rest, I'll understand."

"No," she whispered. "I want you. I want you to fuck me."

No sweeter words had ever been uttered to him, but he didn't want to tax her after the day she had already had. Laying his hand on her thigh he squeezed it gently. "Baby, I would love to do nothing more than make sweet love to you, but you have been through a traumatic time today and you need to rest. I can see it in your eyes."

Bravado leading her, she moved his hand to the apex between her legs. He could feel her heat and the moisture that had pooled there and his breath hitched. Popping the button at her fly, she slowly moved the zipper down, tempting him even more. Remaining still, Trey watched her as she slid her hands up under her thermal shirt and up to her breasts. He could see her hands moving around them beneath the fabric, and he tried to will the straining object in his jeans to rest but it was to no avail.

Standing, he moved to the foot of the bed while unbuttoning the red-and-green flannel shirt he had worn. Toe-kicking off his boots, he pushed the flannel off his massive shoulders, all the while never taking his eyes off hers. Reaching over his shoulders, he pulled the white T-shirt off and tossed it aside before he moved down to pull her jeans off by their hems. Eyeing the red thong he saw the wet spot there at the edge of the triangle that met with her ass. He felt a surge in his cock, knowing she was already ready for him.

"Strip!" he commanded as he unbuttoned his jeans, watching her.

He saw the shiver that ran through her body at his dominant tone. As a good sub should, she unbuttoned the few buttons on the V-neck of the thermal. She pulled it over her head and let it loose to fall down her back. Breathless, he watched her undo the clasp at the front of her bra, the material separating and her breasts bouncing from the effect. She let the red straps slide down her arms, wriggled free of it, and then put her hands on the thin elastic material at her hips.

Trey licked his lips as he unzipped his jeans. His eyes followed her hands as they pushed the flimsy material from her hips down her well-shaped, muscular legs. When she got it to her ankles, he took the thong, pressed it to his nose, and growled before tossing it aside. Bending at the waist, he hurriedly removed his socks and then knelt on the bed between her legs. Not having lain back down, she sat spread eagle so he reached out and fondled her breasts gently, surprising her with his actions.

"I love your breasts. They are so big for a little woman like you," he murmured, moving off to her left side.

Guiding her down onto her back, he gazed upon her breasts before lowering his head. Placing a light kiss to her hardened nipple he pulled back slightly and watched it pucker even more from the mere touch of his lips. Leaning forward again, he licked at the dark-pink nub before letting his tongue move down the side of the large globe, a gasp emanating from her. The tip of his tongue met the tongue of the dragon painted on her side, and he began to follow the languid movement of the serpent on her skin. When necessity rose, he gently pushed her over to her left side and continued to follow the ink. As he got closer to the tail, he pushed her onto her stomach. Her legs separated as she turned and the aroma of her arousal filled his senses. His cock throbbed relentlessly and tapped at her leg. Soon, he told it. Soon.

His tongue began the journey up the slope of her rounded derriere, savoring the taste of her and how exotic it felt to trace the trail of the tattoo.

He might have to get a few of his own and have her reciprocate. At the tail, he ended the exploration with a loud kiss and then a nip with his teeth. She shivered beneath him as a breath of ecstasy escaped her. His finger followed the tip of the tail into the crevice between her rounded, fleshy globes, downward past the puckered hole to the moist slit that was his goal.

* * * *

Anticipation shook her as his large digit teased her. When his finger grazed her asshole she had clinched her buttocks together, hoping he would slip his fingers in and claim her there. Once his fingers grazed her pussy lips, she felt the cream leak from within, coating his digits. Slipping two of his fingers inside her he felt her pussy walls contract around him, drawing them in further. She desperately wanted his lips on her and she pushed her hips upward, allowing him to move in deeper.

He chuckled at her movement but didn't oblige at the moment. Turning his palm over so it faced the bed he cupped his hand and began to slide his fingers in and out, rubbing across the soft, spongy area within her dark, moist pussy.

Her legs spread apart, providing the room he needed to maneuver in, as she gasped at the motion he made within her. He nipped at her ass near the tail of the dragon, sending chills through her body. "Do you want me, sweetheart?"

Her breath escaped her lips as his hand ceased pumping into her and stilled, and his callused fingers began moving against her G-spot. "Yes, Trey. I want you so bad!"

Licking the cleft in her ass, he asked, "You want me to do what?"

Aggravated that he would choose this time to tease her, she said, "I want you to put your cock inside me and fuck me with it!"

There was another chuckle from him before he said, "Oh such dirty language for such a sweet, innocent girl. You better not swear in front of Austin unless you're in bed or he'll take you over his knee and spank you."

Pushing the envelope slightly to see what her men were capable of in the bedroom, her voice came out in a whisper of anticipation. "What about you, Trey? Would you spank me? Would you tie me up and fuck me?"

Pausing, Trey became worried that she was fearful of the concept. "Do you want us to? Does it scare you?"

"Yes. It scares me but it also intrigues me. I've seen the girls have it done to them and they seemed to enjoy it, but it looked scary. What if you lose control?"

Trey licked his way down to her asshole, feeling the tremor rush through her body before resting his chin on her soft flesh. "We don't lose control, honey. We are experienced Doms. We know when to give pleasure and when to punish you with pleasure but we never hurt just to hurt you. Austin is the one who speaks the harshest, but the one you have to watch out for is Storm. Once in Dom mode, he takes control until we have all had our fun. We would use safe words to keep you safe so you don't have to be frightened. Let us show you tonight after dinner. We can stop at any time."

* * * *

Pushing her ass back toward him, her breath hitched in desperation. "Okay. You can do what you want to do to me tonight, but please Trey, make love to me right now!"

With the anticipation built up within her and the talk of bondage, she was so close. His fingers moved within her again, striking that special spot within her, and she rose slightly from the bed as she screamed out her orgasm. When she loosened her hold on him, he pulled out and swung himself up between her legs. With his hands on her hips, he pulled her backward so her hips were up in the air. Taking the hint, she rose up on her hands, swaying her hips against his hard, throbbing cock. He groaned at her brazenness.

Lyndee felt his thick cock at her ass and had to wonder what he was planning. Her ass was sore from the ride up the mountain, but if he wanted to take her there she would let him. She felt the tip of him move down and rub through the moisture that was dripping from her, teasing her opening before moving to rub against her clit. Gasping, she bucked a bit and his dick moved back to the slit before he slowly, tantalizingly slid just the tip inside of her. Moving one hand up her hip and then down under her he found the hard pearl within her folds and when he barely touched it she came again. Her pussy clamped down on the tip of his cock and she felt him still.

Relaxing her vagina, she felt him finally push deep into her until his root seemed to open her further. His thighs were flush with hers and she could feel his hard abs against her ass. Then he pulled out until only the tip remained. It seemed like an eternity before he pushed back in. The fullness he created with his cock inside her made it seem as if she felt every vein in the organ as he began to move in and out of her. Her moans filled the room whenever he passed over her sensitive spot. As if he wanted to make sure she was satisfied, he moved his hand around to enclose her clit between his index and middle fingers and squeezed it gently. She bucked her hips at the sensation but continued to thrust back to meet his hips with each inward stroke.

Lyndee felt his other hand move to the cleft in her ass and move lower, swiping at the fluid that escaped her cunt around his cock and glided it up to the puckered hole. A growl escaped her when she felt his thumb pressed against it, anticipation growing along with the sensation building within her pussy. In a moment his wide digit popped through the tight muscle, and he moved it around the rim, giving her time to adjust. She was now panting as all three erotic zones were being pleasured.

The tingling feeling that had begun deep within her shot through her like a bullet from a gun as it travelled to all of the nerve endings in her body. A scream of ecstasy escaped her lips as she bucked back once more and held herself to him as he held her by the hips with one hand and buried his cock deep inside her. His cum jettisoned into her and she felt as if he wasn't going to stop as it seemed to go on forever.

Her arms were shaking and weak, finally giving way, and her upper body collapsed onto the bed, sweat bathing her whole body. Moans continued to emanate from her as her pussy kept contracting around his cock and she continued to feel him throb within her. Finally he pulled his thumb out of her ass with a resounding pop and then pulled his arm from around her hip. Pulling himself out of her he rose and made his way into the bathroom. She vaguely heard water running and then felt a warm washcloth cleaning her, but she was soon drifting off. From a distance she heard Trey whisper, "I love you, sweetheart. You won't be leaving us."

* * * *

Waking slowly Lyndee stretched her body sinuously, her muscles sore not just from the lovemaking with Trey but from the journey on the ATV and the frantic run down the hill and then the climb down and then up the ravine. She needed a hot bath and she really needed to find a gym to work out in. It had been too long without it and she needed to stay in shape. Her job required it. She wondered how the men stayed in such fantastic shape out here on the ranch. Was it all the lifting they did? She would have to ask.

Rising, she realized she was alone. Trey had disappeared and she wondered where he had gone but she would find out eventually. It was the first time she had been alone since her men had found her and now it felt strange. Going into the bathroom she started the water running in the large tub, and for a minute let her mind slip back to the other morning after they all made love to her and all ended up in the tub together. Smiling to herself she took a clip and pulled her braid up and clipped it so it wouldn't get wet. She could already tell that it was still damp from her shower earlier today. That was the problem with long, thick hair. It took forever to dry.

The mirror was fogging up with the heat of the running water. She loved a bath hot enough to leave her red as a lobster. At first it was to clean off all the filth that she was around all day, but she came to enjoy the way her body felt so cleansed afterward, along with being so relaxed. Stepping into the tub, she sank slowly into the hot water, closing her eyes as she leaned back and rested her head against the edge. When the water had risen to her chest she leaned over and turned off the water. Foregoing the jets she lay back again and relished the relaxing moment as she had no idea how long it would be before her men would come to check on her. Yes, she loved all three of the men, but she felt womanly to be able to have a nice, hot bath alone. She did it also to be able to allow her body to feel relaxed for whatever her men would have planned for her.

Wishing she had a book to keep herself company she lay there trying to wrap her mind around the events that had happened in the past few days. The bust had gone down the way she had expected, with them actually arresting Alexander Markova and most of his lieutenants along with several crime bosses from other cities. Minor players within the organization were taken in also. Hopefully the amount of evidence that she had gathered along with some other undercover agents and cops would take these guys off the streets for good. She never expected Philip to make bail so quickly with the bosses behind bars, but she wondered if he got out, were the others out also. Disappointment and anger had her on the edge. She would need to talk to Trey about what they would need to do, but hopefully she would have tonight to be with her men before getting back to work on the case. They'd have to work out the details on location of the job later also.

When the water began to cool down, Lyndee picked up a washcloth and the bathing gel. Pouring the scented gel onto the cloth she heard a light knock on the door. "Come in."

Austin popped his head around the opening door. She noticed the twinkle in his dark eyes as they lit upon her. The image of herself on her knees while water ran in rivulets down her body caused a flush to rise upon her cheeks as she began to soap up her body. For the first time in her life she realized that something so menial as washing could be so sensual when a man watched her. She had so much to learn.

* * * *

The tall Native American man entered fully and leaned against the counter, arms crossed in front of his chest, ankles crossed with lust painted on his face. Oh how he wanted her under him right now, though the trio of men had agreed to hold off until after dinner. While watching the soapy cloth wash each of her breasts he had a mental chat with his stiffening cock, though he realized it wasn't listening. He had to smile, which wasn't missed by his woman in the tub.

"What are you thinking about?" she asked seductively, as if she didn't know. She had seen the bulge in his jeans growing and it pleased her that she had that effect on him, on all of them.

A chuckle emanated from deep in his chest. "You know what I'm thinking, little one. Since we found you, you are always on my mind. You are embedded in my mind and in my heart. You are our woman and none of us will let you go."

The thrill that shot through her went straight to her heart. It confused her that they had known each other such a short time, though they knew they loved each other immensely. However there was still fear for the future, for her at least. She didn't know how this was going to work, loving three men. What if they got jealous of each other? What would other people think about such a relationship? What about her job and her independence? There were questions that needed to be answered and hopefully they would give them to her soon.

Picking up the towel she had laid on the edge of the tub, Austin held it out for her. After rinsing off her body Lyndee stood up and let him help her step over the edge. His large hands wrapped the large towel around her body then let his arms slip around her waist and he held her to him. Leaning his head down, he kissed the top of her head, squeezing her to him.

"I want you to know that I love you with all my heart, little one, and I will be with you through this whole mess. Then you will come back here to us."

Turning in his arms she laid her head on his chest. "I might not be back for a while."

Hugging her tightly, he said, "I'm not letting you go and I refuse to let you go through this alone. I will be going with you."

She tried to pull back so she could look at him, but he held her still so she spoke into his chest. "I appreciate the offer but I can't take you away from the ranch for so long."

Trying to remain calm, Austin breathed in slowly before exhaling. "I'm not offering. I'm going with you, no arguing."

Knowing she wouldn't win, she nodded her head and smiled. "We'll have to get a bigger bed. You won't fit in mine."

Bending her backward he lowered his mouth to cover hers in a soft kiss before letting her go. "Now go get dressed. Supper is ready," he said, smiling before popping her on her terry-covered derriere, "and be quick about it. We men are starving."

Protesting as if he had hurt her, she exclaimed, "Ouch! That hurt!"

Stepping up to her small frame, he put two fingers under her chin and lifted it so she looked into his eyes. "Baby that was nothin'. I'll show you what a real spanking is," he drawled, his voice dropping an octave with his carnal lust. He noticed her shiver at his words but also saw the light twinkle in her eyes. He had been right about her. She was a hardworking cop who needed a break from being in control, and they were the men to control her sexual needs.

"Get dressed," he said with a sigh and then turned and walked out the door, leaving her to stare after him.

* * * *

Drying off she went around to the closet and chose her clothes carefully for the evening. Excitement coursed through her body, her nipples already hard peaks and her pussy moist. A flowing skirt in a sky blue that came just below her knees matched with a red tank top captured the outer image. Beneath that was a black strapless demi-bra that did little to cover the nipples that could be seen through the cotton of the tank and nothing else. Daringly she opted to tempt fate and not wear any panties, which shot a thrill through her body that went straight to her pussy, causing it to weep even more.

Barefoot was the order for the evening as she figured they wouldn't be going outside. Removing the clip from her hair she removed the elastic band from the bottom of her hair and began to undo the braid. Taking a brush, she brushed through the golden strands before returning them to the braid, the easiest style to help keep them from her face. Glancing in the mirror she was satisfied with her look and made her way down the hallway to find her men.

In the living room she found them relaxing, a reality show on the TV. Each had a glass of liquor that they were nursing as they watched the action on the wide screen. From her vantage point where the hallway emptied into the main room, she silently watched her men for a few minutes. Was this the way their evenings would be spent? Or would they be doing something else each night? She had to wonder especially being used to city life.

The tinkling of ice in a glass brought her out of her reflections and a sigh brought all three of their attentions to her. Smiles on their faces, they rose and came toward her. Each kissed her on the cheek, first Storm, Trey, and then Austin brought up the rear. He escorted her into the kitchen where they all sat at the table to enjoy the meal that Martha had prepared for them. Conversation revolved around the trip Trey had made to town while Lyndee slept.

"How long did I sleep?" she asked with amazement as she knew how long it took for them to get to Kalispell the previous day.

"Darlin', you were out for a good four hours. We knew you were tired and needed the rest," Storm said compassionately, patting her hand. Then, with a devilish grin, he said, "I'm glad. You look well rested. You'll relax tonight, but not the way you think."

A blush tinged her cheeks while each of the men watched her and smiled wickedly, and she felt her breasts swell with anticipation, not to mention what was happening in her groin. The men all watched as her nipples strained against the material. Trey swore while his cousin sucked in a deep breath. Storm continued to look at her, his eyes hooded and lust filled. Nervously Lyndee picked at what food was left on her plate, which was most of it, before the butterflies doing the cha-cha in her stomach won out. Standing she took her plate over to the sink and set it down gently, leaning against the sink and taking in a deep breath as she gazed out into the waning light.

An arm slipped around her waist and a light kiss was placed on the side of her neck. She didn't have to turn to see who it was. A smile touched her lips. Trey. "Don't be frightened," he whispered before kissing her neck again. "Remember, we'll stop if you want us to."

He placed his plate in the sink along with hers before slipping his hand away. Another arm slipped around her and she could tell by the strength in it that it was Austin. Placing his dish in the sink, he pulled her braid, forcing her head up to look at him. His eyes were nearly black with desire before he bent down and kissed her lips lightly. A shiver ran through her. Letting go, he too walked away.

The scraping of the chair at the table announced that Storm had risen. His boots sounded like strikes of thunder as he made his way over to the sink, stopping right behind her. Reaching around her petite frame, he placed his plate in the sink on top of the others. One arm circled her waist while the other circled her shoulders, his hand splayed right above one of her breasts. Breathing became difficult for Lyndee as she was pulled back against his body, his hardened cock nudging her back.

Her head fell back against his chest, her eyes hooded with her emotions. He felt her heart beating rapidly in her chest and knew he had to calm her down. Whispering, he sounded like his everyday self. "Breathe, darlin'. We are not going to hurt you in any way that you don't want us to. We provide pleasurable pain. A pain that will bring you to ecstasy. If you don't like something, you have the right to say so. We won't look upon you badly. We know you have been through a horrible ordeal and we don't want you to panic and hurt yourself, or one of us. Do you understand?"

The heart under his hand began to slow down its beating. It wasn't quite normal, but more of a tattoo of desire, not fear. Her breathing had become regular again. Kissing the top of her head, he turned her and pointed at the door that led to the basement. "Go downstairs, strip out of your skirt and top, and leave your under things on. Then go to the bed there, put the blindfold on, and wait for us in the middle of the bed. Understood?"

Nodding slowly, she swallowed the golf ball sized lump in her throat and thought this was the worst time to go without panties. Damn! Making her way to the door that would lead her in a new direction sexually, she went apprehensively. When she got to the door, she turned to each of the men, who smiled at her, before turning the knob. Opening the door, she descended to her fate, her stomach churning in excitement and fear. She knew when she came back up those stairs she would be a different person.

Anticipation filled her on what lay in the room below the house. At the bottom of the stairs there was a "T" section. To the right, where the banister actually opened up toward the bottom of the stairs, was a home gym area. A treadmill and an elliptical lined one wall with a TV in front of each machine. Several weight benches sat around the room while a boxer's bag hung in the corner. The weights themselves sat on shelves beneath the stairs. At least she now knew where they got their fantastic muscles from.

To the left of the stairs there was an open door. The light was already on and as she walked in her breath drew in sharply. A bed was the centerpiece of the room, a recessed light above it spotlighting it. It was a four-poster, though the posts were common four-by-fours with metal loops strategically placed up the length of each of them. Lyndee figured they could tie a woman up at different heights according to their needs. Black sheets covered the bed and pillows lined one end of the bed.

Other items filled each corner of the room but the bed was what caught her attention the most, especially its location. She remembered another bed in the middle of a room and one that she had been held captive in. Panic choked her breathing and she began to shake. Talking to herself within the confines of her mind, she tried to tell herself that this wasn't the same, but fear still held her captive in her mind the same way Philip had physically.

Chapter Fourteen

Overpowered by the sight of the bed she hadn't heard the men coming down the stairs, nor had she realized they had stopped right behind her. Visibly shaking she tried to take a step but her foot wouldn't move more than an inch. She wanted this so bad right now, to show her men that she was brave and sexy, but her mind just wouldn't cooperate. Tears streamed down her cheeks and just when she felt she would turn and run, she felt a hand on her shoulder. It was a light touch so it didn't frighten her, but she didn't want to turn to face the men as it would disappoint them that she couldn't get into the bed where they wanted her.

Glancing down to the hand on her shoulder, it was the one hand she hadn't expected to be there. The hand belonged to the one who was foretold to be the most domineering. Storm gently turned her toward the three of them, though she went reluctantly. Concern and shame was plastered on their faces as they had come to realize what they had just done to her when they told her to go downstairs alone.

Tilting her chin up to meet his gaze with two fingers, Storm whispered, "I'm sorry, darlin'. I wasn't thinking about the setup down here."

Austin, now behind her, ran his arms around her waist and held her back to him. "We promised we would never hurt you and we won't. This is just our fun room, but we haven't brought a woman down here in several years. We've had to do some cleaning."

Lyndee noticed Trey hung back, disappointment etched in his face, and she knew he thought she would bolt if they gave her a chance. Standing tall, or at least as tall as she could with her stature, she smiled softly and opened her arms to her man with the emerald green eyes, and he practically flew into them, her arms closing around him. Austin sighed behind her while Storm's eyes lit up, a smile hidden in their blue depths, though it didn't reach his mouth. Trey's strong arms held her around her shoulders as his cousin pulled back slightly but kept his arms wrapped around her.

Storm took a step backward and cleared his throat. Austin and Trey both let go of her as she whimpered at the loss of their arms. With authority riding in his voice, Storm commanded, "Lyndee, strip!"

Watching the three men as they stood side by side, she swallowed the lump that had returned to her throat. This time she saw lust in the three sets of eyes and lightning seemed to run from her nipples to her ever-moistening pussy. Not wanting to keep these men waiting any longer, she crossed her arms in front of her, grabbed the hem of her tank top, pulled it up over her head, and tossed it aside. Groans emanated from each of them at the sight before them.

Dainty fingers slid beneath the elastic waistband of the skirt and began to push downwards, the material sliding down her shapely hips. Once it was past her womanly curves, she let it tumble to pool around her ankles. Eyes downcast in shyness, she had to fight the urge to cover the nudity of her pussy, as sighs, groans, and growls came from the trio of manliness before her.

Not sure what to do at this point, she kept her eyes downcast, her hands in fists at her sides, waiting. At times she had heard the girls discussing being handled by a dominant man and having to act the submissive with them or even with their pimp, Philip, so she acted the way the girls did. Embarrassment flooded her on how much knowledge she had learned from her friends and here she was a virgin the whole time. Waiting for one of them to speak was downright nerve-racking for her as her nipples hardened even more at their scrutiny, and her pussy lips seemed to flutter in anticipation, a streak of fluid trickling down her inner thighs.

She saw Storm breathe in deeply as if he could smell her arousal. "Get on the bed," he said in an octave above a whisper.

Turning, she slowly made her way to the bed, which she actually had to climb up into as the height of the mattress fit their frames, not her own. She felt exposed as she did so, her ass, and she was certain her drenched pussy lips, on display for their smoldering eyes, as she came to the middle of the large California king-sized bed. Again, unsure of what to do next, she sat down facing them, her hands in her lap, head tilted down submissively.

With pussy clinching in anticipation, she took a chance to glance up and saw the three men huddled together, speaking in hushed whispers. As if football players breaking the huddle for the next play, all three nodded in agreement before turning back toward her. She lowered her gaze again, hoping she hadn't been caught peeking.

* * * *

Moving slowly, the trio began removing their clothing as they walked to the bed. They knew they needed to squelch her fears about what this room represented and make her understand what they wanted to give her. Unconditional love along with pleasure was her future with them and they were more than ready to provide that. They knew she loved them by her actions, and hopefully soon they would hear her say the words, but for now, they needed to show her they were in essence, her men.

Storm was the first to reach the bed. Sitting upon it, he reached out and cupped her chin with one hand, turning her head up and toward him. "You are the most beautiful woman I have ever met," he said, lowering his lips to hers, laying a chaste kiss to them. "I know you are frightened, but you don't have to be. This is all done in the name of love and pleasure. It's not anything like what Philip wanted to do to you. I hope you can open yourself to the experience, to open your mind to what we want to show you."

Watching her iris eyes he saw the fear replaced with longing, with desire as she slowly nodded her head. Her pink tongue slipped out briefly, wetting her lips in anticipation, and he lowered his head. At first his lips touched hers gently, just barely drinking in her essence, but when he heard her moan, he opened his mouth and his tongue thrust itself against the seam of flesh. He felt her open for him, letting him devour her mouth with his own. He swiped at the insides of her cheeks, the roof of her mouth, over her tongue, dragging it into his own. When she began to back away from his mouth, he moved his hand up, cupping it behind the back of her head and holding her to him.

Moaning against him, she began pushing against his chest but he didn't want to separate from her. "Storm," Trey said gently. "Let her breathe. You're crushing her."

Letting up some, giving her some breathing room, he still drank from her lips. His other hand moved up to grasp a breast, kneading at it. Jeez, he needed to hold her, to breathe her, to be a part of her so much, but he didn't want to frighten her any more than she already was. Remembering that the other two wanted her as much as he did, he let up on her. As his mouth pulled away from hers, a moan of disappointment emanated from her.

His hand remained behind her head while he moved the other hand up toward her chest and gently pushed her backward to lay her down. She kept her eyes on his as she took deep breaths as if she was trying to keep herself calm. Her eyes never wavered as Austin joined them on the bed as if she was looking for guidance from him.

"We won't tie you up tonight, darlin', though I promise you it will come soon enough and you will enjoy giving your body over to us. Do you understand that?" Nodding, she smiled tentatively, but that disappeared quickly when he continued. "You need to answer us verbally. There has to be communication between the four of us in all aspects of our lives, but especially in here and while we are making love to you. You have to let us know what you like and what you don't like, if we are hurting you or if you want more of something. We have to hear you say it. We will always be vocal with you on most things. If there is danger and we want to protect you that will usually be the only instance when we may not communicate openly with you. Understood?"

Beginning to nod, she remembered what he had just said. "Yes. I have a question."

"Ask anything you want, little one," Austin drawled beside her.

She glanced around as if looking for Trey. When she spotted him standing at the foot of the bed with his massive arms crossing his chest and his cock standing up at attention against his abs, she licked her lips. Storm was pleased that she found pleasure in looking at a man's naked form.

"I know this room seems to be special, and I don't know what I am supposed to do, what I'm supposed to say. The girls said that when they played these games with their johns that they would call them sir or master. Am I supposed to do that?"

Smiling down at her, Storm shook his head. "We don't require that of you. We are here to please you, not for you to bow down to us or be our total slave. Despite what you see of the devices in this room, these are here to pleasure you, not to totally dominate you, though by the tone of our voice it may sound that way. If we sound harsh, it is for your protection or for your enjoyment. You will have to learn the difference between the two, but down here, it will most likely be for your pleasure."

To her side, Austin began running his hand up and down her arm. "Never hesitate to ask a question of us if you need to, and never, ever hesitate to let us know that we are hurting you beyond the boundaries you are comfortable with. That is why you have to communicate verbally, so we don't go beyond those boundaries. Now, you need to lay back and let us get to know what you like and don't like."

* * * *

Both Austin and Storm lay next to her, rubbing up and down her arms with one hand. Taking in the moment, Lyndee closed her eyes and reveled in the feeling. The bed dipped at the end between her feet and she knew that Trey had joined them. His hands began to caress and rub one foot, slowly making his way up to her ankle. Reveling in the feeling of three men's hands on her body exhilarated her as she had never imagined this feeling even with one man.

Austin leaned over, slashing his mouth over hers, his tongue demanding entry. When she didn't open quickly enough as she wasn't sure what was expected of her, a hand plucked at a nipple harshly. She opened her mouth to protest and he thrust his tongue into her warm, moist mouth. The hand on her breast disappeared and she moaned at the loss. His mouth was brutal on hers, the flesh of her lips smashed against her teeth, his tongue relentless while moving within her depths. She wanted to hold onto him, to run her hands through his luscious black hair, but she gave in to the need to let them run the show.

A tongue began to run up her leg, sending a shocking chill up to her pussy. It began at her ankle and moved slowly upward. The hands on her arms moved up to her shoulders, kneading her muscles there. Moans began to sound from her at the ministrations, her hips beginning to seek out relief from someone or something. Even after listening to the girls, she never imagined feeling this good. Why hadn't she sought out something like this before? But she knew the answer deep within her soul. It wasn't meant to be and she knew that. She was a believer in "things happen for a reason" and she knew deep in her heart that she was meant to fall in love with these three wonderful men and that was why she knew it was all right to be with them so quickly after meeting them.

A hot mouth covered her nipple, drawing it in and up against the roof of the mouth. Storm had a wonderful mouth and he knew how to use it. Actually, she thought with a mental chuckle, they were all talented with their mouths. The pull on the tight bud sent shockwaves down to her pussy. It seemed that everything these men were doing centered at her pussy as if it were the heart of her sexuality.

The mouth on her leg had passed her knee and was moving up her inner thigh. Teeth nipped the tender flesh and her hips rose off the bed. There would be a nip and then Trey's tongue would savor the spot, soothing the slight pain. She felt his hand raise her leg as he got closer to her core. She heard him breathe in deeply before his tongue began the onslaught.

Austin continued his ministrations on her mouth, their tongues dueling together as her lips bruised under his. It seemed as if he couldn't get enough of her, of her taste. His hand made its way down to her other breast and squeezed it. Working the nipple between his forefinger and thumb, he rolled it around, pinched and even pulled at it, spiking her arousal at the onslaught.

Lyndee felt Trey settle between her legs, lifting them up to rest on his shoulders. Her pussy lips seemed to open and close several times in anticipation, knowing he was looking at her open cunt. In her mind's eye she could see the feral look upon his face as he gazed upon her most private area. His hands fanned out to the sides of her lower lips, spreading her open even more as one of his thumbs slid upward through the moist slit. When his digit rubbed across her rock-hard nub she bucked her hips up as she moaned loudly into Austin's mouth. Trey used his thumb to circle her clit slowly at first and then gained speed as he thrust two fingers into her waiting pussy.

The tingling that had been growing between her legs as these men made love to her with their mouths and hands was beginning to spark deep within her core. Shockwaves shot out from her breasts and core both, her breath coming in pants as she felt her body beginning to spiral upward as the pulses in her pussy became electrified. As if a transformer blew out within her, the sparks flew out to every nerve ending in her body as her climax hit. With leverage of her hips on Trey's shoulders, her body arched upward, leaving her shoulders and head on the bed, Trey taking the brunt of her weight. Ripping her mouth from under Austin's, Lyndee let her scream loose as she rode the ecstatic wave.

Trey never stopped pumping his fingers deep into her cunt or stopped stimulating her clit. Storm continued to suck her nipple and Austin continued to pluck her other nipple. The waves of pure ecstasy continued to roll through her, one after another until she felt she was going to die, her screams turning to a heart-wrenching wail.

As the sensations began to wane, her wail began to turn into whimpers as she felt her body relax. Austin gazed down at her. "Okay?"

Nodding, though embarrassed by making such a spectacle of herself, she nodded as she looked up at him. "I'm sorry. I didn't mean to be so loud."

Austin chuckled. "You can be as loud as you want to be, little one. That way we know we are pleasuring you correctly, that you are enjoying what we are doing to you. Did you enjoy that?"

"Yes," she said breathlessly as Storm and Trey continued to play with her body. Her hand caressed his bicep, feeling the strength of it, and marveled at how gentle he was with her.

"Good," he said as he lowered his mouth to her nipple. "'Cause we are going to make you crazy as we make you come over and over again tonight. Tomorrow, we'll start on your pleasurable punishment."

Lyndee gulped in wonder at his words. Could punishment be pleasant? How was that possible? But for now, she let her mind wander back to what her men were doing to her body, her mind, and her soul.

Storm pulled away from her breast, letting go of the nipple with a resounding pop. His mouth moved slowly up her chest, nipping along the way with his teeth. Goose bumps ran along her skin from his mouth and from his mustache. It was an added sensation she found exhilarating. Still on the move, he made his way to her mouth, which he captured as harshly as Austin had.

While his brother took her mouth, Lyndee felt Trey pull his fingers from her depths and then heard him moan in ecstasy. A vision of him licking his fingers sent her arousal up another notch. Then, she felt his hot breath on her wet nether folds. She heard him breathe in deeply, and though it titillated her, she still had a streak of embarrassment run through her. She still didn't understand what they found so intoxicating about the smell of her pussy.

The heat and velvety texture of his tongue grazed up the valley between her labia. Ever so slowly his oral organ moved from her perineum up past her vaginal opening and up to the peak of her sex. The exquisiteness of the action sent her pussy to quivering and she heard him chuckle. A growl emanated from her, which transferred itself to Storm's mouth, causing him to growl along with her.

Trey found her clit with his mouth, nipping at it with his teeth. Between her trying to breathe and kissing Storm, she whimpered at the sensations he was building within her. It was like a construction zone within her, building from the bottom up. She had been so far undercover she never once thought about even exploring her body, though the girls had told her that it was wonderful if there was a man who would suck her pussy and suck her clit. She hadn't believed it then but wished she had at least tried it.

Again she felt Trey sink two fingers into her. He twisted them around and found that secret spot on the front part of her pussy walls. She felt the digits move as if pressing into her and she felt her insides flutter. Copious amounts of cream seemed to ooze from her depths as his mouth began to suck on her swollen clit and his other hand gathered some of her love juice for she felt the fingers of his other hand move through the area then move down toward her anus. The newly added digits began to circle the puckered star a few times and then she felt a finger slip through the ring of muscle that lay just beneath the surface. She felt her hole pull him all the way in, gladly welcoming the intrusion.

Lyndee's brain shorted out when she felt Trey's finger slip into her ass. She remembered the previous morning when Austin had filled her there with his cock, and even though this finger was thinner, it still had the same effect on her. This time there was a tongue and teeth on her clit, adding to the pleasure that seemed to bring out her climax, and as she let go of herself, she felt her cunt explode around his fingers. Her scream ripped from her into Storm's mouth as he thrust his tongue deeper into her mouth, absorbing the sound. All three men remained where they were, doing what they were doing as her body rode out the aftermath of her orgasm, her pussy pouring her fluid from its depths, which Trey tried to capture with his mouth. Her hips kept bucking as she continued to come, the sensations traveling from her core out to every part of her body. Black spots appeared before her eyes before they seemed to engulf her vision and then everything went dark.

* * * *

Trey could feel her pussy still spasming even after her body went limp. Her legs hung from his shoulders as her derriere hit the bed with a soft thud. Looking up he saw his brother pulling his mouth from hers while Austin pulled his own mouth from her tit. All three looked down upon their woman with concern.

"Damn! She passed out!" Trey exclaimed. "I think that is a first for us."

The younger Goodall brother let her legs down from his shoulders, laying them on the bed while the two older men tried to make her comfortable on the bed, placing a pillow under her head and pulling a blanket up over her. Austin and Storm remained by her side, lying as close to her as possible to cuddle her body while Trey remained between her legs and lay his head gently on her stomach. He loved this position as he drifted off smelling her pussy.

* * * *

She awakened a bit later to find all three men asleep. Remembering the explosive orgasms she had by their hands and mouths brought a satisfied smile to her face, and she let her hands seek out Storm and Austin's while she brought her legs together as much as she could to cuddle them against Trey. Reveling in the love of her men, she let herself drift back to sleep, hoping there would be many nights like this in the future.

Chapter Fifteen

The room was still dark in the morning as there weren't any windows in the room. Storm had turned off the light that illuminated the bed sometime during the night, leaving a soft light on in the bathroom where the door was opened slightly. As everyone slept he had realized that the previous day had to have been taxing on Lyndee. The day had started early to make the trek up the mountain and then there was the meltdown when the past came rushing back to her. Of course she had taken a bit of a nap while Trey dealt with her information with Connor Lawson. But then the evening took a bit of a turn when he had instructed her to go down to their playroom and she had found the bed situated similar to the cabin. After they had calmed her down they played with their little sub until she had passed out from her orgasms. They had decided to let her rest as they knew not what was to come with the information that they had discovered from their future wife.

* * * *

Now, his internal clock woke him. He knew it must be six o'clock as that was usually the time he rose, needing to take on the requirements of the ranch. Looking down he found his mate still asleep, her lips parted slightly as a soft, steady breath emerged from them. Her breasts were bare as the blanket had slipped down to her waist. Fighting the urge to touch them he slid from the bed. He noticed Austin was already gone so he shook Trey.

His brother woke briefly and Storm whispered, "Come cuddle with our woman. I'm going out to the barn and check on the animals and the guys then to the office to do some paperwork. We'll be back in a couple of hours for breakfast and then we'll need to set a plan in motion in case someone acts on the information you have out there through Connor."

Trey stood and rounded the bed and laid down beside Lyndee, pulling the cover up over them before drawing her into his arms. Placing a kiss on her head, he breathed her in before drifting back to sleep. Storm dressed and left quietly.

* * * *

Blinking against the overhead lights that had suddenly come on, Lyndee looked around. Surprised they were still in the playroom she looked at the man stirring beside her. Memories of the previous evening flooded her mind as a blush flooded her cheeks. Glancing to the doorway she found Storm and Austin dressed.

"All right you lazy bums. Up out of bed, it's nearly eight a.m.," Storm said. "We have things to do."

Pushing the blanket down Lyndee rose without consciousness of her nudity. If the men made love to her as one, then she had no reason to be shy. Walking toward the duo, she stopped before them, smiling. "Good morning. I am sorry I fell asleep last night. I wish we could have finished what we started."

Storm chuckled. "Darlin', you didn't fall asleep. We made you pass out."

"You gave us pleasure, little one," Austin said, letting a hand raise to cup her cheek.

"You didn't get to relieve your own pleasure, so how did I please you?" Naivety showed on her face when her eyes lowered.

Trey had made his way behind her and he slid his arms around her waist. His naked body pressed against hers while his chin rested on the top of her head. Liking the position, she let her head rest back against his shoulder.

"We strive to give you pleasure. That is our purpose and that is our pleasure," Storm huskily explained. "You are our woman so we not only will protect you but will provide you pleasure. If we know you enjoy us using our cocks to fulfill your pleasure we will give you that, but your pleasure is first and foremost. We want to introduce you to alternative ways of pleasure as you can see by the toys in this room. We hope you will enjoy what we show you and can accept the different ways of pleasure."

The two men knelt down before her, their heads bowed. "We love you and we will honor you. We will protect you to the best of our abilities, and we will please you with all we have," Austin said as huskily as Storm had explained pleasure to their woman. "Will you do the honor of taking all three of us as your husbands?"

Surprise registered on Lyndee's face as she knew they had wanted her as their own, had mentioned several times that she was their woman, but she had never expected them to propose marriage. She had no idea how any of this was to work, though she did trust them with her life. Speechlessness consumed her at the moment, giving cause for the men to raise their heads. Trey pulled away from her and stepped around to stand next to his brother. He, too, appeared to be confused at her silence.

After nearly a minute of waiting, Storm and Austin stood. They could see that she was warring within herself at the question set before her. Trey picked up his jeans and pulled them on while they watched her. Storm finally stepped forward to stand directly in front of her, concern etched on his face.

"Darlin', please talk to us," he whispered. "Please."

His plea touched her heart as did their love. She did want to be their wife, but she didn't know how it would all work. Also, what was to come of her job? Yes, they needed to talk.

Reaching out for Storm's hand, she clasped her hand in his then reached for Austin's. Walking back to the bed she sat them down and turned to Trey and beckoned him to her. Stepping to the bed, he sat next to his brother. Nervously she stood before them, still naked, though she didn't care.

Her hands wrung together in front of her and Trey wanted to make her comfortable. Jumping up, he pulled the tall straight-backed chair to sit facing their side of the bed and motioned for her to sit. He also pulled the blanket from the bed and covered her with it.

Blushing, she took his hand and brought it to her lips and placed a kiss on the palm before letting go and letting him resume his seat on the bed. Looking at her men, she drew in a breath and exhaled. "I have been happy with you, all of you. I am honored by your request, though I'm confused on how it will all work. What are people going to say about me being with three men? What about my job? I work out of Denver."

"We can work out all of the details as time goes by. No marriage is easy. We'll do what everyone else does. Work through the difficult parts, but there will be all of us to help with all aspects of a problem," Austin said.

"As for what people would say," Storm spoke up, "we don't care. Besides, out here, there won't be a lot to deal with, but again, we will work it out."

It was time for Trey to put in his input. "As for work, I'm sure you can try to get a position up here with any police force in the area. Or, we are all set financially here so you don't have to worry about working if you don't want to."

Lyndee sat gazing at all three of her men as they looked back at her with trepidation. Fear consumed them that she wouldn't want to stay with them, the fear that had lain within their hearts from the moment they had found her. They had no qualms about wanting her to stay with them, had even declared their love for her. Perhaps they had moved too hastily for her, and they would regret it for the rest of their lives if they were unable to convince her to stay.

* * * *

The three men that she loved desperately sat before her, causing her heart to flutter in her chest. That happened every time she saw them, or even heard them. She loved the different qualities of each of them, which made the whole package for her. Their bodies were to die for, which turned her on to no end while their adoration of her amazed her. There was an apprehension that reared its little head that they loved her for her body and not for herself that appeared once in a while, but then their words of commitment touched her heart and the fear dissipated. Was it really possible that they loved the whole package as she loved them?

Wow, there it was, the answer to all her fears. She knew she couldn't live without them anymore than they could live without her. Standing, she let the blanket fall to the floor, letting them feast upon her luscious body. Each of them groaned as they watched the material fall, licking their lips in appreciation.

Stepping forward, Lyndee stood before Austin, leaned down, and kissed him chastely on the lips. "I would be honored to be your wife."

Moving over to Storm, she leaned down and kissed him on the lips. "I would be honored to be your wife."

Sidestepping once more, she stood before Trey, leaned down, and kissed him. "And I would be honored to be your wife."

Stunned at their silence, Lyndee looked from one to the next and then the next, worried that they had taken it back since she had hesitated before answering them. Then all three jumped up and gathered around her, arms tangling as they all tried to hug her to them. She was surrounded by all three of her men, their scents mingling around her. Trey's naked chest warmed her back as it was a bit chilly down in the basement, but she cherished the moment that would be etched in her mind forever. Happiness touched her heart and she let her mind soar with the knowledge that these men were going to be all hers.

The growling of her stomach brought a chuckle from each of them as they knew she hadn't eaten well the previous night. Storm slapped her behind gently. "Let's go get breakfast. We need to prepare for what is going to happen next. You need to go get dressed right quick as some of the men will be coming after we eat."

Trey pulled away first, going to retrieve his shirt that he had deposited near the door the night before. "Connor will be arriving shortly also. I asked him to come out this morning."

Lyndee turned to follow Trey, and a hand from Storm found its way to the small of her back while Austin's hand held onto an ass cheek, as they escorted her up to the kitchen. From there, they left her to get dressed while the three of them made breakfast.

* * * *

In the bathroom she quickly showered and brushed her teeth. Stepping into the bedroom she slipped into a pair of black jeans and a black tee. Sitting on the bed she pulled white socks on her feet and then the black pair of boots that the trio had bought for her on their shopping excursion. The brush was run through her long hair and she let it hang loose down her back. Checking the mirror, she found herself satisfactory and then she made her way back to the kitchen.

The men stood when she entered the room and waited until she sat before they returned to their seats. Each one of them served food onto her plate before handing the bowls around to each other. While they ate, chatter was centered on plans for their wedding. It had been decided that she would legally marry Storm but would dedicate herself to Trey and Austin. Since she didn't have any family left to her, there wasn't a problem with her delaying too long with the plans.

When they had finished eating, Storm took her plate along with his and placed it in the sink. The other two placed theirs on top of the others and before anyone could start to wash them, a knock at the front door sounded and then a male voice called out, "Is it okay to come in?"

Austin answered, "Yes. We're in the kitchen. Take a seat in the living room. We'll be right there."

The three of them stood before their woman. Storm took her hand in his. "We need to plan how to protect you with our ranch hands. You can trust all of them to keep you safe. Also, there is no need to worry about them judging you for being with all of us. They will understand."

Nodding, she trusted her men and so she would trust their workers. Also, even though Connor was that evil woman, Angela's brother, she would trust him since the men did. Letting them lead her out to the living room, she was surprised to find five men lounging on the brown leather furniture. Apparently they had all been raised with good manners for as she entered, they all stood and then proceeded to push each other around until four of them sat on the couch under the window and the fifth man sat on the ottoman near the fireplace. Storm and Trey took their regular places in their recliners while Austin sat on the other couch with Lyndee, his arm around her shoulders.

Leaning forward in his chair, Storm began to make introductions. James, a fiery redhead, probably about the same age as the men, was on the ottoman. He was tall and lanky though looked like he could handle any job supplied him. A smile lit on his face as Lyndee was introduced and he seemed happy that all three of the men claimed her.

"Congrats, I'm happy for you guys," he beamed before turning his attention to Lyndee. "I hope you will be happy here with us. As employees of the Circle G ranch, we will all do whatever we need to do to help you adjust."

"Thank you," she smiled, liking him instantly.

Storm motioned toward the others to James's left, going down the line. There was David. He was about fifty years old, blond hair with streaks of gray throughout. A blond mustache topped his upper lip while a scar marred his left cheek. His eyes were gentle, a hazel color, and they held mischief in them. Nodding his head at her, he remained quiet.

Next to David was Kevin. Brown hair the color of chocolate topped his head, messy as if he had run his hands through it many times. He was probably around her age, perhaps slightly younger. His large brown eyes flickered with amusement. "It's nice to meet you, miss."

Her hand went up in a stopping motion. "Please, just call me Lyndee, or Lyn. All of you."

The men murmured while Austin hugged her closer to him. Snuggling closer, she laid her hand on his thigh. The muscle beneath her fingers trembled and she had to smile to herself.

The man next to Kevin was next up for introductions. He was a shorter Hispanic man by the name of Arturo, possibly a few inches taller than her by the looks of it. Dark-brown hair with brown eyes, a bit on the brooding side, but then she didn't know him well enough to tell yet. His smile was genuine as he spoke. "Hola, Lyndee. It is nice to meet you."

Nodding at him as she smiled, she said, "Hola, Arturo."

The last man was a Native American like Austin. His raven black hair was straight and shoulder length. His eyes a bit darker brown than Austin's under thick, dark eyebrows while his lips were thinner than her man's with a scowl adorning them. When his eyes met hers she felt as if he was looking into her soul. His name was Running Wolf.

"Pleased to meet you," he said with a smooth baritone voice. "Just call me Wolf. As Dave said, we will all do what is necessary to protect you. Also, when you are ready to learn how to ride a horse, come to me. I'll get you the right horse."

"Thank you, but how do you know I don't know how to ride?" Her eyes sparkled at the question.

All eyes were on Running Wolf, waiting for his answer. Brown eyes twinkled at her taking up the challenge. "Well, do you?"

Laughter bubbled from within her. "As a matter of fact…" She stopped with a pregnant pause, letting him anticipate her answer. When his eyes blinked, she continued, "No. I don't know how to ride. I will have to take you up on your offer. Thanks."

The men all laughed and waited for Running Wolf's response to her teasing. When his eyes lit up, he began to laugh with them. "You are going to be a welcome addition to our family," he said.

The laughter died as the front door opened without a knock, causing Lyndee to tense under Austin's arm. A brownish-red shaggy head popped around the edge of the door before his body appeared. He was tall, though slightly shorter than the Goodall brothers and Austin, though about as wide through the shoulders. His uniform spoke of his stature in the community along with the badge on his chest and the Glock sitting in the holster around his waist. She relaxed just a little bit as after Philip she wasn't sure who she could trust within law enforcement.

"Calm yourself, little one," Austin spoke lowly. "This is Connor Lawson. He is our neighbor, our friend, and the local Sheriff. He is here to help."

Chapter Sixteen

The tension was thick in the room and all the men watched how Lyndee was going to react to the man. The five ranch hands had been filled in by Austin briefly on what had transpired with their woman, and they knew she would be hesitant around the Sheriff. Connor stepped around the furniture to stand before her and held out his hand to her.

"It's nice to meet you, Lyndee. I've heard a lot about you and I admire your tenacity and your strength. Also, I would like to apologize for the actions of my sister the other day. We don't see eye to eye on things and she can sometimes be an embarrassment."

Appreciation for the man just from his apology for Angela's actions warmed her heart. Looking at his hand, she refused to shake it, but instead stood and threw her arms around his shoulders, hugging him to her. "Thank you. It is nice to meet you, Connor."

Storm cleared his throat. "Thank you Connor for coming this morning. Let's get started."

Lyndee pulled herself away from the lawman and sat back down, snuggling back into Austin's embrace. Connor waited until she had gotten situated before sitting next to her and then they all looked at Storm.

Storm rose from his seat and began the meeting. "We have a potentially dire situation on our hands, men. As you may have heard, we found Lyndee up on the mountain unconscious. She suffered from amnesia for the first couple of days and regained her memory yesterday. Our woman is actually a Federal agent from Denver. While she was undercover, she was kidnapped, drugged, and brought up to my cabin. The people who want her dead are still looking for her, and someone will most likely be coming here to find her. Since Trey and Connor began the investigation of who she is, we're sure it has tripped some red flags around the country on her whereabouts.

We also know that the man who is thought to have kidnapped her was in Kalispell the other day, and sooner or later, he will try to make contact.

"We will need all eyes out for anyone coming onto this property. Every man is to be armed and ready to do what needs to be done. Austin and Wolf will be out in the animal barn working with the horses. James, I want you, Arturo, and a couple other hands back behind the house dealing with the calves since they need to be tagged anyway. Kevin and Dave, we want you situated on each road in and out of the ranch. Just stay far enough off the road so you can't be seen, and radio in if you see anything.

"Trey and myself will be stationed in the office. We want it to seem that Lyndee is here alone in the house. As soon as we know someone is approaching the house we will all converge on the house and catch this motherfucker before he makes it inside the house."

Lyndee watched her man giving the instructions and pride welled within, but she also wondered if she could really trust the men in their employ. She would have to do that as she couldn't run from everyone in her future. Nodding, she agreed with Storm. When he looked at her, he continued.

"Lyndee, I want you to move around the house as you would normally do at home. I want the house to look normal with normal activity. As soon as you hear that someone is approaching the house, you will need to go down to the basement. On the back wall of the playroom next to the bathroom is a secret panel. If the bastard makes it into the house before any of us can arrive, go down, pull on the wall sconce, and the panel will move, and just step in."

As she listened to him, her face heated when he mentioned the playroom. Did all these men know what went on in there? Looking over at them, the only two that seemed interested in her reaction were James and David. Connor did seem to try to look away from her a little too quickly so she was led to believe he knew also. Stiffening in Austin's arms signaled to him that she was upset but that discussion would have to wait for another time. Once Storm had finished with the instructions, the men dispersed, going out to the office where they were to retrieve guns and radios that Connor was providing. The radios were on the same frequency as his office and the State Police so that if something did happen, they would be alerted also to come lend a hand.

As Lyndee tried to rise, Austin kept her sitting next to him by putting pressure on her shoulder. She knew he knew she was upset but it was already out there and she was embarrassed so there was nothing else to say at the moment. When he took her hand in his he spoke with his Dom voice.

"Look at me, Lyndee!"

She refused, keeping her eyes down on her knees. Storm and Trey looked over at the duo on the couch in concern. Storm stepped around the wooden coffee table, past the fireplace, and then up the other side of her on the couch.

"Lyndee, do as he says!" Storm said, towering over her.

She didn't know why her pussy was weeping at the sound of their harsh voices or why her nipples were tightening up, but she was upset and wanted to ignore her body's reaction to them. Stubbornness was a trait that had always gotten her into trouble as a child and even in her job. Knowing it could disrupt her life with these men was dangerous to play with, but then she looked forward to the punishment she knew would come if she disobeyed them. She knew how the game was played even though she had never played it before.

Storm exhaled so hard she felt it on her arms and she shivered. "Lyndee, if you don't look at Austin right now, I will haul you downstairs and paddle your bottom so hard you won't be able to sit for several hours!"

Wiggling out of Austin's arm, she jumped up and came toe-to-toe with Storm. Leaning her head back so she could look into his eyes, she saw his anger there, but she knew he could see hers also. She felt Austin rise behind her and then move against her back. Backing down was not an option right now.

"Go right ahead! Perhaps you would like to invite all the men back to the playroom so they can have a whack at me too, since they all know about it! What, do you guys have orgies down there? Do all the men join in?"

* * * *

Realization hit Storm as if she had hit him. He had been so caught up in trying to protect her that he hadn't realized what he had said until that moment. No wonder she was furious with him and rightfully so. He had been lucky that she hadn't said anything while the men were there. Hanging his head in shame he reached for her hands which she held down at her sides, clinched in fists.

When she wouldn't let him hold her hands he knew he had screwed up royally with her, and he looked from Trey to Austin and then down into the flashing eyes of his woman. Her eyes were nearly black, her lips pursed tightly. Not knowing what else to do, he fell to his knees, wrapped his arms around her waist, and laid his head on her bosom.

"God, please forgive me, darlin'. I wasn't thinking. My only purpose was to keep you safe. I didn't mean to let that out. I'm so sorry."

* * * *

Two strong hands clamped onto her shoulders and she knew that Austin was willing her to forgive him also. Looking down into Storm's troubled face as he looked up she knew that that's all he was doing. Trying to protect her with all the means at his disposal and that meant his men. The people he entrusted their ranch to. So what if they knew they had a playroom. They knew that they were in a ménage relationship, so was it that bad? They would just know that they had a very active sex life and enjoyed it.

Wrapping her arms around his head, she held him to her breast. Sighing, she let go of the fear of the others knowing. "I'm sorry I got upset with you. I should have been more understanding."

Austin's arms returned to her shoulders, pulling her back against him, her head nestled on his shoulder. Trey, feeling left out, came over and captured her mouth with his, communicating his love for her also. When he pulled away, he and Austin took a step backward and Storm stood, kissing her chastely before he looked down at her.

"I really need you to listen to what I told you though. You need to hide in the playroom wall if they make it into the house."

Nodding, one thought struck her mind. "It's not bulletproof though, is it?"

"Soundproof, yes. Bulletproof, no. You just have to make sure they don't know you are down there at all."

At least now she knew that no one could hear them when they played down there. No wonder Austin had told her last night she could scream all she wanted. The side of her lip slid up as she looked at the man in front of her.

"You guys need to make sure you are safe also. Don't go getting yourselves hurt just trying to protect me. I could never forgive myself if anything happened to you because of me," she said sadly. She didn't think she'd survive without them in her life. They were in her heart and her soul.

"Yes, ma'am," Storm drawled with a smile before he left the house. Trey kissed her again before he walked out and she was surprised when Austin picked her up by the waist, turned her around to face him, and slashed his mouth across hers. He kissed her for a few moments and then let up after first kissing the tip of her nose and then her forehead. He started to walk away from her but she reached out and grasped his hand in hers, stopping him. Pulling his hand up, she kissed his knuckles one by one before releasing him. Remaining where she was, she watched the last of her men leave and stood there for a few minutes more, as if expecting them to come back to her, before turning toward the kitchen.

Looking at the sink she knew that the dishes from the previous night still sat there and she knew she was going to be there for a while. Running water in the sink, she looked out the window at the brown fields that spread out before the house. Behind them, rising to the sky were the Rocky Mountains. Soaring up to the heavens with snowcapped peaks, they were majestic and beautiful. This place must be beautiful in the spring and summer and in the winter while snow fell silently upon the land.

The front door opened and panic set in. Stepping over to stand in front of the double oven, she flattened herself against the appliance as she heard footsteps coming toward her. When the footsteps stopped at her side, she swung her body around and brought her foot in contact with the hard abs of a man, knocking him backward. Flailing, he tried to keep himself from falling backward. He didn't try to retaliate but spoke through his motions.

"Whoa, there, Lyndee!" he said as he righted himself. "It's me, Connor!"

Rushing forward to help the man, she placed her hands on his forearms. "Oh God! Connor! I am so sorry!"

Touching his stomach, he rubbed it as if to feel the pain this small woman had caused him. Raising a hand before defending her actions, he said, "No, it's not your fault. I should have announced myself. I must have frightened you. I know I'll never do anything to make you mad."

A light laugh emerged from her as she continued to hold onto him. For a brief second she looked into his face and found him to be a very good-looking man. His light gray eyes gave a mystical look to him that was astounding. She had never seen gray eyes on someone with brownish-red hair. A blush lit her cheeks as she let go of him. Stuttering, she asked, "Are you…are you all right? Did…did I hurt you?"

"No," he said shaking his head to confirm. "I'm fine, or I will be once this pain goes away."

"Jeez, I am so sorry. Do you need some ice?"

"I'll be fine, though I hope you didn't dislodge any vital organs I might need to live," he jousted with her, trying to make her calm down. "I brought you a radio so you can be in on the sting."

Taking the palm-sized black device, Lyndee turned it on and could hear the chatter from the men as they began to report on their positions. Looking up at Connor, she said, "I have one question. What if whoever is looking for me is monitoring the radio frequencies?"

"We hadn't thought of that. We'll just have to be more prepared than they are, but I will let Storm and Trey know of your concerns."

Nodding, she watched him leave through the front door and returned to the sink just in time to turn off the water before it overran the edges. Deciding to let the dishes soak for a few minutes, she made her way to her bedroom and retrieved a light jacket to keep her warm as the temperature was a bit on the chilly side this morning. Or was it her nerves? As she passed the mirror, she grabbed an elastic band and braided her hair down her back to keep it out of her face. Grabbing a few other things, she made her way back to the kitchen.

Beginning with the sink full of dishes, she washed them, leaving them in the dish drainer to dry. Tackling the table, she cleaned that off, placing the napkin holder along with the salt and pepper shakers in the middle. She took a moment to gaze out the window toward the west, again appreciating the scenery. Once finished with the table, she cleaned down the counters and the stove. The men may make a mean breakfast, but they also made a helluva mess. Remembering dinner, she removed two casseroles from the freezer and set them out on the counter to thaw, as the others would probably be eating with them tonight.

After sweeping the kitchen floor, she found a dust rag and a can of furniture polish under the sink. Going into the living room, she began to dust. She had to wonder if she hadn't arrived, what the house would look like when their housekeeper returned home. The woman would be petrified at what the house looked like at the moment. What would it look like after being gone for two weeks?

As she began to dust the coffee table, which looked like a large slab of a tree cut vertically and then set on legs, the radio began to squawk. Kevin, on the north road, reported that a car with government license plates just passed his vantage point, which gave them about twenty minutes before arriving at the house. Connor answered him, as did Storm, Austin, and James, as if it was a normal conversation that kept them abreast of activities on the ranch. Apparently Connor had spoken to them about the possibility of an intrusion on the frequency.

Deciding her options at the moment, she went into the kitchen and opened the door to the basement. She wanted easy access to where she needed to go if necessary. Opening the door next to it, she found a small utility closet. Inside she eyed the mop bucket along with the mop and the broom. Grabbing them, she thought of how she could use them to her advantage. Moving into the living room, she looked around before moving down to the bedroom.

Looking around the room, she eyed the stereo. Turning it on, she knew the men would flinch if they heard what she tuned it to. Classic rock. She grew up on the music as her parents loved it. Creedence was playing at the moment and she wiggled her ass to the beat before sashaying back to the kitchen. There, she took the broom and ran it through the handles on the cabinets on both sides of the doorway. The handles were about one and a half feet off the floor so whoever was to try to enter the kitchen would get a helluva whack in the shins. Briefly she thought of her reaction when Connor entered a few hours ago but this was different. This was life or death time.

By lifting herself up onto the counter next to the sink she gave herself an excellent vantage point through the window. She had a perfect view of the rounded driveway in front of the house. It wasn't too long before a trail of dust appeared above the horse barn before it got closer. The silver sedan with extremely darkened windows pulled up from the road and turned in the drive, stopping in front of the house.

Noticing her heart pounding in her chest, she was certain it could be heard if anyone were in the room with her. Reminding herself to breath as she waited for the occupant of the car gave her a brief respite until the doors opened and she gasped. She was expecting only Philip to show his treacherous face but five large men exited the car. The long, black-haired man that emerged from the driver's seat was one person she had hoped she would never see again though he was expected.

Besides Philip, the others were obviously Russian musclemen. Tall, muscular, and blond, each man wore a business suit and dark sunglasses, looking conspicuous out here in Montana country. Lyndee was certain that under those coats each man had at least one gun if not more. She knew they were all in for a hell of a fight and she hoped her men and the others were up to it.

Watching for a few more moments, she watched as two men stalked off toward the closest barn, which was the horse barn. She prayed that Austin and the others were prepared for what was about to happen. Philip and the two others looked at the house with determination. He thrust his chin out in her direction and the three started walking toward the front porch. Jumping down from the counter, Lyndee went to the basement door. Closing the door behind her she disappeared to the basement.

* * * *

Philip drew his gun before he reached for the front door. He had come with the resolve that he was going to kill the woman that had been the bane of his existence for the past several years, and he didn't care if he had to kill the three men that owned this ranch. Anxiety rushed through his veins as he felt the prize was within his reach this time. Indicating that one of the men remain at the front door, he indicated the other one come with him. Knocking at the door to appear on the up and up he waited briefly for an answer. When none came, he turned the knob and found it unlocked. Holding his gun up in a normal police stance, he glanced around the living room and noticed the dust rag and furniture polish on the coffee table. Wondering if it was left in haste, he listened for any movement or sound.

Hearing the music down the hall he motioned for the Russian to follow him. Making their way down the hall, they cleared each room along the way for anyone hiding in them. Reaching the master suite, they found the stereo playing music and they checked the closet, the bathroom and all the nooks and crannies but found the room lacking of a female occupant.

* * * *

In the horse barn, the two foreign men entered through the large door that led into the wide aisle between all of the stalls. They were both holding Glocks in their hands, prepared for any encounter with anyone who would deter them from performing the job at hand. Collateral damage was expected with this job even out here in the middle of nowhere.

Horses neighed and whinnied in their stalls as they watched the men slink through their domain. Mirrored images moved with grace down the aisle in their dark-gray suits, white shirts, and black silk ties. Their black dress shoes clicked softly upon the cement walkway as they neared the other end of the barn, not finding anyone. Turning around at the other end, they moved back toward the entrance. When they were near the entrance, the back door slid shut loudly, causing the two men to turn quickly. As the door had closed, the barn had darkened considerably since the morning sun had been streaming in and the entrance was still cast in shadows.

"Toss the guns toward the open doorway!" A loud baritone voice sounded through the barn. The men looked around trying to find the source of the order. "Do it! We have guns trained on you right now and are ready to use them!"

One man trained his gun at waist level while the other one waived his around as he turned looking in the rafters, toward each end of the barn or anyplace he could think there would be a person. Both whipped off their shades as they couldn't see anything in the barn. Letting their eyes adjust, they tried to find the disembodied voice but no sound or visual of anyone appeared.

Rustling from the stalls continued as the horses ate from their mangers of hay that had been filled earlier, unaware of the danger that was evident. Their tails swished as their heads moved around. The normal sounds of the barn continued as the men continued to make their way back to the entrance.

Turning to the large opening they found themselves face-to-face with five cowboys holding shotguns. Menacing, the five men didn't budge while the two Russians stood their ground, guns aimed back at them. Nerves rattled the two men when the disembodied voice sounded again.

"Now one more warning. Slide the guns toward my men and then raise your hands! I have a gun aimed at your backs so unless you want to die in the next thirty seconds, do as I say."

Glancing at each other, the two men nodded before leaning down and slid the Glocks to the five men. The next few seconds became a blur for everyone involved as the two men went to stand. They both reached for the small guns they had hidden in their socks under their trouser legs while dodging to the sides of the aisle. Shotgun blasts sounded before the handguns could be fired. The sound was deafening as the horses panicked within their confines. The two men fell, blood covering their thousand dollar suits from the front and back. The five men slowly advanced on the two, guns still aimed at them cautiously.

Two of the men stepped toward one while Wolf and the other two headed for the other. Austin swung down from the rafters on a rope, landing a few feet behind the two Russians, a shotgun slung on his shoulder. Austin and Wolf checked for pulses, the former finding one while the latter looked up and shook his head.

"This one won't last long by the looks of him," Austin said, standing back up to his full height. Looking at the two men standing next to the man, Austin gave his orders. "Stay with him. Make sure he doesn't go anywhere. Wolf, you and the others come with me."

A gun cocked behind them and the six men turned slowly toward the sound. Austin was surprised to find another Russian man, dressed the same as the other two standing in the doorway, gun pointed at them. No words had to be spoken, just a gesture of the ominous gun toward the ground. Each man slowly laid their shotguns down on the cement and kicked them toward the tall blond man.

Standing back up, Austin caught a slight movement from Wolf as he tumbled to the ground, rolled, and grabbed the concealed weapon from the dead man's trouser leg. Taking quick aim, he shot at the enemy at the door but not before another gunshot sounded. The Russian grasped his chest, just to the left of his sternum, blood appearing quickly, spreading out across the dark material of his suit. Austin, as a backup, fell to grab one of the disposed shotguns, aiming at the man, though by that time the man was on his knees and within seconds falling face-first onto the floor of the horse barn.

Looking over to give his man a nod to say well done, Austin noticed the pain-stricken look on Wolf's face as he clutched his blood-soaked shoulder. "Shit!" the foreman said before rushing to his ranch hand's side. One man had already removed his shirt and was holding it up to the injured man's shoulder. As Austin knelt down, he noticed the blood splatter along with the bullet that had lodged in the four-by-four post behind Wolf. Looking behind his man, he saw the exit wound and quickly removed his own shirt. Giving it to another man to hold, he barked orders. "Hold this on the back of his shoulder to staunch the bleeding. I'll call for the ambulance then go help out at the house. Keep your guard up. Only five arrived but we don't know if they have backup waiting out there."

Anger flashed through his eyes, his mouth set in a straight line as he grabbed the gun that Running Wolf still held in his hand. Standing, he grabbed a shotgun from the floor, pulled shells out of his pocket, and began to reload the weapon as he exited the barn, making his way toward the house. Halfway there he met up with Trey and Storm, the latter carrying a Winchester rifle. Trey carried a shotgun but had his revolver in its holster strapped around his shoulders. The two eyed their shirtless cousin, his chest and shoulders bronzed in the sunlight, as they made their way toward the danger that presented itself.

"Wolf got shot," the Indian said grimly. "Took one to the shoulder, in and out, and it's bleeding a lot."

"Fuck!" Trey exclaimed while his brother just shook his head. Marching toward the house, their gait along with their attitudes expressed their anger and determination to end this nightmare that Philip had brought to their peaceful, tranquil life. If anyone had come upon the scene at that moment, they would have thought they had traveled back to the Old West.

Chapter Seventeen

The two strangers in the house heard the gunfire erupting outside, confident that their cohorts were handling the situation. Making their way back to the kitchen, the tall Russian started in first, handgun raised to chest level, looking for a sign of their prey. Taking a step he felt the blockage at his shin the second he felt himself falling forward. As his two-hundred-thirty-pound-frame hit the floor with a thud, his gun skidded across the floor under the table.

Watching the large man tumble, Philip scoffed at the action when he saw the broomstick across the doorway. Amateurs. Kicking his foot out, he broke the stick in two before checking around the kitchen, behind the island, in the larger cabinets. If she was naïve enough to think a stupid trick with the broomstick would stop them, she'd be stupid enough to hide in a cabinet.

"Come on Lyndee or Lisa or whatever you want to call yourself! Stop playing these games," he shouted in frustration. "Your friends are dying out there and that will all rest on your shoulders. You're killing them! Do you want that on your conscience?"

Standing silently, he watched the large blond man haul himself back up to his feet. Going over to the table he searched for the runaway gun. Philip eyed the two remaining doors across the kitchen. She had to be in one of them. Stalking over to them, he first opened the pantry door and found it filled with food stuffs and a few cleaning supplies. No petite woman in there. Smiling maliciously, he opened the second door and found it dark. Flipping the light switch, nothing illuminated. As if he thought flicking it a few more times would help, he tried. Still nothing. Not sure where it led, he took a step tentatively. Taking another, he felt his foot roll out from under him, and before he could right himself, he hit the rolling bucket before toppling down the stairs into darkness.

Righting himself he swore softly as he searched the walls around him and found a light switch. Flicking the small rectangular protrusion on the flat plastic panel, the basement illuminated. Looking around, he found his gun, which had skidded near one of the weight benches. Picking it up, he surveyed his surroundings. Skipping over the exercise equipment, he eyed the door furthest from the stairs and cautiously opened it, gun ready for action. Finding the laundry room empty he moved to the one remaining door. Trying the knob, he found it locked.

Irritation ran rampant within him, his heart seemingly beating in his ears. He had had enough of this woman and what it was costing him. "Damn it, Lyndee! When I get through this door, I am still going to feast on that wonderful body of yours before I kill you!"

Stepping back, he raised his foot and kicked open the offending object, sending it shattering to the side. A moment of déjà vu struck him as that was how they had started this little journey. Finding the light switch, he flicked on the bank of four switches, letting his eyes adjust to the bright lights and the vision that lay before him.

Smiling, he thought he may hate the men that lived here for they had taken his bit of heaven from him, but he liked their taste. Letting his eyes go from one BDSM device to the next, he was envious that he didn't have the same setup at his home or his office. Perhaps when the smoke cleared, he would claim the ranch as his own and entertain his women here. The thought appealed to him.

Remembering the reason he was there, he looked around. Skirting the perimeter of the large room, he admired the apparatuses while looking for the one woman that he wished was attached to any of them for his pleasure. Placing his large hand at his crotch, he readjusted himself as he had grown hard thinking about the conquest at hand. Eyeing the one door left in the whole house that hadn't been checked, he held his gun against his chest as he softly made to it. Turning the handle slowly, he opened it knowing she was a sly, conniving woman. Lowering his gun, he began to shoot randomly, though saved the majority of the bullets for the shower curtain, certain she was hiding there for there was no other place for her to be.

After the barrage of gunfire that destroyed the bathroom, he threw open the white shower curtain that now looked like Swiss cheese and found the stall empty. Disparaged, he shouted as loud as he could, "Lyndee! You fucking bitch! Show yourself!"

* * * *

Trey entered first as was his right as a police officer. They wanted this to go down as swiftly as possible and by the book so if Philip did manage to come out of this alive, they had evidence against him. As he entered the living room, Austin and Storm were right behind him. Spotting a shadow coming from the kitchen, Trey motioned for the two to stay put. Flattening himself against the wall near the doorway, he held the shotgun to his shoulder. As the finely dressed Russian exited the kitchen, he was expecting trouble, but by the look on his face, wasn't expecting to come face-to-face with the shotgun.

"Don't make any sudden moves or you won't have a face left," Trey threatened. "You're going to go to your knees slowly while my brother takes your gun. Do you understand?"

The man nodded slowly before lowering his large body to his knees, his grip on his gun loosening. Storm stepped forward, grabbing the firearm quickly before stepping back. The man knew the routine and placed his hands behind his head without being told. The entire time Austin had his own shotgun trained on the man, anger still flashing through him. His finger was itching to put a bullet through this son of a bitch as he was sure this man had done many times in his career, but he reined in the control that was set to let loose.

"Check his legs for a hidden gun," Austin said harshly. "They seem to conceal them there from what we discovered with the others."

Handing the shotgun to Storm, Trey pulled the concealed weapon from the man's ankle, removed a zip-tie from his back pocket, and pulled one large hand down behind the man's back and then the other hand. The zip-tie was pulled tightly against his wrists, but that wasn't enough for Trey. Undoing the clasp on his belt, he pulled it through the loops on his jeans and proceeded to wrap the leather strap around the man's ankles, pulling it tight. Using the excess he pulled on it and looped it through the zip-tie and then let the prong slip into one of the holes before cinching it tight. He wasn't going anywhere.

A noise behind them caught their attention. Relaxing when they saw who had arrived, Trey motioned for James and Arturo to take the Russian to the barn with the others. The shouting from downstairs was becoming desperate and then they heard the door to the playroom being kicked open. The three men looked at each other, all thinking the same thing. They were going to have to do some work down there quickly.

As they started into the kitchen, Connor and Lyndee came through the front door. Their woman looked frightened, and rightfully so, but a twitch of a smile was on her lips at the discovery of their secret. Trey cocked his head toward the basement door and the five of them made their way down to the subterranean vault.

Before they were halfway down the stairs they heard the gunshots as Philip massacred the bathroom. At the bottom Connor pulled out his revolver and entered the playroom first. The other three men entered next standing beside him, making a force of four for Philip to get through before getting to Lyndee. She entered last, standing behind Austin and Connor. Lifting the backside of her shirt she pulled out Philip's Glock that she had retrieved from the ravine.

As the criminal in the bathroom shouted out, "Lyndee! You fucking bitch! Show yourself!" she pushed her way through the wall of men and stood between them as they moved to the side just a bit.

"Okay," was all she said, aiming at the doorway to the bathroom as did the four men. There was no way that Philip would get out of this and live. It was all or nothing and they all knew it. Lyndee was proud to be standing with these strong, virile men whom she could trust with her life. At that moment she knew everything was going to work out the way it should. Since everything did happen for a reason, she now knew the reason for the kidnapping.

* * * *

Philip was hesitant as he exited the bathroom, gun held out in front of him. "You bitch! What the hell..." His voice trailed off as he saw the partition of flesh before him.

The four men were angry as they held their guns aimed at him. Lyndee was beautiful as she stood amongst them. Even when she was just one of his whores he thought she was beautiful. He hated it when she piled on the makeup. It made her look cheap. The slutty clothes and jewelry didn't help much either. When she was herself, like she was now, was when he felt his cock rise to the occasion. He had wanted her from the first day she came to work for him though she shunned him. This was his woman and as he looked at the four men he wondered which was defending her honor and which ones were just helping out. Then he remembered what that slut Angela had told him, about all three men taking her.

He cringed at the thought. The petite woman before him had a look to her that screamed she had been fucked but good. That was supposed to be his job before he killed her. Now he just wanted to kill her. It was an old-fashioned showdown amongst the St. Andrew's Cross, the penance table, and the whipping bench that the room held. He couldn't help but chuckle at the thought. He would love to have tied her to the penance table and teach her a few lessons.

The small group watched as he laughed to himself, fearful that he had lost his mind, but then he sobered up. "I can't believe that you did this to me, Lisa. Oh, sorry, Lyndee. I know that you're a Fed. Boy you had me fooled. Right down to the men you fucked. You know you can't testify against me after you did that, right? You broke the rules."

"No," she said softly. "I never slept with anyone. I made friends with a hooker that looked a lot like me and she was the one who did my job."

Maniacal laughter erupted from him. "You expect me to believe that? You would lie on the stand? I can bring in many of our clients that can testify that you fucked them."

"She was a virgin when I made love to her a few days ago," Trey said proudly. "And I don't appreciate you calling my woman a liar."

Philip's mouth dropped open at the declaration and the smug look on the petite blonde's face made him face the truth. He also knew he wasn't going to get out of this alive so might as well make the best of it. "So that bitch Angela was right. You are fucking all of them, but wait. I thought there were only three of them. That's what she told me when she told me where to find you."

Gasps and groans were heard from the group, and Connor raised his gun even higher, aiming for Philip's head rather than the torso. "What did you say about my sister, Angela?"

Philip couldn't believe this. How had this gone so horribly wrong in such a short time? The Sheriff was the brother of the woman who had tipped him off? Was this a setup even from a few days ago? He wondered as he recognized the three men from the store on the same day he met Angela in the parking lot. Shit!

"I met your sister at the store the other day," the nervous man began, beginning a sidestep toward the broken door. "She informed me that Lisa was shacking up with three men on this ranch. She was more than talkative about the living arrangements here."

Smugness overwhelmed him as he felt he was making headway toward the door. The group was turning as he moved, though they still had his head in their crosshairs. "I find it interesting, Lisa, that you say you found your old job not to your liking but you would sleep with multiple men at the same time. Seems you really did like your job. Apparently Angela enjoyed sleeping with the same men also. Perhaps it's the men who are the whores instead."

* * * *

By this time Philip was at the door, but before he could turn to run, two guns exploded their gunpowder, expelling the bullets from their chambers. The tall, dark-haired man's body jerked before stumbling to the staircase. Lyndee was the first to the door, Glock still aimed and ready for danger. The four men rushed up behind her, and as they all exited the room they found Philip laying on his stomach, trying to pull himself up the stairs.

The injured man chuckled before speaking weakly. "If I had been a straight cop, Lyndee, I wouldn't have minded having you for a partner. Sexy as hell and a hell of shot."

Trying to take one more stair, his body shuddered in pain as a horrible bubbly wheeze emerged loudly from the hole in his chest. One more wheeze escaped before his body collapsed on the staircase and slid down a few steps before going still. The group stared for a few more moments, knowing this man couldn't hurt Lyndee anymore, before Connor kicked the man's boots. When there wasn't any movement from him, he stepped up a few steps and bent to check for a pulse. Shaking his head negatively the others followed the Sheriff up the stairs and out into the kitchen.

* * * *

Storm, Trey, and Austin circled around Lyndee, hugging her to them and telling her how thankful they were that she was all right. When the shrill of a siren got closer, they all made their way out to the driveway. James and Arturo waved down the ambulance to stop at the horse barn while everyone made their way over to it.

The paramedics pulled the gurney out of the back of the vehicle and rushed it into the barn, sidestepping one body. Sidestepping another body they stopped where two men were applying pressure to Running Wolf's wound. The Native American was pale and shivering as the medics checked him out. The shirts being used to staunch the flow of blood were soaked in the sticky fluid and the sight was upsetting to Lyndee. This was all her fault and these men had put their lives on the line for her.

Looking around the barn, she had seen the two dead men as they came in, and as she turned her head she saw one more Russian man half lying and half leaning against a stall across the aisle from Running Wolf. James noticed her looking. "He didn't make it. He died a few minutes before the ambulance arrived. The only one who survived is trussed up in Vixen's stall since she's at the vet's."

They all turned their attention back to Running Wolf. One of the medics was inserting a needle into one of the veins on the back of his large hand. The other medic was preparing a drip line and then attached it to the needle already placed there. On his other hand they repeated the motions, though this time, they placed a bag of blood onto the drip line instead of medication as Doc Anderson had told them it was all right to do it. James and another one of the hands helped the paramedics get the Native onto the gurney while another ranch hand held the bags with meds and blood. Strapping the man down, they popped the moving bed up and rolled it to the ambulance.

Sliding the gurney into the vehicle, one of the medics climbed in and sat next to the patient. James stepped up to Storm and Austin. "I'll go with him, make sure he's all right."

The two bosses nodded at him as he climbed in the back and sat next to the medic across from Running Wolf. In a flash Lyndee jumped up into the ambulance and knelt down next to the injured man, taking his hand in hers.

Tears filled her eyes. "I'm so sorry this happened to you, Wolf. I want to thank you for your bravery in trying to protect me."

Grinning while grimacing, he said, "I'll be back, boss lady. I still have to teach you to ride a horse."

"You better," she whispered before leaning over and kissing his cheek. "You better."

Accepting the hands of two of her men, she let Storm and Austin help her down from the ambulance before the other medic closed the double doors. As the vehicle circled the driveway to make its way to Kalispell, a sedan pulled around the corner of the barn followed by another one.

* * * *

None of the men had relaxed fully after the ordeal they had already been through so nerves were still high as was their adrenaline. Before the two automobiles could come to a stop, guns rose from every man and the only woman in the vicinity. Again, Austin along with Storm and Trey tried to shield her, as did Connor, but as soon as the first man burst from the driver's side of the first car, she pushed past them. They all tried to grab her but missed as she ran into the man's arms. Growls emanated from the group of three at the action but she ignored them.

Austin watched as the tall man with short black hair hugged her before pushing her slightly away from him. Turning her around full circle, he frowned at the wound on the side of her head, which was healing nicely. Shrugging, she said something to him before she removed the sweater and showed him her other wound. Hugging her again he looked over at the men hesitantly. Taking his hand, Lyndee led him back to the defensive group.

Car doors opened and men in suits began to pile out of them. Seven in all emerged after the first one did, but they all stayed where they were until an order was given for the ranch hands to stand down.

Lyndee and her guest stood before Storm, Trey, and Austin, a smile on her face. "Gentlemen, this is my real boss, John Drake. John, this is Storm and Trey Goodall and Austin…" Blushing, she realized she had slept with the man several times and didn't even know his last name.

Austin lowered his gun and shook the proffered hand that John had already put out there. "Lighthorse. Austin Lighthorse. Pleased to meet you."

Storm and Trey shook hands with him before Lyndee moved on to Connor. "And this is Connor Lawson. The local Sheriff."

Putting his revolver back into his holster, Connor accepted the man's hand in greeting. The two law enforcement agents stepped away from the group as Storm called out to the ranch hands. "It's all right, boys. Let's get this place cleaned up. Cooperate with these men, answer all their questions."

Guns lowered slowly as if they were still untrusting of the government men as they had already failed the boss lady once before. Kevin arrived on an ATV from his vantage point, looking around at the Armageddon he had missed. He knew Dave was going to be a bit upset also when he arrived back here. Austin made his way over to the barn with his men as four suited Feds joined them for their part of the investigation.

* * * *

Trey used a finger to lift Lyndee's chin up to gaze into her eyes, "Are you sure you are all right with this man?"

Nodding, she looked over at John as he and Connor stepped into the house. "Yes. He is the only one I could trust while I was deep undercover. We'd meet every few weeks for coffee or lunch so I could give him my report. He always acted like one of my johns so as not to attract attention to himself."

Storm chuckled unexpectedly and Lyndee looked over to him. "What?"

"A john named John." He chuckled again.

Trey and Lyndee both stared with open mouths at his pun as Storm was not the one to make light of anything. That was Trey's personality.

"Oh, come on now. You have to admit that's funny." He laughed. It was then that Trey knew his brother's lighter mood matched his for the first time in the past four days. Was that all it had been since this little bit of heaven had entered their lives, changing it forever?

Trey and Lyndee did have a bit of a chortle at the jocularity of the statement before the blonde woman became serious. "You better not let John hear you say that. He didn't like what he had to do, posing like that. He is married and yet when he was with me, he had to stroke my hair, hold my hand, or touch my arm like we were intimate. He would even kiss me on the lips. We had to make it look good"

Becoming serious, Storm looked down at his woman. "Well, he won't be doing that anymore."

She nodded as a sadness seemed to shroud her. Trey knew Storm noticed her change in mood and that they both felt a twinge of guilt over the circumstances. She knew they wanted her to stay with them and hadn't balked at the idea, but she would be leaving her life behind and they never really asked if she wanted to do that. Sadness settled over them as they glanced at each other, knowing what the other was thinking.

They were really going to need to sit down and talk about their future. Watching Lyndee as the action built up they knew that she loved her job and now they didn't want to take that away from her. Did they want to be selfish and have her stay with them and make her miserable, or could they let her go to do what she enjoyed the most?

* * * *

From the horse barn Austin stood in the doorway as the Feds took pictures and questioned the other men. Watching his cousins he knew that something was wrong as dejection appeared on their faces. It had happened moments after Lyndee became sad. Even from a distance, he knew that something had happened that could destroy their future together. Running his hands up over his face then down the backside down his hair he became frustrated. He just wanted this whole ordeal to go away so they could fully enjoy their woman.

Connor called Trey and Lyndee to the house and Storm turned and caught Austin's eye. Shrugging, he followed the requested people to the house.

Chapter Eighteen

After several hours, what seemed like thousands of questions and a visit from the coroner, who retrieved four bodies, the Feds were waiting around to leave. A tow truck had also retrieved the sedan that Philip and his cohorts had arrived in to be taken to the local impound yard for evidence.

John, Connor, Lyndee, and the three ranch owners walked down the steps from the porch. Lyndee looked around at the four local men. "I'd like a word with John alone, please."

Deflated, they nodded. She and John started walking toward his car when he put his hand on her elbow as they walked. Stopping at the driver's side, John leaned against the door, crossing his arms across his chest. "You did a wonderful job, Lyn. There will be a promotion for you when you get back. You practically undermined the mob in Denver by yourself."

Kicking the dirt with the toe of her boot, Lyndee blushed at his kind words. Then she looked up at the man who had pretended to be one of her lovers in the past several years. "After the trial I don't think I'll be coming back to work."

John's right eyebrow rose in amazement but the knowing smile caught her eye. "So," he started, "which one is yours?"

The blush rose even higher on her cheeks. Stepping forward so none of the other agents would hear, she still whispered, "The brothers and the cousin."

Chuckling, John looked down at her in amazement. "For what you did, you deserve to be happy. You put your life on hold for the past five years on this, so I say go for it."

"No judgments?"

Shaking his head, he unfolded his arms and patted her arm, "None. I mean it. I'm happy for you."

Throwing her arms around his neck, she kissed his cheek before stepping back. "Thank you, sir. I'll be in the office next week and stay until the trial is over. Then I'll submit my resignation."

"Okay. I'll still have some time to try to work on you to stay, but from the looks I've seen being thrown your way today, I'd wager I'll be barking up the wrong tree. I'll see you next week. Have a safe trip down."

"You too. Make sure that asshole makes it to Denver in one piece," she said, motioning to the Russian in the backseat of the car. Tears welled in her eyes as one big chunk of her life was coming to an end and she was going to miss her friend.

Surprise struck Lyndee when as was his custom when they had parted in the past when they were alone, John leaned over and kissed her forehead. He had come to be more than just her boss. He was more like a father to her and she was going to miss their weekly meetings. Climbing into the car, he turned the key in the ignition and waited for everyone to pile into the car before driving off. The second sedan followed his, leaving Lyndee to stand in the driveway, her arms wrapped around her waist, trying not to let the tears fall.

* * * *

Feeling the awkwardness of being a fifth wheel, so to speak, Connor cleared his throat, "Well, I think I have seen enough excitement for a week this morning. You guys really know how to throw one helluva party. I'm going home to have a chat with my sister. I'll call you tomorrow."

Lyndee's three men listened to him speak but didn't take their eyes off of their woman, standing alone in the driveway. He wasn't offended as he knew how much these three had fallen for her. He just wished at that moment that he could find a woman that could fill his heart and emotions the same way she filled his friends'.

Walking around the side of the house back to the equipment barn, he straddled his Harley. Turning the key in the ignition he felt the rumble beneath his thighs and relished the loud sound coming from the pipes. Pulling on his leather jacket and his helmet, he rode out through the open door, down the side drive and out past the house onto the dirt road toward home. Lyndee waved at him as he passed by and he waved back.

Perhaps he should offer her a job. She was good at hers as was shown by the respect the agents had given her, and if he did so, she would stay and make those three lucky louts happy. He would have to think about it, but right now, he thought about how he was going to handle his kid sister. She had gone too far this time, nearly costing Lyndee her life, and no telling what was going on with Running Wolf yet. Once he handled Angela, he was going to have to go to the hospital to check on the injured man and to get statements from him and James.

Opening the throttle, he picked up speed, enjoying the freedom his bike gave him. At least for the next half hour it would take him to get home, he could have a bit of enjoyment after the morning they had all had. He would have a bit of enjoyment before confronting Angela and then going back to work. Yes, he would be offering Lyndee a job. Trey was a big help to him, but he felt the little woman would be a great asset to the small force and perhaps give him some freedom to have a social life.

* * * *

The three men remained rooted on the walkway from the house to the driveway. They had wanted to give her the privacy Lyndee deserved with John but now that he had left, and the sadness was written all over her, they didn't know what to say. One thing they did know was they needed to talk, but for right now, they needed to hold her, love her.

Watching her, they waited for a sign that they could approach her. The last thing they wanted to do was rush her. Patience was never something that the men had, but with Lyndee they were learning that virtue quickly.

Looking at the house, Lyndee found her three men watching her. She noticed the worry on their faces and she hoped they didn't think she was having second thoughts. She never wanted them to think she didn't want them. The adrenaline rush was beginning to wane and the guilt that she had brought all this violence to their lives, to the lives of the others, was beginning to build. Tears that had abated a moment ago began again. She began to shake as her emotions overwhelmed her, and as she felt herself slipping to the ground there were hands to hold her up.

With emotions warring she hadn't heard the ATV arrive right behind her. David had stopped to ask about news on Running Wolf but he had seen her tears and knew something was wrong. Seeing her knees buckle he reached out and grabbed her before she could hit the ground, and he slowly cushioned her as he himself sank to the ground. Cradling her against his chest he absorbed her tears with his shirt as he tried to control her trembling.

Three sets of boots rushed up to the duo and David looked up at his employers. Not certain whether he should give up their woman, he saw them each shake their heads as they knelt down around him. Their hands rubbed her back, her arms, and her legs as they all tried to soothe her. Each man, including David, spoke softly, encouraging her and saying everything was going to be all right, and after a couple of minutes her tears slowed down to an occasional sob. Her body ceased its trembling and she became pliant in the ranch hand's arms and her breathing became steady and shallow. She had cried herself to sleep.

Standing, David looked to the three men for what to do with the sleeping beauty, as handing her off to one of them might wake her up. The men knew what they needed to do and that was to check on Wolf at the hospital. Austin nodded his head toward the back of the house where they all headed. Entering the garage, Austin held the backdoor of the black pickup as David slid in. Storm climbed in the driver's seat while Trey took the front passenger side. After closing the door for David, Austin went around to the other side and got in.

The three cousins knew that it was a big step, letting David continue to hold their woman, but as he was more a father figure to them they didn't mind. As they drove away, the man smoothed her hair and the large Native American pulled her feet over to his lap and stroked her calves. They sat this way until they reached the hospital in Kalispell then Austin reached for his lady.

"Lyndee," he spoke softly. "You need to wake up. We're at the hospital."

* * * *

Iris eyes fluttered open as she adjusted to her surroundings. She had heard Austin say they were at the hospital, and she tried to remember why they would be there, then the morning's activities came rushing back to her. Sitting up she looked up at David and smiled. "Hello."

"Hello, yourself." He smiled. "Hope you had a good nap."

Blushing, she nodded then looked around. Catching a glimpse of herself in the rearview mirror she grimaced. The men didn't miss the action and chuckled.

"You're fine." Trey smiled. "We can stop at a restroom if you wish to wash up."

They piled out of the truck and headed into the emergency room entrance. Four, tall muscular men and a petite blonde woman were hard to miss as they entered through the sliding automatic doors. Nurses stopped to stare at the four-pack of eye candy that had entered. There was no shortage of cowboys in the area, but to have four of them enter at once, especially the variety that sauntered through the halls, was too much overload for many of them. Several men stopped to stare at the small group, ogling Lyndee.

Making their way to the waiting room, they found James. His head hung in frustration as a toddler wailed on his momma's lap while a man was softly snoring a few chairs down from him. Lyndee slipped into a chair next to him and put her hand on his upper back. He jumped at her touch as he hadn't seen any of them arrive. Putting her arms out, he fell into her arms, burying his head into her shoulder.

"He was so bad by the time we got here. They had to bring him back twice," James said sadly. "I thought I was going to lose a good friend."

"Any news yet?" Storm asked, sitting on the other side of him, next to the snoring man.

Looking up, James shook his head. "No. He's been in surgery since we got here. Doc Anderson arrived a little bit ago and is looking for answers."

Austin and Trey found seats across the room from them while David took the empty seat beside Lyndee. Long legs stretched out in front of all the men, which seemed to take up a lot of room, their presence overwhelming the size of the room. The baby had stopped crying and was looking between all the men in wonder. Storm smiled at the little tyke and the child hid his face in his mother's chest.

"I feel he is going to be all right," Lyndee said. Inside she prayed. He had to be.

Removing the elastic band from the bottom of her braid, she combed out her hair with her fingers. Lifting his butt, Austin pulled out a comb. Motioning for her to come to him with a crooked finger, she rose and went over to him. Starting to kneel on her knees between his legs, he patted his lap and she sat there spreading her legs to either side of his. All the men growled, including James and David. Austin began running the comb through the long, silky blonde hair while everyone in the sitting room except the snoring man watched the erotic gesture. Taking his time, he smoothed her hair down until it was snapping with static electricity. Pulling her hair back, he began to braid it. Entranced by the deft hands of the large Indian as he twisted sections of hair back and forth, each man had to reposition their legs a few times or clear their throats.

Lyndee was well aware of the men watching her as she enjoyed the attention Austin was giving her hair. She loved having her hair long. The girls she had worked with had been trying to get her to cut her hair but she resisted and Philip had often told her that foreign men requested blonde women with long hair. She was a commodity for him. Now, she was free. Both Trey and Austin seemed to love her hair, tending to it, but Storm never really made mention of it or expressed an interest in working with it. She had to wonder about that.

Watching the three men opposite her, she could see the desire in Storm's eyes, as they were now cobalt blue instead of the sky-blue they usually were. She was amazed how much of a change of emotion there was in those eyes. James was watching her with turquoise eyes, amused at the little woman in the lap of Austin. Desire was in his eyes also and she blushed. David's emerald green eyes were filled with desire also. She knew that Trey and Austin would have noticed their intense desire for her and she feared for them as she knew how jealous her men could get.

The sexual tension was thick in the room by the time Austin finished braiding her hair and she started to get up, but his hands sliding around her waist stopped her. Leaning back against him, she felt comforted in his arms, though nervous with what was going on behind those silver swinging doors. Nurses and doctors passed out in the hallway, tending to their business, their other patients' business. Every once in a while someone would look in the room to check the activity there, but mostly it was nurses to ogle the cowboys, Lyndee's cowboys. She felt proud.

Finely, unable to stand the silence, she looked at the woman with the toddler. "Is your little one sick?"

Shaking her head, the woman looked at Lyndee with sad eyes. "My husband was seriously injured in a logging accident this morning. He was flown in by helicopter and is in surgery."

"I'm sorry to hear that," Lyndee said with genuine concern, especially after watching the little boy in her arms with the mop top of brown hair. She knew what it would be like for the youngster to lose his father at such a young age if the outcome was grim. "Is he your only child?"

"No. I have six-year-old twins. They are still in school. My mother will get them when she gets off work. She works at their school," the woman said sadly.

"I'll pray for your husband and your family," Lyndee said, trying to fight back her tears.

The rumble from Austin's chest was comforting when he added, "We all will keep your family in our prayers."

Lyndee let her eyes drift closed as she relaxed against Austin's chest. She felt Trey's hand find hers and let him interlace his fingers with hers and rest their hands on his thigh. For the first time that day, Lyndee felt at peace. She knew that Running Wolf was going to be all right, and she was surrounded by the men who loved her and by friends who put their lives on the line for her. Sighing heavily as the sense of tranquility settled over her she felt Austin's arms tighten around her waist.

"Are you all right?" he whispered in her ear.

"Yes," she said as she nodded.

"Then what's wrong, darlin'?" Storm asked from his chair.

Opening her eyes, she looked over at his concerned face. "You've all made me so happy today. I don't know how to thank you all for what you did for me. You all risked your lives to save me. I won't ever be able to thank you enough."

"You don't have to thank us, sweetheart," Trey said next to her. "We love you and it's our duty to protect you. All of us."

"Yes, ma'am," James said. "We don't take kindly to people coming around here trying to hurt one of our own, especially women."

"That's right, boss lady," David grinned. "I'm just sorry I missed all the action."

Smiling at the two men who were now her friends, she said, "Well, thank you for all your help. When I get back from Denver after the trial I'll treat you guys to a big meal."

"Thank you, ma'am," they both said in unison.

"And don't call me ma'am," she said laughing. "I already told you that."

Everyone's attention was drawn to the double silver doors as they opened and Doc Anderson walked through them. Lyndee jumped off Austin's lap to rush to the doctor as the five cowboys stood and gathered behind her.

"How is he, Doc?" she asked quietly.

The older man ran his hand through his hair before speaking. "It was touch and go there for a while. He's a fighter. He's going to be all right, but he'll need some rehabilitation on his shoulder. The bullet tore through some muscle and nicked an artery. That's why he bled so much. He'll probably need to go to Helena for physical therapy."

"We'll make sure he gets the help he needs." Storm spoke above Lyndee's head.

"Perhaps he can go to Denver with me while we await the trail. I have an extra bedroom he could stay in," Lyndee offered innocently.

Growls emanated above her and she realized she had misspoken. They could discuss it later. "When can we see him?"

"They're just finishing up with the surgery then he'll go to ICU. Once he's settled there, a nurse will come and let you know when you can go in," Doc explained. Then looking down at Lyndee, he said, "Little lady, I heard you went through an ordeal this morning and I would like to do a little exam on you to make sure you are all right."

Nodding, she looked at the men. "I'll be okay. You guys really need to relax."

* * * *

They watched her follow the doctor, watching her ass sashaying before it disappeared behind the swinging doors. Even after she was gone, they continued to watch for a few more seconds as if she was going to come back. Finally, they all returned to their seats.

"Damn, boss. You got mighty lucky." James smiled for the first time since he got up the morning.

"We all got lucky," Storm said, a bit nervous about the one conscious person in the room besides them. "We all did."

Glancing over, the woman gave a little smile before shrugging and saying, "It's all right. I understand. Right now I wish I had what you have. At least if something happens to one, there are others left to help out and love you."

The men were just as choked up as she was at the moment, as they knew she was right. If anything happened to one of them, there was someone else to carry on for Lyndee. David got up and made his way over to the chair next to hers and pulled her against his chest as she broke down and began to cry. As she broke down, the little boy became fussy. James went over and took him from her arms as she slid her arms around Dave's neck, holding onto him as her life seemed to fall apart. James sat a few chairs over from the boy's mother, letting him ride his knee like a horse. The boy laughed, not knowing his life was about to change forever. Trey took his hat off and placed it on the boy's head, and the boy held onto it so he could see out from under it and said, "Cowboy!"

Chapter Nineteen

Twenty minutes later Lyndee exited the emergency room and was about to walk back into the waiting room, but her heart soared when the scene inside stopped her in her tracks. Trey and James were on the floor playing with the little boy. Trey was on his hands and knees and the boy was riding on his back. You could barely see the boy's face under Trey's hat but he seemed happy. Dave was sitting on one side of the lady and Storm was on the other side while Austin had pulled a chair in front of the woman. They were consoling her, talking to her.

Lyndee knew her men were compassionate with her but didn't know that it extended outside the ranch. This was the first social interaction she had seen them in and she was so proud of them. Today had been an eye opener for her as to their abilities and the abilities of the ranch hands. She had found a new home and she knew in that instant she wouldn't miss her old job.

The boy had spotted her first, pointed, then giggled. When James looked up to see what he was pointing at, he tapped Trey on the shoulder and nodded toward his lady. Trey turned his head, careful not to dislodge the tyke. He smiled happily at her. Stepping into the room, Lyndee knelt down next to him and lifted the hat slightly to look at the beaming face of the boy. "Are you having fun?"

Nodding, he spurred on his horse and Trey whinnied and rose slightly, sending the boy into more laughter. He leaned over and gave her a chaste kiss and they both heard the boy say, "Yuck," and they both laughed. Looking over at the boy's mother then back to Trey, he shook his head and frowned. Lyndee knew that this lady and her family were going to need all the help they could get, and she knew she wanted to give her all the help and strength she could for she knew what the kids were going to have to deal with. Placing her hand on one of Trey's she tried to fight the tears again as her heart broke for them.

Trey looked into her eyes questionably but she shook her head to indicate it wasn't the place and he accepted that. He went back to play with the boy until boots approaching the room then stopping brought all their attention to the doorway.

Austin, Storm, and Lyndee stood quickly to face the new arrivals. Lyndee's fists clinched next to her when she recognized Angela standing next to Connor. Austin and Storm both stepped in front of their woman as protection, though they clinched their fists as much as she had. Storm and Austin's faces showed their hatred for the woman as they remembered she was the one who had told Philip where to find Lyndee.

"How's Wolf?" Connor asked, trying to break some of the tension.

It took a moment to drag their attention from their friend's sister, the bane of their existence at the moment. They could see she had been crying as her eyes were red and she couldn't look them in the eye. They had to wonder if Connor had done anything rash to her that could jeopardize his job, but then that wasn't their business.

Storm spoke up finally as he dragged his eyes from Angela's face to her brother's. He thought Connor looked defeated and he shouldn't have to. "He's going to be all right. Doc came out a while ago and said he'll be out of commission for a while and will need extensive therapy to get his shoulder to working again. According to James he flatlined twice on the way in."

He knew he sounded harsh, but he said it to emphasize to Angela that there were consequences to the actions one takes and sometimes they could get someone killed. Angela sobbed as she covered her face with her hands then blindly turned and rushed from the room. Storm and Austin looked at Connor to see what his reaction would be. The man shrugged but stayed put.

* * * *

Lyndee pushed her way past the wall of protection her men tried to present and rushed after the woman she had despised until that moment. Turning the corner into the hall she stopped for a moment to listen to see if she could hear the other woman's high heels on the laminate floor, and when she heard them, she followed suit. Her own boots thudded loudly in the halls of the hospital as she turned this way and that until she stopped outside the small chapel. The swinging wooden doors were still moving slightly from being opened and closed.

Pushing the door open slightly Lyndee stepped into the dimly lit room. The quietness was overwhelming as she had to look around for the person she sought. Angela was in front of the alter kneeling, her hands on the floor in front of her. Walking around the back of the pews and then down the small aisle to the prostrate woman, she knelt next to her. Laying her hand on the Angela's back, she wasn't expecting her to flinch.

"Angela," Lyndee spoke softly in reverence for their setting. "It's all right. Wolf is going to be all right and I'm sure you didn't know that Philip was going to try to kill me."

Angela moved up so she was kneeling before she looked at Lyndee. "I'm so sorry," she cried. "I was so jealous of you that when he stopped me in the parking lot I gave him the information he wanted. He said he was a cop and that you were a prostitute. I was so angry that the guys had chosen you over me."

"Did Connor explain what was going on?" Lyndee asked hesitantly.

Nodding, Angela's breath hitched. "He was so angry when he came home today. I thought he was going to hit me as he yelled at me. He told me what happened out at the ranch. I'm so sorry. I didn't know anyone was going to get hurt. I just thought if you were a prostitute you didn't deserve the guys so I told him where to find you. Can you ever forgive me?"

Lyndee's hand was still on the woman's back so she pulled Angela to her to hug her. "Yes, Angela. I forgive you. I know we all do things in the heat of anger and you didn't know the situation. I want you to know that I love them with all my heart and I will not hurt them."

Pulling away slightly, though still in the embrace, Angela looked into Lyndee's eyes. "I see that in your eyes. I also saw how they looked at you and tried to protect you and I know they love you. I thought I loved them, but once I saw you with them, I knew deep down inside, I didn't. I just wanted them to love me."

"I know. It's easy to fall under their spell. But we are going to make this work. I don't want you to ever think you aren't welcome at the house. Once this all blows over, we will all be friends," Lyndee tried to assure her. "It'll take some time for the men, I think, but I forgive you."

Angela pulled Lyndee to her to hug her one last time before standing. Rising next to her, Lyndee reached over to the altar, where a box of tissue sat and pulled several out. Handing them to Angela, she escorted the woman back to the waiting room, with directions from Angela. Walking back into the room, silence fell and everyone looked to the women.

Angela looked at Lyndee for support and with a nod gave her solidarity. Casting her eyes down in guilt that everyone was watching her, Angela started to speak but found she had to start over as her first words weren't audible. "I'm so sorry that everything happened because of me. I was jealous of Lyndee and I was mad at the three of you and I wanted to hurt you. I didn't know anyone was going to get hurt. I know you won't be able to forgive me, but I ask for forgiveness anyway."

Connor got up and went to hug his sister as the Goodall brothers and Austin looked at Lyndee for support. One slight nod from her blonde head told them that she already had so they knew that was the right thing to do. The three men stood, their muscular bodies taking up a lot of space in the room, and went over to the weeping woman. Each one hugged her, assuring her that she was forgiven.

A nurse entered the room and interrupted them, telling them that they could go see Running Wolf but only for a few minutes. Excusing themselves from Connor and Angela, the foursome made their way to the ICU to see the injured ranch hand. True to the nurse's prediction, they were only allowed a few minutes with him, assuring him they'd be back the next day to visit.

When they were finished they went back to the waiting room to say their good-byes as they had all had a stressful day and needed rest. Dave was going to stay to offer James some company as they had all become like brothers while working at the Circle G and couldn't leave their wounded comrade without some kind of company. Also, he had bonded with the woman, Anita, and had offered his assistance should she need it.

Lyndee hugged Angela and whispered, "It's going to be all right. We've forgiven you. Now you have to forgive yourself."

Pulling away, Angela nodded. As the foursome exited the building, nurses lined up to appreciate the sight of the three men walking away as much as they had enjoyed the sight of them arriving. Walking out to the truck, they all piled in and headed home.

* * * *

Lyndee squealed as she landed in the middle of her bed. Storm had carried her in from the truck fireman-style to her room then tossed her gently onto the mattress. Before she hit, he was pulling his shirt off, and as she looked toward the doorway, she found her two other men rushing in, already ridding themselves of their clothes. Licking her lips, she watched them strip before her as they never took their heated eyes off of her. She scooted back until her back was up against the headboard as she enjoyed the striptease, her nipples pebbling as moisture seeped from her cunt. She wanted them so badly.

Storm knelt on the bed to her left, smiling maliciously. "You've been a bad girl, darlin'. You need to be punished."

A thrill shot through her body, straight down to her pussy at his words. Glancing over at Austin and Trey she saw the raw hunger in their eyes and knew she was in for a long night. Storm grasped her wrist and slipped a silk rope around it before tying the other end around the post on the bed over to her right, twisting her body. Pulling on her right wrist, he brought her around and pushed her facedown onto the bed, tying her right arm off to the other bed post. Looking around, she eyed his hard cock just inches from her face and tried to move to lick it but wasn't able to move to the side. Looking further back, she could make out movement but not enough to get an idea what the others were going to do.

The bed dipped behind her and she felt knees separating her thighs. Large hands slid under her legs, lifting her while a pillow was shoved under her stomach and then another. The hands settled her down, leaving her pussy exposed and her ass sticking up in the air. A silk rope was wrapped around her left ankle and then her leg was tied to the post at the end of the bed. Anticipation filled her that her other leg was going to be tied next. She slid her other leg out to the side and she heard three chuckles.

With a whisper just inches from her ear, Storm asked, "What are you doing, darlin'? Are you in a hurry for your spanking?"

Her breath hitched at his words and she felt her pussy swell and weep. Her ass undulated a bit at the thought and she felt a large hand slide gently across one of her soft fleshy globes. Austin.

Storm slid a hand under her, found her hardened nipple, and pinched it between his thumb and forefinger. Her gasp brought out another chuckle from the man as his tongue licked at her shoulder before sliding up her neck. Austin's hand lifted from her ass cheek as Storm's mouth found her ear and licked at the shell of it, sending chills down her body.

Smack! Austin's hand came down on her ass, which surprised her even though she had been warned.

"Ouch!" she squealed.

"Quiet!" Storm whispered. "You were warned and I don't want to hear anything until your punishment is over."

"But I don't understand why I am being punished," she said as she tried to process the pain that still sent tingles through her body, though it sent shocks to her pussy.

Storm stretched out next to her, letting his head rest on his hand casually to the side of hers to look into her eyes. "Oh, my love, we told you we would protect you. This morning, you were told to wait behind the panel of the playroom until we came for you, but you didn't."

"But Connor came for me behind the panel and took me up the back stairs. I went with him and then came to help you guys out," Lyndee said trying to defend herself, holding onto the black silk rope around her wrists.

Storm glanced down at Austin and nodded.

Smack! The large tanned hand came down on her ass again. Austin began to rub the pink spot as she rose up into the caress and she took comfort in the action. After a few seconds, the next smack came before the next caress. This was repeated seven more times before Storm looked into her eyes again. Tears had formed there as the pain turned into pleasurable sensations radiating from her derriere, her bottom undulating in an invitation.

"Hush. Connor came and got you but he told you to wait in the office, which you refused to do, putting yourself in danger. You didn't listen and Philip could have shot you down in the playroom. He had the means. That's why you are being punished," Storm explained. "Do you understand that?"

Lyndee didn't agree with his logic but she understood he was trying to protect her. And if truth be told she had enjoyed the spanking very much. Her ass burned but there was a pleasant sensation running through her. She would enjoy this activity in the future.

Trey had moved to her other side and was fondling her left breast, his callused fingers running across the tight nub on the tip of it. His teeth grazed her shoulder and back, sending electrical currents through her body. She trembled under his ministrations.

Teeth grazed her ass cheek as a hand reached under her and stroked a finger through her moist folds. A sigh escaped her lips as the finger circled her cream-laden labia before going lower to find the hardened nub at the top of her slit. The mouth on her bottom opened up and began to suck on the flesh, pulling it into his mouth. Austin's mouth suckled on her as his finger ran under the hood of the woman's most precious sensitive spot and began to rub in circles. Her gasps came between pants as her breathing came in short bursts as copious amounts of cream leaked from her depths.

Their hands teased and fondled her as the temperature in her body seemed to rise from her core. The finger on her clit circled faster while her nipples were pinched harshly. The tingling within her cunt increased as did her juices and she knew she was close. The mouth released her globe as Austin's other hand ran down to her pussy, gathered some of her cream on two fingers, and pulled it backward up to the puckered hole of her ass. They moved around the outer rim of her ass, lubricating the way. She relaxed for she knew what was to come. One finger pushed its way through the tight muscle of the outer edge and pushed in further, causing her to cry out.

"Relax, little one," Austin said huskily. "You've accepted your punishment, now accept your pleasure."

His finger moved around inside her forbidden channel a couple of times before he pulled out. She cried out at the emptiness before he reentered, though with two fingers. His other hand continued working her clit. He had turned his hand and rammed two fingers into her vagina and placed his thumb on her clit and began to rub even harder. She was filled in her pussy and her ass and the whimpers escaped her lips as she moved her hips to fuck his digits.

Storm leaned forward and slammed his mouth onto hers. As she gasped with the effect, he thrust his tongue inside the dark depths there. Her pussy, ass, and mouth were filled, but not with what she longed for, yet her mind slipped into overload. The tingling in her core shot outward, her limbs going stiff as wave after wave clinched up her pussy and she screamed into Storm's warm mouth. Trey pinched hard on her nipple and she climbed even higher through the orgasm as it throbbed through her entire body. Electrical pulses shot out to the far reaches of her body, down to her toes to her fingertips to the top of her head.

Pulling her mouth away from Storm's she breathed in deeply as her breath had left her as she came over and over again. She was lightheaded as she descended from the pinnacle she had climbed with the assistance of her men. Little ripples of aftershocks kept pulsing through her cunt, causing whimpers to escape her as her teary eyes drifted closed.

Untying her arms and legs, Storm and Trey each took an arm to massage. Austin rose and made his way to the bathroom, washed his hands and then returned, climbing between her legs again. Using both hands he started on her ankles, a soft squeezing that a one-handed massage would give, but she flinched as his cold hands touched her. "Cold," she murmured.

The three men smiled at each other. "Sorry," Austin said lowly.

"You all right, darlin'?" Storm asked, concern mixed with lust as he continued to knead her flesh.

"Yes," she sighed. "Wonderful."

"Good, because we aren't done with you," he whispered. "We all have hard cocks and you are going to relieve our balls of this hot cum we have just for you."

Pushing herself up onto her hands, she looked at his cock, long and thick, rising from the nest of dark-blond curls. Leaning over, she ran her tongue across the tip, taking the drop of pre-cum that sat upon the tip with it. She heard him groan as his hands tightened around her arm. Turning, she did the same to Trey, savoring his flavor in the small droplet. Glancing around to the large man behind her, she noticed his hard cock throbbing, tapping against his taut abdomen. At the tip was the glistening drop of man dew that she wished she could taste. She licked her lips, which wasn't missed on the man.

"Lay back down, little one," Austin said, pushing down on her derriere. "Let us work out your arms and legs. You came hard and probably tensed up in the restraints."

Doing as she was told, she let the men minister to her needs as she relaxed. It was astounding that one minute they could have her tied up, bringing her to an explosive climax, and then treat her like a fragile piece of china the next. Reveling in the feel of their hands, she let herself drift on a cloud of luxury.

When the brothers were finished massaging her arms, they moved to her neck and shoulders. Austin's hand moved up to within inches of the V of her legs. She was surprised when he spoke, jumping slightly as she must have started to doze.

"Why do you shave your pussy?"

It felt as if the blush spread through her entire body with that question but uncertainty arose also. "Do you not like it?"

"It's amazing." Austin's husky voice filtered up to her ears.

"It's not shaved," she stated lowly. "It's waxed."

A gasp from all three men resonated through the room before the groans began. With her eyes closed, she pictured all three of them grabbing their balls in protection. She smiled.

"It may hurt a little bit, but it lasts longer than shaving, and I love the feel there, even if I didn't have anyone to touch me there." The last bit brought a bit of a lump to her throat and the men noticed.

Storm leaned over lower and kissed her ear before whispering, "You now have three men to enjoy your naked pussy. We love it."

Running his tongue around the shell of her ear, she shuddered in pleasure at his soft touch, his mustache tickling the outer edge. "Why did you start doing it?"

"The other girls took me to the salon that does it and insisted it was the thing to do. I tried it."

Whispering again in her ear, he asked, "What about this sexy tattoo? Why'd you get it?"

"I got that as a present to myself when I graduated the police academy. I loved the design."

Her breath was short as Storm continued to tease her ear with his mouth and he stroked the dragon with his fingertips.

"I love your tattoo," Trey said. "I love anything about your sexy body. I could spend all day fucking you and never get tired of it."

Sighing heavily, she said, "You guys could spoil a girl."

"We enjoy spoiling you, little one," Austin said. "And if you want sex all the time, we will try to accommodate you as much as possible, though we do have jobs to do."

A giggle escaped her. "I don't expect it all the time but you have started a hunger in me that I have come to enjoy."

Storm's whisper in her ear caused fresh nectar to seep from her pussy. "Then let's see if we can satisfy some of that hunger for you."

Chapter Twenty

Callused fingers ran up both sides of her pussy lips, up and around the top of her slit, not touching the part she wanted to have touched the most. She groaned in frustration. As the fingers repeated the path in reverse, she tried to push back against them to no avail. Austin's fingers continued up the cleft of her ass, past the rosebud there on up to where the cleft ended at her back. He chuckled at her motions, knowing what she wanted.

Removing his fingers, he placed his tongue at the top of her crack and slowly began to slide it downward. Arriving at her forbidden entrance, she clinched her cheeks together as his tongue circled the puckered hole.

"Relax," he murmured, knowing she could hear him. "Relax."

Doing as she was told, she relaxed her ass cheeks, letting Austin master her body. Storm and Trey were back to fondling her breasts with one hand while rubbing lightly with their fingertips down both sides of her spine. Letting her inhibitions go with their ministrations, her ass relaxed under Austin's hands and he separated the cheeks and let his tongue circle her little rosebud again.

After rimming her several times, Austin moved his mouth lower, swiping at the copious fluid at the opening of her slit. Her hips bucked up at the sensation of his velvety organ licking at her then trying to scoop out her cream from its depths. He seemed to be trying to suck the juice from within her, which caused more of her juices to flow.

"Damn, woman, you are leaking so much. I love it," he said, pulling his mouth away from her briefly. Setting his mouth back against her he licked her opening, savoring the taste of his woman. Wanting more, he left her pussy briefly, flipped onto his back and pushed her knees further up under her, raising her ass up in the air.

Resting his head under her pussy his mouth went to work on her slick folds. His wide, flat nose rubbed on her clit, heightening her arousal as moans escaped her mouth. He wrapped his muscular arms around her thighs, holding her down to him while spreading her ass cheeks.

Storm, kneeling next to her, with one hand fondled her breasts as they hung down from her chest, and the other one made its way over her back. Rounding the flesh of her derriere, he squeezed the globe as he inched his way down to her pussy. Pulling her sweet cream back up to her puckered hole with two fingers, he moisturized the area before pushing one finger in past the tight muscle there.

A shudder flowed through her as all three men administered their affection upon her. Trey fondled her other breast, pinching the nipple there between his finger and thumb as he laid kisses on her shoulders and neck. Storm slipped another finger into her anus and pumped in and out, readying her for the tryst that was about to happen. Austin continued sucking her cunt, letting his tongue glide in and out of her opening and then moving up to her clit. There he sucked on the hard nub. Her womb seemed to coil up within her body, tighter and tighter until it sprung, currents racing through all her nerves while fluid gushed onto Austin's mouth and chin. Her scream was long and soulful and she hoped it touched each of her men's hearts, letting them know they had brought her to this moment. Lapping up her juices, Austin gathered all she had given him as she felt her arms nearly give way under her.

Lyndee felt Austin move his head out from under her as Storm pulled his fingers from her ass, her body immediately missing the intimacy. She felt Trey's hands at her waist, a whimper escaping her when she thought he was pulling her away from the other two. Austin laid fully on his back in the middle of the bed as Trey held her as if she weighed nothing before he sat her on the large Indian's abs. She felt Trey move in behind her and a thrill ran through her.

"Lay down on me, baby," Austin said, seeing she was still shaking from the aftermath of her orgasm. "Let us love on you."

Doing as she was told, she lay down upon the mattress of muscle under his hot skin, her knees on both sides of his waist. Trey rubbed her derriere, kneading at the flesh he loved so much. Leaning over, he kissed the tip of the dragon's tail of her tattoo, letting his tongue follow it into the cleft before swirling it around her rosette. Her hips shifted slightly before his hands held them still. Continuing to lave attention on her puckered hole, he pushed the tip of his tongue into the tight muscle, causing a gasp to escape her.

Leaning up, Austin tipped her chin up with a finger and captured her lips in his. His tongue plied for entrance, which was granted as her mouth opened to his. His tongue swept the inside of her mouth, not missing an inch as if he was trying to memorize her. Behind her Trey's mouth left the rosebud of her ass and warm lube was being applied to the area generously. A finger slipped in through the tight muscle and moved in and out several times before another one was added. Austin absorbed her moans in his mouth as he wrapped his large arms around her waist, holding onto her tightly.

Being held in this large man's arms made her feel so secure, and she loved how all of them were so protective of her but also so tender and loving. They made love to her as if she was the only woman in the world, and after watching prostitutes getting screwed by man after man she cherished their attention and love. She only wished every woman could feel like this.

Lyndee's tongue danced with Austin's as Trey's fingers disappeared from her rosebud, and she felt the hard tip of his cock at her entrance. Knowing now what to expect, she bore down on him as he slipped through the pink ring of muscle that was exposed after his ministrations with his fingers. Inching his way in, she pulled from Austin's mouth and arched her back, savoring the feeling of her dark channel's invasion.

Trey inched his way in as his hand grasped her cheeks, holding onto them tightly. When he was fully seated Storm raised her slightly in his arms as Austin held his thick, hard cock up to line up with her weeping pussy. Letting her down easy, he still held her so she wouldn't take him fully at once, letting her get used to the full feeling of two hot cocks in her. When each cock was filling her beyond belief, she sighed contentedly as she laid her hands on Austin's defined chest to hold herself up while Trey grasped her braid and pulled on it.

The men began to move, seesawing in and out of her holes while Storm pulled her head over and ran his hard cock across her lips, painting them with his pre-cum. Licking her lips of the proffered taste of Storm, she heard him growl as the other two fucked both her nether holes. Her tongue shot out and caressed the V of underside of the mushroom head at her lips before moving upward to the hole at its tip. He hissed at the touch of her tongue as it tried to dig into the hole before she pulled back and let her tongue run down the length of his hot swollen cock.

"Oh, geez," Storm hissed before he aimed his dick at her mouth and shoved it in until it touched the back of her throat. Surprise registered on her flushed face and she swallowed around the girth of it and she heard him hiss again. Glancing up at him, she saw that his head was thrown back in his ecstasy, his eyes closed. Moving her head back and forth, she fucked his dick as Austin and Trey moved in her tight holes.

Her pelvic bone felt as if it was being split but the pressure and the heat there began to build as the men moved within her depths even faster. Panting was coming from all four of them as they were building toward that epic release. Austin reached down and found her clit, squeezing the swollen nub. The dam burst within Lyndee's pussy first as her climax rocketed through her body, causing it to become rigid, her cunt clamping down on their cocks as she screamed out around Storm's dick.

Austin shot his seed deep within her pussy, scalding her depths with the heat of it. Trey was next to cum as he shot hot streams of jism into her forbidden hole. The heat of both men's seed caused her orgasm to continue as Storm released himself, his thick cum flooding her throat. She tried to swallow as much as she could as she rode the tidal wave of orgasm, though some leaked around her lips.

Pulling himself from her mouth, Storm collapsed onto the bed next to his cousin as Trey lay upon her back, his sweaty chest and abs covering her nakedness. Austin pulled her down gently to lie on his chest, holding her as close to him as possible with his cousin still on top of her, surrounding her with his body, arms, and legs.

Trey laid kisses along her shoulders and neck. Austin covered her lips with his gently, licking at them while Storm played with the nipple that was closest to him. Lyndee felt surrounded by their love and knew that she was going to miss all of them when she had to go back to Denver. Sighing, she laid her head on Austin's chiseled chest.

"Are you all right, little one?" Austin asked, kissing the top of her head.

Lifting her head to look at him, she smiled. "Yes. I was just thinking how much I was going to miss all of you when I have to go back home."

All three men stilled, Trey in the midst of pulling his flaccid cock from her ass. When no one moved, she looked from Austin to Storm and glanced back at Trey, each one wearing a solemn look upon their faces. Storm was the first to come out of the shock she sent them into as he leaned up on one elbow and reached out to cup her cheek.

"You are coming back, darlin'. Aren't you?" he asked, frightened of what her answer would be.

Confusion crossed her features. They had wanted her to stay, or at least that's what she thought they had wanted. Was she not clear on that in the past? Or had they changed their minds? Lowering her eyes, fighting to keep back the tears, she whispered, "Only if you want me to."

Storm's thumb moved to her chin and pulled her face toward his. She knew he saw the tears that had welled in her eyes, though she still looked downward. "Look at me," he said sternly, and she knew he, Trey, and Austin were barely breathing in anticipation.

Rising up on her hands against the hard chest beneath her, she looked up at the man she had come to love in such a short amount of time and saw the concern in his eyes. Licking her lips with a suddenly dry tongue, she hoarsely said, "I know you had said you wanted me to stay, but I didn't know if you really wanted me to."

"Of course we do!" Storm practically snarled, causing her to jump. "What would make you think otherwise?"

With one blink of her eyes, the tears fell. They ran down her cheeks and rained onto Austin's chest. The copper man beneath Lyndee covered one of her hands with his as it pressed into his chest. Trey withdrawing fully began rubbing his fingertips up and down her spine while kneeling between his cousin's legs. Storm moved quickly to his knees and pulled her into his arms, apparently forgetting that Austin was still lodged within her pussy. Austin moaned.

"Oh, darlin', did we hurt you?"

Trying to shake her head, she ended up rubbing her face on the tanned, hard pecs that adorned Storm, the light blond patch of fur between the bulging muscles becoming damp. Pure masculinity invaded her senses as she breathed in sweat, a bit of his musky cologne that lingered from his morning shower and a light scent of fabric softener. Funny, she hadn't noticed the scents of the other men before. Perhaps she was trying to memorize them before she had to leave for a while. A deep sigh escaped her and she pulled slightly away, though relishing the feel of being enveloped in his arms.

"No, you didn't hurt me. When you asked if I was staying, I thought perhaps you really didn't want me to. Also, when you tied me down, you didn't..." She sniffled as she let her sentence trail off, hiding her face again in his chest.

"We didn't what?" Storm asked, his voice tinged slightly with irritation.

"Never mind," she murmured into his chest.

Moving slightly away from her, Storm moved a hand up to her neck and pulled on her hair slightly to cause her to look up at him. Feeling vulnerable as each man stared at her, she flushed. Laying her hands on Storm's chest for support, her eyelids lowered in embarrassment.

"I'm sorry, I've never been in a relationship before, so I'm not good at this." She tried to smile but failed for fear of their answers. "You didn't tie me up all the way and not tight, so I thought perhaps you changed your mind or didn't want to play with me like you did others."

Storm's mouth dropped open and Austin somehow managed to rise to his knees next to her without knocking his cousins or Lyndee over. His hand went to her upper back while Trey's sat at her hip on the opposite side. With their actions, she felt nervous, her stomach fluttering in anticipation of their responses.

Austin was the first to recover from the shock of her words. "Little one, we have never told you we want you to leave. We have loved you from the first time we saw you lying on the ground on that mountain, unconscious. You have our hearts, all of them. We never intended to let you leave here permanently. I will be going with you to Denver to help you move and deal with the end result of this mess."

Trey kissed her cheek before turning her to face him. "We meant it when we said we loved you."

Storm tipped her face back to him with a finger under her chin, sighing before speaking, as if he was choosing his words carefully. "We didn't tie you up completely because we were afraid you might freak out because of what happened with you being kidnapped. We wanted to gauge your reaction."

Nervously her teeth worried her bottom lip as she lowered her eyelids in embarrassment. She had really blown this whole evening. "I'm sorry," she said softly. "Sometimes I can be a little unsure of myself with people. I know you said you wanted me to stay with you, but when you asked again if I was staying, I really thought you had changed your minds. Especially after what happened earlier today, I thought perhaps I was too much trouble for you. That I brought too much baggage."

"Don't ever think that, little one," Austin said to her left. "We all have baggage but we move past it. If we didn't care about you do you think we would have gone to the trouble we did this morning to protect you? We protect what's ours. You belong to us and there is no more talk about us not wanting you. We love you and you are coming back here and marrying us."

Turning to face him, surprise registering on her features, she asked breathily, "You do know that's illegal!"

It was time to look at Trey as he spoke. "You'll legally marry Storm since he's the oldest, but Austin and I will commit ourselves to you as your husbands in a separate binding ceremony that a friend of ours from Texas will oversee."

"But what will people think? What about Martha and the men who work with you? What about Connor? I knew that you shared women in the past but I just didn't think you'd marry one of them. All of you."

Storm raised a finger to her lips as she was rattling off questions as a display of her nerves getting the best of her. "Hush darlin'. You're thinking too much. There are more of us out there than you think. There are many places out there that it's the norm for our lifestyle. You don't have to let your job influence your thinking. We love you and you love us, so there is nothing that will stop us from living life our way. The guys know about us. They're fine with it. Martha has known us since we were kids so she knows what we are looking for. She's going to love you as much as we do."

Austin chuckled. "Well, maybe not as much as we do, but she'll still love you. Even Doc understands our lifestyle. There are more people out there that accept us than you think."

Having to switch from man to man as they spoke she was beginning to feel like she was going to get whiplash. She turned to Trey again as he spoke. "Did you not think it odd that the nurses at the hospital didn't think twice about us showering you with attention at the hospital? Or that Anita wasn't surprised? She even told us that she wished she had what we had so she wouldn't be alone now that her husband was gone. Does that sound like there is going to be a problem with this relationship?"

Taking one last look at each of her men, she saw the love that emanated from them and knew they were right. This was something that they would make work and she would do her damnedest to make them all happy. Tears began to fall again but this time they were happy tears. Throwing her arms around Trey's and Austin's shoulders, she drew them together against her and Storm rested his forehead on hers, breathing a sigh of relief.

* * * *

Three days later, Lyndee walked down the hallway into the living room and found her men standing near the front door waiting for her. She was dressed in a black long-sleeved dress that was belted at the waist. Its "A" style skirt hung to just below her knees over the black stockings she wore, tipped by the black heels she wore on her feet, her big toes showing through the peepholes there. Her hair hung down her back, the ends curled while a slight trace of makeup adorned her face.

The three men sucked in a breath as she appeared, their woman looking beautiful and they were all proud she was theirs. They each wore a suit. Austin wore a white shirt beneath his black jacket with a black tie, while Storm and Trey wore light-blue shirts and dark-blue ties with their dark-blue suits. Black cowboy boots, shined, were upon their feet and each of them held a black felt cowboy hat. Storm and Trey's hair were slicked down while Austin's hung shiny down his back.

They were all handsome as Lyndee had never seen them dressed like this before. They were all the epitome of sexiness but it was a shame the reason they were all dressed so elegantly. They were heading into Kalispell to the funeral of Anita's, the woman from the hospital, husband who had succumbed to his injuries. The men had offered their support to the woman and Storm had even paid for the funeral since they didn't have any money.

James and David seemed to have taken a shine to the woman, even though she had just lost her husband and they would bide their time before approaching her. For now, they were friends offering their help.

Trey stepped forward and took Lyndee's hand. "You look beautiful."

Blushing, she smiled. "As do all of you."

Storm stepped forward smiling. "Darlin', men are handsome, not beautiful. But Trey is right. You are beautiful. You make us proud to stand by you."

Austin smiled and stepped forward, though didn't say a word. To Lyndee's surprise, all three men got down on one knee. Storm took her left hand in his. "Lyndee Dwyer, we would officially all like to ask for your hand in marriage. We promise to love you and protect you as a trio and make you our one and only wife. Will you marry us?"

Sinking to her knees, tears in her eyes, she nodded, "Yes! Yes, I will marry each of you! You have made me so happy!"

She watched Storm slip a ring on her left ring finger. When he pulled his hand down to just hold her fingertips, she saw a one-carat diamond on her finger with two smaller diamonds on each side on a ring twisted of Black Hills gold.

"It's beautiful," she exclaimed.

"Not as beautiful as you are, honey," Trey said as he turned her toward him for a kiss.

"Nothing can ever be as beautiful as you, darlin'," Storm said before he kissed her.

Austin placed a hand on each of her cheeks and drew her to him and covered her lips passionately before pulling back. "You have made me the happiest man on earth."

Tears still glittered in her eyes at the love they showed her and she giggled as she looked at the ring. The three men stood and each helped her to her feet. When she looked at them, they were looking at her quizzically.

"I love the ring, guys. I just thought I'd never see one there. I was beginning to wonder if this case was ever going to be cracked or if I was going to be some aged undercover prostitute. By then my chance to find a guy would have passed."

Austin pulled her small left hand into his large one, the skin color contrasting. "Everything happens for a reason, and though I regret you had to go through so much pain and suffering, I'm glad Philip brought you here for us to find you. You have filled our hearts with love and joy."

His words touched her heart, and she raised her other hand to his cheek and laid a gentle caress upon it. Swallowing the lump in her throat, she whispered, "Me too."

The three men stared at their woman for a few more seconds before Storm cleared his throat. "We need to get going. It's going to be a long day."

Escorting Lyndee out to the pickup truck that was waiting in the rounded driveway, they met James and David, who were dressed in their Sunday best also and all crowded in. Once everyone was situated, they headed to the C.E. Conrad Memorial Cemetery in Kalispell.

Chapter Twenty-One

Two days after the funeral, Austin and Lyndee stood in the living room for a tearful good-bye. The suitcases had already been taken out to Austin's black pickup along with a cooler full of sodas so they wouldn't have to stop on the road too often. She had been crying since they had tucked her into bed after a long session of lovemaking. She would miss the two men that were staying behind as they had been with her since they had found her and all her emotional baggage.

Austin hung back by the door, giving Lyndee a bit of room to deal with Trey and Storm since he was the one going as her bodyguard. Storm stepped up to her and pulled her into his arms, holding her against his chest where she buried her face in his blue plaid flannel shirt. They both breathed in each other's scents, trying to memorize them. Their hands roamed each other's backs and sides, frantic to feel as much as possible of each other. After several minutes of this, Storm pulled a hand around and tipped her chin up with his fist before his mouth descended on hers.

It was a carnal kiss as his lips slashed over hers, both of them seeking out the other's tongue. Lips smashed and teeth clicked as they tried to memorize the feel of each other's mouths, inside and out. Their tongues swirled together or licked at the interior, not leaving a spot untouched. They ravished each other's mouth before finally coming up for air. Storm supped at her lips a few more times before pulling back slightly.

"Ah, darlin', I'm gonna miss you. But we'll be down in a couple of weeks to visit or hopefully bring you guys back home," he whispered as he wiped her tears away with his thumbs, but couldn't seem to catch them all.

Nodding, she gave a weak smile. "I'm going to miss you, too. I love you."

"Love you, too," he said as he pulled her in for one last hug. Letting her go, he turned her to his brother, who was waiting his turn.

Trey draped her with his strong muscular arms, drawing her to him and held her. Her arms slid around his waist, trying to pull him closer to her, though they were as close as two people could get. He was wearing his uniform as Connor had told him that he'd had enough time playing with his woman and needed to get back to work, though he had been officially on duty since the day after they found her. He was protecting a victim of a crime and Connor could spare him to do so.

Lifting her head, Lyndee smiled through her tears. "You look very handsome, Officer Goodall."

Chuckling, he looked down into her soft iris eyes. "And you look very beautiful, Agent Dwyer. I love you."

He didn't have to hear the words from her. He knew she loved him and he knew this was hard on her. Leaning down, he laid his lips gently on hers and drank from them. He didn't have to be as dominant as his brother but kissed her in his own way to let her know he was going to miss her. When he pulled back, her eyelids were lowered as she licked his flavor from her lips. They untangled their arms and she stepped over to Austin.

The Native American escorted their woman out to the truck, his hand on the small of her back. Storm and Trey followed somberly. Austin opened the passenger door and helped the petite woman into the seat and waited until she had buckled her seatbelt before shutting the door. The window was down and Lyndee reached her arm out and clasped the two hands that came up to hers.

"I love you both so much," she said, trying to fight back the tears. "Take care of each other."

Each man took her hand and kissed her palm before declaring their love for her. As they looked at each other Lyndee noticed a secret smile pass between them. "What was that?"

The driver's side door slammed shut as Austin adjusted himself in the seat before putting the gear shift into drive. He chuckled at his cousin's perfect timing. Lyndee whipped her head around to glance at him and knew something was up, looking back out the window as the half-ton vehicle began to move slowly.

"Why are you smiling like that?" she asked Storm and Trey.

Shrugging then grinning, Storm nonchalantly said, "When you get home there will be a surprise for you."

Before she could ask what it was, Austin sped up and pulled around the circular drive to the road that would lead them off the ranch. Twisting around, she watched two of her men waving and smiling until the truck passed the horse barn and she wasn't able to see them anymore. Tears slipped down her cheeks as she turned back to face the windshield. Austin reached over and wiped them away before patting the seat next to him. Unbuckling herself, she slid over to the middle and buckled up. The large man's arm slid around the back of the seat and hugged her to his side. They drove like that in silence until they got to the Kalispell hospital.

Wolf had agreed to go to Denver with them for rehabilitation on his shoulder. The doctors had referred him to a physical therapist there and that way he had Lyndee and Austin to help him while they awaited the trial.

Once all the paper work was finalized, the two lovers helped the injured man into the truck and set out on their journey to Denver. Austin had planned on a two day trip since it would take about sixteen hours to get to their destination. Lyndee had volunteered to do some driving also, and Austin had told her he was anxious to see her petite form at the helm of his truck. Then he went on to say that since she had harnessed the power of the three of them, it would be interesting to see if she could handle the power behind it.

Wolf settled in the backseat. Blankets and pillows had been placed back there so he could rest when he got bored or tired. He had told them that being able to look at the scenery and not have to lie in bed all day was fine with him, though he didn't last an hour before his painkiller kicked in and he laid back, his eyes drifting closed.

As his soft snores sounded, Lyndee unbuckled and climbed onto her knees, her ass in the air in full view of passing vehicles, to reach back and pull a blanket up over the man and tuck it under his chin. Austin reached his hand around and caressed the denim-clad bottom and thigh before she could turn around.

"Hey," she hissed lowly, as not to wake Wolf. "Keep your hands to yourself, mister!"

Climbing back into her spot next to her man, she leaned into him as his arm came around her shoulder again. Giggling when his hand brushed her breast she looked up at him and saw the slightest smile on his face under his dark aviator shades. Taking his hand, she kissed the palm before holding it in her hand. Watching the beautiful scenery roll by, she marveled at the mountains surrounding them, knowing this was going to be her new home and the man next to her was all hers for the taking. After a while she dozed next to him, his clean scent wafting through her nose, a content smile on her face.

* * * *

Austin couldn't be happier then to escort their woman to Denver. To have her to himself was going to be heavenly, though they would have to be quiet since Wolf was going to be around. He and Storm had talked about taking her to the BDSM club they belonged to while they were there just so she could get an idea of what was going to be in store for her, but he opted to wait until his cousin arrived. If they were going to be teaching her submission, they might was well all be there. Perhaps when he and Trey came down in a few weeks they could go then.

Looking down at his lover, he saw the contentment in her face as she slept against his side, one hand on his thigh, the other clutching his other hand near her shoulder. The hand on his thigh seemed to burn through the denim of his jeans at the near proximity of his cock, which he tried to talk down from its arousal. It was going to be a long two days he smiled, thinking to himself.

* * * *

After spending the night in Buffalo, Wyoming, the trio was back on the road. They would hit Denver late in the afternoon, taking Lyndee back to her home and her job for the time being, something neither she nor Austin really cared to do. Wolf was on his way to restart his life after the injury he took in her defense. It all led back to Denver.

* * * *

It was near six in the evening when Austin pulled his black pickup into the parking lot of a restaurant in the downtown district where Lyndee had directed him. Wolf protested his involvement with dinner but both his employer and Lyndee insisted he was going to enjoy a nice meal before getting settled in at the apartment. As Austin got out and helped Wolf down from the back, Lyndee quickly ran a brush through her hair, letting it fall freely down her back and then applied a layer of lip gloss. She had applied some makeup as they had maneuvered through traffic.

Scooting over past the steering wheel she swung her legs around and let Austin lift her down from the lifted vehicle, setting her down on her feet. After closing the door the three of them made their way through the parking lot to the front door. They made an odd-looking group. One tall Native American that looked like a wrestler with his large, muscular frame and long hair, the other several inches shorter but still muscularly built, though the sling on his arm showed his vulnerability. Both wore black jeans and T-shirts that looked like the seams would rip at any minute while cowboy boots and hats adorned the polar ends of their bodies. Dark sunglasses shaded their eyes as if protecting them from the elements of the city instead of the ball of fire in the sky.

The woman that walked between them, at least a foot shorter than each of them, wore blue jeans, a white blouse over a spaghetti-strapped purple tank, and her new black cowboy boots. Her long blonde hair shone in the late afternoon sun as it hung down her back, swaying with the movement of her ample hips that Austin liked to look at while she walked away from him. Her face was relaxed for the first time since she had been rescued, but her nerves were evident when she slid her small hand into Austin's large one for comfort.

Austin opened the large wooden door and let Lyndee and Wolf enter first before stepping into the dimly lit building. Surprised to see a long bar down one side of the room while booths lined the other side of the room with tables set up in between, Austin just stopped inside the door. The restaurant was teeming with men in suits, casual wear, and even jeans and T-shirts. Women in dresses and jeans and T-shirts milled around also, though the majority of the patrons were men. The din of voices and laughter died out quickly when they looked up to see who had entered their haven, which caused the two men to become nervous.

Possessiveness gripped both men as they grasped Lyndee by the arms and began to pull her back toward the door. All of a sudden John was before them, a glass of beer in one hand as he reached for Lyndee with the other.

"Lyndee! I'm so glad you were able to make it for happy hour!" he said exuberantly, giving the petite woman a hug. Looking over at Austin, he put his hand out in greeting. "Austin, wasn't it?"

Grasping the man's hand, Austin shook it. "John. Good to see you again."

Chatter picked up again throughout the restaurant as people milled around or made their way over to the threesome. Several men threw their arms around Lyndee's shoulders and hugged her or shook her hand, all congratulating her on busting up the crime ring. Jubilation was the order of the evening as this was a celebratory dinner for all the law enforcement involved.

John escorted the trio over to the bar where several men cleared the area for them while everyone turned to watch them. John shouted, gaining everyone's undivided attention. "We would all like to welcome Lyndee back, though we know she won't be staying. And I'd like to introduce you to two of the men who helped take down five members of the Markova gang. Welcome Austin and Wolf. Wolf took a bullet during the incident and he's here to get some therapy." Turning to face the trio, he added, "We will all be at your disposal for any help you need, rides to the hospital, errands, and food deliveries. Don't hesitate to call us."

The bombardment of bodies pressing up to them to congratulate the men and offer assistance, handing them business cards, was nearly too much for the two cowboys. Their world was quiet with only a few people around at a time. Six or seven dozen people or more was too much for them. When the barrage finally settled, they each ordered a drink, a beer for Austin while Lyndee and Wolf took a soda before finding a booth. Austin scooted in and left Lyndee on the end as he knew people would continue to come over and talk to her, and he didn't want people talking over him. Wolf scooted as much as he could to put himself in the corner, leaving an empty spot, which John filled rather quickly.

"I want to thank you guys again for stepping in like you did to help out Lyndee. My wife would never forgive me if something had happened to her," John said before taking a swig of his drink.

Austin's irritability was evident as he glared at Lyndee's commanding officer. "Something did happen to her. If we weren't lucky enough to have found her, she would be dead."

Lyndee covered his hand with hers trying to calm his anger. It dawned on her that of the three men, Austin was her protector. Storm was her strength, the one who kept her in line and honest with her feelings, while Trey was the one who kept everyone grounded, even though he had his mischievous moments.

John raised a hand as if trying to defend himself from Austin's anger. "I understand you're upset Austin. You have no idea how angry I was when we found out that Philip had made bail. I immediately went over to Lyndee's to take her home with me, but by the time I arrived, he had already been there. When I found the blood on the couch and the floor I thought the worse. God, I wish I could have been the one to have killed him!"

Lyndee's other hand covered John's soothingly. "It wasn't your fault. I never dreamed he would have gotten out either. Plus I didn't even know he had my address. I should have been more prepared for it and I hate that I wasn't."

"The way I see it," Wolf started, "is that Philip would have found a way to hurt you no matter if you had been prepared or not. His life was at stake. Sometimes when that happens people seem to have extra strength, mentally and physically, to do things we don't expect. Everything happens for a reason. We know the reason for what happened to you. Blaming each other or yourself for what happened is wasted time. Grab the moment, learn from it, and go on."

Austin, Lyndee, and John looked at each other before nodding. Austin extended his hand to John. "I'm sorry. After having Lyndee in our lives even so briefly, I don't know what I would do if we lost her."

John took Austin's hand graciously. "I'm sorry too."

Lyndee smiled at Wolf, who sheepishly smiled back. Austin gave the recovering man a smirk. "What are they giving you in those pills? I've never heard you speak so much in one day and now you're talking like a shrink."

Shrugging, Wolf smiled, opening the menu with his one hand. "Someone has taught me how to live recently and I am going to do just that. Now what's good here?"

John and Lyndee looked at each other for a moment before laughing. In unison they both said, "The drinks!"

The rest of the evening was spent enjoying the company of Lyndee's fellow officers of the law. Austin eased up a bit and actually began to relax, enjoying himself by the end of the evening. At Lyndee's insistence, he even joined a few women on the dance floor, noticing his woman wasn't jealous of them at all.

Wolf had a steady flow of women flaunting themselves at him, fawning over his injury, offering any assistance he needed. One woman, an agent with the DEA, dressed in a woolen pencil skirt along with a blazer over her white blouse, offered to help him with showering or dressing if he needed it. Lyndee had to contain the laughter that wanted to bubble up from within her as Wolf explained that he was perfectly able to tend to his bathing needs. He raised his eyebrows to Lyndee for help when he saw the tears in her eyes along with the laughter. Finally, Lyndee touched the woman on her hand. "Jenny, Wolf will be staying with me so he won't need any personal assistance. But we appreciate the offer."

Flabbergasted, the woman looked at Lyndee, back at Wolf, and then glanced at Austin before returning her gaze to the petite blonde across from her. "Both of them? Damn, you are one lucky lady!"

Standing on shaky legs, Jenny turned away and walked with a stagger to the bar. "Have another one, Jenny," Lyndee had to say under her breath as she began to laugh. Looking over she saw that Wolf was trying not to laugh, but wasn't succeeding. Soon they were doubled over and with a glance at Austin, Lyndee could see he was concerned, excusing himself from the fifty-something woman he was dancing with to a Kenny Chesney song.

"What the hell is wrong with both of you?" he demanded lowly, arriving at the table.

Lyndee had scooted over to the wall and sobered a bit. Wolf was still chuckling as Austin scooted in next to him, eyeing both of them. "Can someone please tell me what is going on?"

"Later, babe," Lyndee said, catching Jenny trying to size up the two men. "I've really had enough socializing for one day. Can we go home? I'm tired."

Standing, Austin stepped over to help Lyndee from the booth, and they both stood by to help Wolf to his feet if he needed them. Good-byes were said before they were able to escape the gathering and head out to the truck. A chill was in the air as they walked and Austin looked up. Lyndee knew the sky here was much different than back in Montana. He must be looking for the stars. Piling into the truck, they were off to what would be their home until the end of the trial.

Chapter Twenty-Two

Before they had left the restaurant, John had given Lyndee her purse along with her gun and shoulder holster. She was afraid she would never see either one of them again just a little over a week ago.

Once they parked in front of her apartment building Austin could see how someone could break in so easily. It was a U-shaped building with the parking in the middle. The doorways opened right to the parking lot, windows looking out onto the cars also. Lyndee's apartment was at the end on the bottom floor. Austin was glad she was moving in with them.

After fishing the keys from her purse, she opened the door and took a moment to look around after switching on the lights. Lyndee was surprised to find her apartment immaculately clean and the door had been repaired. There was a new door along with new locks for her future safety. She knew John had been the one to have taken care of everything in her absence. She also saw she had a new sofa. It warmed her heart that he had done all this for her, though after looking around the place she had called home for the past five years, sadness consumed her that she would miss this place and her friends a bit. The moment wasn't missed by the tall, muscular man behind her, though he would let it go for now.

Arms wrapped around her from behind, one around her waist and one around her shoulders, drawing her back to him. He knew the turmoil that circulated through her but he knew she would be happy with them. She already had a good start on making friends and she was loved by everyone she had already met. All three men loved her so much they knew they would work hard to make her content for the rest of their lives.

A groan behind them made them remember they weren't alone. Stepping inside, Austin placed his suitcase and Lyndee's on the couch. "Where's Wolf's room?" he asked, taking the man's suitcase from him. The evening had been too much for him and he was pale and in pain.

Lyndee escorted the two men to the small hallway and showed them which room was Wolf's. Austin set the suitcase on the chair near the closet while the other man sat on the bed. Lyndee had left the room and quickly returned with a glass of water. "John said he stocked the fridge and put up other supplies so don't hesitate to help yourself to anything you need. Your bathroom is just in there," she said pointing to the door, "though you'll have to use the shower in the bathroom in the hallway."

Austin opened the orange prescription bottle for his friend and laid a pill in his hand. Wolf drank down the painkiller while Lyndee stepped out of the room to give them privacy while Austin helped him change into something more comfortable. Taking her suitcase into her bedroom she laid it on the bed and began to put her stuff away.

Stepping to the closet, she slid open one of the doors to grab some hangers when a large arm slid around her waist. It was the first time she had jumped since the incident with Philip and the motion wasn't missed on Austin. Pulling her back to the bed, he sat on the edge of it. Using his large hands, he turned her to face him and saw the fear in her eyes.

"What's the matter, little one?"

Shrugging, she tried to step away but he grabbed her hands in his and pulled her back. Opening his legs, he had her stand between them and he held her there. She knew he wouldn't let her go without confessing her fears to him, but she really didn't want to speak of them. They were in the past and she now had three wonderful men to love her.

"Lyndee!" he said sternly, causing her to jump slightly again.

Tears welled in her eyes as she looked up at him and saw the tenderness in his eyes. She felt ashamed that she would be afraid of him. Trying to turn away from him, he held strong and had her rest her bottom on his knee.

"Trust and honesty," he simply said as he cupped her chin and turned her to face him again. Even in this position, he still looked down at her, though it wasn't more than his eyes at the top of her head instead of when they were standing.

A sniffle and then a wipe of the hand on her cheek before putting it back in her lap, she nibbled on her lower lip before beginning. "I was lost in my thoughts when you came in. I didn't hear you. I flashed back to the night Philip broke in here. I'm so sorry."

Seeing her burst into tears, Austin wrapped his arms around his woman, pulling her to his chest. Her head rested on his chest as his hands soothingly ran up and down her spine as he let her cry. Dropping kisses on the top of her head he rocked her back and forth.

He let her cry for he knew she needed it. They had come full circle of her abduction and she needed to face her fear of her home, or at least temporary one, so she could move on. Austin had discussed with his cousins before they left that perhaps they should put up in a hotel during the trial but they agreed she had to get past this. Also, Wolf needed a stable living arrangement without the expectation of having everything done for him such as housekeeping or room service. His rehabilitation was going to be right down to everyday chores.

Wolf appeared at the door as he had heard Austin's commanding voice and the bosses' lady crying. Seeing Austin's nod that he had everything under control, the man turned to leave, closing the door behind him and giving the two the privacy they needed. Austin sighed as he held Lyndee, thankful that her tears were beginning to abate and her body began relaxing against him. Reaching around without letting go of Lyndee, he pulled the comforter back on the bed. Lifting his bundle in his arms, he scooted around and placed her on the bed, positioning her head on a pillow.

Hooded eyes looked up at him as she reached for him but he pulled away briefly. Moving the suitcase from the bed he turned off the light, leaving a soft glow behind the curtains at the window. Removing his boots and jeans on his way back to the bed, he laid down next to her. He undid her jeans and removed them for her along with her boots before removing her blouse. Turning her over, he spooned her from behind, her head resting on his bicep and his other hand resting around her waist.

She was asleep within a minute. He lay there in the dark, listening to her breathe and feeling the rhythm of it from her stomach and chest. With all the loss that he and the cousins had had over the years, he thanked the Lord above for the woman in his arms that she would bring a fresh ray of light into their lives and keep it there for the rest of his life.

* * * *

The next day Lyndee rose to shower first before making breakfast for the men. Needing to be at work by nine, she left by eight to fight the morning traffic, leaving the men to their own devices. Austin cleaned up the breakfast dishes and the two sat around watching TV or playing cards with a deck they had found in a kitchen drawer. Wolf wasn't scheduled to see his new doctor until the next day so there wasn't much for them to do.

While Wolf napped in the afternoon after taking a painkiller, Austin walked around the apartment complex, scanning the area for insecurities. When the manager found the intimidating man looking around he became suspicious and confronted him, though Austin could tell the short Hispanic man was quaking in his shoes. After obtaining a guarded explanation of the situation, the manager had to go call Lyndee to verify the validity of it. He had known about the break in and was concerned for her safety, but he wanted to make sure Austin was who he said he was. After verifying the information with his tenant, the manager returned to Austin.

"I'm glad she found a man to help her out. She lived here for five years and never went out on date. She works too hard," the man said in broken English.

"I am here to do everything I can to protect her," Austin said sternly to the man. "Our friend Wolf will be staying here with us while he recuperates from a gunshot wound, so you will see him around also. As soon as the trial is over, Lyndee will be moving up to Montana with me. I appreciate you keeping an eye out for her all these years."

The man shifted from one foot to the other as he gazed up at the man who stood at least a foot taller than him, intimidated by his size. "Lyndee is like family, though she needs a man to love her."

The two men shook hands before Austin returned to the quiet apartment. He felt as if the walls would close in on him so he took a kitchen chair out to the front of the apartment and sat in it next to the front door. Through his dark sunglasses, he watched kids playing soccer in the parking lot since school had let out for the day and he had to smile.

Things were so much different in the city. When he was a kid, they had chores that needed to be tended to before they even did their homework. There was little time for play after school let alone on the weekends, but they had a full childhood. Watching the kids he wondered if any of them would amount to much given the freedom they had from parents who worked full time or just didn't care that their kids weren't doing their homework.

The front door sat open in case Wolf needed him. Plus he had left the stereo on a country station to fill in some of the quiet in the house. A car was approaching the back alley that led to the parking lot, and he noticed a silver four-door sedan start to pull in. Four large men sat in the car. Dark suits and dark glasses were predominant through the tinted windows. Austin stood cautiously, making sure the men saw the gun tucked into the waistband of his jeans. Wolf at that moment chose to step out the door, his stature as dominating as his friend's.

"Feds?" Wolf asked, leaning against the doorframe.

"Nope," Austin said, never looking away from the car as it stopped, but kept an eye on the kids as they took their ball and moved out of the way of the vehicle. "Got it?"

"Yup," Wolf said, his hand on the other side of the wood.

Four doors opened simultaneously and the occupants stepped out, though shielded by the doors themselves. Austin whipped his gun out while Wolf moved nonchalantly away from the doorway, bringing up his own Sig, aiming it at the silver car. Sneers marked the four Russians' faces, anxious for a fight while Austin and Wolf smiled back at them. Glancing over, Austin made sure the kids were now gone as if they knew of the impending danger, which he was thankful for.

"Bulletproof glass?" Wolf whispered.

"Wouldn't doubt it."

"Good. I want some revenge," the injured man said.

Chapter Twenty-Three

A gun appeared above the driver's side door a second before Wolf's gun erupted. The Russian got off one lucky shot as Wolf got off four before anyone else got a shot. The two men from the front seat howled in pain as their legs went out from under them, one shot to each calf. Ducking into the car they tried to pull their legs in behind them. The two from the backseat let their guns ring, a shot barely missing Austin's shoulder as he stepped behind the post that held up the balcony above them. Wolf stepped inside the doorway to avoid getting hit. He and Austin got off a couple more shots before the Russian's continued shooting, but then more gunshots rang out and the two large blond Adonis dropped to the ground next to the car. The two in the front seat threw their weapons out, yelling in broken English, "Surrender! Surrender!"

Austin looked around the corner as Wolf came out the door to find Lyndee and John along with several other agents making their way toward the sedan, guns drawn. Lyndee sidled over to the passenger side of the car, leaning down and making sure the one man lying on the ground was dead or alive while John did the same to the other side of the car. Moving around to the front seat area, each one picked up the guns that the survivors had tossed. Austin and Wolf kept cover for them from the porch of the apartment while the other agents came around to handcuff the two men in the car and then try to stop their bleeding.

Holstering her Sig under her left arm, Lyndee made her way over to her men. "You better put those away. Neither one of you are licensed in the state of Colorado to carry a weapon."

John walked up behind the petite blonde woman as people started to emerge from their domiciles, the children curious of Lyndee now along with her two men. Before, she was someone who left in the early afternoon and came home at all hours of the night. She was considered a loner as she never had very many visitors. Now, here she was a gun-toting agent with two gorgeous men as her bodyguards.

Sirens were approaching the scene as the other agents surrounded the silver sedan. Police arriving on the scene cordoned off the area with yellow crime scene tape as they began to talk with John, who easily slipped into SAC mode.

Austin gathered Lyndee into his arms, holding her close after a scare like this one. Even Wolf leaned in close and gave her a quick hug while Austin held her before an agent came over to the trio with notepad in hand. He was tall and lean, though muscular. A swimmer's body. Light-brown hair streaked professionally with blond highlights topped his head while thick, dark lashes rimmed his nearly golden eyes. If he wasn't wearing the dark-blue suit, Austin would have figured him for a surfer from California instead of an FBI agent.

Lyndee extracted herself from the embraces of the two men, though she kept her right arm around Austin's back. Wolf went back to leaning on the doorframe, his face noticeably paler than usual, while a twinge of pain teased the side of his mouth. In the past few days, Lyndee had begun to read Wolf like he was one of her men since they resided in such close quarters.

The ambulance had arrived and while the paramedics dealt with the two wounded Russians, Lyndee introduced the men. "Lawrence Whitaker, this is Austin Lighthorse and his cousin Wolf. They are my friends from Montana."

Lawrence reached out and shook both men's hands in greeting. Austin was a bit taken aback that he didn't remember seeing the agent at the party last night and wondered why if this case was such a priority that John and Lyndee had made it out to be. Wolf exchanged a glance at his friend over Lyndee's head, and Austin knew he was thinking the same thing.

"Nice to meet you both," Lawrence said, looking the men up and down. "We appreciate what you have done to help Lyndee out. We're all going to miss her when she leaves."

Clearing his throat, Austin spoke. "We would do anything to protect our little lady here," he said, hugging her closer to him. "Sorry we didn't see you last night at the party."

Shrugging as if he wasn't happy about the party, he said, "I don't tend to socialize outside of the office."

Rather cryptic, Austin thought.

"So," Lawrence began, pen ready to write. "Can you tell me what happened here today?"

Austin described what events had taken place and Wolf filled in his part of the story. He noticed Lawrence look up at the latter when he had described shooting off the four shots that had hit each calf of the wounded men. Admiration was in his eyes as he took in the sling on the left arm, and Austin knew he was amazed that the Indian would be able to function properly himself. When Wolf was beginning to waver in place, he watched as Lawrence quickly moved to the man's side and held him up. Austin immediately came to his friend's side and he and Lawrence helped the man to the couch in the living room. Lyndee went to get a glass of water for Wolf as the men continued to talk.

Walking back into the room, she watched Lawrence's demeanor with Wolf and had a fleeting thought before making her way to Austin's side. Handing the water over to Wolf she noticed his hand shaking before he downed the contents and set the glass down on the glass coffee table. Lyndee knew Lawrence Whitaker's secret and why he didn't attend social gatherings that included his fellow employees. But she wasn't sure what was going through his mind about Wolf. As far as she knew, Wolf wasn't Lawrence's type, but she could be wrong. Glancing at Austin she noticed him watching her. He shook his head slightly as if telling her not to say anything. Sitting on her man's knee, she listened as the three men talked.

The ambulance's siren shrieked its exodus out of the parking lot while people murmured and milled around out there. Several kids, about five and six years old stood at the doorway of Lyndee's apartment, all trying to get a look at the two men with the guns. Giggles and whispers were heard from them as they watched intently the interrogation Lawrence conducted.

Guilt ate at Lyndee that she had lived here for five years and never once had spoken more than four or five words to a neighbor. She had seen the children playing in the parking lot and never talked to them. No wonder these kids were gawking at her and the men. They didn't know their neighbor at all. She never gave them a chance.

John came to the door and slipped in past the kids, who were eyeing his holstered gun and badge. Pulling out the coffee table, he sat in front of the small group, resting his elbows on his knees, his hands hanging down. "Who shot the vics?"

Austin chuckled at the term since in all actuality he and Wolf were the victims here, though he answered, "Wolf did."

Leaning forward, Wolf removed the gun from the back of his jeans and handed it to John. The lead investigator dropped the clip and removed a round for ballistics before replacing the clip and handing it back to the injured man.

"Pretty good shooting," John said, smiling at the man.

"You have to be a good shot when hunting game. You usually only get one shot to take down an animal. I took two per animal today," Wolf said proudly though wearily.

"They of course all worked for Markova. We were given notice today that Markova is demanding his right to a speedy trial so we are going to trial on Monday. I think if he thinks he can catch us off guard with the speediness of this, he can try to get at Lyndee. I'm glad you guys are here for her, but I would feel much better if the agency puts you up in a hotel."

Lyndee and Austin glanced at each other as he took the opportunity to glide his hand up and down her back. "I would normally say that I could handle her safety, but after investigating the exterior of this place, there are too many variables for someone to get to her. We'll take you up on your offer as long as Wolf and I still get to keep our weapons."

John nodded as did Lawrence. The two men stood and John walked into the kitchen to make his call. Lawrence left the apartment and Lyndee looked at Wolf. "Thank you for doing what you did. You could have gotten hurt more because of me."

Wolf leaned forward, a bit of anger glinted in his eyes. He covered one of her hands with his large one. "You need to stop thanking me for doing what any friend would do. I would gladly take another bullet for you or for any of my friends if it meant saving their lives. I know you are thankful and I know you are worried about me, just like I am thankful you are my friend and that you are alive and well. Do you understand?"

Looking into his rich chocolate-colored eyes she nodded slowly, fully understanding the true extent of friendship for the first time in her life. She had lived with her grandparents while a teenager so she never had friends, and since graduating the police academy she had been so intent on building her career that she never made time for friends. As with her relationship with the three guys being a new experience, she was finding that dealing with the new friends in her life was as much a new experience. Feeling ashamed for hurting his feelings, she lowered her eyes so he wouldn't see the tears there.

Laying her head on Austin's chest, she felt as if she was messing everything up with everyone. She was putting everyone she loved and cared about in danger, including John and the team. She didn't know if she should continue to stay with Austin and Wolf or go into hiding in a safe house. At least if she were tucked away, she knew they would be safe.

"You're doing an awful lot of thinking there, little one," she heard Austin say quietly. When she opened her eyes she saw Wolf watching her as if he knew exactly what she was thinking. Had Austin known also? Glancing up at him, the intense gaze he gave her, she knew that he did. Squirming on his lap, her nerves about to shatter, she tried to stand, but he moved his arms around her waist and held her still.

John came back into the room, replacing his phone into the hip holster he had for it. "We've got you set up at a hotel downtown. There will be an officer outside your door at all times. An officer will escort you wherever you need to go, and Wolf, that includes your appointments."

The two men nodded in understanding while Lyndee was still trying to process her feelings. Both men sheltered her, moving in closer as they expected her to bolt, which wasn't missed on John. Looking first at Austin and then to Wolf, he surmised what was taking place and asked, "Lyndee, can I talk to you in private for a moment?"

Knowing it would give her a moment to regain her composure, she nodded. "Sure."

Austin and Wolf headed for the door and stepped outside. The kids followed them as if they had found new heroes. They chattered away with the men, tossing endless questions at them. John motioned for Lyndee to sit, which she did, nervous at what her supervisor would need to discuss with her at this particular moment. She had seen the glances between the three men and she knew that perhaps even John knew what she was feeling or thinking.

John returned to his place on the coffee table across from Lyndee. Drawing in a deep breath, he looked at her seriously. "Lyndee, you know how I feel about you. I took you under my wing when you came to the Bureau and have been there since. I know that being undercover can be frustrating on a family and I was thankful you didn't have one while you were. I missed one important thing. Do you know what that was?"

Thinking it was a rhetorical question, she didn't answer until she realized he wanted her input. Shaking her head negatively, she glanced down at her hands as if the answer was there. Noticing the ring, she knew the answer. Five years of her life had been put on hold. Her life was in constant danger. She had no friends. She couldn't get close to anyone for she would either endanger them or she didn't know who she could trust. Now, she felt she couldn't trust the people she was supposed to and she still felt she was endangering them. She didn't know how to cope with the enormity of the situation this danger had set her in.

Starting to stand, John pulled her back down, holding her hands in his. "Look at me," he said gently.

"I'm not a rookie, John! I know what this is, but I don't know what to do about it." Tears began to fall and her body began to shake.

"I shouldn't have let you stay under so long. I felt you were our best bet to get to Markova. I couldn't figure out how every time we went in for a bust they knew about it. If I had known Philip was a cop, I would have pulled you out a long time ago," John said, sympathy lacing his voice. "They love you. I saw that when I was there. Wolf was right about friendship and you've been so far under for so long, you don't have any friends, do you?"

Shaking her head, she avoided looking at him. He had been her only friend but she hadn't realized it until then. He was her boss, but he was a friend also. Moving over to the couch, he gathered her against him, holding her in a fatherly gesture, which made her cry more.

"I'm happy that you are moving on, that you have people who love you and will do anything to protect you. I saw that in the aftermath last week. I'm going to miss you like crazy, but I want you to go on and love your men and have many babies. You deserve that happiness."

Throwing her arms around him, she felt whole for the first time in ages. She knew he was right about everything. Perhaps when they got back home she could go for some therapy for she knew the PTSD was going to eat her up if she let it. She had seen it happen to many people before. "Thank you."

"As Wolf said, you don't have to thank me for helping you."

"I know, but thank you for all the understanding also. It's not every day a woman is going to have three husbands and an FBI agent is giving his blessing."

He laughed as he wiped tears from her cheeks. Glancing over, he saw two men scowling at him. Standing, he helped Lyndee up before turning to the doorway. "Oh, get over it. She needs her man and her friend to help her now."

Austin and Wolf made a beeline for Lyndee, the former gathering her in his strong arms while Wolf stood next to them, caressing her back. John stepped away. "We're leaving in half an hour."

* * * *

The next week was spent sequestered in the suite the Agency had set them up in. Wolf left each morning and returned late in the afternoon, usually too exhausted to get past dinner. Therapy was difficult on him, more his mind than his body. He was used to physical labor, but it frustrated him that he wasn't able to make his body work the way he wanted. Usually after he ate he retired to his room, which was across the suite from Austin and Lyndee's.

John had insisted Lyndee stay and work on paperwork from the suite, which she could transmit directly to him online. Austin was bored, she could tell, for he, too, was used to manual labor and being outdoors.

The second day of their captivity, they sat at the small table in front of the window overlooking downtown Denver, eating breakfast that had been brought in by room service. Wolf finished eating before Austin and Lyndee so when the knock at the door sounded, he went to answer it. Lawrence stood there in his dark suit, light-blue shirt, and a red tie. His streaked hair was slicked back from his morning shower, and his eyes were hooded as he took in Wolf's appearance. Wolf grabbed his duffle bag from next to the door and the two were off.

The two occupants stared at the closed door before turning their attention back to each other. A smile lit Lyndee's face when she saw the desire darken Austin's already dark eyes. They looked black now as she was sure hers did too. Being bold, she untied the robe she wore, letting the belt and the lapel fall away, revealing her naked body. Her hands rose to her breasts, and she began to rub her nipples lightly, causing them to pucker tightly and turn a dusky rose color, all the while watching Austin.

His breath was shallow as he watched her. His tongue darted out to wet his lips as he felt his cock firming within his jeans. Admiration and disbelief filled him. Admiration that she felt comfortable enough to play with herself to please him, and disbelief because he couldn't believe that she had calmly sat there and eaten breakfast, naked under that robe, while Wolf was in the same room. A growl emanated from his chest. Stretching out his legs in front of him, he leaned back in his chair, crossing his arms across his chest, and watched his woman.

Lyndee looked up at him through half-open eyelids as she spread her legs open to his gaze. The table was slightly in the way, but it was a glass-topped table so he was able to view her ministrations without any difficulty. Tweaking her nipples, she pulled at them, elongating them between her fingers and thumb and then letting them snap back into place on her ample globes. After doing this several times, she let her right hand lightly glide down over her abs while her left hand continued to play with her left turgid nipple.

Her hips moved forward as her right hand was now at the beginning of her slit. Splitting her hand into sections, she let her middle finger slide into the moist folds that lay beneath her nether lips while the other parts of her hand slid down the slick outer part of her mons. As her finger rubbed across the hardened pearl that lay beneath its hood, a shiver shot through her as a moan escaped her. Rubbing back and forth a couple of times, she threw her head back against the top of the chair before moving her hand lower. Her finger slid smoothly into her pussy while the rest of her hand cupped it and she moved the finger back and forth against her G-spot, gasping as the tingling began.

Raising her left hand to her lips, she slipped her index finger into her mouth and sucked on it as if she were sucking on Austin's cock. Sucking it in as far as it would go then bringing it back out before sucking it in again was a rhythm she repeated about ten times before she removed it and moved it down to her cunt and onto her clit. The finger moved in circles at the nub at the top of her slit as her other finger in her pussy pumped against the tender spot within her dark, moist cavern of love. Her hips began to undulate as her finger rubbed at the hard nub and her G-spot was massaged, everything picking up speed.

The pulsing from deep within her was getting stronger and stronger, little electrical currents shooting out to all parts of her body. Her breaths were coming in short pants. She was ready to ride the wave until she heard Austin's voice sternly call to her. "Lyndee!"

Opening her eyes she looked at his through her lashes, her hair falling back down around her shoulders. Moaning her disappointment, she stopped her hands, though didn't pull them away as she waited for him to say or do something.

"Continue," he said, his eyes wide with lust, "but don't close your eyes. Watch me while you play with yourself. Make yourself come for me."

Unaware she had become so preoccupied with her own ministrations that she had closed her eyes, she began to move again, watching him as he tensed, trying to keep from pouncing on her. Inwardly she smiled that she could make him squirm like a teenager watching his first porn movie. Knowing that he wanted her so much caused her clit to stand erect so she flicked it with her fingernail, gasping at the sensation it shot through her body. Tapping her finger at the interior of her pussy, she continuously hit the soft spot that she had discovered was not a myth as many women had come to believe. Her men had shown her that spot and she relished the feelings it provided her.

It was so hard to keep her eyes focused on Austin as she teased her clit and G-spot as she got closer to her climax. Letting another finger slide into her and join the first one she pumped harder as sparks seemed to ignite within her pussy. Her clit throbbed under her other finger. Sensations built up from her core as she watched Austin's hand move down toward the bulge in his jeans. Licking her lips in anticipation of the taste of his pre-cum, she squeezed her clit between her forefinger and thumb. Hips bucking out beneath her, electricity shot out from her, sizzling to every nerve ending in her body. Her keening was long and soulful as she rode her orgasm, her eyes hooded but still on her man, though she didn't really see him. Black spots appeared in her vision and her breath was so ragged she thought she might pass out, but she let the aftershocks tease her pussy as the rest of her body tried to calm itself.

* * * *

Moving quickly, he was there in front of her before she slid off the chair, his arms grasping her waist. Hauling her up against him, he stood and strode to the closest sofa. Turning her around, he bent her face-first over the back of the piece of furniture, her ass an open invitation to him. With one hand on the small of her back he held her down while the other hand undid the buttons on his jeans, freeing his throbbing cock. Widening his stance, he separated her legs as he bent at the knees. His free hand guided his penis toward her core, the dripping hole that it sought out. Its mate.

In one thrust, he was deep within her cunt, her hips being pushed up with each one. Bracing her hands on the sofa she held herself so he didn't buck her over onto the floor. Her tits swung with each thrust, hitting her in the chin. The excitement of watching her pleasure herself had sent him over the edge and now he was ruthless with his fucking. A sheen of sweat settled on his features, a grimace on his face as he watched himself sink into her pussy over and over again, needing to fill her with his sperm, to mark her as his.

He could feel her vaginal walls begin to pulse and knew she was close as she hadn't fully come completely down from her first orgasm. Moving his free hand around her hip he found her clit and began to rub it, her hips beginning to push back against his. His cum boiled in his balls as her sheath squeezed him and he felt the viscous sperm shooting its way to his cock and it would be only moments before it reached the tip. Pumping himself into her two more times, he slammed her hips into the back of the sofa as he let his cum expel at an alarming, nearly painful rate as he felt her spasm around him. He shouted as he released himself. At the same time she screamed her own release, each of them lost in their visceral orgasms.

Austin's senses surfaced first as a pounding on the door caught his attention. Looking down at Lyndee, who was still dazed as she rode the aftershocks of her orgasm, he knew she wasn't coherent enough to move yet. Quickly he picked her up and laid her on the sofa, laying the red throw over her naked body. Buttoning up his jeans over his quickly diminishing cock he ran a hand through his long black tresses as he strode over to the offensive object.

Pulling open the door in irritation, he found the officer on duty standing there with gun in hand ready to kick the door in. Surprise registered on both men's faces.

Chapter Twenty-Four

"I heard a lady scream," the young officer said, looking up at Austin.

A flush stole to Austin's cheeks, embarrassed that he would have to explain the scream his lady emanated in her orgasmic state. Shifting from one foot to the other, the Native American man, who in the past never cared about his partner's comfort, had to protect his woman's integrity. "I'm sorry if we scared you. We were playing around and I tickled her. She's very ticklish."

The officer looked past Austin and saw Lyndee on the couch smiling. "Sorry about that," she called out. "My fault."

Nodding his head, he waved slightly at Lyndee before stepping away from the door, holstering his gun. "Sorry about that," he said hesitantly. "I'll be right out here if you need anything."

"No problem, officer. Thank you. You're doing a very good job." Austin closed the door, making sure it was locked before walking to the sofa. He sat down at Lyndee's feet, drawing them onto his lap before he burst out laughing, trying not to be overly loud with his jocularity. Lyndee giggled but then as she watched Austin she sobered. Concerned, he asked, "What?"

"I have not seen you so relaxed that you could laugh and enjoy it," she said. "You've always been so serious with everything that has happened that that was the first time I have seen you laugh."

Austin knew that he had made her happy as he broke out of his comfort zone briefly but he also knew a war waged within his woman. He knew she still blamed herself for falling into their lives with all this danger attached to her, but he knew she still needed to learn to understand it wasn't her fault and she had to come to terms with that. As Wolf had said the other day, she was surrounded by people who loved her and who would protect her no matter what.

Taking one foot in his hands he rubbed the ball of her foot with both thumbs, watching her as he did so. Her eyes closed at the sensation of someone taking control of her but not in the usual sexual nuances they had in the past. "I can laugh because of you. You have to remember that we are going to take care of you, little one, whether it's providing for you, protecting you, or giving you our love. Your friends will protect you and provide their own form of love for you. You don't have to shut us out or try to do things yourself. Let us fill your heart with love, comfort, and peace of mind."

"I know," she said with a sigh. "I have been on my own for so long and responsible for so much in the past few years, it's hard to let go and trust other people."

"I hope you can trust us to let go of your responsibilities and let us tend to you?"

It was a rhetorical question but she nodded her head and murmured, "Uh-hum," before she sank further in the sofa, drifting off to sleep.

Austin let her sleep as he knew the previous night she hadn't slept much due to nightmares. He hoped he would be able to calm her down enough to where she could sleep through the night without waking up unless it was at the hand of one of the three of them. He smiled as he watched her sleep, content to sit there with her feet in his lap.

A vibration in his pocket caught his attention. Pulling his phone from his pocket, thankful it was on vibrate, he read the text from his cousins wanting to know why there had been no contact in the past two days. Looking down at his sleeping beauty, he knew the outside world beckoned so he gently stood and laid her feet on the couch, covering them with the throw. Making his way out the sliding glass door, he stepped onto the balcony that overlooked the busy city. Dialing Storm's number, he waited for the connection.

"Well, it's about time!" Storm practically yelled at him. "What the hell is going on?"

After explaining what had transpired two days ago, both Storm and Trey cursed, letting Austin know he was on speaker phone. "Do you want us to come down?" Trey asked.

"No," Austin sighed. "There isn't much that can be done. We are pretty much on lockdown here at the hotel. Wolf is the only one with in and out privileges but that is with a bodyguard. We have an officer at the door. He got scared 'cause I made Lyndee scream when she came. He thought someone had gotten to her."

"How's she liking lockdown?" Trey asked.

"She's not. Though I think we are getting through her defenses of blaming herself for everything that has happened at the ranch. Wolf went off on her the other day then John talked to her. I think she has PTSD. We may need to get her a shrink to talk to when we get home."

Storm sighed strongly. "We'll work it out buddy. Any news on the trial?"

"Yeah, John said that Markova has expressed his right to a speedy trial. It starts on Monday. Until then Lyndee does not leave my sight. You guys gonna be here for the beginning?" Austin asked.

Whispers on the other end of the phone meant the two men were quietly discussing it amongst themselves. Trey spoke first. "Yes. We'll fly in Sunday night."

"Tell John we're coming in and have him meet us at the airport. We need to go over security for Lyndee without her being there. We don't need to add more stress onto her than needed," Storm practically ordered his cousin, his need to protect their woman strong.

"I will. I'll have her call you after her nap."

"No. Just tell her we love her and we'll see her Sunday. We need to keep things as low key as possible," Trey said, the cop in him knowing what was best. "I'll text you the info on the flight."

After ending the call, Austin slipped back in quietly and began putting the breakfast dishes on the cart. When he was finished, he set the chairs to right at the table and wheeled the cart to the door. Pushing it out into the hall, he caught the officer's sheepish grin from the chair he sat in. Feeling bad for the man, he nodded then closed the door, locking himself and Lyndee in for the day. He knew she had paperwork to do but he wanted her to sleep so he picked up a book he had brought with him and sat in the chair across from the couch and began to read.

The days following were pretty much the same. Breakfast and then Wolf would be escorted to therapy by Lawrence and Lyndee and Austin would make the best of the day. Austin felt guilty about making love to her every day as it wasn't fair to his cousins who couldn't. Lyndee understood, though she did manage to entice him several more times, one of them from the spa tub in their room.

Wolf came home around four every afternoon and napped until supper. They partook of their evening meal together as a family, talking and joking, and then afterward they would watch television or play cards. John had told them not to go online to any of the social networks as they could be located that way, which didn't matter to any of them since Austin and Wolf hadn't managed to get that into them being isolated on the ranch and because of long hours they put in. Lyndee never got around to putting a profile together on any of them since she was so far undercover. She hadn't realized how much she missed out on until then.

Austin didn't tell Lyndee about Storm and Trey coming. He thought it would be a good surprise for her.

Saturday and Sunday were boring for all three of them. There wasn't any therapy for Wolf, which was good for he was quite sore from the ministrations of the therapist, though he missed getting out of the hotel room. He couldn't see how Austin wasn't climbing the walls by the end of Saturday, as he himself he was about to go batty. But Austin and Lyndee had each other to keep themselves occupied.

* * * *

Sunday after breakfast Wolf's phone rang and after looking at the display he became worried. After sliding the bar to answer the device, he asked, "What's up?"

Austin and Lyndee both watched him, perplexed at the emotion they saw before answering the phone. Nerves stood on end briefly until they saw him relax. "Yeah, buddy that would be great. What about…" he didn't get to finish as he glanced up at the other two occupants of the room. Indecision flashed across his features as he listened to the caller on the other end. "No, I understand. I just don't want them to feel left out."

Lyndee stood and walked over to Wolf and laid a hand on his forearm. "Don't worry about us. I can't be seen out in public so you go and have fun," she said as she smiled at him. "And tell Lawrence hello for me, since he doesn't want to seem to speak with me when he comes to pick you up each day."

Guilt consumed Wolf, that he had possibly come between whatever friendship Lyndee had with his escort, but when she smiled the way she did, he knew she was being genuine with her feelings. She really did understand him and what was happening to him. Tears stung his eyes and he had to turn away from her and Austin, not wanting his vulnerability to show. Sighing he responded to Lawrence on the other end of the connection. "I'll meet you in the lobby in twenty minutes."

Regaining his composure, he turned to smile tentatively. "I feel guilty that you guys have to stay locked up here all the time. I know it must be killing you, Austin."

"It is," Austin sighed, repositioning Lyndee as she came back to sit next to him on the couch, folding her legs under herself. "But, I do have great company. Where is Lawrence taking you?"

A genuine smile lit up Wolf's face. "Bronco's game at Mile High. I've always wanted to go to a live game. He has season tickets."

"Great!" Austin exclaimed. "I know you're a big fan."

Wolf disappeared into the bedroom that had been assigned to him and then reappeared with his coat and a baseball cap in hand. Shyly he stopped in front of them, an action Austin had never seen before in his friend. "I hope you don't think any different of me. I mean…"

Both Austin and Lyndee glanced at each other for a brief second before both of them stood up and, each going around opposite ends of the glass and chrome coffee table, they stopped in front of their injured friend. Austin carefully threw his arms around his cousin's shoulders, drawing him into a hug. "No one will judge you, buddy. Follow your heart. You are still my brother in my heart."

Letting go, he stepped back. Lyndee let her arms slide around the man's waist, letting her head rest on his chest. "We are in no position to judge you. You are meant to find your happiness wherever you can find it. Like Austin said, follow your heart. I did and I ended up with three men. I know I will be judged for that by many people, but I don't care what they think, just like you shouldn't care what others think. Screw them all. I just hope that Lawrence likes the country, because I know you aren't going to stay here," she said, pulling herself away to look up at him. "Are you?"

Chuckling, he said, "No, Lyndee. I will be coming home to my family and friends. We will have to see where this thing with Lawrence lies."

Nodding, Lyndee hugged him again before pulling away. "Go have fun. Enjoy yourself."

Wolf nodded slightly before disappearing through the door.

* * * *

Austin pulled Lyndee into his arms, "When did you get to be so smart about everyone's feelings?"

Wrapping her arms around his waist, she laid her head on him. "I've learned a lot from some new friends of mine. They keep telling me that they are here to help me, so if I can return their help just by understanding them, then I know I've done a good thing."

"I love you, Lyndee Dwyer," Austin said, kissing the top of her head. "You've been so open-minded about everything that has happened with us. You've accepted each one of us with open arms and shown your love to us. I know that we all love you, including our friends. You have brought sunshine to a bunch of cowboys."

The blush stole over Lyndee's face as she leaned up to kiss her man, her hand caressing his cheek. "You have shown me a whole new world, you and your friends. I am happy to be a part of it. I love you all so much."

Grasping her ass in his hands, he hauled her up against him, her arms sliding around his neck as his lips slanted down over hers. He tried to drink in her essence as he carried her to the bedroom where they spent several hours showing each other their love.

* * * *

It was late in the day when they wandered out of the bedroom and dinner was ordered in as usual. Lyndee was clothed in her robe and Austin in just a pair of black jeans as they supped on steak, baked potatoes, and a salad. They had worked up quite an appetite, though Lyndee felt she could easily work off those calories in short time as she worked over her man. If she had had to be sequestered in that hotel room without Austin or one of the other men, she thought she would have gone crazy.

As she finished the last bite of steak, she glanced up at the glorious man sitting across from her. Seeing a smirk on his face, his eyes lit with a smile from deep within, she had to grab up her napkin and wipe her face, thinking she had something on it. Leaning back, Austin crossed his massive arms on his chest and just watched her as nerves began to overtake her.

To avoid his watchful eyes, Lyndee stood and began to put the dishes on the cart. This was the first time he didn't jump up to do it for her, which she found odd. Skepticism swept through her for a brief moment that perhaps he was tired of her, of protecting her, but then she pushed that thought aside. She knew he was in love with her and he showed her over and over especially in the past week, but right now he was gloating and she was anxious to find out what that was.

When she finished, he stood, towering over her. His hands came to her shoulders and slipped under the collar of the robe. "Undo the tie."

Doing as instructed, she undid the belt on her robe, standing there still and quiet for his next command, watching his face. Running his hands down her shoulders to her upper arm, he let the cottony robe flutter to the floor, pooling around her feet. Standing before her lover, naked as he gazed down at her with love and lust flashing in his eyes, she stood with her shoulders back proudly. She was proud to be his, Storm's, and Trey's and that was the only part that made her sad, that they weren't there with them.

Austin noticed the bit of sadness that crossed her features briefly before it disappeared. Letting his hand rise and graze her cheek, he became serious. "What just made you sad, little one?"

"I miss Storm and Trey," she said quietly, though never taking her eyes off of his. "I miss home."

Joy swept through the muscular Indian at her comment of home. She knew where she belonged and they would accept her with open arms. When this mess was over, they were going to take their woman home with them and make her their bride and make babies with her. Smiling down into her iris eyes, he let his callused thumb slide across her lower lip. Her tongue swept out quickly to lick it before she sucked it into her mouth, letting her tongue continue to circle it, her eyes never leaving his once. His breath hitched at the action.

God, he was wonderful. He was a manly man, a man used to hard work. He played hard, she thought, and he fucked hard. Her eyes lowered in shyness at that thought as a smile played at her lips. All three of her men were of the same cloth and they were all hers.

Sighing, Austin pulled his thumb from the hot, moist mouth that had captured it. "That's enough for now, little one. I have a surprise for you and it will be here shortly, so I want you to go relax in the hot tub for me. You are not to come out until I come to get you. Do you understand?"

Gazing into his deep-chocolate eyes she saw excitement nestled in there and she herself became excited. Nodding, she ran her hands across the wide expanse of his chest, leaned up, and kissed each flat disc before turning to do his bidding. With a sashay in her ass, she walked proudly naked across the room to their room, disappearing from Austin's view as he watched her with a hunger not associated with the meal they just ate.

Wheeling the cart out to the hallway, he nodded to the guard on duty before retreating behind the door. Straightening up the dining area, he made sure it was clean as he heard the water running in the other room. When he was finished he sauntered into the bathroom where he found Lyndee sitting in the tub, her back to the door while her arms laid out on the top of the tub, her head lying back. Her hair cascaded down the side of the tub to the floor, and Austin bent to pull it together and took the elastic band on the vanity and wrapped her hair up in it.

Watching her breasts bob up and down on the surface of the water, generated by the bubbles the jets fed, he was mesmerized. Her nipples were dusky pink, looking like rosebuds floating there. His attention was drawn when he heard her ask lowly, "Are you going to join me or just stand there watching me?"

"I'll join you in a minute, love," he said, letting his hand slide along her neck to her ear. "I have to wait for your surprise to arrive."

She knew better than to question him on what it was. She had learned that with all three of them. It was part of their dominant nature. The sub doesn't question the master. She couldn't imagine what it was but she hoped it would something to alleviate the boredom that had engulfed them. At least the next day they would be in the courtroom, breaking up the monotony that surrounded them.

"Mmm, I can't wait."

"Well, you'll have to. I'm going to blindfold you, little one," he said, pulling a black silk scarf from his back pocket. "Will you be all right with that?"

The thrill that ran through her body caused her to shiver with delight. Her nipples hardened into sharp points while her pussy creamed. Their sex had been pretty much vanilla since that first day Austin took her on the back of the couch after she had gotten so worked up. They had to remember there was an audience, one with Wolf around, and two with the guard outside the front door. This was going to be good, she thought to herself.

"Yes, sir. I'll be fine with it," she said meekly, trying not to show her excitement.

A chuckle resonated from Austin's chest as he bent over and tied the cool strip of material around her head, covering her eyes. "Not too tight?" Negatively shaking her head, she sighed. He saw her hand move so he whispered in her ear, "And no playing with yourself."

A growl of frustration emanated from the lovely lady in the tub and Austin had to chuckle. "I promise I will make this extra special for you, little one. Just relax."

Leaning her head back again, Lyndee sighed and tried to relax, though the anticipation kept shooting electrodes out to her nipples and clit. Trying not to squirm, she was unsuccessful as she knew that Austin hadn't left the room yet. Another chuckle rumbled from him before she heard him exit the room, or had he?

Chapter Twenty-Five

A featherlight touch on her lips brought her attention to the present. Had she dozed off? She must have, she thought. Trying to be still, she felt the touch again. It was skin brushing across her lips with a bit of hardness behind it. As it came across her lips again, she felt a pearl of moisture there as the skin branded the bead of moisture to her lower lip. Breathing in, she smelled a familiar muskiness so she let her tongue touch her lips and she tasted pre-cum. It wasn't Austin's though. Were they actually here? A bolt of anticipation shot straight to her pussy and she could feel the cream ooze through her tunnel there.

Reaching up she tried to pull off the blindfold but strong hands stopped her. Storm, she smiled. Fur touched her right wrist before she heard the click and then the same happened to the left wrist, trapping her hands together. One hand held onto the small chain that connected the cuffs as another hand slid down over her shoulder and captured her breast. The hand squeezed tightly at her ample flesh as the cock at her lips pushed for entrance. Opening her mouth, she felt the silk-covered piece of steel push through to the back of her throat. Savoring the feel and taste of the cock as it slid in, she knew it was Trey.

She found it amazing that she could tell who they were just by their taste, smell, and the feel of their hands. Even blindfolded as she was she could tell. Storm's lips came down on her neck, nipping at the skin as his hand continued to squeeze her tit. Her moans began to fill the room at her men's ministrations. Trey's cock, hot and velvety, pistoned in and out of her mouth as his hands came around her head and held it in place. Water sloshed around her breasts as the thrusts became more violent, his legs moving within the water as Storm nipped his way up to her ear.

Lyndee wanted to move, to love on her men, but this was their moment to relish and she would cede to them. Trey's cock was beginning to pulsate and his movements became more jerky and quicker and as he began to shoot his cum down her throat, Storm bit her earlobe. Swallowing the bounty that Trey gave her, she licked him clean before he pulled out of her hot mouth. Storm let go of her ear and her breast and she felt hands slide under her knees and around her back. She felt herself lifted out of the hot water and carried, the cool air of the room brushing skin that had been heated by the water and from their loving. She was stood on her feet and a soft towel began to dry her off. The cuffs remained.

Again she was picked up and she felt the coolness of the sheets beneath her back and bottom. Her hands were pulled up over her head and attached to a rope that had been tied under the mattress. She felt Storm's hand on her left ankle as he pulled a loop of rope around it while Trey's hand did the same to her right one. Being spread out openly on the king-sized bed made her pussy weep and her nipples harden even more. She didn't think her breasts could become more aroused, but they did. They were tight and ached while her pussy clenched and longed to be fucked.

Once she was spread open for the pleasure of her two men, a feeling of pride enveloped her as she felt them watching her. She remained still and quiet, sensing their arousal as their heat and musk filled the room. She had to wonder if Austin was there for she hadn't felt his hands on her, but she knew that the two brothers would be able to please her.

Light pieces of leather stroked at her skin. She could tell it was real leather for the aroma of it assaulted her senses as much as the aroma of the men had. At first she wasn't sure what it was, but when the tendrils began to swish against the skin of her abs she knew it was a flogger. After a few moments, the strips began to come down harder upon her, striking her abs first so she could adjust to the erotic feeling. Ten strokes on her abs, each getting harder with each infliction, before they moved on, and when the first one hit her breasts, her body bowed off the bed as much as possible and a moan escaped her lips.

The leather sent zaps of sensations throughout her body, but they all led to her cunt. Cream oozed from her as her nipples hardened into nubs that ached and moans continued to emanate from her. Her breathing came in short pants as her head moved from side to side.

The flogger came down again but instead of stopping this time to let her adjust, it came down repeatedly on her breasts before moving down to her thighs. It struck the tops of them and reached to the inner thighs, moving closer to her pussy. Her body anticipated the blows and her body kept bowing into them. When the first strike of leather hit her pussy, she pulled against her bonds as her orgasm shot through her with ferocity. Her limbs seized up as electricity zinged to every nerve within her body, her scream caught silently in her throat, her breath held in her lungs. Bursts of color appeared within the darkness of her vision before they went dark and she began to drift.

The blows came repeatedly upon her, striking swiftly and across the entire expanse of skin open to their viewing pleasure. She felt the blows but she seemed to be floating out of her body as if she was watching the whole experience from above herself. She could see the men perfectly as they stood beside the bed, Storm being the handler of the whip. Being the alpha male he was, she knew it would be him. Not that the others didn't have it in them, just that Storm seemed to be the more experienced of the three.

When her pussy was struck again, she came again, this time crying out loud, and she felt a hand come down on her mouth, pulling her back into reality. Her pussy clenched and released over and over again as the cream gushed from her. Again she pulled against her restraints, gasping for air, still crying out. She was thankful she was blindfolded because she didn't think she would be able to see clearly anyway with the dark dots that seemed to encompass the space behind her eyes.

Lyndee knew the flogging had ended when she felt the bed dip at the end between her legs, and as she anticipated the next move, a mouth covered her pussy, suckling at the juice that she had so freely given when she came. Crying out at the sensation, the hand on her mouth moved, and she felt a mouth replace it, capturing her sobs of ecstasy.

Contentment began to overtake her as she came down from her orgasmic high. Two sets of lips were hungrily dining on both sets of her lips and she moaned against the ones on her mouth. If she could move her legs she would have captured Trey's head between her legs for she knew he was the one that was drinking her cream that her body provided for all of her men. He was her pussy man, though all of them seemed to like to eat her pussy. Austin liked her ass, but she felt he wasn't there to share with his cousins this time, so she was content with the two making love to her right now.

The bed moved again and this time she felt the body between her legs rise up over her and felt the hard, wide cock at her cunt, demanding entrance. Even if she hadn't been tied down, she would have granted him openly as that was where she wanted them, where she had ached for them for the past week. Even though Austin fulfilled her needs, they were all a part of her now, and she literally ached for them each day. She didn't know how it happened that they had consumed her, body, heart, and soul, but they had. She loved each of them with her whole heart. They completed her, filled her with joy and happiness that she had never known, or thought she ever would.

Trey slid in to the root of his cock, filling her until his balls hit her ass. Air hissed through her teeth at the invasion. She loved the way all of them filled her pussy to capacity. It was enlightening that they could do that for she had heard stories from the girls of the johns that they had slept with who had very small cocks that barely fit just inside their cunts. She now felt sorry for those women and a fleeting hope went out to them that they would possibly find what she had found.

* * * *

Trey didn't move. He relished the feeling of being inside his woman, their woman. He had missed the hot, moist pussy that fit him like a glove. He missed the feel of her, the taste of her. He missed the unconditional love she showed them, and most of all, he missed her company. She had embedded herself into their lives since the moment Austin brought her up from the ravine.

Slowly he began to pull out and stopped short of pulling out altogether. Thrusting back into her he filled her up and she cried out. In and out, in and out, his hips pistoning in and out, thrusting harder and faster. The root of his cock rubbing the turgid nub of her clit with each stroke driving her closer and closer, and when he thrust once more, he hit her cervix with the head of his cock and her clit at the same time, which set off her climax.

Somehow she had forgotten about the mouth that was drawing hers into his, his tongue assaulting hers. Storm's hand was on her breast, squeezing the nipple between his forefinger and thumb driving her orgasm further up the scale and then the red-hot cum shooting out of Trey's cock shook her while the darkness behind her eyes enveloped her into unconsciousness.

* * * *

Featherlight touches of callused fingers rubbing her belly and her hip, drawing her out of her orgasmic bliss, as light began to invade her sight. Kisses were laid upon her neck on one side and her shoulder on the other as she moved her arms to grasp both hands in hers. Smiling, she realized she was no longer bound. Opening her eyes, she found Storm to her right and Trey to her left, both smiling down at the center of their new family. Pulling each of their captured hands up, she kissed the palms of each of them then held them both close to her heart.

"I've missed you both so much," she whispered.

"I've missed you also, sweetheart," Trey said, kissing her lips chastely.

"I have missed you too, darlin'." Storm smiled. "Was I too rough on you?"

Blushing, she shyly closed her eyes. When a hand slapped her thigh on her right side, she snapped her iris eyes open to look into Storm's cobalt-blue eyes, a touch of anger along with the lust settled into them.

"Remember, little one, you are to answer when you are asked a question," Austin said from the doorway. "It is not only for us to know the answer, but it is also so we know that you are comfortable and content. That we aren't hurting you."

"I know," Lyndee whispered, looking first at Austin, then Trey, and then finally Storm. "I didn't mean to be disrespectful, Sirs, but I am embarrassed to say that I enjoyed it immensely."

Rising to his knees, Storm looked down at her in disbelief. "Why would you be embarrassed about something that gives you pleasure along with us?"

"I wasn't sure if I was supposed to be enjoying it," she said meekly.

All three chuckled, the sound joyous. "Oh, little one," Austin said sauntering over to the bed. "A flogging will bring you pleasure. A paddling will give you pain that will turn into pleasure. You still have a lot to learn, but you have all three of us to teach you."

Leaning up to her, Trey smiled before kissing her again. "And sweetheart, we are all going to enjoy teaching you."

"I'm sure you will," she sighed as she felt their hands and mouths begin to pleasure her again.

They each took their turns with her, the two brothers showing her how much they missed her, but they didn't want to overindulge as their woman needed her sleep to be ready for court the next morning.

* * * *

The next morning the foursome rose early and had a hearty breakfast, and while they were finishing up, Wolf's door opened and Lawrence walked out followed by the man himself. Both looked over at the table when they realized they weren't alone and both men blushed, though it was harder to see on Wolf. Lawrence glanced between Wolf, the small group now standing, and the door, as if he was deciding what he should do at the moment.

The decision was removed from him when Lyndee stepped forward in the dark-blue suit she had chosen to wear to court. The skirt was a pencil skirt, accentuating her rounded ass, and the blazer strained at the buttons a bit to keep it closed over the red blouse she wore. She had remained barefoot as she was dreading wearing the heels she was going to need to wear with the outfit and would only put them on when she had to leave.

"Lawrence," she said as she made her way over to both men. "You should have said you would be here this morning. We would have ordered breakfast for you also."

Looking down into her eyes, he smiled. He reminded her of a high school kid when he smiled, he looked so young then. "Thank you, Lyndee. You are so kind. I think it's best if we forget I was here this morning. But I appreciate the offer."

"Nonsense," Storm said cheerfully, stepping over to the group. Holding out his hand to the younger man, he drew him in with his smile and dominant form. "I'm Storm Goodall, Wolf's employer. It's nice to meet you."

Glancing at her, Lawrence saw her smile never faltered. Taking Storm's hand in his, he shook it. "Lawrence. Lawrence Whitaker."

Trey, dressed in his sheriff's deputy uniform, stepped forward next and took the young man's hand and shook it also. "I'm Trey. Storm's brother."

Lawrence was still hesitant around them, even with Austin and herself, which was surprising to the woman since she knew him from work. They all seemed to understand then what was going on between the two men, and the Goodalls and Austin didn't seem to have a problem with it, though Lawrence and Wolf seemed to. It would work out for them as it did for the brothers and cousin and herself.

Clearing his voice, Lawrence shifted from one foot to the other. "I will wait for you in the hall with the guards. We need to leave in five."

The tall blond agent walked through the room and exited the door. They all stood watching him for a few moments longer before everyone began to move around. Trey double-checked his Glock in its holster on his hip while Lyndee checked her Sig Sauer in its shoulder holster. Guns wouldn't be allowed in the courtroom but at least they would be able to keep hold of them until security was reached. The guys had told Lyndee at breakfast that the guns in the truck had already been loaded and locked in the toolbox in the bed of the truck. Parking had been permitted for them since Trey was a police officer, letting them park closer to the building in case the vehicle was needed quickly.

Austin and Storm both wore dark jeans and a sports coat over a black long-sleeved T-shirt. As Lyndee slipped on her shoes, adding three inches to her petite height, she looked over her men, all tall, muscular, and handsome, and pride consumed her that they were hers. Wolf was as handsome as her men in his dark jeans and a dark-blue T-shirt, the blue sling marring the overall image of the masculine man. Both his and Austin's hair were both pulled back in leather bands while Storm's hair hung still damp down to his shoulders. Trey let his hang down below his ears.

When Lyndee stood before them, each man stepped up, gathered her in his arms, and gave her a long kiss. Wolf stepped forward and hugged her also, pressing a light kiss to her forehead. No words needed to be spoken as she knew they were all being encouraging and supportive so she just nodded and smiled. Together they walked through the room to the door and stood before it. Trey opened the door to find John, Lawrence, and four uniformed police officers standing in front of it.

John stepped forward and took Lyndee's hands in his. "Are you ready for this?"

Her body betrayed her nervousness but her men showed their support. Austin was behind her and his hands sat on her hips, and Storm and Trey's hands lay at the small of her back, one above the other, giving her a mental nod that they were there for her.

Looking directly into her eyes, John let his hand come up and caress her cheek. "I know this is going to be tough and that Markova's attorney will say some things that will be hurtful even though they might not be true, but you have all of us to protect you. Use us to keep you calm. Don't let them get to you. You have a wonderful future ahead of you. We'll make sure you get through this so you can get on with the rest of your life."

Stepping forward, she threw her arms around his shoulders, hugging him close to her. "Thank you," she whispered. "I trust you."

Letting go of Lyndee, John pulled back and with authority he issued the command, "Let's go!"

The four uniformed officers walked down the hallway toward the elevator while the four men belonging to Lyndee followed to the rear while Lawrence walked to her left and John to her right. They kept her close as they waited for the elevator and then they all stepped into it, stepping into accept the fate that was to become the next step in Lyndee's life.

Chapter Twenty-Six

The high profile of the case caused a media frenzy, which meant a blitz of reporters, mics, and cameras awaited the arrival of any person significant or insignificant, for that matter, involved. The arrival of the woman who pulled down a top mob figure along with her ten-man entourage sent all media scrambling to get the first interview with Lyndee. The officers tried to clear the way for everyone, but as they passed anyone, others came around shoving microphones and cameras in the remainder of the group's faces. The four cowboys practically growled each time they had to push away the media electronics and even a few reporters themselves away from their woman. Several reporters found themselves on their asses as there was no uncertainty that Lyndee was unapproachable.

Stepping into the building came with no less aggravation than the media circus out front. Having to stand in line to get through the metal detector was frustrating for the four cowboys as it wasn't something they were used to, and they had all worn their big belt buckles and boots with the silver tips on the toes. Lyndee, John, and Trey had to relinquish their weapons, which caused further irritation, but they knew it had to be done. Since this was so high profile, the group was assured that the amount of Sheriff's deputies had been increased, though it didn't provide much comfort to any of the men.

* * * *

Approaching the double doors to the courtroom assigned to the case, a tall blond man with Slavic features stepped up to the group. His steel gray eyes were sharp and unfeeling. Not as muscular as the cowboys, he still commanded a presence. His body was still intimidating but his beautiful face showed his confidence and oozed sex appeal and charm. His grayish-blue thousand-dollar suit hung on his delicious frame as it had been custom made for him as were all of his clothes. Women would usually be hanging off his arm, but this morning, he had two men who stood behind him in their own dark suits and again, the telltale shades that everyone that had come after Lyndee had been wearing. Storm actually thought they must have stock in the sunglasses company.

The man stuck his hand out to Lyndee, who looked at it with distain. "Miss Dwyer, it's good to see you again. I hope that the business we have conducted in the past won't be held against me. But of course, things you did are considered inappropriate to your position and could result in corrective action against you."

The smooth baritone voice with the Russian accent was contemptuous and condescending, but the growls from her four cowboys caught the man off guard. He knew about them from Philip but he was surprised that these fine paragons of American culture would take up with a prostitute. Pulling his hand back he took one step backward.

"I hope there will be no hard feelings when this is all over, Miss Dwyer," Markova practically purred, noticing the frustrated looks on the cowboy's faces. "Perhaps when this is over, we can find another position for you within one of my business ventures. Perhaps we can find you a spot on the Governor's reelection committee. I'm sure you would be an asset to it."

Though size wasn't his friend amongst the four cowboys and Lawrence, his speed took John front and center, his hands out at forty-five degree angles to keep them from attacking the bold Slavic. His voice was low and tight as he tried to restrain himself from attacking the insulting man. "You are not to approach or speak with Miss Dwyer during or after the trial. She will never go back to work for you, for when this is over, you will be spending the rest of your life in prison. Is that clear, Markova?"

The tall blond glared at John, then Lyndee, and then the rest of the men before he threw his head back and let loose his laughter. His confidence was running high at the moment, which caused nervousness to run roughshod over everyone in the FBI's group.

"I will get a restraining order for you if you come near her again," John threatened. "And don't bother sending any more of your goons after her. They just make good target practice for her friends here."

Still smiling though coldness touched his eyes, Markova stepped closer to John then lowered his head and spoke slowly and low. "I wouldn't get too comfortable, John. We wouldn't want your wife to know of the feelings you have for Miss Dwyer. We have pictures and they will be used."

Indignation struck John as his fists rolled up at his sides at the insinuation voiced. "My wife knows Miss Dwyer and I have had to work closely with each other." Storm and Austin reached for John as the agent grasped Markova by his tie but weren't able to pull him away quick enough before he pulled the tall blond down closer to him by his tie then whispered venomously. "Don't ever threaten me or my family again, Markova! You get near them before you are locked away forever I will personally take care of you myself."

* * * *

Lyndee watched as this all unfurled before her. Surreal. That was the only word she could think of. The officers had her backside as Trey held her hand. Wolf stepped forward, stepping between John and Markova, a sneer on his face that frightened Lyndee. His shoulder twitched as if it knew that the man confronting them was the one responsible for the injury it had obtained. The two men were equal in height but Wolf outweighed Markova by a good thirty pounds of raw muscle. A nerve twitched in the Russian's jaw as he readjusted his expensive tie.

Wolf's words were low and calculating. "Stay away from Lyndee. Do not look at her and do not ever speak to her again. She is part of our family now and will be protected by us. The same goes for John and his family. If I ever hear of you threatening any of my friends or family again, I will find you and slit your throat. I will even go to prison to do it if I have to. Beware of the darkness, comrade, for you don't know what lurks within it!"

Austin and Storm pulled John and Wolf away from the Slavic mobster and ushered their group through the doors to the ominously chilled courtroom. Taking the bench along the back wall to their right, they sat, Lyndee between Trey and Storm while Austin and Wolf pulled up the outside of the threesome. Lawrence sat next to Wolf while John took the end at the aisle. The men didn't remove their cowboy hats so their presence drew a lot of stares and hushed comments from people already sitting in the gallery.

Markova and his misfits trailed in a few minutes later. Looking around he eyed the group at the back of the room before he went through the swinging gate at the front. Waiting for him there was a rotund man about five feet eight. He was bald except for a strip of brown hair around the bottom of his plump head and he had a small mustache, which made him look devious, and his small, beady eyes within his puffy face caused him to appear shifty. He greeted his client enthusiastically, letting the tall man hug him. They made a spectacle of themselves with their greeting, but everyone in the Goodall-Dwyer group knew it was a rouse to make them nervous.

The prosecutor was at his desk reading over some papers. Lyndee had met with him a couple times during the week via Skype on her computer since she wasn't allowed to leave the hotel room. They had gone over her testimony, which seemed simple enough, though he had warned her of a few things Markova's lawyer could try to embarrass her with or degrade her with. She didn't care. She wanted the scum to go to jail. It didn't matter what image the slimy lawyer painted of her as long as those who knew her well knew she wasn't that person. She would be gone from Denver soon enough.

As if he could tell she was there, Prosecutor James turned around and nodded to her then he noticed the group she was with and his left eyebrow rose in curiosity. He gave a nod to John before his eyes skimmed the rest of the courtroom. There were others to testify, those who had been undercover as Lyndee had been and others who had been affected by the mobster.

Storm and Trey held her hands while Austin had his arm around the back of Storm's shoulders so he could keep a hand on his woman also. They had to all show her they were there for her. They all noticed there were seven Sheriff's deputies in the room in full uniform. Two stood at the back door, one in each corner at the rear of the room, two up at the front on opposite sides, and one near the judge's podium, to the right. A male court reporter sat to the left of the judge's podium opposite the jury box ready to start his day. Anxiety seemed to weigh down upon the room.

The door to the left of the judge's podium opened and the deputy standing before it stood straighter. "All rise. The United States District Court of Colorado is now in session. The Honorable Judge Martin Scott presiding," he seemed to shout. Everyone rose. Waiting for the judge to enter and then be seated in his chair, the deputy waited for a nod from the judge. "You may all be seated."

At that point, the jury was brought in. There were eight men of different ethnic backgrounds in different forms of dress and the four women were dressed nicely in dresses. There were three Caucasian women and one Hispanic.

Judge Scott looked over some papers before looking out into the crowded courtroom. There wasn't a vacant seat in the room. His eyes moved over Markova before moving on to the prosecutor. Looking back at the shifty lawyer in his shabby suit sitting next to the pristine Alex Markova, he asked for his opening argument.

The stout man stood, straightened his tie, and pompously walked to the jury box. Looking at the members of the jury, he began his speech. He went on for about an hour, defending his client, and unfortunately Markova was getting his money's worth. When he was finally finished he started back to the defense table, but before he sat down, he let his little beady eyes scan the crowd before lighting on Lyndee. Holding her gaze for only a moment, he sat and leaned toward Markova to make a comment.

Lyndee fussed in her seat, irritation eating away at her. Her three men tried to calm her but she was so fidgety after that visual exchange with the lawyer, as if he was challenging her. They all knew that that's what Markova was trying to accomplish in the lobby but now his attorney was doing it also. Now they were beginning to feed off of her irritation. Lunch time couldn't come fast enough for them. They needed to get her out this place for a while to calm her fears.

The prosecutor stood and began his opening arguments, listing all the crimes against Alexander Markova and the manipulation of political figures along with officers of the law and businessmen. He offered insight to the criminal behavior that the foreign man had brought to the State of Colorado and the illicit dealings the man had worldwide, especially in countries cowering in drug wars. The promise of evidence into such despicable acts caught the jurist's attention as they all looked over at the distinguished man sitting at the defense table. When the prosecutor was finished, Judge Scott called for recess for lunch and announced that court would resume in two hours.

After everyone rose while the judge exited the room and the dismissal was granted, the row of Lyndee's entourage made their way out of the courtroom. As quickly as possible, John, Lyndee, Trey, and Lawrence retrieved their weapons from lockup and holstered, giving them a sense of security. Exiting the building they came face-to-face with the media again and they pushed their way around people to get to the truck.

With all six of them piling into the dual-cab, the four officers assigned to them got into their patrol car and followed them away. Lunch was eaten at the hotel, giving Lyndee a little time to rest before they had to head out. She was to be the first witness when court reconvened. After they had dined and Lyndee had napped while the men talked quietly, they headed back to the courthouse. After they ran through security, they took their places on the back bench again.

When Lyndee's name was called, Markova and his lawyer looked back at her as if challenging her to remain seated. Her men all smiled at her and touched her hands as she made her way to the aisle. With her head held high, she walked up to the swinging gate and let the prosecutor hold it open for her before she made her way to the witness stand. Raising her right hand, she swore to tell the truth, the whole truth, and nothing but the truth, the whole time glaring at the beautiful mobster sitting off to her right. She sat down.

The prosecutor asked her to start at the beginning when she first went undercover. Explaining all the ins and outs and details of her undercover work, she outlined the five years she had been working within Markova's organization and the heavy hand Philip used to keep his girls in line. Objections from the defense attorney flew repeatedly until Judge Scott finally told the man to sit down until it was his turn to cross-examine the witness. The beady little man sat down in a huff, pouting as he did so.

Lyndee explained in detail about the party she and the other girls were expected to work that night and provided names of men, very influential men throughout the state, who were in attendance at the party, and how the bust went down. She detailed the events leading up to her kidnapping and how she was rescued by the Goodall brothers and their cousin and then how Markova's men showed up to kill them all so there wouldn't be any witnesses.

By the time she had finished, it was late in the day. Court was convened for the day and she would be drilled by the defense the next day. Stepping down from the witness stand, she was visibly shaking as she made her way back to her men, Storm gathering her in his arms. Markova and his attorney were walking by at that point and the men glared at Storm who didn't back down at the visible showdown. Finally the two criminals walked out. Lyndee was led out by her men and taken back to the hotel where she went to bed without any supper, saying her head hurt.

* * * *

The next morning the process started all over again. This time Lyndee wore a pair of slacks with a blazer that again seemed too small for her over a dark-blue blouse. The men wore their ever-present dark jeans, dark shirts and boots. The Stetsons were black also, causing them to stand out in any crowd, and not just because of their size. Trey of course wore his uniform but donned a Stetson also, which Connor didn't care that he wore.

Upon arriving at the courthouse, they were surprised to see Connor and Angela there to greet them when they got out of the truck. Connor wore his Sheriff's uniform while Angela wore blue jeans and a red shirt with western stitching on the chest. She was shy when she stepped up to Lyndee, who opened her arms to her and welcomed her openly, proving that the woman was her friend. The men shook hands and each took their turn at hugging Angela in a sisterly fashion, which earned them a smile from their woman. Connor hugged Lyndee before being introduced to John and Lawrence. As they headed toward the front doors of the courthouse, Connor spread his arm wide. "Quite a circus going on here."

The men chuckled before bowling their way through the crowd, leading Lyndee and Angela to the safety of the lobby. After going through the harassment of security, they made their way into the courtroom, taking up their spot they had the previous day. All the men gave her words of encouragement. *Don't let him goad you. Don't make eye contact with Markova. We love you. Be strong.*

As the court was called to order and Lyndee resumed her seat on the stand, she was reminded she was still under oath. After acknowledging that she understood, she took a deep breath when the defense attorney stood and approached her. She had to stifle a giggle for she knew the kind of money that Markova was throwing toward the lawyer to defend him, and yet here he was again, wearing a threadbare, shabby, wrinkled suit. Some people have no class, she thought.

The attorney started on her, not even dishing out any pleasantries that some defense attorneys partake of to trip up the witness. Lyndee answered all the questions quickly and honestly, and when the questions became too personal, she struggled a bit. She knew what this was leading up to.

The question finally came and she looked at the prosecutor for reassurance. He nodded to her, letting her know she had to tell the truth, no matter how embarrassing it would be for her. The defense attorney smirked as he approached the witness stand, though looked at the jury.

"Miss Dwyer, you state that you worked as a prostitute undercover, is that correct?"

"Yes, sir."

"And can you tell me how many men you have slept with throughout this supposed undercover operation?"

"None."

Still smirking, he said, "So you are telling this court that you posed as a prostitute for nearly five years and had a known client base and yet you didn't have sex with any of these men?"

"That is correct," she said, looking straight at the shifty man.

"Don't you think that the men that supposedly paid you for your 'services'"—the man chuckled as he used air quotations around the last word—"would really have paid you for not having sexual relations with them?"

Smiling sweetly at the man, she said confidently, "No, sir. They wouldn't and you would know about that since you didn't pay me for my services. You paid the woman that worked as my double. You remember her, long blonde hair like mine? She said you have a mole shaped like Mickey Mouse on your left hip."

Gasps erupted in the gallery as the beady little eyes widened at the statement before changing back to being beady. The gesture wasn't missed on Lyndee and she hoped it wasn't missed by the judge either as the lawyer was facing her at the time.

"I have no idea what you are babbling about, Miss Dwyer. I have never used a prostitute before."

Snidely, Lyndee smirked. "Of course not."

The unruly man was flustered as the crowd snickered behind him.

"So, Miss Dwyer, you are saying under oath that you never had sexual relations with any of your clients?"

The deep voice from the back of the room soothed Lyndee's spirits, though caused a flush to spread through her. "She just said she didn't have sex with any of the men!"

The attorney, surprised at the outburst, turned to the man standing in the back in a peace officer's uniform. Knowing it was totally out of the line of questioning, the stout man asked the man anyways, "And how would you know that, sir?"

"Because after we found her unconscious in the woods we took her home with us and as she recovered I took her virginity from her." Trey proudly made the announcement as gasps traveled like wildfire through the expansive room and people turned to stare at the Sheriff's Deputy. He smiled at Lyndee to give her comfort even though her cheeks flamed red.

The gavel hit the podium several times as the judge called out "Order!" several times. When he finally had what he was seeking he looked at Trey, who had remained standing. "Another outburst like that, young man, and you will find yourself in a holding cell!"

Smiling, Trey nodded. "Yes, sir."

The attorney turned to Lyndee, anger flaring his nostrils and his eyes even darker and beadier than before. They reminded her of beads on a stuffed animal. "I have no further questions at this time. I would like to reserve the right to question the witness again if needed."

"So be it," the judge said.

The attorney sat down and quietly held a discussion with his client, who seemed to be just as furious. Markova glared at Lyndee as she began to step down from the witness stand until the prosecutor stopped her.

"I have another question for the witness, your Honor," he said as he stood. Walking around the table, he leaned back on it. "Miss Dwyer, would you elaborate on this new development please?"

Lyndee explained how Philip had kidnapped her and that the brothers Goodall and their cousin Austin had rescued her when she escaped. She did explain about the misconception of her belief she was a prostitute because of her memory loss and subsequently how she had lost her virginity to Trey, though she did leave out the tidbits of Storm and Austin joining in. The prosecutor thanked her and dismissed her.

Steel gray eyes bore into Lyndee as she walked back to her seat. She knew he was furious with her as she had just blown his defense sky-high. A chill shot through her as he sneered at her and she hurried to return to her seat surrounded by her men.

Lunch was the same as the previous day. Lyndee slept, though Storm insisted she eat more than she had. The cross-examination was stressful on her as was the whole ordeal, and she hoped it would end soon so she could go home. She wanted to be able to have sex with her men without worrying what the neighbors or guards on duty would think of them. She was anxious to start her new life.

Walking back into the courtroom sent chills up Lyndee's spine again. Something was going to happen and she was anticipating it. Looking around at the guys, she knew they felt it too. Even John and Lawrence seemed edgy.

One by one, Storm, Austin, Trey, and then Wolf were called to the stand. They gave their versions of finding Lyndee and the shootout at the ranch when Markova's men stormed the place. Also, Wolf and Austin gave their versions of the shootout at the apartment. The defense attorney tried to discredit their testimony by trying to trick them, but it didn't work. By the end of the day, the attorney was frustrated and Markova looked ready to kill, and Lyndee knew who he had in his crosshairs.

After retrieving their weapons from the lockup, they stepped out into the sunshine amongst the media that wanted a statement from the key witness. The men tried surrounding her as best they could for this time the reporters were pressing forward to get any kind of a statement or picture, especially after Trey's outburst. As they reached the end of the steps and the media mob had thinned out, the groupings shifted as Connor and his sister headed for their car while the four officers headed for their squad car. As the six remaining people reached the pickup, a flash struck the driver's side window.

Trey instinctively pulled his gun and tried to push Lyndee to the ground. "Gun!"

Chapter Twenty-Seven

Austin and Storm tried to cover her, Storm reaching in Lyndee's blazer and pulling out her Sig. "Where?" he asked his brother.

"Flashed from the rooftop across the street."

The men stayed crouched down, aiming at the roofline, waiting. The sun struck a piece of metal as it edged over the center of the roof and a shot was fired, breaking the glass on the driver's side front window. The gun retreated from the roofline but the men knew danger was still present. People in the vicinity were screaming and scrambling for cover, chaos ensuing.

The high-powered rifle barrel appeared again, this time further to the right of where it had been before. Another shot rang out and Trey tried to shoot right above the end of the gun itself hoping it might strike part of the maniac shooting at them. The gun retreated again. Storm saw Wolf stand and Lawrence help him into the truck bed where the injured man quickly unlocked the large metal toolbox that spanned the back of the pickup under the window.

Opening it up, he began to pull out weapons. A shotgun went to Austin, who preferred it to a rifle. Storm took the Winchester rifle with the scope on it and he handed the Sig back to its rightful owner, though they weren't going to give her much of a chance to use it, while Wolf chose his own handgun.

The priceless look on John's face at the firepower emptying out from the truck would have been amusing if it wasn't for the situation. "Is there an army in there also?" he asked jokingly. "After he shoots next, cover me, I'm going over there. I'll take a couple of the uniforms with me."

"Got it, boss," Trey said, crouching down next to Lyndee. "You okay there, baby?"

"Yes," she said tensely. "I would appreciate it if I could get up though."

"No!" was shouted in unison from seven men. Seven, where had he come from? Connor had run over and grabbed a Winchester from Wolf and stood next to John. "I'm coming with you."

The barrel of the rifle had moved again and the shot rang out. Storm felt the intense sting and then burning as a bullet embedded itself into his left bicep while the impact sent him falling against the door of the pickup. "Fuck!" he shouted as he grabbed the wound instinctively, feeling the blood ooze from it. As he fell against the truck Lyndee pulled out from under him. Looking him over, he knew she saw the blood darkening the already dark shirt on his left arm. They heard her name called, and as she looked over to see who had called her a large object was coming at her. Grabbing it, she pulled open the first aid kit and pulled out the gauze pads and spool of tape. Helping him out of his shirt, she placed the pads on the wound and then wrapped tape around it.

"Keep pressure on it!" she demanded and started to pull away but he grabbed her arm and pulled her back to him.

"You are not going out there!" he ground through his teeth. "We will handle this!"

Exasperated Lyndee pulled against him. "I'm protected. I'll be fine."

His hand gripped tighter and he growled. "If you defy me, darlin', you will be punished and it won't be the pleasurable kind."

Kneeling back down, she stayed at this side and handed him her Sig.

* * * *

Sirens began to fill the air as reinforcements came screaming to a halt on the street and parking lot. John, Connor, and the uniformed officers had taken off as soon as the barrel of the rifle had been pulled out of sight and Trey and Austin stood in front of Storm and Lyndee. Wolf had hunched down in the bed of the pickup while Lawrence stood next to it, protecting his man.

Another shot sounded, this time hitting the ground about five feet away from Trey and Austin. This time, the rifle didn't retreat but another shot sounded, the bullet hitting another car behind the truck. A woman's scream came from the vehicle and Lawrence glanced over to see that Connor's car had been the one hit and Angela was crouching in the backseat.

Running in a zigzag pattern, he ran over to the car to the driver's side, which was the protected side, and pulled her out. They sat on the ground, letting the car protect them from the barrage of bullets as the windows shattered above them.

* * * *

Pistol shots erupted and then another shot rang out from the rifle and yet the bullet didn't strike in their vicinity and they had to wonder where it had landed. Storm and the other men stayed alert and then screams could be heard from the front of the courthouse. Trey and Austin took off running toward the front of the courthouse to see what was going on there while Storm continued to cover Lyndee's body with his.

When Trey and Austin reappeared, Austin's phone began ringing. Pushing the button to answer it, he listened for a minute before he turned to look up at the rooftop across the street and waved at John who was standing at the edge. Disconnecting the call, he put his hand out to Lyndee. "It's over. John got the sniper. Markova won't be bothering you anymore."

Lyndee pushed against Storm to dislodge herself from under him, which wasn't hard since he was getting weak from the loss of blood. Standing up she helped Trey get Storm to his feet. He was a bit unsteady for a moment before he leaned against the truck. "Why won't he?" Lyndee asked hesitantly.

"The last bullet apparently found Markova in the head instead of one of us. Apparently when John and the guys shot the gunman, his finger was still on the trigger and when the rifle moved, the bullet caught Markova."

Storm watched as a smile and tears appeared on his woman. Lyndee's shoulders sagged in relief, and he, his brother, and cousin surrounded her as they hugged her, murmuring their love. Wolf came over to give her a hug also and soon the media was surrounding them again. John arrived along with two of the uniformed officers and was able to disperse the crowd by promising a press conference the next morning. He reminded the reporters that Lyndee had just spent a whole day in court and had been shot at so she needed to get some rest and tend to her friends. Grumbles and murmurs sounded through the crowd though they finally began to go their separate ways.

The medics who tended to Storm wanted to take him to the hospital via ambulance, but he refused. He let Lawrence take him and Wolf in. Lawrence just wanted to make sure that Wolf hadn't torn anything open while climbing around in the back of the truck. When the threesome arrived back at the hotel Storm found Lyndee asleep and Austin and Trey playing cards. When they walked over to the table, Austin and Trey stood to greet them. Wolf was fine, no damage done. Storm had to have the bullet removed but there would be no lasting damage. It was time to put this mess behind them.

* * * *

Two weeks later, the last box was packed into the trailer that was attached to Austin's pickup. Lyndee stood at the doorway of her apartment and took one last look around at the emptiness that engulfed it. It represented her past and the man that had come up behind her and wrapped his arms around her waist represented her future. Childish giggles caused them both to turn around to find several small children watching them. Smiling at each other, Austin leaned down and kissed his bride-to-be gently before several snickers sounded and then running feet. They had to laugh.

Wolf stood near the truck along with Lawrence. They both looked sad as Austin and Lyndee made their way to them. They had all gotten closer in the past few weeks and Lyndee knew she was going to miss Wolf terribly. He wasn't wearing his sling now. The doctor said he could go without it. He needed another month of rehab on his shoulder, and she had offered her apartment, but Lawrence said he felt better if Wolf wasn't alone so he was staying with him. Plus it was closer to the rehab center.

Pulling her into his arms, Wolf buried his face in her hair. "I'm going to miss you. You have become a great friend," he said.

"No," she said stepping away from the man. "We are family. We expect to see both of you in a month. Don't make us come down here to get you. Though, I wouldn't mind seeing that club that Storm keeps talking about."

Lawrence's face flushed at the mention of the club and now Lyndee's curiosity was peaked. Perhaps they did need to go. She hugged Lawrence before Austin swung her up into his arms and placed her on the front seat of the truck. Turning around, he shook Lawrence's hand and then hugged

Wolf. No words needed to be spoken. They would be missed but seen again soon. Climbing into the truck, he started it up and drove away. Heading north, Austin was going to take Lyndee to her new home and her new life.

Epilogue

The homecoming that awaited Lyndee and Austin as the truck rounded the horse barn and turned into the circular driveway surprised her. It was actually as if she was truly coming home. The ranch hands, sans Wolf, were all there along with Anita and her three sons, as were Doc Anderson, Martha, though she hadn't met her yet, and her two other men. Throwing the door open and jumping out as soon as the vehicle stopped, she was running to Trey and Storm.

Storm got to her first as she threw herself into his arms, holding her to him as she kissed him furiously. Trey brushed up against her and she turned to him, letting him take her as she kissed him as she had his brother. A throat clearing somewhere had them pulling away from each other and Trey set her down, turning to face the small crowd.

"Lyndee, I would like for you to meet our housekeeper, Martha. Martha, this is the lady we are going to marry, Lyndee Dwyer." Trey made the introductions.

Surprise lit on Lyndee's face when Martha grasped the petite woman into her arms and against her bosom as she gushed, "I am so happy you have made my boys so happy. It'll be a pleasure having you around."

When the woman let her go, Lyndee smiled at her, feeling the woman's maternal nature emanate from her. "Pleased to meet you too, Martha, I've heard a lot about you."

The older woman looked at each of the men and then groaned a, "Hmph!" as if she knew exactly what these men were like. Lyndee had to laugh. She was going to like Martha.

Doc Anderson was next to gather her in his arms to welcome her home. "I'm glad that whole mess is behind you now. I hope I won't have to come out here for any more mishaps. Perhaps I wouldn't mind coming out here to deliver a baby or two though."

Everyone laughed. All the ranch hands came over to give Lyndee a hug to welcome her home and then Anita came over, shyly though. The two women hugged and then Lyndee was introduced to the little men. James, Dave, and Kevin were all very protective of the woman and the kids, and Lyndee knew the family was going to be all right. Anita blushed when James and Dave held her close and Lyndee knew how she felt.

Since it was late in the afternoon, Doc announced he would walk Martha to her cottage before heading home, while the three men with Anita said they were going to drive her home. Arturo headed back to the bunkhouse. That left four people standing on the porch. The three men were fidgeting in nervous anticipation, which wasn't missed on Lyndee.

"Ok guys, what's going on?"

Storm, who was usually so centered and serious, grabbed her hand and practically dragged her into the house and down the hallway to her bedroom. She remembered his parting words as Austin drove away toward Denver, that there would be a surprise for her when she returned. The door was closed and Storm stepped behind her, covering her eyes with one hand while he opened the door with the other. She giggled as she heard Trey and Austin come up behind them. Gently pushing her inside, he stopped her. "Are you ready?" he asked.

Nodding, she whispered, "Yes."

Pulling his hand from her eyes, she had to blink to take in the remodel that had been done. The outer walls had been extended out and where the walk-in closet had been that had been extended also. There was a fireplace on one wall and opposite that was the biggest bed she had ever seen. The bed was made up with a blue-and-white wedding ring quilt, which shone stark against the dark wood of the four posters and other furniture in the room. The wall to the room that had been next to hers had been knocked out, which extended the room also, but also gave room for the new closet. Where the walk-in closet used to sit was a sitting area with a loveseat and a chair along with a low table with a lamp sitting upon it. Further back from that was the top of a spiral staircase leading down.

The men watched their woman's expression at the revelation. Her smile said it all as she touched the furniture and even tested the bed. As she tried to settle back on it, Trey stepped forward and scooped her up. "Not right now, sweetheart. We have another surprise for you."

Squealing as she was lifted into his bulging muscular arms, she saw they were heading for the spiral staircase. Down they went and she saw they came out in the playroom, which had received a makeover also. Trey set her down so she could explore. The bed was bigger and there were more devices sitting around the room. The bathroom had been completely renovated since Philip had demolished the small one. This one had been enlarged and a large hot tub had been installed.

As she moved back toward the three, muscular men who seemed to dominate the room, she felt the mood of the room had shifted. Her nipples puckered and she felt wetness flood her panties as she looked up at her men. They stood with arms crossing their chests, their legs apart with their hips thrust forward. The bulges in their jeans were evident and she licked her lips in anticipation. Austin had been teaching her about the lifestyle in which she was entering into, not just the polyamorous one, but the D/s side of what the men expected of her.

Slowly she removed her shirt, pulling it up over her head then tossed it onto the bench near her. Reaching behind her she undid her bra, letting her breasts fall clear of their confinement. Her nipples were a deep, dusky rose and puckered and her breasts were beginning to feel heavier than before. Aware that all three of them were staring at her, she felt self-conscious, though she knew she shouldn't. She loved them and they loved her. Boldly she undid the button on her jeans and then slid the zipper down slowly, teasing them. A growl sounded from one of them. She wasn't sure who, but it didn't matter. It achieved what it was meant to. Sliding the denim material down her legs, she kicked them off along with her tennis shoes. Then hooking her thumbs in the tiny band of her thong panties, she slowly slid them down and kicked them off.

Lyndee Dwyer stood proudly naked before her men. Each of them stepped forward and took a turn around her as if examining her before returning to their original spot and stood over her. Storm breathed in and then out audibly before issuing his first command of their woman, their sex slave. "Position!"

Lyndee sank to her knees in one fluid motion. Back straight, knees shoulder-width apart and head bowed. She placed her hands on her thighs, palm up. She was relaxed in this pose as she knew she was pleasing her men.

* * * *

Storm stepped forward and bent down in front of her, the back of his hand grazing her hardened nipple. A tremor flashed through her but she didn't make an audible sound. He was pleased. Slowly moving his hand down over her abs, he moved to her newly waxed mound, reveling in the smoothness there before slipping his hand further down. Sliding into her slit, he felt the involuntary muscle twitch as he passed over the hardened pearl at the top, but he continued on, finding what he wanted. Her pussy was slick with her juices. Removing his hand, he licked her cream from his fingers. Growls came from the other two men.

Standing, he resumed his spot between Trey and Austin, just watching their woman. Finally, Storm had had enough. Growling, he commanded, "Get on the bed!"

Rising, she moved quickly to do his bidding. Finding the middle of the bed, Lyndee knelt again in her submissive position and waited for her men. The bed was made up with a bottom sheet, a top sheet, and one blanket. There was no comforter to make it pretty. It was simply made to protect the mattress from the decadent acts that would take place upon it and the bodily fluids that would most likely wind up on it. Still bowing her head, Lyndee's eyes darted around, glancing at the objects in the room, excitement racing through her veins, her cunt pulsating at the thoughts that ran through her head.

The three men slowly made their way over to the bed. Trey climbed up from the foot of the bed and knelt before Lyndee. With his fist under her chin, he lifted her face up to look at him. His green eyes were a dark emerald, filled with desire. She gasped. Reaching out, he whipped an arm around her back and hauled her up against his chest, her breasts smashed against the hard cut muscles. His chest hair tickled her skin but she didn't mind that. She minded the mouth that smashed down upon hers. His tongue pushed through her lips, demanding entrance as his other hand caught her ponytail and pulled back on it. He followed her mouth, his tongue lashing against hers, as if he was trying to swallow it.

Lyndee had to put her hands on Trey's biceps to keep from falling backward from his assault. She marveled at the raw power that lay beneath her fingers as she squeezed them. Her moans became louder and finally Trey pulled his mouth away, both of them drawing in deep breaths. He smiled down at her, "God. I love you woman!"

"I love you too, Trey."

There was no timidity to her voice. It was strong and filled with the love she had spoken of. She may be submissive to them in all things, but she would never shirk from their love.

"Undo my pants, love," he said breathlessly.

Looking down, she let her fingers follow her gaze slowly down his chest, over the ridges of his abs, and then down through the V of fuzz of brown hair that pointed down into his jeans. When her fingers lit upon the button on his jeans, she flipped it so it sprang free of the hole. Knowing he went commando, she slipped her hand inside the material to shield his cock as she pulled the zipper down with the other. He hissed at the touch of her hand and her eyes lifted to his in concern. His eyes flashed his lust and desire as she pushed his jeans down over his hips to the bed. When she wasn't able to push them down any more, he began to push her to her back. As he lay upon her, her legs splayed out and she felt the hot, bulbous head of his cock tapping her slit. She sighed.

"I've waited too long to sink my cock into you, love. I'm sorry I can't love you properly right now."

"It's okay," she responded, smiling wickedly. "I just need all of you to make love to me."

Leaning over the petite body beneath him, Trey tried to contain himself. He felt his jeans being tugged away from his body so he spread his knees out, spreading out Lyndee's thighs even more, opening her cunt wide. She never took her eyes off him. When the head of his dick found the slick, hot opening to her hidden pleasures, he moved his hips back and then thrust deeply into her until his root was smashed against her. A cry of ecstasy escaped her lips as his pubic bone ground into her clit, which sent off sparks to the rest of her body. Pulling back, he slammed back into her, causing her to cry out again. He performed this maneuver several more times before he gathered her up in his arms and turned over onto his back, letting her straddle his hips.

Lyndee lay down on his chest and she felt the bed dip behind her. She knew it was Austin when she felt his large hand on her back before she heard him say, "Cold." His other hand slid along the crevice of her bottom, and he slid the lube along the puckered rosebud there. She groaned. His finger entered her and slid in and out several times before he added another finger. Lyndee clutched at Trey's hard chest at the sensations Austin was conjuring within her ass and she began to move back against his hand.

Removing his fingers from her ass, more lube was added before she felt the head of his hot hard dick at her entrance. Instinctively her hips moved back against him as her forbidden hole pushed out, welcoming the invasion of the velvety piece of steel that was about to enter her. Austin looked down and saw the pink rim and he began to push his cock in. When the head slipped past the ring of muscles she groaned and her pelvic muscles contracted around both cocks. Both men growled at the action as their cocks twitched inside her.

Austin continued to sink his dick into Lyndee's behind as she bent to lay kisses on Trey's chest. With both hands on her hips now, Austin felt his balls hit against her and he sighed. Pulling out until the tip was just inside her entrance, he heard the hitch in her breath and then he pushed back in and Trey pulled nearly all the way out. A rhythm was set with the two men, and they fucked their woman, driving her arousal higher. Trey squeezed at her tits, pinching her nipples, which sent electrical shocks to her clit.

A nudge at Lyndee's cheek caught her attention. Opening her eyes, she turned to see Storm's long, wide cock staring at her. A drop of pre-cum had oozed from the slit there and she licked her lips. Storm reached over, grabbed the back of her neck and pulled her face toward his cock.

"Open, darlin', and suck my cock!" he said forcefully. "Make your Masters proud of you!"

His words thrilled her and she felt them all the way down to her pussy, which caused her to tighten up again. Both men hissed at the reaction and they both had to will themselves to keep from coming right then. Even though they had pounced on her as they had gotten her down to the playroom without any foreplay, they wanted to make it last until they all came together.

Lyndee opened her mouth and licked the drop of man dew from the tip of Storm's cock and then opened her mouth wide as he slid it into the warm depths he found there. It kept sliding until it found the back of her throat and then he held her there for a moment before pulling nearly all the way out.

He guided their movements with his hand at the back of her neck, which she didn't seem to mind as she willingly took what he gave her.

Storm's hip began to thrust faster, feeding her his cock and then pulling out as Trey and Austin began to pick up the pace. Lyndee began to moan from their ministrations as her pussy was shooting sparks out to the rest of her body. Her breasts felt so tight she thought they were going to burst, and her turgid nipples ached so much, but she loved the way they felt. Her pussy and ass were filled so much but she wouldn't have it any other way at the moment. Her body was filled with her men as they pleasured her and she pleased them. This was her place and she would relish each and every time they made love to her.

Austin reached around and slid his hand into her slit and placed his index finger on her clit. Beginning to rub at the hard nub he knew she was close as her breathing came in short pants and her cunt and ass clinched and then relaxed.

"Lyndee, are you ready for your men to come inside you?" Austin asked breathlessly. He saw her head nod. "All right guys. Let's fill our woman with our cum. She's ours. All ours!"

Trey and Austin pumped into her at the same time now, totally filling her with their flesh, while Storm fucked her mouth faster, hitting the back of her throat each time. Lyndee readied herself as she felt his cock begin to swell even more, and his balls were hotter and harder when they struck her chin. His hand tightened in her hair and he held her still as he began to pump his seed down her throat. She drank down all he gave her and as she pulled her mouth away and licked the head one last time, Austin pinched her clit and she came. Her scream seemed to echo throughout the room as her orgasm tore through her core, her cunt contracting around Trey's cock tightly. He came hard within her, shooting his hot cum deep into her womb as she milked him dry. Austin's cock went off as her tight muscles squeezed his cock at the root, his seed finding its way deep within her ass.

Her vaginal walls continued to contract as the pulses electrified her body, her screams turning to hoarse moans, and her body twitched between the two men. Having lost her strength she lay down on Trey, his heart beating beneath her ear, his breathing as erratic as hers. As she came down from her orgasmic high, her pussy continued to spasm lightly, her body following every so often.

Storm lay down next to his brother, his face even with Lyndee's. He watched as bliss settled upon her face and he leaned over and kissed her gently on her lips. Her eyes fluttered open and she let her hand reach up to caress his cheek.

"I love you, Storm Goodall."

"I love you too, darlin'," he said, smiling at her. "You've made me one of the happiest men in the world by accepting to be our wife."

"You've all made me so happy. I will gladly be your wife and serve as your sex slave for the rest of our lives." She smiled genuinely.

Trey and Austin chuckled, but Trey, being the residential smart-ass was the one to retort, "Can we have that put in the wedding vows?"

THE END

ABOUT THE AUTHOR

Eileen Green lives in the beautiful state of Washington after recently relocating from California. What started out as the most dreaded time in her life, moving away from all of her family and friends, turned out to be a new beginning for her, as she submitted her first erotic novel for publishing and she also found the love of her life. Falling in love after reading her first romance novel, she knew was hooked from that moment and knew writing was embedded in her. Being able to create interesting characters and provide them with love, lust, and mind-blowing sex along with those unexpected twists, is like welcoming new family members into the fold.

Writing is Eileen's main hobby though she enjoys the outdoors when she can find spare time away from the computer. She enjoys finding the beauty in things, whether it is in nature or even the human body. A people watcher, she admits to enjoying just watching people and their nuances in the one place people can really be themselves…Disneyland, for even in the Happiest Place on Earth, she is unable to turn off the creative switch in her head. Many a character has been created in her mind while people-watching.

For the quirkier side of Eileen, anytime of the year you can find her watching Christmas movies or even singing Christmas carols. If her family didn't threaten to commit her, she admits she would have Christmas decorations up all year long. How does she get away with some of those decorations sticking around? Coca-Cola decorations adorn her kitchen, and what are Coca-Cola decorations without a few Santas on them?

Now, Eileen would like to welcome you, the reader into her family of characters, to let them come alive for you in your own imagination and mind's eye.

Siren Publishing, Inc.
www.SirenPublishing.com